SPELL CASTER

REBEKAH OLSON

SPELL CASTER

ISBN: 978-1-7349262-2-4

Formatted by: Heather Dowell, Unicorn Nightporium, LLC
unicornnightporium.com

Cover by: Betibup33 Design
thebookcoverdesigner.com/designers/betibup33

Edited by: Philip Athans

Chapter 1

ERRYCK STEPPED out of his tower where his charms would not alert him if someone approached. This particular corridor of Coraline Palace was usually vacant, which would have suited his present state. At the moment, Magician Masorno was lodged in one of the rooms as a guest. With all the doors closed, there was not a way to tell if he was in his room or somewhere else.

Normally Jerryck took no thought to his steps when he moved up and down this well-lit corridor. He didn't care. Now, with how much his heart ached from recent death, he didn't think he would be a good host for company. He eyed the doors. He hadn't bothered learning which one was Masorno's.

The numbness had set in, overwhelming and pushing aside some of the hurt. Experience told Jerryck it would wear thin after a week or two. In the meantime, it made the grief more bearable.

For the most part, he had holed up in his tower avoiding everyone. But when the king sent a summons for his court magician, he expected an appearance, no matter how much more lenient he ruled than his father had. So Jerryck went. Focusing on keeping his feet to the runner carpet in the center where he would make less noise and draw less attention, he nearly ran into Tajor, the one elite guard who made himself so annoying he was impossible to forget.

Jerryck drew up short, taking a step back. "What are you doing here?"

"Here in this corridor?" Tajor grinned at him, blocking his way forward. "Here in this palace? Here in the nation of Brend?"

Jerryck stepped around him and continued on. Tajor followed. "Did I not broaden that enough?"

Jerryck didn't bother looking at him. "If I ask what you want, will you just play head games with me?"

"You make it so easy it's difficult not to." Tajor walked a few more paces with him. When Jerryck didn't respond, Tajor spoke again. "General Heston wants you to know that Magician Masorno is causing problems."

"I didn't invite him here." Jerryck's voice sounded dull to himself, almost monotone.

"Do you ever?" Tajor walked beside him now instead of following. "He's spreading rumors."

Jerryck rolled his eyes. "He always spreads rumors."

"This time he's telling people that your brother-in-law died last week because the medics in the infirmary killed him."

Jerryck's feet stopped working and he stumbled. Tajor caught his arm and steadied him as Jerryck said, "It's not their fault."

"I know that. You know that. Heston knows that. Do you think everyone else knows that?" Tajor moved forward again, drawing Jerryck along. "He's getting people to say they'll back you up when you ask King Terrance to turn out all the medics and staff the infirmary with healing magicians instead."

"I'll do no such thing." Jerryck got his feet back under control and pulled his arm away. "There aren't enough healing magicians to staff that infirmary, even if I wanted to ask for it."

"I didn't say people were giving it much thought. Just that Heston wants this stopped."

"Later." Jerryck said. They went down a flight of stairs to a corridor with more traffic. "Why hasn't Heston done anything to stop Masorno?"

Tajor smirked at him. "Besides sending me to tell you? He also assigned an honorary escort guard. Two of them, actually. Except that one stays out of the way until Masorno causes problems. Then they both intervene."

2

People moved aside as Jerryck walked up the corridor grumbling. "He's not stupid. And he's never had an escort guard before. He'll probably try and demand they leave him be."

"What makes you think he didn't? We told him that as an important foreign minor noble, he deserves the escort."

Jerryck snorted. "He's not a noble."

"He's as much a noble as you are. Or did you forget that again?"

Jerryck said nothing. He felt the eyes of the people they passed and avoided looking at them. Tajor chuckled. "You've had the position that makes you a minor noble for how long now? Nearly a decade? Longer than I've been at this palace at the very least. How do you keep forgetting this?"

"I don't think about it," Jerryck said.

"Obviously." Tajor stopped chuckling, but his smirk remained. "So... About your guest. Heston wants to know how soon you can take care of this. Unless you think he'll be satisfied with just later?"

"Right now I have to answer a summons from the King," Jerryck said. "So... Later."

He stopped walking. They had come to the landing of the busy flight of stairs going down to the floors that contained most of the working offices of the palace. The landing he had to cross to get to the king. People sat so thick on cushioned benches it was a wonder they didn't fall off. Spring flowers sat trapped in large vases between the tall windows that exposed the courtyard below.

Masorno stood from one of the benches with his usual patronizing smile. Jerryck glanced at the people traversing up and down the marble stairs, to and from the corridor on the far side of the wide landing. Normally he avoided rivers of people threatening to swallow up anyone who got too close. This time the river backed away from him, refusing to diminish his exposure. Masorno approached.

Tajor leaned close to Jerryck's ear. "Maybe now is better than later?"

"There you are." Masorno held his arms out wide, regardless of anyone else around him. One of the elite guards, Tajor's friend with a crooked nose and permanent scowl, followed him closely. He didn't seem to notice. "If I didn't know how you isolate yourself to deal with grief, I'd think you were avoiding me."

Tajor cocked his head. "Are you sure that's it?"

A muscle twitched in Masorno's cheek. He didn't even glance at Tajor. Exaggerating his Shontese accent by over-rolling his R's and clipping his consonants too short, he said, "It's a good thing I come every year around this time, even though I don't get the respect I deserve. Otherwise I wouldn't be here to help you out when you so desperately need me."

"I don't need your help." Jerryck turned away, heading for the other side of the landing.

Masorno followed. "Not precisely. You could finish your apprenticeship with someone else to become legitimate."

"A private conversation in a room full of people..." Tajor tapped his chin with a finger, as if musing. Then he cocked his head at Masorno. "Are you trying to embarrass him into doing what you want? Or are you just showing off what you know?"

A few people snickered, including another of Tajor's elite guard friends, the one with the cleft chin. Masorno glared around at them. Then said to Jerryck, "You shouldn't allow common people to speak to me this way."

Tajor smirked. "Common? Does that mean the general lied when he said I was elite?"

Masorno looked down his nose. "You're not a nobleman. At my home, you would be flogged for this disrespect."

"Are we at your home? Or the home of King Terrance?" More people snickered at Tajor's questions.

Masorno's face reddened. He reached for Jerryck's arm. "We need to speak privately."

Tajor inserted himself between them. At the same time, the honorary guard pulled Masorno's upper arm drawing it back and away. The cleft chin guard stepped in closer too.

Masorno lifted his double chin. "Every time. No matter how often I come here to try and help you. Every time you rebuff me. Ignore my help. Now you try to embarrass me publicly? I've never been anything but a friend and mentor to you. And this is how you treat me?"

"You've never been my mentor," Jerryck said. "And as long as you're spreading lies, you're not much of a friend either."

"What lies?"

"What you've been telling people about medics." Jerryck tried to keep impatience out of his tone. He must not have done a good enough job. Everyone stopped to watch them.

Masorno drew himself up, speaking more clearly now without over-accentuating. "It wouldn't have happened if your sister's husband had gone to a magician instead of a medic."

"Yes, it could have," Jerryck said. "If the magician he went to didn't know the severity of his ailment, just like that medic didn't. They would have treated it the same. Lightly. He still would have died. You can't go around telling people otherwise. The fact is, I was unavailable."

Masorno's eyes glinted maliciously. "You would have been available if you already had your license and could do your job properly."

Jerryck's vision narrowed. Everything in the periphery went dark, leaving only Masorno's face. If he wasn't so numb from the loss of his brother-in-law, he might have had a magic accident.

"You think I don't do my job." The words came out of Jerryck's mouth, even though he didn't feel his tongue moving. "Yet here you are, in a different country, ignoring yours entirely."

"My job is secure," Masorno said. "I have a license."

"Go home." Jerryck turned his back and walked away. "Get out, and stop lying to people. And don't come back until you can use your manners."

"You ungrateful brat." Masorno spoke so quiet he probably wouldn't have been heard if everyone else on the landing hadn't gone silent. "At your age, you have no business acting like such a child."

Jerryck kept going. He turned his head just enough to address the elite guards. "See to it he leaves the premises."

Whispers raced ahead of him. By the time he reached the reception area outside the king's office, everyone was staring at him open mouthed. The king's aide sent him directly into the office.

Jerryck stepped inside, closing out all the snooping eyes and ears. His shoes clicked on the wood floor by the door, announcing him. Then he stepped onto the thick rug that covered all but the edges of the room.

Kellos, the head medic, was there. He stared at the wall to the right, where a portrait of the princess was framed with drapes of crimson and gold. King Terrance stood in front of his cluttered desk, as he often did when addressing an issue personally. He looked calm as ever. As thin as ever. A half-eaten plate of food sat in its usual corner of the desk. His crown rested in its normal spot on a bow-legged table beneath the portrait of his daughter. Since losing the Queen, he had never worn it outside of court.

"Jerryck," Terrance said. "Do you need more time before you talk to anyone about what happened?"

"I'll manage," Jerryck said.

"You're sure?"

Jerryck took a deep breath. Lavender. The king still kept dried lavender petals on the shelf, scenting the air with his late wife's favorite flower even after all these years. Terrance was as intimate with death as Jerryck. As intimate at dealing with it and moving on. He would understand. Jerryck nodded. He was up to answering questions.

Terrance looked back and forth between him and Kellos. "Then how about we start with the two of you explaining this to me."

"It was my fault," they both said at once. Kellos didn't look the king in the eye. He turned his face to Jerryck, not looking directly at him either, and said, "It wasn't your fault Chev died. It was mine."

"No, it was mine." Jerryck said.

Terrance crossed his arms. "I appreciate that neither of you are looking to blame someone else, but that doesn't answer my question."

Kellos looked around the room, anywhere but at Terrance. Jerryck didn't know what to say. Terrance blew out his breath. He leaned his hips back on his desk and raised one hand to pinch the bridge of his nose.

"Kellos," he said. "My infirmary is turning away anyone who isn't a regular patient for fear of misdiagnosing them and providing insufficient treatment. When that happens, people question whether or not medics can be trusted. It creates a rift between them and coworkers who distrust healing magicians, like Jerryck."

"Right now," Kellos said, staring at Terrance's feet. "I question whether or not my medics can be trusted."

"That isn't the only problem," Terrance said. He lowered his hand and looked at Jerryck. "My kitchens are falling apart because they're arguing about who's going to replace Chev as the chief food stocker. The scullery maids are all fighting with each other without your sister's influence. Everyone's meals are late. When that happens, no proper work gets done. I need this resolved. Tell me exactly what happened with Chev."

"Sometimes his lungs and throat would close up," Jerryck said. "He couldn't breathe."

"I thought spring was the worst time for that," Terrance said. "We're almost into summer."

"He's had breathless attacks other times of the year," Kellos said. "Not just spring. People do when they have this ailment as severely as Chev does... did..."

"The worst danger is still springtime," Jerryck said. "And since most of spring is passed, I thought the worst danger had too. So I asked not to be disturbed so I could handle a correspondence. That's why he didn't come when he needed me."

Terrance turned back to Kellos. "And when Chev entered the infirmary? Didn't you usually treat him personally when Jerryck was unavailable?"

"I was also unavailable," Kellos said. "I was writing a personal correspondence. One of my junior medics treated him without knowing how severe his ailment was."

"He wasn't just a junior medic," Jerryck added. "He was the newest medic on the staff. He hasn't been here long enough to know individual patients that only come intermittently. And he gave Chev a potion that would have worked for the average person."

Kellos held his hands out, fingers splayed in confusion. "Why are you defending me like this. Why do you keep saying this isn't my fault?"

Jerryck sighed, tired of the argument. "It's not your fault."

"Tell that to your sister," Kellos said.

"I have."

"And their children."

"Them too."

The King cut them both off. "I'm not holding either of you account-able. Sometimes these things happen. We'll sort this out. I just need the details. Now we can figure out how to prevent something like this from happening again."

"I'll extend the trial period for new medics to six months." Kellos finally looked Terrance directly in the face. "Even if they have prior experience elsewhere."

Terrance nodded approval. "Reasonable. Come up with other measures. Get back to me. And stop your medics from turning away patients. Immediately."

Kellos bowed his head. "Yes, sire."

"Jerryck," Terrance turned back to him. "Were you unavailable because you were trying to draft a response to the Gathering of Seats?"

Jerryck looked at Terrance in surprise. "You knew about that?"

"You get a letter from them at the end of every spring." Terrance leaned his hands on his desk behind him. "I watch for it. Are you finally going to let me help you respond to them?"

"No need," Jerryck said.

"Really?" Kellos asked. "You already responded?"

Jerryck nodded. Terrance said, "Kellos, thank you for your time. Please go fix my infirmary."

Kellos bobbed his head in deference, like most people did when they left the king. He closed the door behind him on his way out. Then Terrance gave Jerryck a long, searching look.

"It normally takes you days before you come up with a draft you're satisfied with," Terrance said. "You already sent one? When?"

"Six days ago."

Terrance leaned forward slightly. "The same day Chev died?"

"That evening. Yes. I portaled it through to their post."

Terrance's eyebrows now shot straight up. "You *portaled* it? And you did all the scrying you say is necessary without any problems or anything?"

"I had the same problems." Jerryck shrugged that away. "They don't make it impossible to open portals. Just difficult."

"What did you say to the Gathering?"

"I told them since I've had my position as your court magician for almost a decade, I don't need a license from them," Jerryck said. "If they send any more letters harassing me about it, I'll ignore them. I'm not going to make myself unavailable just to respond if people are going to die because of it."

The corner of Terrance's mouth twitched upward. "You blamed them? You told them someone died because you were responding to their letter?"

"I specified that it was my brother-in-law."

Terrance pressed his lips together, but a slight chuckle escaped him. Jerryck frowned. There was nothing funny about this.

The King dug out a parchment from the mess on his desk. He added to the notes scribbled all over it. "You do realize this could cause problems in foreign relations with Kemetulla."

Jerryck wasn't sure exactly how. For him, yes. For Terrance? Kemetulla was two nations to the south. Far away. He shrugged again. "It's not like they have an official representative here to stir up trouble."

"They would, if you'd get your license from them." Terrance set down his pen. "You really think they're just going to give up on you?"

They didn't have a representative because Terrance had refused one nearly a decade ago, though it probably wasn't prudent to bring that up. Anyone who brought it up only ever got cold responses from him. He crossed his arms. "I shouldn't have to remind you of their history. When was the last time they ever gave up on a magic user refusing to obey them?"

"When the Chemwanitz Shamans nearly destroyed them by erupting that volcano on their city," Jerryck said.

"And nearly destroyed themselves in the process," Terrance said. "That wasn't giving up. That was acknowledgment of mutual destruction if they continued to war. I'm talking about individuals, like you."

"There were the Ahnjwat Summoners in the south."

"They warred," Terrance reminded him. "And eventually capitulated to the Gathering."

"My mentor refused to take up one of their seats."

"And yet he still took their oaths and had a license from them," Terrance said. "On top of that, he didn't defend alchemical medics the way you do. Not that I disagree with you, but you need to be more careful. In this particular situation, any other magician would be screaming for me to get rid of those medics and hire magicians in their place. Like Masorno's doing."

"That's not going to be a problem anymore."

"You told him to stop?"

"I told him to stop lying and go home. I left him with some of the elite guards to escort him off the palace grounds."

Terrance stared at Jerryck for a moment. He opened his mouth as if to say something. Then he closed it again, pursed his lips, and ran a hand across his short-cropped beard.

"Did I do wrong?" Jerryck asked.

"Did you do this privately?" Terrance asked right back. "Or in a room full of people?"

"It was on the landing outside your reception area," Jerryck said.

"So in a room full of people." Terrance paused and sighed. "He's going to go home to Shontarra and tell Prince Sanbralio that you publicly embarrassed him. I'm going to get a formal complaint from the crown and a demand for an apology to his court magician."

"So I did do wrong." Jerryck shook his head at himself. "I'm sorry."

"I'll deal with it by sending a counter complaint," Terrance dug his note riddled parchment back out and added more to it. "Considering how Masorno has been acting, it wasn't what you did so much as your method of implementation."

"So... I did right and wrong at the same time?" Jerryck frowned with confusion when Terrance nodded. "I really don't understand that."

A shadow of a smile slowly spread across Terrance's face. "You don't understand that you created two foreign relations messes in one week?"

"Social nuances make no sense."

"They do to most people, Jerryck. Just not to you." The smile now spread to Terrance's eyes, something that didn't happen often enough. "Go back to your tower. I'll take care of these messes for you. As always."

Chapter 2

ERRYCK PUT the corner of a cheap parchment into the flame of a candle. When it caught, he dropped it into the stone mortar he had set on his worktable. He focused in as it burned, getting a feel for the natural magic in the flame.

Fire consumed. Why couldn't that trait be altered? What if it consumed other magic instead of physical materials? Like Tajor's curse. And if so altered, what would it have for boundaries? There would have to be boundaries, or what would keep it from consuming every last bit of magic in its vicinity? A boundary on Tajor's curse was that he had to come in contact with the magic. But it had to be more refined than that, because he could walk through ambient magic without absorbing or disrupting it. So, was it really like consuming fire after all?

Jerryck lit another parchment and dropped it in the mortar atop the ashes of the first. In the three years since he'd met Tajor, that curse had presented an ongoing enigma. A puzzle that his mind screamed to figure out. He had tried disruptions, alterations, transferences, all kinds of different magic. Nothing he did came close to the sophistication or function of what was woven into Tajor's aura. He didn't expect that altering what fire consumed would come close either. But it might be fun to play with. And it would keep his mind off of other things.

He created a spherical shield made entirely of magic around the burning parchment, just like the bubble he used to contain energy when he opened a portal. With his finger he snagged hold of the flames, drawing it all outside the bubble. He cast an inane spell on the parchment that would turn ink invisible. At least, it would if it had been written on. Then he focused on the flames again dancing off the edge of his fingertips, thinking of which spell had the best chance of getting the fire to eat the magic he had just put on the parchment, rather than the parchment itself.

The chimes attached to the underside of his high cupboard rang a warning that someone had entered the tower. Startled, his hold on the fire slipped. It dripped off his finger back down into the mortar basin. The parchment re-ignited, ruining his experiment. Jerryck frowned at it as it burned.

He wiped the frown from his face when footsteps thumped on the landing at the top of the tower stairs. He wasn't supposed to be playing around with magic anyway.

An elite guard entered the workroom. Without preamble, he said, "Tajor's sick."

Jerryck put a stone lid over his mortar to snuff the fire. "Tajor doesn't get sick."

"He's sick now," the guard replied, lifting one shoulder in half a shrug. "Not sure why I was sent to fetch you. General Heston always makes us guards go to the infirmary for healing. No magic allowed. Too quick. Says a little pain is good for us. Makes us hard."

"Hard to what?" Jerryck asked.

"Just hard, I guess." The guard looked around the workroom.

The place would likely seem cramped to someone seeing it for the first time, despite the rafters above that vaulted the roof to a cone. The guard glanced at both the windows on either side that let in light and a cross breeze. He moved on to eyeing the shelves full of jars and books, his gaze passing across the worktable taking up the middle of the room, and finally resting on the curtain to the storage area in the back. He didn't stare at the view of the palace rooftops below the windows as some did. And he never once looked Jerryck in the eye.

Jerryck nudged the guard back out of the workroom, then passed him and headed down the narrow stairs of his tower. "Tajor doesn't go to the infirmary."

"I've been told he doesn't get sick, either." The guard followed, running his hand along the inner wall that enclosed the other floors of the tower.

"What are his symptoms?" Jerryck passed by one of the outside windows and the beam of light it cast on the steps.

"He won't say. But he's acting like he's hurting, curled up in a ball, gritting his teeth, shivering some." The young man didn't look out that window any more than the ones in the workroom at the top.

"Is it constant? Or does it come and go in waves?"

"It comes and goes. It's pretty weird seeing him like this. I figured him for the type that wouldn't even flinch if you cut off all his fingers and toes."

Jerryck stopped. He grimaced up at the guard a few steps above and behind him. The guard gave him a confused look. "What?"

"How long have you been with the Elite?" Jerryck asked.

"A few months now." The young man beamed. Jerryck nodded and continued down. The guard hurried after him. "Why? Does it show? Did you guess because I'm doing a page's job? I was told that's common for rookies in the Elite."

"Is it? I never paid attention."

"Deek says I talk too much. Is that it? Did that give me away? Please. I want to know."

"You don't have any stripes on your upper sleeve," Jerryck said, pointing.

They exited the tower into the corridor. A woman cradled a whimpering toddler, pacing back and forth in front of the door. She froze when she saw him.

"Lord Magician?" She said, a tremor in her voice. "I was wondering if you would, please… If you have the time, could you… If it's not too much trouble…"

"What do you need?" Jerryck asked.

"My baby has a fever," she replied, glancing down at the little girl she carried. "All the medics are busy. My friend told me you could help."

"All of them? Busy with what?" Jerryck put his hand on the child's skin. She burned under his touch. Whimpering again, she turned her face to her mama's neck and batted away his hand.

The woman caught her child's hand and said, "People started getting sick after lunch."

"Sick from what?" Jerryck probed with his fingertips under the girl's chin. The glands under her jaw were swollen.

"I don't know," the woman said.

Jerryck gathered energy around his right hand, just enough to shape into a probe for health. He muttered the word that severed it from his aura and directed it at the little girl. The results came back befuddled and confused, giving him both healthy and sick readings at the same time.

"The magician is needed elsewhere," the guard said.

"I'm sorry." The woman backed away staring at his uniform and the gold star pinned to his collar, indication of Elite status.

Jerryck frowned at the guard. "Part of my job is serving the residents of the palace. You really think I'm going to refuse a sick baby?"

"You're busy." The woman nearly whispered. "I'll go. I'm sure the medics will get to her if we wait long enough."

Jerryck caught the woman's arm to stop her. "I'll use magic to reduce her fever. It'll only last a few hours. If a medic hasn't seen her by then, bring her back to me. I'll do more to try and figure this out."

The woman barely stayed long enough for Jerryck to apply the magic. Casting nervous glances between him and the guard, she left the moment he finished. He went with the guard to the elite barracks, scolding him along the way. "You can't try to scare off the people I'm supposed to help."

"I'm sure your own reputation had nothing to do with her being nervous." The guard rolled his eyes. "Nothing at all whatsoever."

"What reputation?"

"Well, you…" The young man spluttered. "I mean, just that, um… Never mind. Maybe Deek is right. I do talk too much."

He closed his mouth and didn't open it again. All the way down to the ground floor, through the bustle of the bailey, to the four-story building that provided housing for the elite guards, separate from the barracks for the rest of the guards. Rumor had it there was a tunnel that led from here to the palace proper and to several of the other buildings. But then, rumor also had it that there was an entire labyrinth below the dungeon level too. If that were true, the palace would collapse under its own weight.

The young man marched right in, past the two guards manning the entrance, and through a low-ceilinged common room were several men lounged. Jerryck followed him, his eyes adjusting to the close dimness after the open light of the bailey, up a flight of stairs and turned left down a narrow corridor. Identical doors lined it on both sides. There the young man stopped, pointing to where another elite stood blocking most of the light from the window at the end.

The young man headed back down the stairs. Jerryck went up the corridor struggling to put a name to the man's face, with his crooked nose and scowling eyes. How many times had he been told it? The man was one of the guards with Tajor when Jerryck tossed out Masorno. He really should know the name.

"Took you long enough." The man's voice was gravelly.

"I had to stop to help someone along the way," Jerryck said.

Tajor's voice in one of the rooms was too muffled to make out any of the words. General Heston's response was much louder. "Just answer the question. And stop giving me riddles."

Jerryck blinked in surprise. "He won't answer Heston?"

"Tajor doesn't answer anyone," the guard said.

"I know, but, not even the general?" Jerryck squeezed past the guard and knocked on the door. It was so thin the light rap jostled it on its hinges.

It jerked open from the inside. Heston, teeth bared, saw Jerryck and dropped the snarl. "There you are."

Jerryck stepped back, making room for Heston's large frame to fit in the corridor. He asked, "What exactly happened?"

"Deek." Heston looked over at the crooked nosed guard, reminding Jerryck of the man's name.

"He took a drink of water," Deek said. "He collapsed."

"Was he alone?" Jerryck asked.

"In the common room." Deek said.

"No one sent for a medic, did they?" Jerryck hadn't seen one on his way in, but it was better to make sure.

"Is it tattling if I tell you Deek punched the person who tried?" Tajor asked from inside his room.

Heston glowered at Deek. "Did you?"

"I don't want to know about this." Jerryck entered the tiny room. Tajor sat on a bed almost as narrow as he was, leaning back against the wall. His gray eyes were open and alert, not squeezed shut against waves of pain. His skin looked almost as ashen as his hair. He clenched his jaw and trembled some. But he wasn't hugging his arms over his belly or doubling over into a fetal position.

"How bad was it?" Jerryck asked.

"Can you specify?" Tajor asked right back.

"I really don't want to play this game right now," Jerryck said with a sigh. "It makes it really difficult to help you."

Tajor smirked at him. "Help me with what?"

"How bad was your reaction to whatever magic you came in contact with?"

"I don't react to magic."

Jerryck let his mouth hang open for a few moments. Then said, "I do believe that's the first lie I've ever heard come out of your mouth."

"It's not a lie. I don't react to magic."

"You feel pain every time you come in contact with magic," Heston said from the doorway.

"Not from the magic." Tajor's smirk grew. "Would this be an argument of technicalities or semantics?"

"If you don't come in contact with magic, the curse weaved into your aura doesn't punish you," Jerryck said. "The initial cause of your reaction is contact with magic, whether that's directly what causes you the pain or not. How bad was your reaction to the magic? And what magic was it?"

"So, semantics then?"

"Would you stop that!"

"Why?" Tajor smirked again. Then he ground his teeth, his eyes unfocusing.

"You're still hurting," Jerryck said.

"You can tell?" Tajor spoke through a clenched jaw.

"Tell me what magic you came in contact with," Jerryck said.

"Here's the problem…" Tajor relaxed again, his eyes refocusing. "I can't specify exactly."

"You always know every magic you come in contact with. How can you not specify?"

"It was diluted."

"How diluted?"

"It was diluted enough I doubt anyone else will be affected by it." Tajor stretched out his legs, jostling the narrow bed just enough that it creaked. "Unless its instability plays a factor. I suppose that's a possibility now that I think on it."

"What kind of magic was it?" Jerryck asked. "Break this down for me so I know what to look for."

"Elemental with a cover," Tajor said. "Beyond that, I'm embarrassed to say, I honestly can't tell. What I caught was too minuscule."

"You don't react this way to minuscule elemental magic. If you did, you'd collapse every few seconds because it's everywhere." Jerryck spread his hands out above his head.

"Did I mention that it was unstable?"

Jerryck dropped his hands. Unstable. He pulled his lower lip. Elemental. Covered. With these factors, could it affect other people? The woman with the toddler had said people were getting sick. When had Tajor taken the drink? After lunch?

"Did anyone keep the water Tajor drank from?" Jerryck asked.

"Deek." Heston leaned to look back in the corridor. "Get it."

Jerryck let go of his lip and asked Heston, "Are any of the guards sick?"

"A few took ill after lunch," Heston said. "I have a medic looking in on them."

"What are their symptoms?"

"They vary. Why?"

"Because unstable magic reacts disparately with minor variations in minute details on the subject it affects."

Heston scowled at him. "Speak plainly."

"Everyone is different. So unstable magic will affect them differently, if it affects them at all."

Deek returned with a bucket. Heston passed it into the room. Jerryck took it and looked at the water in it. There was nothing abnormal. He used the same kind of magic as he had on the girl, except shaped to detect other magic rather than physical ailments. It gave him negative results. With a word he altered his sight, giving himself the ability to see the colored auras of magic. Still, there was nothing abnormal in the water.

"I don't see anything wrong with this." Jerryck let his sight fade back to normal. "No magic at all."

"Are you going to discount evidence simply because you can't see what it's pointing to?" Tajor asked. "Besides, there are ways to hide magic."

"Covered," Jerryck mumbled. He looked up from the bucket. "Where did this water come from?"

"The vats," Heston said. "Same as always. And since you didn't think to ask, no one tampered with the bucket before Tajor drank. Whatever affected him is in those vats. It could very well be affecting everyone. Go check them."

"Everyone?" Jerryck couldn't examine every individual in the palace. And even if he could, it wouldn't do much good until he figured out exactly what the magic was.

Heston gave him a droll look. "The vats. Not the people."

"Oh, right." Jerryck nodded. "Of course."

Heston stepped aside, letting him out of the room. He walked up the corridor as Heston demanded of Tajor, "Why did you make us drag this information out of you? You could've just told me and saved a lot of time."

"Where's the fun in that?" Tajor asked.

Jerryck headed back down the stairs to unintelligible shouting in the common room. Tables and chairs scraped across the floors, shoved about violently, crashing into each other. He came off the last step just as several men separated two combatants. One of them was quickly hustled up the corridor. The other was pushed into the nearest corner. One of the men holding him shouted in his face, "What is wrong with you? Why are you acting so hot tempered?"

Hot. Fevers. Jerryck looked around at the men. Some of them were flushed. A couple were dripping in sweat. One man sat fanning himself with a piece of parchment. How many people were affected by this throughout the palace?

Chapter 3

ERRYCK HEADED straight for the kitchens to check on his family. Leanne, his wife, had come to the palace as a midwife and worked in the kitchens between caring for pregnant women. His sister Kendra directed all the scullery maids, and often had her children helping out. The two older ones would still be in class at this time of day, getting the education the king provided to all the children dwelling in the palace. They would come to the kitchens afterward to do their daily chores.

He nearly ran over Leanne as she came out of the wide, main doors to the kitchen. She smiled and said, "I was just coming to find you."

He grasped her hands. "Are you all right?"

People swept around them, passing in and out of the kitchens. He drew her off to the side, out of the way. Her skin had her normal pale tones, no flush. She wasn't overly warm. Her pretty blue eyes didn't have any dark circles under them, like they got when she wasn't feeling well. A few wisps of her black hair had escaped where she pinned it back that morning, as usual. Nothing pointed to anything abnormal. He asked, "What's wrong? What do you need? Why are you coming to find me?"

"A couple of people in here need help." She led him into the heat of the kitchens. In the spacious main room, she raised her voice to be heard above the clatter of all the workers. "All the medics are busy."

She stopped by one of the scullery maids, sitting on a stool near an outside door where the temperature was somewhat cooler. She hugged her knees to her chest and wore a look of misery. Leanne said, "She's got heat rash all over her body. She's especially prone to it. We try to keep her away from the ovens during the worst of the summer heat."

"We're not really into summer yet," the woman said, stating the obvious. "It's not all that hot yet. I don't understand why this happened."

"This is the worst I've ever seen her." Leanne gently prodded the woman, turning her left and right, peeling back clothing to show the rash. "It's under her chest, inside her elbows, the backs of her knees, around her neck, all over."

"I usually get a cream from the medics," the woman said. "I'll be fine when I get that."

"You should go somewhere private you can take off your clothes." Jerryck examined what was exposed without making her indecent. "Make sure any affected area is dry. Don't rub it. Just blot it with a clean towel or dry cloth. Do you have any powder to put on?"

The woman's eyes widened. "You sound like a medic. You're not going to throw magic at me?"

"Not if there's a treatment that doesn't warrant it. I could make you a cream which I'd use magic on to promote healing, aside from the natural medicinal properties in the ingredients. But it might be faster if you wait on the medics for what you normally use. They've probably got some on hand and I have other things to do first."

She stared at him, her mouth hanging open. Jerryck asked, "What?"

"I thought alchemical medics and healing magicians hated each other." "So?"

"So, you just told me to go to them. After you said exactly the same thing they usually say."

Leanne looked a little smug. "I told you he was just as good or better than any medic."

Jerryck looked around. "Did you say there was more than one person who needed help?"

A couple of people watched him while standing at a counter chopping vegetables. Several scullery maids marched through wearing their white aprons and their arms full of clean plates. A couple of young men hauled wood and charcoal from the door to the bailey. Off in one corner, Kendra kneeled beside her crying younger daughter Marla.

"What's wrong with Marla?" he asked.

"She had another bad dream," Leanne said. She hadn't cried over a bad dream since a couple of days before her papa died. Jerryck headed in her direction. Leanne stopped him with a hand on his arm. "Let Kendra finish calming her down."

"Did she talk to Zev yet?" Jerryck asked. Talking to her older brother usually helped calm Marla down.

"Yes, right before she asked for her mama." Leanne tugged him in a different direction. "Let Kendra handle it for now. The head chef needs you too."

Marla saw him and wiped some of her tears away. Kendra turned and made eye contact with him, despite all the busy people between them.

A month had passed since the death of her husband. She pulled her hair up into a knot on her head, a custom she had taken up after that first wretched week of mourning. Her eyes had their normal hue, a brown so light they were almost golden, the same as his. They weren't bloodshot, red, or puffy from weeping. She still had baggy, dark circles under them. The last time he'd offered her a sleep spell to help out, she nearly sliced off his ears with her words. Other than that, everything was normal. She showed no signs of undue heat.

Jerryck let his wife lead him through one of the side doors, into a much smaller room where prepared dishes were normally laid out to go into either the banquet hall or the common dining hall. At the moment there were only stacks of dirty dishes from lunch. The head chef sat leaning far back in a chair, his head tipped up to the low ceiling with a wet cloth over his forehead.

He opened one glassy eye for Jerryck. He took off the cloth, opened the other eye, and sat up a little. "Oh, good. Your sister said you'd come."

"What's this?" Jerryck took the cloth. It dripped over his hand onto the floor.

"My head hurts bad," the chef said. "Feels like there's a fire behind my eyes. Making me want to throw up. Bad for a kitchen."

"Okay, but what's that got to do with this?" Jerryck waggled the wet cloth.

"I thought a damp cloth would cool the fire."

"This isn't damp." Jerryck watched it drip onto the floor. "It's soaked."

"Damp didn't work. So I made it damper. I think it made it worse, not better."

If something in the water had given him the headache, then he had absorbed more through his skin, and yes, that would make it worse. Not better.

Marla came in, followed closely by Kendra. The little girl asked, "Jerryck, are you making all the sick people better?"

"Trying to." He dropped the wet cloth onto one of the stacks of dirty plates.

What exactly was causing this problem? There had to be some way past the cover Tajor had mentioned. He knew of one simple method that might work. He'd discovered it during youthful experimentations. He sent it to the Gathering of Seats for approval and checked on it every few years. The last several times, they had informed him that it was "under review." That was a step up from "pending" which meant they'd at least looked at it. They hadn't rejected it. He could probably get away with using it. Probably.

"I'm sorry," Marla said with a sniffle.

"For what?" He got down on one knee beside her to put himself at her eye level. "You didn't make people sick."

"Then what did?"

"I think something is wrong with the water."

The chef sat up a little more. "You do?"

"I need materials to put together a test to make sure," Jerryck said. "Simple things. Like either sugar or salt sprinkled on parchment."

"I'll get them." Marla ran from the room.

"Thank you for that," Kendra said. "When she gets past the crying, the best thing for her is to feel useful."

While they waited for Marla, Jerryck worked magic on the chef for pain relief. It didn't nullify the headache completely, but it helped enough that he went back to work.

Marla returned with some sheets of parchment and two clay jars. She set them down in a clear spot on one of the tables saying, "This one's sugar. And this one's salt."

"I didn't need both." Jerryck laid one of the parchments flat. "Just one."

"Sugar and salt aren't substitutes for each other," Kendra said.

"They are if all you need is something granular that dissolves quickly in liquid." Jerryck unlatched the lid of the jar closest to his hand, the sugar.

"You're not using the whole thing, are you?" Kendra picked up the salt.

"I only need about a teaspoon." Jerryck scooped some out and sprinkled it on the parchment. "Or less. This'll do."

He drew energy around his hand yet again, this time forming it into something that would temporarily make auras visible to everyday sight. Marla grinned when it made his hand glow. He ran his left hand through the energy, tweaking it to make it passive and latent, unless there was an opening for the energy to release through. The glow subsided, and he tuned what he had shaped to the sugar sprinkled on the parchment. Finally, he spoke the words that severed the energy from himself. The magic did exactly as he intended, attaching itself evenly across every sugar granule.

"Are you going to give that to the sick people?" Marla asked.

"No." Jerryck pinched a few granules onto the wet cloth the chef had used.

When the sugar dissolved, it left an opening for the magic to release through, activating it, funneling it through what had dissolved the sugar. It lit up in a colorful glow. The bold blue of water. The silver of his own work. There was also a thin layer of navy blue, most likely some sort of manipulation magic. Under that was an even thinner, sickly layer of red and blue bound together with black.

The off-color slowly faded, still affecting the water, growing weaker and weaker. Whatever had contaminated the water wasn't caught in the cloth, just the effects of it. Heston was right. Jerryck had to go test the vats.

"Don't let anyone drink any water," Jerryck said. He folded the parchment around the rest of the magicked sugar. "Don't cook with it or put it in any food."

"What do I tell people?" Kendra asked.

"Tell them I'm doing more tests," Jerryck said.

Chapter 4

E LEFT the kitchens and went straight to the vat chamber. There, about half a dozen men worked winches, pulleys, and buckets to bring up water from the canal chamber directly below. They kept full two wooden containers, each the size of a small room, that people could draw water from simply by working a spigot at the bottom.

One of the men drank from a large mug. His head and shirt were soaking wet. His face dripped. He drained the mug and refilled it from the spigot.

Jerryck snatched the mug before the man could drink. "Let me see that."

"I need it." The man panted while he spoke. "I'm burning up. I can't stop sweating."

"Something might be wrong with the water," Jerryck said.

All the men paused their work, instantly focused on him. He took the parchment with the magicked sugar and dropped a pinch into the mug. He got the same result as the wet cloth in the kitchens, even the gradual fading effect of the colors that weren't supposed to be there. He hadn't gotten the particle of the contaminant this time either. Just the tainted aura.

Navy blue was the right color for some of the covering magic he knew. If it was the kind that took on the appearance and attributes of whatever it was in, concealing what it covered, that would explain why he hadn't been able to find it earlier. He could run further tests later to verify. For now, he needed to catch a particle of the actual taint. And whatever that was, lay in the vats.

How could it have gotten in there? Each vat stood twice as tall as the average man and just as wide. Open at the top, the length was twice that. A narrow, wooden walkway surrounded the tops for maintenance, accessible by a single ladder built into the wall.

Jerryck pointed to the tops. "Has anyone been up there recently?"

"Not since the last weekly maintenance and inspection a few days ago," one of the men said.

A string of buckets on a vertical rope made a pillar in the narrow space between the vats. Down below, the gurgle of water echoed up from the canal where water was channeled underground from the river then back out again. Was the contaminant diluted enough that it could be in the river itself?

Jerryck dumped the water in the mug. He cast one regretful glance at the vertical shaft. If he'd known he'd need water directly from the canal he'd have gone down there. Instead, he climbed the ladder and navigated the narrow walkway to the string of buckets.

He refilled the mug directly from one of them. He took it back down to the floor and repeated the sugar test. This time, the colors of the contaminant didn't fade. They stayed strong and constant. In fact, they radiated outward, pushing, contaminating everything around them. He'd caught a piece of it.

"Well?" Heston's deep voice growled from behind him.

"Oh!" Jerryck spun around, nearly spilling the water in the mug. "I didn't see you come in."

"Obviously." Heston crossed his thick arms. "What did you find?"

Jerryck lifted the mug, still glowing. Heston shook his head. "I don't know what that means. Just tell me whether or not the water is drinkable."

"I wouldn't drink it." Jerryck looked into the mug. He pointed at the colors. "See this—"

Heston held up a hand. "Not here. We take this to the king."

Jerryck folded the sugar back into the parchment and stuffed it in his pocket. King Terrance ended court at noon. He should have finished lunch along with everyone else. There were no group meetings scheduled for today, so he was likely in his office meeting face-to-face with whoever was on his schedule.

"Don't let anyone draw from the vats," Heston said to the workers.

"For how long?" one of them asked.

"Until you're told otherwise by a member of the core staff," Heston said. "Get the hoses ready in case we have to drain them."

He and Jerryck went to the reception outside the king's office. By the time they got there, the magic had worn off the water in the mug. The glow disappeared. They crossed the floor between the chairs and benches of waiting people to where the king's aide was now arguing with Head Medic Kellos.

"I don't make the rules," the aide said. He stood between his chair and his desk, nose to nose with Kellos.

"What about his next appointment?" Kellos tapped the schedule book. "That can be delayed."

"That's someone who came in three days ago." The aide moved Kellos' finger off the book. "He's already been delayed. More than once. I already told you. Write a note, I'll take it to him in between."

Heston slapped his hands down on the book, interrupting them. "Who's in there with him now?"

"Chamberlain Malk and Priad Lalven," the aide said.

Heston took his hands off the book. "Perfect. Summon the rest of the core staff and send them through as soon as they get here."

Heston barged into the office. Jerryck hung back, not quite so bold. Kellos started in. The aide held up a hand to stop him. "You're not part of the core staff."

"We need him," Jerryck said. Since Jerryck was one of the five men on the core staff, the aide couldn't really argue with that. Jerryck and Kellos both went in.

Stacks of papers still littered Terrance's busy desk. In two armchairs before it sat Lalven and Malk. Terrance stood by them and looked up at the entry. "We have an emergency?"

"People are sick," Kellos said.

"Sick people?" Lalven scowled. He sat slumped in his seat, his soft paunch sticking out, one hand absently rubbing the center of his chest. "We're making plans for when the Shontese delegation arrives and you interrupt because a few people are sick?"

"Is your heartburn bothering you again?" Kellos asked.

Lalven jerked his hand away from himself. "Something I ate for lunch is bothering me, that's all. What difference does that make?"

"So far," Kellos said, "every person affected by this ailment is experiencing heat in some way or another."

Lalven sat up straighter. "I'm not sick."

"Jerryck," Heston said. "Show them what you found."

"Whatever's causing this is in the river." Jerryck set the mug on the king's desk. He snagged another pinch of the magic sugar and dropped it in.

Except for Heston, everyone leaned in to the mug. Terrance asked, "What are we looking at here?"

Jerryck waved a hand through the glowing colors. "This is the aura of the water in the mug. I made it so you can see it — temporarily."

"I thought pure water was supposed to be just blue," Kellos said. "What magic did you use to get this effect?"

"Just a little trick Old Heldavio taught me a long time ago." Jerryck stretched the truth. Heldavio, the previous court magician and Jerryck's mentor, hadn't taught him to link to an object that would melt, leaving an open end for the magic to latch onto something else.

"What's this thin layer of black?" Kellos ran his finger through it.

"That's what's making people sick," Jerryck said. "I haven't yet identified exactly what it is. I'm fairly sure it's elemental, fire probably. I do know that's our contaminant."

"Magic might explain the variety of symptoms." Kellos withdrew his hand from the mug. "Everyone is reacting to this differently."

Terrance stood straight. "You said they're all experiencing heat?"

Kellos nodded. "In varying forms. Hot tempers, heat rashes, searing headaches. Lalven isn't the only one with heartburn. A lot of people are feverish, and more are sweating and flushed."

Lalven drew in a breath and opened his mouth. Before he could speak, Terrance said, "How would something like this get in the river? Could there have been some sort of accident?"

"You see this?" Jerryck stuck his finger in the navy-blue layer. "That's a concealing manipulation spell. Again, I'd have to run more tests, but it's likely what we call a chameleon. It appears to take on the aura of whatever it's in, to cover what it's hiding."

"Not an accident," Heston said. "I'll collect information from upstream, find out if this was put directly into the main body, or if it's feeding and from a tributary river."

Lalven sank into his chair and went back to rubbing his chest. "We need to get the rest of the core staff in here and plan damage control."

"I already sent for them," Heston said.

"We can't have this here when the Shontese delegation arrives." Chamberlain Malk leaned back from the desk and drummed the arm of his chair with his fingertips. "Jerryck, how long before you can clear it out?"

"I don't think I can," Jerryck said. "I haven't definitively identified it. I can barely even isolate it. We'll have to wait it out."

"We can't wait it out." Malk stopped drumming and gripped his chair. "This delegation is headed up by the grandnephew of their prince. If word gets back to them, if they even think he could be in any kind of danger from this…"

"He's still a couple weeks away," Terrance said. "We'll deal with that situation if and when it becomes a problem."

"I'd worry more about the local populace and the Brendish nobles." Lalven stood and paced. "We'll need a cover story. If anyone thinks this is some form of sabotage, they'll cry for blood before asking who's guilty. Also, you may need to put tight controls on all consumable liquids to prevent merchants from price gouging."

"Heston, get your searches started," Terrance said. "Then come back as soon as you can. We'll need you for planning control. Malk, start coming up with contingency plans regarding the Shontese delegation. Jerryck, if you can't clear the water, I want it monitored. Test it three times daily until it's clear. Kellos, do you need Jerryck's help caring for the ill?"

"We're overwhelmed," Kellos said. "At least half the patients prefer a magician over a medic, since one's available."

"Then, Jerryck, you're dismissed to assist him, just remember — *everyone* remember," he may have addressed everyone, but he stared right at Jerryck. "Outside this room, we put up a good appearance. Act as if everything is under control. Go about your daily activities and routines as best as the situation allows. No one says anything about magic tainting the water."

Chapter 5

TESTING THE WATER was more of a chore than anticipated. Obtaining it was easy. The testing process was easy. But the household steward wanted the results. Getting through the chaos and mess of people outside his office to hand him the test took far longer than suited Jerryck. And that was when people didn't try to waylay him to ask for information, opinions, favors, or make requests. So when he received a summons from the king, he nearly leaped at the opportunity to escape.

He quickly made his way to the White Room, so called for the lack of color in the decor. That was where the king formally greeted important guests, even if the visit was an unscheduled surprise. Jerryck wasn't usually summoned for it, unless the guest was a practitioner of some sort of magic or had one with them.

Terrance, Heston, and Lalven were already there, in the middle of a discussion. Lalven had his nose tilted up. "I still say you ought to throw them into dungeon cells. They're just here to survey their handiwork."

"I want to talk to them." Terrance dressed in dark velvets, a stark contrast to his surroundings. White furnishings. White plaster on the walls. Rugs bleached to match. The only colors were the light fixtures, the scene outside the large windows, and the people.

"They'll lie," Lalven said with a sneer. He glanced over at Jerryck's entrance. Then his eyes shifted back to the door as Princess Nita entered.

"I apologize for the delay," she said to her father. "I was in the middle of dealing with a minor situation."

"It's taken care of?" the king responded.

"Yes," she said. "Jerryck, I'm glad you're here. Zev and Darren will bring you water to test from now on until it clears. Don't be nice to them."

"Were they fighting again?" Jerryck frowned. Zev had been finding every excuse possible to punch people over the past month.

"It's taken care of." Nita folded her hands primly in front of herself. "This is their punishment."

"Coming up to my tower is punishment?"

"No," she said, then smiled. "Well, it kind of is for Darren, since his parents are some of those silly people who don't trust magicians. They'll likely make him sorry for it. The real punishment is when they try to hand over the water test. Everything's a mess in the household offices right now. Too much chaos. If they want to cause trouble, they need to help smooth some of it out."

"Very good." Terrance nodded approval. Then he turned to the general and said, "Heston, if you please."

"I got reports from upstream," Heston told everyone. "We traced the poison to a tributary that comes from the Chemwanitz Mountains."

"This quick?" Jerryck was surprised. "It's only been a few days."

"People drinking from the tributary have more severe symptoms," Heston said. "Open burns and blisters on their skin. The farther east you go, past other smaller tributaries, it gets worse. Word was already headed our way before we started looking."

Nita paled at the description of increased severity. "Have we sent them aid yet?"

"A caravan is already being put together to leave," Lalven said, turning his sneer on her. "As if that's any of your concern. Your duties are to play hostess."

Nita sneered right back at him. "I know my duties better than you."

"Stop, both of you." Terrance used the same tired tone that parents did sometimes when their children bickered.

"Maybe you should relieve her of this particular hostess duty," Lalven said. "Even I wouldn't want her to have to entertain some Chemwanee shaman and a couple of hunters."

"Shaman*ess*," Terrance said. "And her two sons. Heston, would you mind fetching them please."

Nita watched Heston leave and asked, "Not a page?"

"He asked to escort them in," Terrance said. "It shows more intimidation in case they really are here for nefarious reasons."

"This shamaness," Jerryck said. "She's the reason you summoned me?"

"My suggestion." Lalven's sneer finally relaxed, letting his small jowls sag back into place. "I know the shamans use magic differently than you magicians. But you can tell us if she's trying to pull any shenanigans of a magical nature."

"I'm not supposed to associate with any practitioner of shamanism," Jerryck said. "The Gathering of Seats hates them."

"Your first duty is to your king, not the Gathering." Lalven's face flushed. "Your insight and advice could be valuable here. Besides, this saves you the trouble of having to allow that woman up in your tower out of protocol if you just meet her here and have done with the formalities."

Heston returned so quickly they had to have been waiting in the next room. With him came Chamberlain Malk, a gold haired woman, and two fair featured men. The latter three wore the leathers and furs that enhanced most people's impression that the Chemwanee were all barbarians. At least their weapons were absent. Normally they carried bows, knives, and spears the way some people wore necklaces, rings, and bracelets.

"Your Majesty, Your Royal Highness," Malk said, keeping the introductions to the king and his daughter formal. "I present to you her ladyship, the Shamaness Sakila of the Chempagquin, translated as the tribe of the jagged finger peak, with her two sons, the hunters Arlos and Shagiro."

"Welcome to Brend," Terrance said to them. He sat on one of the couches, turning the situation casual. Everyone except the guests also took a seat, Nita right beside him. Then he skipped most of the regular pleasantries. "Now then, what brings you to my palace?"

"We came to bring bad news." Sakila did not speak with the accent most Chemwanee did. She gestured to the older looking of her two sons and continued. "Arlos was leading a hunt when they found two strangers walking our land. They did not make any trouble. The hunters followed them in secret to make sure they were just passing through. They stopped and poured water into a small river from a jar they never drank from."

Lalven snorted with derision. "That sounds rather ridiculous."

"Arlos thought it strange and ridiculous too," Sakila said. "He and his hunters took the two strangers and brought them to our tribe. I used magic to try to see what they had carried in the jar. I only found water. I asked them why they poured water into the river. They did not answer. I thought perhaps they did not understand. I asked them in two other languages. Still, they did not answer."

Jerryck leaned forward. If he could get his hands on that jar, he could run all kinds of tests. Sakila continued on. "The hunt chief became angry. He had the jar refilled, and ordered the men be made to drink from it. They grew afraid and asked him not to do that. So they understood my question. I asked again why. They still did not answer. They just cried and begged."

Jerryck sat back again. Terrance frowned. Nita stiffened beside him. Everyone knew that a Chemwanee never made idle threats.

"What happened when they drank?" Terrance asked.

"They burned." Sakila held out a hand to her sons. The younger took a leather bag from the pouch on his belt and gave it to her. She presented it to Terrance. "We bring you their ashes to do with as you please."

"They were actually on fire?" Jerryck burst out as Malk accepted the leather sack for Terrance.

"Yes," Sakila said. "They burned. Then I saw there was bad elemental magic. I have not figured out why I could not see the aura of the element magic before that, while it was still in the water."

"Do you still have the jar they used?" Jerryck asked.

"I am sorry, no," Sakila said. "When the men burned, there was much chaos. The jar fell and broke."

Jerryck struggled not to show his disappointment. He sat back, swallowing, gripping the arms of the chair. Lalven leaned forward, eyes narrowed at him. He pursed his lips. Did he want something of Jerryck? Perhaps something should be said. Jerryck had no idea what.

Lalven cleared his throat and glared at the shamaness. "Perhaps, if you had nothing to hide, or if more care was taken in concern for us here in Brend downstream—"

"Have you ever seen someone burning?" Jerryck clenched his teeth. "Even an animal? It's not something you can calmly stand by and watch. It's terrifying. I somehow doubt they broke the jar out of maliciousness or lack of concern for us."

Lalven sat back. The shamaness stared open mouthed. Jerryck avoided her eyes, avoided looking at anyone in the room. He didn't like reminding people how he had discovered he had magical capabilities. Terrance glanced at him. Then he crossed one ankle over his knee, stretching out his arm across the couch. That drew all attention back to him.

"The Chempagquin tribe..." he said. "Isn't that near the district of Tarn?"

"Yes," Sakila said. "I know your family ties there. I bring you a letter from your Premiere Grinnald. He told me to deliver my entire message to you first. But if you want it, I will give you his letter now."

"Is his water affected by this?" Terrance asked.

Sakila shook her head. "This river is north of him."

"Is he aware of what happened?"

"Yes."

Terrance held out his hand. "The letter, please."

Without hesitation, she pulled a letter from her own belt pouch that bore the seal of the premiere of Tarn. She didn't ask if she could finish her message. She didn't try to add any caveats like most nobles would. She simply handed it over without a word.

She waited politely while he read it. She didn't interrupt or distract. She stood still as a stone, asked nothing, did nothing, until Terrance handed the parchment to the princess, who had been trying to read over his arm.

"We do not have enough gifts to pay you for letting this happen," she said. "We in the Chemwanitz Mountains do not keep what you here in Brend think of as wealth. So we offer you our people and our land."

Terrance smiled at her. "You owe me nothing."

Sakila's eyebrows drew together in confusion. "We brought you bad news..."

"You brought me good news."

"How can this be good?"

"We discovered the problem with the water a couple of days ago," Terrance said. "We've been trying to figure this out. The information you bring helps. It's good. Thank you. In fact, by your customs, I should be offering you gifts in gratitude."

"I'll make certain they have appropriate gifts," Chamberlain Malk said.

Sakila wore astonishment so openly even Jerryck would have been hard put to miss it. Her elder son said something in their language. She blinked like someone coming out of a stupor and gave him a short response.

"Would you like one of your sons to take the gifts back to your people with my thanks for the good news?" Terrance asked. "I will extend an invitation for you and your other son to stay in my home as my guests. That way, you can bring back word to your people as soon as the water clears, if that will ease their minds."

Sakila stood gaping for a few moments longer before slowly saying, "Your brother was right about you."

Terrance raised an eyebrow. "Brother?"

"Premiere Grinnald."

"Oh." A flash of sadness passed through Terrance's eyes, then was gone as quickly as it appeared. "He was my wife's brother."

"Yes, your brother," Sakila said. "He insisted you would treat us like family and make everything right. I feared to believe him. He is your family, so I have no doubt you treat him as such. You had never met us."

"Not even Nita?" Terrance looked at his daughter. "She goes to visit at least once a year. More if she can manage it."

"I have always stayed away to let Grinnald enjoy his time with his niece without extra guests," Sakila said. Her face softened, the astonishment all but gone. "Now that we meet, she looks much like I remember of her mother."

The sadness flashed again in Terrance's eyes, even as Nita's lit up with delight. She said, "You met my mother?"

"Long ago," Sakila said. She looked at Terrance and added, "You need give us no gifts. You treat us as family, we will treat you the same. And I will send Arlos. Shagiro and I will accept your invitation to stay as guests."

36

"Promise me one thing," Terrance said, holding up one finger. "If you need or want anything during your stay, you'll ask."

"May I have time with your magician?"

"Of course," Terrance said.

Jerryck caught his breath and clenched his teeth to hold in his excitement. He wasn't supposed to speak to magic practitioners other than Gathering-sanctioned magicians. Even speaking with the summoners of the southern continent was hardly tolerated, despite the treaty that had been signed during Jerryck's youth. He should say no. He should tell Terrance he couldn't do it. He should find some excuse to back out. He should. But the prospect of asking questions and learning new magic was just too tempting.

Priad Lalven clenched his teeth too. He evidenced his irritation by using formalities, "Your Majesty, you're going to just let her run around sightseeing in the palace with someone like Jerryck?"

Terrance didn't look at him. "Is there a problem?"

Lalven leaned in and whispered, just loud enough for Jerryck to hear. "We're still dealing with the mess he made with the Shontese court magician. He's too inobservant. She could be seeking weaknesses in our defenses and he'd never know the difference."

Terrance uncrossed his ankle and put his foot on the floor. "Go help prepare lodgings for our two guests and see that their accommodations are appropriate for foreign nobles."

"Malk is much better at choosing the servants to oversee such details," Lalven replied, glancing over at the Chamberlain.

Terrance turned his head just enough to look Lalven square in the eye. "I didn't tell you to pick servants to do the job. And don't worry. Malk will still help you make sure everything is up to the standards I require."

"Absolutely." Malk stood, beaming from ear to ear. "Lady Shamaness, do either of your sons speak Brendish? Or should I provide an interpreter for them?"

"I speak little Brendish," the older son spoke up.

"Shagiro is learning." Sakila touched her younger son's arm. "No interpreter please. It will make learning slower for him."

"As you wish," Malk said as he headed for the door. "If you'll please follow Lalven and I, we'll get everything prepared for you."

Sakila hesitated. "May I go with the magician now instead?"

"Of course you may." Terrance answered before Jerryck could say a thing.

Chapter 6

AKILA FOLLOWED Jerryck out of the room. What exactly was he supposed to do now? Visiting magicians always came to him in his tower, if he couldn't get rid of them first. But all magicians were men. Would his wife be all right with him taking another woman up to his work room? Even on a professional basis?

Princess Nita came out of the White Room. She giggled at Jerryck. "What are you doing just standing out here?"

"I... Um..." Jerryck stammered. How did he explain uncertainty to someone who always knew what to do with guests?

"Have you ever been to Kershet City?" Nita asked Sakila, who shook her head. "The day is clear enough, we should have a wonderful view from some of our higher outside balconies. Jerryck, why don't you go and show her that?"

"Good idea." Jerryck beamed at the princess. "Thank you."

He headed for a wide set of stairs that went to the floors that housed important guests. Large, glass-paned windows let in light that toyed with crystal-hung chandeliers lining the vaulted ceilings. The thick runner carpet muffled their footsteps. The walls were softened with painted artist renditions of people, landscapes, and historical scenes. All this was a vast contrast to the tighter, dimmer back corridors used by most of the workers and residents that Jerryck normally went through.

"This is Amaryllis Hall," Nita said.

39

"I know that," Jerryck said. Why was she still following them?

Nita smiled at him. "Your guest doesn't know."

"Oh, right," Jerryck said. He waved at the corridor as they passed by some of the paintings and told Sakila, "This is Amaryllis Hall. A lot of these art pieces are historical people, or stuff that happened in the history books."

"I'm certain you'll be given a room here," Nita said. "We reserve these rooms only for the most important people and their families."

Sakila's mouth quirked the way Tajor's did sometimes when amused. "You think I am important enough to stay in a place name for a flower?"

"Named for a queen, actually," Nita said. "My step-grandmother. She's the one who decorated this hall the way it is. Except for the family portraits. My father had those put here."

They went up another couple flights of stairs. Nita kept up a running commentary the entire way. They reached the door to the outside balcony on the south side of the palace that would give a good view. There, Jerryck stopped.

He studied the charm placed above the door. Sakila stopped and looked at it too. She pointed at it. "This is some of your work."

"I have one over every door to the outside," Jerryck said. "Some over the wall gates, and on the outbuildings too. They're supposed to alert me when a magic practitioner enters or exits."

"Did they?"

"No, I need to adjust them to recognize shamans," Jerryck said. "I have them adjusted for hydromancers. They come through every once in a while."

"From the coast? Or all the way from the archipelago?"

"Both," Jerryck said.

"This is very interesting." Sakila stared intently at the charm. "I may have to use something similar at home. How do you adjust it so finely so that it detects people who actually use magic, instead of just anyone with a strong aura?"

"People who use magic…" Jerryck said. "Their aura tends to fluctuate more than most others. Because they use it, then regenerate it at greater capacities. That variance and the vibrations that accompany it is what the charms pick up."

"I don't think she's understanding all the words you're using," Nita said.

"Why not?" Jerryck asked.

"Because I don't understand exactly what you're talking about," Nita said with a giggle. "And this isn't a second language to me."

"That is all right," Sakila said. "I will figure it out."

They went out onto the balcony. From this height they could see easily over the wall, down the hill the palace was built on, all the way to Cham River and the capital city. On the lower levels of the palace all the outside balconies had stone balustrades at their edges. This high, balconies had wood railings that were lacquered against the weather. Jerryck had never asked why.

Sakila went to the railing and put both hands on it, looking out across the view. A slow smile grew on her. "Almost like standing on a low bluff."

She walked to the right, her hand brushing along the rail. She pointed to the city. "That is the capital?"

"Kershet City, yes," Nita said, following at Sakila's pace.

"And the big, tall, black building in the center?"

"That's Bershent Fortress," Nita said. "It was built by my ancestor who brought all our districts together to form a unified nation. All of our kings lived there until the palace was built."

"You named your fortress." Sakila looked to her right, up at the palace towers that still stood taller than the high balcony. "Did you name your palace as well?"

"It's called Coraline," Nita said. "My great-grandmother. It was built for her. There are a lot of people who say that's appropriate, since a lot of the stone for it was quarried at the coast, even though there was no coral there."

They rounded the curve of the balcony and Aconi Grove came into view, upstream from the bend in the river were most of the city's docks were built. It was closer to where the river split to go around Unification Isle, where the nation had officially been born. Sakila pointed at the green mass of thick trees. "Did the builders use magic, that they did not have to use all the trees for their wood?"

"Yes," Jerryck said. "They did use magic. The canal beneath the palace—"

"Not that," Nita interrupted him. She said to Sakila, "He means magic was used in some of the planning stages."

He hadn't been talking about just the planning. He tried again. "And in the spells that—"

"—like the charms you use," Nita interrupted him again for some reason. "Over the doors."

Jerryck frowned. Was he committing some kind of social blunder in talking about the details of magic in the palace? He didn't want to create another foreign relations mess.

"Most of the lumber came from other areas of the country," Nita said. "This area used to be mostly forest, but a lot of it was harvested when Kershet was built. These trees were left because a dryad lives at the center. Aconi Grove is named for her."

"Wise to leave the grove," Sakila said. "Dryads do get rather violent when you try to take trees too close to theirs."

"There's a pond in there," Nita said. "A lot of our most famous artists have done their greatest works on its banks."

She took a breath to say more, but stopped when a page came and found them. The lad nodded acknowledgment to the princess then turned to Jerryck. "Lord Magician, Lady Leanne requests your assistance with one of her charges in the infirmary."

"Thank you for helping me with the guest," Jerryck said to the princess. Then left the balcony and went to the infirmary.

The reception room was lined with cots. Groaning people filled them. All the benches that people normally used to wait were pushed up against the walls. Still more sat or lay on the floor, filling nearly all the space available.

"No! No! No!" One of the medics in the room came forward, fury on his face. He pointed behind Jerryck. "Get out! We don't have time for this chicanery. Out. Begone with you."

Jerryck glanced back. Sakila had followed him. She watched, completely nonplussed, as the medic waved his arms and shook a fist at her. Whispers rippled through the reception room, across the cots and benches, everyone staring at the shamaness. She didn't grace them with acknowledgment.

"She's with me," Jerryck told the medic just as Kellos entered the reception area from the back of the room.

"Shows what kind of person you are," the medic said with a snarl. "Keeping that kind of company. Maybe this will finally open people's eyes to how worthless you are."

"That's enough." Kellos came over to them. He stood in front of the medic. "You don't talk that way about a member of the king's core staff."

"The king should get rid of this charlatan and put you in his place."

"Go back to your quarters," Kellos said. "I'm relieving you of duty."

"*What?*"

"You're obviously overworked and too tired to think straight, or you wouldn't be spouting such nonsense. We can't have someone in your condition attempting to triage the patients that come in. We need someone with a clearer head."

The medic stood staring at Kellos, not moving. Kellos nudged him away. "Go. Now. I'll find someone to cover your shift."

"He brought a Chemwanee woman in our infirmary." The medic bared his teeth, but stepped back. "We don't need that kind of trash in here with our patients."

"She speaks Brendish," Jerryck said. "And Terrance wants her treated like visiting nobility."

"And you shouldn't talk like that about anyone who comes to us," Kellos said. "If I have to tell you again to go back to your quarters, I will relieve you of your position permanently."

The medic closed his mouth and set his jaw. He stomped out, glaring back at them every few steps. Kellos said to Jerryck, "My apologies for that. Now then, is she sick? Chemwanee generally prefer their shamans for healing services."

"She's a shamaness," Jerryck said. "She's not sick."

Kellos' face darkened. He stepped closer and whispered in Jerryck's ear. "What are you doing with a shamaness?"

"Protocol," Jerryck said.

"What are her intentions? How do you know she's not going to hurt you?"

Jerryck lowered his voice to match Kellos'. "She came to help us figure out the water. And I only came here because Leanne asked for me. Where is she? And what does she need?"

"She's this way." Kellos turned and headed into the corridor at the back. He frowned when Sakila followed a step behind Jerryck, but his voice stayed calm and measured. "One of the pregnant women is refusing to eat. Her paranoia and emotions are going to her head. She's terrified she'll poison her baby with whatever's in the water. We tried showing her there's nothing wrong with her baby and insisted she eat. She demanded we get you."

They stopped at a room about midway up the corridor on the left. The door was open. Inside, Leanne sat by a cot bearing a woman rubbing her swollen belly. Leanne smiled at them and said to the woman, "There he is. See? I told you he would come as soon as he could."

"Took long enough," the woman said.

Farther up the corridor, one of the other medics called to Kellos. At the same time, one closer to the reception chamber beckoned him with a wave.

"Excuse me," Kellos said. He headed for the one that had called from up the corridor. The one from the reception chamber ran after him, whipping past Jerryck and Sakila as if they weren't even there.

"Are you going to help me or not?" The pregnant woman was scowling at Jerryck. "Didn't I wait long enough just for you to come?"

"Sorry that took some time," Jerryck said. "I was in a meeting with the King. Then he asked me to see to a guest."

The woman blanched for some reason. Her belly wriggled. She absently rubbed that spot. Leanne patted her arm. "I'll just step out and let him know what your concerns are."

Jerryck stepped back to let Leanne out, and nearly tripped over a page running up the corridor. Leanne shut the door. Jerryck said, "Kellos told me she's afraid to eat."

"She has to eat." Leanne kept her voice quiet. A blush crept up her neck and she stared at the shamaness.

"This is Sakila." Jerryck quickly introduced the shamaness to stave off his wife's bashfulness around strangers and nobility. "She's not a noble. We're just treating her like one. It's okay, she's not even Brendish."

"You're silly sometimes." Leanne smiled at him, her blush subsiding. "Anyway, my patient. She's used to medics. Right now, she's just scared. She thought she'd hear your opinion, give you a try."

"I'm not sure what I can do," Jerryck said, holding up his hands in puzzlement. "If she's used to medics and she won't believe what they tell her..."

Leanne's face brightened up like an idea had just struck her. She pointed a finger at him. "Your water test! Can you do that with her food so she can see that it doesn't have that black part?"

Sakila cocked her head. "Black part?"

"I'll show you as soon as I get a chance," Jerryck told her. Then he said to Leanne, "I don't have the materials here to do that. They're all the way up in my tower."

"Didn't you say it's just sugar with a spell?" Leanne asked. "There's sugar here in the infirmary. Do you need anything else beside that?"

"No, I can do it with just sugar," Jerryck said. Kellos and the waving medic came down the corridor in their direction. Jerryck pressed himself against the wall to make room for them to pass. "You think that'll satisfy her?"

Sakila also pressed against the wall and said, "If it does not satisfy, it may distract. That may be enough."

"We can try it," Jerryck said.

Leanne left to fetch the sugar. Sakila watched Kellos and the medic disappear into one of the rooms. She said, "When you are done here, can you show me this water test with a black part, somewhere with less happening?"

"I can show you here," Jerryck said. A child wailed somewhere, momentarily distracting them both.

Sakila shook her head. "I have too many questions. It will take longer. There are too many people here and we are in their way."

Three more people traversed the corridor before Leanne returned. After that, it was a simple matter of putting on a demonstration for the pregnant woman. Jerryck did it first with water, pointing out the black color. Then he did it with a plate of food, pointing out the lack of the black color.

The woman pointed to the small amount of sugar he had magicked but hadn't used. "Can I keep this?"

Jerryck shrugged. "I guess so, if you promise to start eating again."

The woman sat up straighter. "I promise."

"You can start right now," Leanne said. "Eat what's on that plate."

The woman took her first bite, and Leanne stepped back out of the room with Jerryck. She said, "Thank you so much."

"Yes," Jerryck said to Sakila. "Thank you."

"I was talking to you," Leanne said, leaning in close to him. She looked at Sakila. "But he's right. Thanks to you too. Are you going up to the tower with Jerryck?"

"Is that all right with you?" Jerryck asked.

"Is she not a magic practitioner?" Leanne blushed. She looked away. "I'm sorry. I assumed, because she was with you…"

"She is," Jerryck said. "But she's a woman. I wasn't sure you wanted me to do that."

"I trust you," Leanne whispered in his ear, her shy blush fading.

Chapter 7

SAKILA FOLLOWED Jerryck back down the corridor. They passed by Kellos again, who frowned once more at the shamaness. Then out in the reception chamber, the replacement medic there scowled at her too. A couple of people reached out to Jerryck as he wended his way through the rows of cots. They stopped when they saw her following him.

Inside the palace proper, more people stopped him in the corridors. Most of them asked for advice on caring for family members or friends with symptoms too mild to send them to the infirmary. They all eyed the shamaness with suspicion. When he led her to his tower and shut the door behind him, he leaned against it and breathed a sigh of relief before climbing the four flights of stairs to his workroom.

He offered Sakila one of his three pine stools. She sat at the worktable and asked, "What is this water test you do with a black part?"

He took out the sugar he used on the daily test and put in front of her. He didn't have any of the tainted water on hand. He should have thought of that on his way to the tower. Too many distractions. He glanced around his workroom for a little something that would work for a demonstration.

Sakila stared hard at the sugar on the table. "What magic is linked to the sugar? And why? If the sugar melts, will that not leave one side of the link open?"

"Yes," Jerryck said.

How had she figured that out so quickly? There was no flair in her aura, so she hadn't used magic. Was she more sensitive than he? So much so that she could actually feel out the magic on the sugar? Just how powerful was she?

She looked up at him expectantly. "What does it do?"

"It makes magic glow so you can see its colors."

"You cannot see magic's colors by adjusting your sight? Like when you see a person's aura?"

"That's different." Jerryck sat on another stool opposite the table from her.

"Why?" She leaned her elbows on the table, one on each side of the sugar. "A spell is just a piece of the aura of the one who cast it. Why is it different?"

He shook his head. "Magic has its own aura."

"It looks that way because the color is usually different from the strongest color of the caster. It does not have its own aura. If you read the waves, you read the mark of the caster."

"Waves?" Jerryck gave her a confused look. "I've never heard that term in reference to magic."

"Perhaps I have the wrong word." She tapped a finger on the table momentarily, like some people did while they were thinking. Then she said, "When water shakes, it gets waves on its top. Perhaps shaking is the right word. What do you call it when something shakes so much that it seems to buzz, like the hum of a bee?"

"Vibration?"

"Yes, vibration, that is the word. Vibration makes waves. And all energy is vibration."

"Huh?"

"All energy is vibration," she repeated. "Magic is energy. It vibrates. Vibration makes waves. And no two waves are the same. Every spell you cast will match the wave for your aura."

"You're talking about signatures." Jerryck leaned forward, drinking in the new angle of thinking. "I know about signatures. I've just never heard them described like that."

She smiled. "How many shamans have you spoken with?"

"You're the first."

"We do use magic," she said. "Though we prefer to study it. This has led us to use it differently than you magicians."

Jerryck frowned. "That doesn't make sense. The more you study it, the more that should lead you to doing it the way we do."

"Why?"

"The more you study, the more you understand how dangerous magic can be. We follow specific safety rules because the more complex and difficult the spell, the more dangerous it is." As soon as he said it, he realized he was feeding her the teachings the Gathering of Seats put out. Perhaps he was more influenced by them than he thought.

"Not if you study enough to know what you are dealing with, how to avoid the dangers, and how to avoid what you are weak with."

"Magicians have tried doing it that way in the past," Jerryck said. "They ended up dead."

"Is that what you're Gathering told you?"

"Yes." The word left a bitter taste in his mouth. His mentor had expressed no love for the Gathering and he had instilled that disdain on Jerryck during his apprenticeship. It felt wrong to admit that he was spouting off their claims without even thinking about it.

"And these magicians who ended up dead," Sakila said. "Were they studying shamanism?"

"Of course not."

Her smile turned a bit smug. "That is why they ran into danger. Studying magic the way we do makes us more careful. We learn exactly what the dangers are so we can avoid them, instead of following silly rules imagined up by other people that keep us blind to the real problems we face."

"Is that what you think the Gathering is good for?" He half smiled with bemusement. "Keeping magicians blind?"

"They keep people from even looking." Her smile disappeared. "No one can tell if they would be good at anything other than spellcasting, like you magicians."

Jerryck leaned forward again. "Do you look for any abilities beside shamanism?"

"Of course," she said. "And when we find someone so gifted they cannot stop themselves from using magic, we send them where they can learn. A boy from my village went to study with a summoner in Ahnjwat almost 10 years ago. My chosen brother, before he died, knew of a young set of twins who always received anything they put effort into praying for. He sent them far to the east to study with a priest."

Jerryck rested both his elbows on his sturdy worktable. "How would you tell if someone is able to do shamanism?"

"I give a little test," she said. "Then I can tell if they have the ability and they can see if they actually want to study more."

"What's your test?"

"I have never heard of a magician asking this many questions." She sat a little straighter, looking rather pleased. "I thought none of you would even speak with me at all."

"Don't tell anyone," Jerryck said, smiling sheepishly. "With the history of past conflicts between shamans and the Gathering of Seats, none of us are supposed to talk to any of you."

"I will tell no one. Would you like me to give you the test? Just for fun?"

He sat up, spine straight, shoulders back. "Absolutely."

"I normally use tea—" she looked around the shelves in the work room— "but since the water is bad, do you have something else here that uses every element?"

"I have some clean water." Jerryck got up and snagged his teapot. "One of the privileges of being on the king's core staff."

He poured two cups and magically heated them. He added the tea and set them on the table to steep. Sakila held her palm just over the lip of the cup nearest to her, the steam from the water curling around her hand. "Can you feel an aura without casting a spell?"

He opened his mouth to tell her no, but hesitated. That was what he would tell other magicians. She wasn't a follower of the Gathering. She certainly wouldn't report his answer to them. He said, "I think… Sometimes? I've never done it on purpose."

"You have never felt your own aura on purpose?"

He shrugged. "With magic, lots of times."

"Can you clear your mind?"

"I do every time I prepare to cast a difficult spell," he said.

"When you do that, do you feel energy around your body like a cloud?"

"Yes." That was another thing he would never admit to other magicians. His mentor had advised him to keep that information to himself. Very strongly advised.

"That is your aura," Sakila said. "Clear your mind until you feel that."

Jerryck did so. He had practiced and done it so much throughout his career, it took him very little time. He was just about to tell her he was ready, when she pushed his teacup closer to him and said, "Now, put your hands just over this and feel its aura combined with yours."

Jerryck placed his hand over the cup without touching it, just as she had. Steam from the hot tea warmed his palm. The sensation of his aura now came in contact with a foreign energy. Everything about it was alien. He began to withdraw.

"Wait." She pushed her own hands near his. Again he came in contact with a foreign aura. This one, a little less alien. She said, "The aura of a live being is always moving, like fire. No two flames are the same. Each one dances around, never making the same move two times. That is the nature of your aura."

She placed her hand just above her cup again. "The aura of a thing not alive is like rock. It moves only when something makes it move. That is the nature of the aura of the cup."

Jerryck put his hand back over his cup. Comparing it to rock made the sensation easier to tolerate. The aura of the cup lay about its surface like sediment on the bottom of a pond. The outer edges were so light, he could barely perceive them. Further in it became dense, pressing its weight against his hand. Then a different aura inside the bowl of the cup caught his attention.

"Liquid," he said. This aura had a smooth, definite surface. "Is the aura of any liquid like water?"

"Water moves by how it is held," Sakila said. "Sometimes it is still. Sometimes it moves gently. Sometimes it moves with great strength."

Another aura brushed against his, the way a gentle breeze would whisper on his skin. "There's something else in this. It feels like air."

"The tea herbs. Plants are like air. It can be still. It likes to move. Sometimes it moves in a pattern, like wind in a cave. Sometimes it moves with no pattern, like wind in a storm. Sometimes the movements are soft. Sometimes they are strong."

The concept was so simple. This was like seeing without using his eyes. If he got really good at this, he could probably move around in complete darkness and not bump into a single thing.

He closed his eyes and stretched out his aura. The aura of the worktable lay still about it, solid and stable, unless something moved nearby. Then it swirled and eddied like dry leaves in the wind, only to settle back down like sand rolling down the mound in the bottom of an hourglass, leaving little trails that were like the grains of wood, putting it back into the same stable, reliable form it had been in before. On the opposite side of the worktable from him, Sakila's aura radiated out, licking at everything around her.

He expanded some more. His aura swept across the floor. Crept up the walls. Flowed around his bookcases, cupboards, and shelves. The paper and the leather of the books, scrawled with dried ink, their aura lay about each one with a definite surface, but swirled inside itself like wind in a bottle. Every once in a while, a tiny particle would burst out, the way a fire would throw off sparks when hit with a blast from a bellows.

The jars on the shelves varied. Some of them were glass. Most of them were fired clay. All of them had an aura like rock. Their contents varied. Some mimicked their containers, still as rock. Others stirred in response to the touch of his aura, as if he opened a long-forgotten closet and disturbed the air in there. If they responded this way just to his touch, could he manipulate or make use of them this way? He gave a little push of energy, just to test.

"Jerryck?" Sakila's voice had a hint of trepidation, a hint of warning.

The dried herbs and powders swirled inside their containers. The jars vibrated and rattled. The shelves cracked along the wood grains, splintering.

Raw magic burst out of him without warning. The window glass flowed out of the panes and piled up on the floor as sand. Books fell. The cupboards creaked, leaning crooked. Their doors opened and disgorged some of the items stored within. The jars imploded, disintegrating into dust. Their contents exploded, flying all over the room.

Sakila slapped her hands on Jerryck's temples. "Be calm!"

Placating energy flowed from her, into him. It soothed all the raw magic, calming, giving him enough pause to get hold of it again. He drew in a ragged breath. The room shuddered one last time, and the magic dissipated.

Exhaustion crashed over him. His eyes rolled up even as he fought to remain conscious, terrified of the void that always loomed when he passed out this way. Sakila's magic continued to flow. Now it invigorated just enough. Remaining awake became less of a struggle. He took deep, even breaths, stabilizing further until the danger of fainting faded away.

She removed her hands. The magic flow from her ebbed to a trickle and tapered off. On his own again, his weariness weighed down. He would need food and sleep. And even still it would take him a couple of days before he got completely back to normal.

"I am so sorry," Sakila said. "I did not expect that. I have never seen anyone do that before."

"It's not your fault," Jerryck said. "I know better. I can't play around too much or accidents happen. Please, I beg you, don't tell anyone of this either. If the Gathering ever found out about this weakness of mine..."

"Weakness!" She surged to her feet with the biggest grin she'd worn yet. She made a fist and flexed her arm muscles. "This was strength! You would make a wonderful Shaman. You would just have to learn control."

Chapter 8

SOMEONE SHOOK Jerryck by the shoulders. "Wake up. Wake up!"

"Huh?" He pried his eyelids open to slits. Zev, his fourteen-year-old nephew, stood over him.

"Why are you in bed?" Zev stopped shaking without letting go. "Is that why you didn't come to supper? Mama's mad at you for that. So's Aunt Leanne."

"Tired," Jerryck mumbled.

"How can you be tired? It's only sunset. Darren and me need the sugar stuff and we couldn't find it."

"Darren? He's not supposed to come up to the tower. His parents don't like magicians."

Zev let go and looked at him as if he were daft. "We have to do the water test."

"Water test," Jerryck repeated. Some of the sleepy cobwebs in his head parted just enough. "Oh. The water test! Sunset."

"Duh." Zev stepped back, rolling his eyes. "That's what I said. And we can't find the sugar you use for it."

"Were you in my workroom without me?" Jerryck sat up in his bed. He looked around his room where he had crashed after sending the shamaness on her way. "Where's Darren?"

"He's looking at some pictures in one of your books."

Jerryck jumped up. "Zev!"

54

He took the stairs two at a time up a flight to his workroom. He stepped inside and nearly tripped over the mess he'd left. Darren looked up from where he sat innocently thumbing through the pages of Jerryck's magical fauna compendium. Then he grinned. The innocent look vanished.

"Did one of these swirly cloud things come in here?" Darren pointed to an illustration of an air elemental. "It says they leave behind destruction and a terrible mess."

"If one of those came in here—" Jerryck picked his way across the room— "there probably wouldn't be any room left to contain this mess."

"What did you do?" Zev barreled his way to the remains of the shelves, stepping on whatever debris was in his way.

"Doesn't matter," Jerryck said. He reached Darren and retrieved his book.

"It was over here." Zev shoved broken things aside with his hands.

"Some of those pieces are sharp." Jerryck set his book on the unfazed surface of his worktable. "You're going to cut yourself."

"What happened to your jars?" Zev kept rummaging through the shambles. "I can only find bits and pieces of them. Oh, look. This one didn't break."

Jerryck lunged. "Give me that."

He tripped over something, fell to his knees, stretched out his arm the rest of the distance, and snatched the jar. "Stop touching things you don't know anything about."

Zev pouted. "I'm just trying to help."

"I know." Jerryck sighed and examined the jar. The runes still held. Nothing had even cracked. The creature within was still bound. He tucked the jar safely under his arm. "Not everything in here is safe. You're going to hurt yourself. Both of you, out. Now."

"What about the test?" Darren picked up a cup of water between his feet.

"We'll go to the kitchens and get supplies to make more sugar to test with," Jerryck said as he shooed them both out. "Give me a moment."

The boys started insulting each other and headed down the stairs. Jerryck would probably have to break up another fight between them before they got to the bottom. He set the jar on his worktable beside his compendium and scolded himself for overreacting. Of course the runes had held. They always held. Jerryck left it there and went to follow the boys.

Zev and Darren were already scuffling on the next landing down. The cup went flying, spilling water and clattering around their feet. The boys grappled for a better grip, trying to shove each other down to the floor.

"Stop!" Jerryck grabbed them both by the collar. "You're on stairs. This has got to be the worst place for you to do this."

"But…" Both boys spluttered. "But…"

"You want to fall and break your necks?" Jerryck marched them down. "Is this the real reason you got in trouble with Nita? Why you have to bring the water for testing? You were fighting, weren't you."

"No!" Zev shifted his shoulders, wriggling under Jerryck's hold.

"Nita's just bossy," Darren said. He marched sullenly, much more submissive. Jerryck let him go.

"She's the princess. She's supposed to be bossy." Jerryck shook his nephew to get him to stop trying to get free. "Why have you been acting like this? You've gotten into more fights this past month than you ever have in your entire life."

"He says he's standing up for his sister." Darren rolled his eyes and snorted.

"Which one?" Jerryck asked.

"Chandra!" Zev grabbed Jerryck's arm, trying to pull it away. "Everyone's flirting with her."

"She's flirting with them." Jerryck shook him again. "Not the other way. Your mama's trying to get her to stop. You're making things more difficult for her."

Zev stopped resisting. Tears welled up in his eyes, though none of them fell. "I'm supposed to defend her. I'm the man of the family now. It's my job."

Jerryck put his hands on his nephew's shoulders and looked him square in the eye. "No, you're not. I am. It's my job. Stop trying to do it for me."

"You don't even notice half the things that go on around you!" Zev shouted.

"And that's where your mama and Aunt Leanne make up the difference," Jerryck said. "Let them. Quit giving us all more problems than we're already dealing with."

Neither of the boys said anything more the entire rest of the way to the kitchens. Most everyone had gone outside in the bailey for the evening's dancing and socializing. Jerryck sent his nephew to hunt up some sugar.

"Keep complaining." Kendra's harsh scolding came from one of the adjoining washrooms.

Jerryck slipped in there. His sister stood with her hands on her hips, intimidating one of the scullery maids who was elbow deep in a washbasin. "I told you they weren't clean yet. You want to make more people sick by putting unwashed plates in with the clean, you'll wash every single one. We've got too many sick people right now as it is."

"The water will just make the plates carry the sick," the scullery maids said.

"No it won't," Jerryck said. "Not according to my tests. It has to reach a certain temperature for activation. And once everything's dry, so is the taint. It's really no problem. Unless it's a living body ingesting it. That would give it so much moisture to interact with, adding in the temperature factor that's required for activation—"

"Jerryck," Kendra interrupted. "We don't need a full explanation. Thank you. How about instead, you explain your absence at supper."

"Hi, Mama." Zev came in with a sack of sugar on his shoulder, Darren right behind him.

She pointed at the sack. "What do you think you're doing with that?"

"Jerryck needs it for his test," Zev said. "We can't find what he had because he blew up his workroom again."

"What?" Kendra stiffened. So did the scullery maid before she paled, turned her face away, and scrubbed furiously at the dishes.

"I did not," Jerryck said, giving Zev a dirty look.

The scullery maid dropped one of the plates. The anti-shatter magic on it pinged. Good thing the head chef had talked Jerryck into putting the spell on all the dishes, not just the finest sets.

Kendra hustled them all out of the room, away from the scullery maid. Zev thumped the sack down on one of the counters. "Oh, and I found out why he missed supper. He was taking a nap."

Kendra tensed even more, scrutinizing Jerryck. "You were sleeping?"

"I'm fine," Jerryck said. "Just my workroom isn't."

"He told me he was tired." Zev bobbed his head while he talked. "The next time I'm too tired to clean up a mess and just need to sleep—"

"Don't even try it," Kendra interrupted, shaking a finger at him. Then she whipped that finger around to point behind herself and shouted, "Get back to work."

The scullery maid had sneaked over to the door and stood listening. She scurried back in. Jerryck shook his head. He never had figured out how his sister knew what was going on when her back was turned. The scullery maid hadn't even made any noise.

"Your mama's a little scary sometimes," Darren whispered to Zev.

Jerryck snickered. "Be glad you didn't grow up with her."

"Jerryck!" Kendra scowled at him. "Do whatever it is you do for these two and get them out of my kitchens."

Jerryck separated out a small portion of sugar from the sack and magicked it. He let the boys drop a pinch in some water. He declared it still tainted. Then Kendra shooed them out while he folded the rest of what he'd made into a parchment to keep.

Kendra whirled on him, keeping her volume just low enough the scullery maid in the other room wouldn't hear. "You had another accident."

"I don't want to talk about it," he said.

"You don't have a choice."

He tucked the sugar into a pocket. "I'm fine."

"What were you doing?"

"Nothing."

"Don't give me that." She crossed her arms, narrowed her eyes, and hunched forward. "You were playing around again. Weren't you? You know you can't do that. What were you thinking? How many times can you do this before you really hurt yourself?"

"Apparently at least one more time."

"This isn't funny!" With that yell, she glanced at the door to the other room. She took a moment and composed herself. Then asked, "Did you dream?"

"No," he said.

That's what had her so worried. The first accident he'd ever had, the one that had unlocked his abilities as a child, he'd fallen into a dream-like state that trapped him. She'd had to get help from a more experienced magician to pull him out of it. For a week, he slipped and slid around near the edge of a void, more real in that dream state than anything else he'd ever known in waking life. He'd been near it several times since. Never so close. Never again in such danger of going over the edge. And the place still left him shaky with fear if he thought about it too much.

"Please be more careful." Kendra closed up the sack of sugar, her hands trembling.

He nodded and left the kitchens, thinking he should avoid the shamaness. That created a dilemma. It was his duty to tend to the needs and questions of visiting magic practitioners. He couldn't just shut Sakila out and avoid her entirely. Not unless he left the palace. For that, he needed a reason while they were in a time of difficulty.

He headed for Terrance's private rooms. The king usually liked spending a little time with his daughter in the evenings. They would likely be in there with a smattering of people waiting for his attention out in the parlor.

The guards posted outside the double doors to the parlor let him right through. He didn't even have to say a thing to them. Inside, he stopped and raised his eyebrows. No one sat gossiping or sipping wine on the sofa or chairs. No one preened in the floor-to-ceiling mirror dominating the far wall. No one stared at the blue and white drapes around it, complaining that the king favored the late queen's home district of Tarn with that color scheme. The room was empty, except for General Heston. He stood near the doorway to the bedchamber, which was closed off by a crimson curtain with gold filigrees stitched all through it.

"What do you need?" Heston demanded.

"I, uh, I need to speak with Terrance."

"Why?" Heston stepped sideways, in front of the curtain.

"Isn't that between him and me?"

"He's worked himself to exhaustion today," Heston said. "Give him some time to take a rest."

Jerryck cocked his ear at the voices on the other side of the curtain. The privacy magic was in good shape. He couldn't make out a single word they said. "Is Nita in there with him?"

"Don't try using her as an excuse to go in," Heston said. "I've already sent away five people, gave them jobs to do just to get rid of them for using that excuse."

"I'm not using her as an excuse." Jerryck moved aside some of the cushions on a chair to sit.

He focused on the muffled voices and the charm he kept attached to the wall above the curtained doorway. He had to strain just to figure out which voice belonged to who. He wouldn't need to do any maintenance here for at least another month.

"Whatever you need to talk to him about," Heston said, "can it wait?"

"Wait for what?" Jerryck asked. "Do you really think I'm going to interrupt his time with his daughter?"

"I suppose not." Heston moved from the doorway and sat on the edge of the sofa opposite Jerryck. "Not you. Others would."

Curious, Jerryck said, "If I did insist on talking to him now, would you stop me?"

Heston narrowed his eyes. "No one's supposed to block members of the core staff from getting to the king."

"Oh, right," Jerryck said. "I knew that."

"Sure you do," Heston said. "That's why you never use it to your advantage?"

"Am I supposed to?"

"No."

Heston turned his head to watch the double doors that led out to the corridor. Over the next half an hour, a couple of people made it in past the guards. Both times, Heston found out what they wanted, then redirected them back out.

Eventually, the curtain to the main chamber whisked aside. Terrance and Nita entered the parlor. Jerryck and Heston both stood respectfully. Terrance looked back and forth between them. "Just the two of you? I expected a slew of people wanting something or another from me."

"Not tonight," Heston said.

"They had other things they needed to do," Jerryck added.

"Is that so?" Terrance leveled his gaze at Heston, who gave Jerryck an impatient glance. "If someone needs something truly important from me, they should be allowed through.

"Except for Jerryck," Heston said, "they all told me what they needed before they found other tasks to occupy their time. I'll give you a list when you're ready."

"What do you need?" Terrance asked Jerryck.

"I need to go to Kershet," Jerryck said.

Heston shook his head. "Not a good idea. The city's chaotic right now."

"I have to stay away from the shamaness," Jerryck said.

"Why?" Terrance asked. "Did she do something inappropriate?"

"No." Jerryck sighed. "I did."

Heston frowned. "Did you blow up your workroom again?"

"Sort of?" Jerryck said. Heston, Terrance, and Nita all knew about his occasional accidents, just like his wife and sister. Unlike his wife and sister, these three didn't get so worried over it.

Nita snickered. "Again."

"How many workers do you need in there this time?" Terrance covered his mouth with a hand, but his eyes crinkled up. Evidence of a smile.

"I need to do some initial cleaning first," Jerryck said.

"That's not what I asked." Terrance lowered his hand. The corners of his mouth were still slightly upturned. "What kind of damage do you need repaired? What workers are necessary? Or should I just send someone up for assessment?"

"That might be best," Heston said. "The last time Jerryck tried to assess was disastrous."

"I need to replenish my stock," Jerryck said. "Most of my jars broke, and all my powders are mixed together."

Terrance sobered. "So you really do need to go to Kershet. You're not just trying to get away from Sakila."

"Don't you use a lot of the same materials the medics keep in the infirmary?" Heston asked.

"Some," Jerryck said. "But they're kind of hard pressed right now. I doubt they're going to want to share. Especially with me."

Terrance pinched the bridge of his nose between his thumb and forefinger. He put his other hand on his hip. "Heston, arrange an escort of some of your finest elite for him."

"I can take care of myself," Jerryck said. He'd gone to Kershet lots of times without escort.

Heston crossed his arms. "This isn't a good idea. I'm the finest. And I'm leaving tonight to go upstream, not toward the city."

"I know you trust your men to do this." Terrance took his hand away from his face. "Or are you just looking for an excuse to go to Kershet yourself to check on certain people?"

"If he waits until I can go with him," Heston said. "I can help him get a search started."

"I don't need to search for my supplies," Jerryck said. "I know where to buy them."

"Search for whoever made what poisoned the river." Heston only moved his eyes to look at Jerryck. The rest of his body remained perfectly still.

"I thought you were doing that search," Jerryck said.

Heston clenched his jaw, released it, then said, "I'll set up an escort for tomorrow morning."

Chapter 9

JERRYCK WENT up to his tower to get some cleaning done. He found his wife and sister already there. They had somehow brought a little organization to the room and had started getting rid of some of the broken bits and shards.

"Don't go crazy on us," Kendra said the moment he entered the room. "I know you don't like people in here without you, and we know what you don't want touched. We left them alone."

"We also know what's most valuable to you." Leanne pointed to all his books carefully stacked in a clear corner. She spread her hands to cover the rest of the room. "Most of this, we're unsure of. You'll have to help us go through it."

Jerryck knelt by Kendra to dig into the debris. "I thought you were standing over a scullery maid."

"She finished," Kendra said. "Did you think it would take her all night?"

Jerryck sorted through what they had left for him. Then he repaired the damage he'd done to the charms that let him know when certain things were happening, like someone entering his tower. The women continued sweeping out the bulk of the mess. Altogether, it took far less time than he had expected. Then Kendra left, swearing that if her kids hadn't stayed in bed where she'd put them, she was going to tan their butts.

"When are you going to Kershet?" Leanne asked. He stared at her. How had she known? He hadn't mentioned anything about it. She laughed and said, "Don't look at me like that. You always go when your supplies are low. And right now they're definitely low."

"Tomorrow morning," he said.

"That soon?" Her face drooped momentarily. Then she straightened up and headed to their bedroom one floor below. "I'd better pack you some things."

"I can pack," he said, following her.

"The last time you packed for yourself—" she took at his travel bag and opened their bureau— "you only took one change of clothes for a three-day stay."

"So?"

She wrinkled her nose at him. "So that's disgusting."

"I had them laundered. And I bought another change there."

"That's my point. You have plenty. You shouldn't have to buy a change. Besides, I like doing this for you."

It was pointless to argue. Just as it would've been pointless to ask her to come with him. Every time he did ask, it only upset her. She didn't like leaving the comforts of the palace. She didn't like meeting new people. And she certainly didn't want attention from some of the people his position would require him to interact with.

He half listened while she chatted idly. Soon, his eyelids drooped and he started yawning, despite the sleep he'd gotten that afternoon. He lay down thinking just to rest a bit. He was vaguely aware of Leanne blowing out the lamp and climbing into bed at some point.

He woke to someone tapping his shoulder and whispering his name. He opened sleep-gritty eyes. Someone with a shaded lamp stood in the doorway, giving light to the elite guard standing over Jerryck. It was the one with the cleft in his chin, one of the three who was often seen with Tajor.

"What?" He tried to whisper to keep from waking Leanne. In his grogginess, it didn't come out as quietly as intended.

"There's a quepota outside." The guard whispered much quieter than Jerryck. "Sergeant of the watch wants your advice."

Leanne stirred. She mumbled something unintelligible and snuggled in closer to him. Jerryck rolled his head, popping his neck. He gritted his teeth against the temptation to just hand out some flippant advice and go back to sleep next to her.

"I'll come take a look," he said.

He shoved his feet into his boots and went out onto the landing. The man holding the lamp was another elite guard, the one with a crooked nose.

Once the door to the bedroom was closed, the guard took the shade off the lamp. All the way down, they kept quiet. That gave Jerryck time to mentally review what he knew of quepotas. If the sun was up, they could see the creature and just shoot it, since it had no natural camouflage. Some people theorized this was why quepotas were nocturnal. They covered themselves with the dark of night. Jerryck had never paid much attention to such debates. He studied more on the methods of dealing with the things.

Known to burrow into holes near rivers or creeks, Jerryck was fairly certain there was one on Unification Isle. Eventually he'd have to go and take care of it, if a magician from Kershet City didn't do it first. It wasn't urgent until an event was planned in the location. Quepotas were more of a problem further south. This far north, they were much sleepier and lethargic than in the warmer, southern climates.

Ships traversing the waterways, or caravans traveling roads near them, tended to keep lamps blazing. Quepotas instinctively avoided well lit places, unless especially determined. In Jerryck's magical fauna compendium, there was an example of a village wasting away because they couldn't get rid of one. A female had dug into a hole under one of the houses. She never came out or caused any problems. They didn't even know she was there until it was too late. A male sniffed her out and wanted to mate. Every night he would come to the edge of the village, latch on to whoever was nearest, and drain their aura. Sometimes it was just one victim. Other times, it would partially drain several people.

Every morning, the villagers rose to see which family had lost one of its members in the night. Everyone took ill. They grew too weak to light fires and lamps at the village perimeter. The male found its way to the female and they nested. They both latched onto the entire village with that, draining every person to expend the energy in mating. The next person who wandered through found all the bodies and a diary describing the entire ordeal.

The Gathering of Seats claimed that if they'd just gotten a magician in there, the village could have been saved. They had schools in their city of Kemetulla, where dealing with magical fauna was formally taught. Jerryck had attended some classes with the few conventions he'd gone to. His mentor had taught him a few things here and there. But most of what he knew to do, he'd only read in books.

The guards escorted him outside one of the gates in the wall surrounding the palace and its complex of outbuildings. Bonfires were lit at the perimeter all around. Between each fire stood men waving around torches and lamps. Jerryck's escorts went directly to the sergeant of the watch.

He was holding a bucket of water and standing with a knot of guards, some elite, some regular. Tajor was among them. He must have been acting up again, because the sergeant was busy yelling at him. "You're not going out there like that. You try it again, and I'll have you thrown into a dungeon cell."

"I'll agree to that," Tajor said with a smirk. He reached for the bucket. "You have a deal."

The sergeant jerked the bucket out of his reach, slopping some of the water on the ground. Jerryck asked, "What's going on?"

"Looks like Tajor's going on," the cleft chin guard said with a snicker.

"A quepota isn't enough trouble?" Jerryck glared at Tajor. Then he turned to the sergeant. "Where is it?"

The sergeant pointed out into the darkness. "Over that way. We think it skirted around the city, heading upriver. At first, I hoped it would head for Unification Isle, or Aconi Grove. Instead, I think it's looking for a drink. Every time we've taken a water bucket out to the men, the thing attacks. We're trying to figure out how to leave one out there to draw it into the light where we can shoot it, without endangering whoever's carrying the bucket."

"It might have been skirting Kershet to get to the pond," Jerryck said. "That water is awfully clogged and stale, though. If it smelled fresher, clean water here, it absolutely would try to get some if it was dehydrated enough."

"I guessed as much," the sergeant said. "That doesn't solve our dilemma. I've tried three times to put the bucket inside the perimeter and then withdraw from around it. The cursed thing comes on too fast. It starts killing anyone between it and the water before we can get out of the way."

"I offered to take the bucket," Tajor said.

"You offered to run right toward it with no defense." The sergeant snarled, his volume rising again. "No man in his right mind would be that suicidal."

"We all know Tajor is not in his right mind," the cleft chin guard said with a laugh.

The sergeant snapped at him. "You're not helping!"

Magic flared in the dark, directly out from where they stood. One of the men holding a lamp between them and the flare let out a strangled cry of agony. The lamp fell. The cry tapered off, gurgling into silence.

"That makes eight," the sergeant said.

"Give me the bucket," Jerryck said, reaching for it, keeping his eyes peeled for any movement out where the magic flared.

"You're not going out there by yourself." The sergeant held the bucket out of Jerryck's reach.

Tajor grasped the bucket handle. "I'll go with him."

The sergeant refused to relinquish, pulling on the bucket, slopping more water. "You're too reckless. You're staying here."

Jerryck looked at the sergeant, aghast. "We don't have time to argue this."

"We have enough time for me to pick who to escort you," the sergeant said, still wrestling over the bucket.

"Just give it to Tajor," Jerryck said.

"I'll decide who to give it to." The sergeant leaned close to Jerryck, his face just a couple of inches away. Tajor twisted the bucket in the sergeant's grasp. The man grabbed it with his other hand, keeping his grip. He turned to snarl at Tajor. "Back down!"

Tajor squatted down. The cleft chin guard laughed. The sergeant threw a kick at him. "Don't think I won't report you to General Heston when I report Tajor."

"Why isn't he out here?" Jerryck looked around. He should have noticed the absence of the general before this.

"He went upriver earlier this evening," Tajor said. "Something about deflating noble egos north of the tainted tributary so they stop inhibiting the transfer of clean water downstream."

"He's investigating the taint." The sergeant leaned back in to Jerryck's face. "I'll pick someone else to escort you."

"I'll take Tajor," Jerryck said, staring out into the darkness. The magic was pulsing out there, going back and forth like the creature was pacing just beyond the light.

"You can't override my decision on this," the sergeant said.

"Yes he can," the crooked nosed guard said. "And you may as well stop posturing. It doesn't work on him. He doesn't pick up on it."

The sergeant glared at the guard and let go of the bucket. Tajor headed off with it out into the dark. Jerryck hurried after him.

"Wait," he called to Tajor. He hadn't put up any shields, or defensive magic, or anything.

Tajor stopped. He looked back at Jerryck and cocked his head. "With the way you use your aura, you light yourself up like a beacon for anything sensitive to it. Won't that make you especially susceptible to this creature?"

"I'm also the best able to counterattack it." Jerryck caught up.

An unfamiliar aura brushed up against his, licking at it the way a flame would lick at someone's hair or clothing. A tongue of that flame aura licked at the water bucket. Then at Tajor. He tensed up, his shoulders going rigid in the little light that spilled their way from the torches now behind them. The curse weaved into his aura swirled and eddied around the unfamiliar touch. Whatever it was jerked away in recoil, as fast as a hand burned on a hot stove.

Jerryck mentally followed the tendril of aura until it withdrew all the way back to the quepota. If he gathered up energy to put up a shield now, the creature would latch on and suck it all away before he could get the words out of his mouth. It turned its head in Jerryck's direction and sniffed. It took a step forward. Jerryck stepped back.

No one had been able to determine if the quepota was more like a hairless dog or cat. Some even argued that it was a hairless, miniature bear. Either way, it had teeth and claws. Its magical abilities weren't the only threat, as if that wasn't enough. Jerryck took another step back.

A tendril of the creature's aura snaked out again. It carefully went around Tajor, avoiding contact, inching ever closer to the bucket. Tajor set it on the ground and backed away. The tendril hovered over it. Then snaked its way over to Jerryck.

Magic flared at the end of the tendril. Hooks shot out of it, piercing into Jerryck's aura. Weakness buckled his knees and nausea punched him in the stomach. He bled energy out of the piercings. The creature's aural tendril sucked it up like a leech.

Jerryck pulled his aura in so hard his arms curled around his chest, the one reflex his mentor had cautioned him to avoid. It pulled the quepota's hooks in. They dug deeper, widening the piercings.

He was supposed to do the opposite. A sudden influx of energy without resistance would throw the quepota off balance, make it flinch. That was supposed to give Jerryck enough time to get off an attacking spell, if he was quick enough.

Jerryck pushed his aura away from himself, directly at the quepota. He flung his arms wide, his back arching with the effort. His energy surged out in front of him, tipping over the bucket and ripping up the ground. The quepota tumbled away, clawing at the ground and snarling as it was flung end over end.

Blackness encroached on the edges of Jerryck's vision. Either that or the lamps and torches behind him all went out at once. The rabid snarls of an angry animal rushed at him. Finding himself on his hands and knees, Jerryck raised his head. The lamps and torches still burned behind him. They cast just enough light to see the hairless monstrosity bearing down, leaping at him. He gasped. Behind it, the energy Jerryck had flung out surged and rebounded, looping back around and heading for him in a flood.

A blur of motion came from behind. Tajor tackled the animal in the middle of its launch, driving it to the ground. The creature's magic flared. Tajor grit his teeth, hissing in pain. Despite that, he took the quepota's head in both his hands and twisted it backward. The bones snapped with an audible crack.

All the energy from Jerryck's aura washed over both of them. It reattached itself to Jerryck and nearly washed past him, pulling him backward. It rebounded again, pulling him forward in the tide, then back again to finally settle.

Men ran toward them with bobbing lights and indistinct shouts. Tajor lay on the ground, curled in on himself and shuddering. His two friends passed Jerryck and knelt by his side. The sergeant stopped at Jerryck and shouted, "Get them both to the infirmary."

"No!" Jerryck and Tajor's friends all said at once.

"You don't want to go, that's your choice," the sergeant said to Jerryck. He pointed at Tajor, telling the two guards, "Take him."

"No," the crooked nosed guard said with a sneer.

The sergeant glared at him. "Are you defying me again?"

"I'm all right," Tajor wheezed.

"I'll take care of him," Jerryck said.

"You're the one who got him into the situation." The sergeant's snarl was almost as ugly as the quepota's.

"I'm the one who treats him when he gets like this," Jerryck said, crawling over to pat Tajor on the shoulder.

"You don't treat any of Heston's men," the sergeant said.

"He treats Tajor," the crooked nose guard said.

"I've never believed that rumor."

The guard raised his fist. "You calling me a liar again?"

"Deek!" The cleft chin guard pushed the fist down. "Stop. Don't get yourself in trouble again."

"Heston's not here," Deek said. He raised his other fist.

"Fine!" The sergeant started walking away. All the others followed him except Tajor's two elite friends. "Do what you want. You will no matter what I tell you. Just keep in mind what he did the last time you interfered with my job."

Deek lowered both his fists. Jerryck tried to shoo both the men away from Tajor before they learned too much about the man's affliction. "Go back with the others. I'll take care of him."

"We know about his curse," Deek said, pointing to himself and the other guard. "Garret and I. You don't have to make us go away to try and hide it. Besides, Cade will want every detail we can give him when he gets back from upriver with Heston."

"Cade?" Jerryck mentally searched through faces, trying to attach the name to one of them.

Garret smirked for some reason. "Nevermind."

"Who else knows?" Jerryck asked.

Garret ticked names off on his fingers. "Tajor, of course. You, Heston, Terrance... I'm not sure if Nita knows or not. I haven't been told about anyone else."

"Cade knows," Deek said.

Garret smirked again. "That won't do Jerryck any good if he can't remember which of us is Cade."

Tajor shuddered and let out a long, measured breath. The very fact that he hadn't laughed at the ribbing, or added to it, was evidence of just how much he was hurting. Deek asked, "You want us to carry you in?"

Tajor clenched his teeth. "Could you please not ask stupid questions right now?"

"You ask stupid questions all the time." Garret poked him in the shoulder. "Just answer for once."

"No, I don't want to be carried," Tajor said. "Just give me a few minutes. Then I'll walk."

Chapter 10

JERRYCK SAT on the edge of his bed scrubbing sleep from his eyes. He needed a full night of sleep, not a disturbed half night. He had waited until the soldiers had collected the body of the quepota and disposed of it, waited until Tajor was well enough to walk back to his room unaided. Then he'd gone back to bed.

Leanne puttered about the room, chatting idly. He only half listened to her. He dragged himself off the bed and slowly paced the floor to get his blood circulating better, driving away more of the grogginess.

On days he had to leave, she was always given time to spend with him until his departure. At nine years his junior, he still marveled that she would even have him. She had come to the palace pronouncing her name Loo-ee-ahn-eh. In her shyness, she had dropped the first and last vowel sounds instead of correcting anyone who pronounced it wrong.

When he never forgot her name, even though he forgot most others, Kendra had pushed her at him. He balked because of the age difference. It wasn't right to impose that on someone so pretty. Until another man started flirting with her, driving him into fits of jealousy he hadn't even known he was capable of. Then she pushed that other man away and pursued Jerryck as aggressively as he wanted to pursue her.

72

Voices wafted up the stairs, ripping him from reverie. Zev and Darren were bringing the morning water for him to test. He went out to greet them and led the way up the last flight of stairs to the workroom.

"Just to make sure," Zev said, grinning and bouncing on the balls of his feet. "We don't have to do this while you're gone. Right?"

"Correct." Jerryck put out the sugar for them to drop some in the water. "I'll do it myself in the city."

Darren stuck his nose up in the air. "Did you know there are some people so stupid they can't spell Kershet?"

"That's not stupid." Zev rolled his eyes instead of watching the glowing color change in the water. "You're stupid."

Darren punched him in the shoulder. "I'm not stupid."

"Stop." Jerryck separated the two before they could start fighting.

"I'm not stupid." Darren repeated, backing up a couple of steps. "That new kid in class is stupid."

Zev balled his fists. "She is not."

"Here." Jerryck picked up the glowing cup of water as a distraction. "The test is still bad. Take it to the household office and report it."

"There's a new family at the palace," Darren said, ignoring the cup. "Came in just last week to work in the kennels. Their oldest girl is stupid. She doesn't know how to read or write. Not even the names of important places, like Coraline Palace, or Kershet, or Bershent Fortress."

"She's not stupid!" Zev shouted. "She's pretty."

"Being uneducated isn't stupid," Jerryck said to Darren while pushing Zev's fists down. "It's ignorant. There's a difference."

"Besides, I'm helping her learn." Zev brought his fists right back up. "She's smart enough she'll pick up on it right away."

Darren snorted. "You just like her because she's pretty."

"All right." Jerryck put a hand on both boys' shoulders, maneuvering them back to the landing and the stairs. "Pretty girl. Needs better education. I get it. Neither of you will impress her by neglecting your responsibilities. Take the water test."

They started down the stairs and got just out of sight when Zev shouted, "What are you doing here? If you've flirted with my sister again, I'm going to smash your ugly face."

Jerryck leaped down the stairs, rounding the curve of the tower, bringing them back into sight. "Zev!"

The boy jumped, nearly spilling the cup in his hands. Below him and Darren was a zit-faced page. He looked up at Jerryck and spoke so fast his words were jumbled together, "His Majesty summons you to the royal chambers."

He turned and ran, nearly tripping over his gangly feet. Zev and Darren laughed. Jerryck shooed them on their way again. Then he quickly dressed and went to the king's private chambers.

Terrance was eating breakfast in the corner by the open doors to his balcony. He sat with his back to the doors, facing the wall where he had hung portraits of family members dead and gone. His crimson and gold canopied bed looked like it had not been slept in. His food was only half eaten. Several reports were strewn around his plate.

"Good morning," Terrance said. He looked up at Jerryck and set down his fork. He waved the parchment he'd been reading from. "I hear there was some excitement last night."

"We took care of it," Jerryck said.

Terrance set down the parchment and sat back in his chair. "The guards needed your help?"

"I helped."

"I'm rescinding permission for you to leave." Terrance pushed away his plate. Jerryck's mouth opened. He closed it again with a frown. Terrance said, "You don't have to look so worried and flustered. I know your concerns. I'll tell Nita she's excused from all tutoring sessions. She'll be more than thrilled to spend that time playing hostess instead. She'll keep the shamaness entertained."

"And my supplies?" Jerryck asked. "I need to restock."

"A lot of the materials you use are also purchased by the medics." Terrance picked up a list from one of the stacks of documents. "I'll have Kellos open his stores to you. And you won't even have to go yourself. Send a page directly to him. That way the other medics won't give you a hard time. Plus, I know you have things stored away. You always do. You're not really hurting for supplies. You mostly just want to get away from the shamaness. I've covered that. And this keeps you away from the chaos presently outside the palace walls."

Terrance's personal servant came out of the wardrobe room. He strode across the floor. Like so many other people, Jerryck couldn't remember the man's name no matter how many times it was given to him. Thin, aging, the man had nothing but wisps of gray hair. In public, he was very prim and proper. In private, he hovered over Terrance like a nanny.

He scowled at the uneaten food as if it was a personal offense to him. "You didn't eat everything again."

"I've had enough," Terrance said, waving a negligent hand. He turned to Jerryck once more. "Mobs have murdered entire families and raided their cellars for anything to drink. Some neighborhoods have hired private mercenaries and barricaded their streets in attempts to isolate themselves."

"You need to dress for court." The servant drew Terrance up from his chair.

"If they're so sick and thirsty they're getting violent," Jerryck said, following them to the wardrobe, "maybe I could help."

"I don't want you there." Terrance stopped just short of the wardrobe door and jerked his arm away from the servant. "Every magician in the city has been pressed into service. Not just the ones that are employed by the capital. All of them. The private contractors, the ones who came for a day of business, even the ones visiting as tourists. Aside from your personal safety, what if we need you here again? I can't afford for you to be stuck there."

"You have your answer." The servant made curt, shooing gestures, much like Jerryck had with Zev and Darren. "Go on now. Terrance needs to dress for court."

Terrance held court for a few hours every morning after breakfast, ending about lunchtime. He insisted on keeping up the formality even during times of tumult, claiming that people needed something steady they could rely on. Jerryck attended as rarely as he could get away with. Every time he occupied Terrance too much beforehand, the servant roped Jerryck into attending. So instead of pursuing the matter further, he left and went back up to his tower.

Marla came bounding down the curve of the steps, leaping at him about halfway up one of the flights. He grunted at her impact. "Oof! You're getting heavy. You need to stop growing."

She giggled at him. "I'm going to keep growing and growing until I'm as big as mama and Leanne, just like papa wanted me to."

"Good." Jerryck set her down and ruffled her hair. He turned his ear to the voices up in his workroom. One of them was his sister. The other was the shamaness Sakila.

Marla pointed up the stairs. "That's a lady from the Chemwanitz Mountains. She has blue eyes like Leanne's. And pretty yellow hair. And she's nice."

"You talked to her?" Jerryck continued up the stairs.

Marla followed. "Is that all right?"

Kendra stood on the top landing with Zech, her toddler, on her hip. "Marla insisted on coming up to tell you goodbye. She was afraid you'd already left."

"I'm not going," Jerryck said.

Marla beamed at him. "You're staying?"

"For now," Jerryck said. Leanne joined Kendra on the landing. He told them, "Terrance wants me here in case I'm needed. Where are Zev and Chandra? They didn't come to say goodbye too?"

"Chandra's mad at you." Kendra smiled. "She says you aren't hard enough on Zev for scaring off all the best-looking lads. And Zev is still trying to deliver this morning's water test to the household steward. That's turning out to be more of a punishment than I first thought. Maybe he'll learn his lesson this time."

"Have you met the nice mountain lady?" Marla ducked through the workroom door. "You met her, right? She's so nice, even Leanne talked to her, and I don't think they've ever met before."

Leanne blushed and ducked her head. She quietly said, "We met."

Sakila was seated on the same stool she'd used last time she visited. Jerryck patted Marla's shoulder and said, "You're in the morning class with the general studies tutor now, aren't you?"

"I'm seven." She put her hands on her hips in the perfect imitation of her older sister and their mama. "I've been in the morning class for two whole years now."

"I know that." Jerryck nodded. "I was trying to be subtle, and suggest you go get ready for it."

"You're about as subtle as a rock through a pane of glass," Kendra said. She herded Marla to the stairs. "If you want us to go away so no one sees you talking with someone who isn't a magician, just say so."

"I'm glad you're staying," Leanne whispered in his ear. She followed up with a peck on his cheek, then silently followed Kendra and the children down.

"You did not send her way to hide that you are talking to me," Sakila said. "Did you send them away so I will not see what the girl can do with magic?"

Jerryck whisked the door shut, hoping no one had heard. "Don't say such things."

"I will never understand why everyone west of the mountains treats women who can use magic the way they do," Sakila said. She clicked her tongue in disapproval. "And you call us Chemwanee barbaric. You should send your sister and her daughter to live with us. We will keep them as safe as every other woman who ever came to us."

"I'm not sending any of my family away," Jerryck said. "I'll take care of her."

Sakila nodded once and rose from her seat. She looked around the remains of the workroom. "You probably do not want to talk to me anymore. I came only to ask if you need payment for what happened here."

"Payment?" Jerryck picked up some of the books set to the side. "What for?"

"For the damage in this room," Sakila said.

"You don't have to pay for that." Jerryck gathered as many of the books as he could carry. They would be safer in his bedroom when workers came in to repair and rebuild. He straightened with the load, facing Sakila. "I did it. Not you."

"If I had not been here, you would not have done it. I should pay you."

"What is it with you and paying people?" Jerryck stepped out of the room, heading down one flight. "Why would you pay something you don't owe? You even tried to pay my king for something that wasn't even your fault in the slightest."

"Your king amazes me." Sakila folded her hands in front of her, gracefully gliding down the stairs behind his lugging clump.

Jerryck nudged the bedroom door open with his foot. "Because he did the right thing?"

"Because he treats me like family," Sakila said. She stayed on the landing while he dumped the books. "I bring him bad news. He refuses payment and makes it good. Are you treating me like family because he does?"

"Is just what decent people do," Jerryck said. He came out of the bedroom, heading back up for another armload. "You didn't really think he'd enslave your people, did you?"

"Perhaps," she said.

He stopped. "And you came anyway? Why?"

"It is just what decent people do." She smiled at him and added, "When they want to make things right again."

"Lady Shamaness?" A page came up the stairs. "Her Royal Highness Princess Nita requests your company."

Behind the page came a couple of assessors with their papers, pencils, charts, and measuring sticks. The shamaness left with the page. Jerryck followed the assessors the rest of the way up, snatching at his books.

Chapter 11

FOR THE NEXT SEVERAL HOURS, Jerryck kept finding things that other people had no business touching. The two men poked about, taking measurements, writing notes, jotting figures and numbers. They asked a lot of questions, half of which he couldn't answer.

Then the rebuilding began. Since he wasn't picky about the materials his furniture were made out of, the carpenters had a lot of the supplies they needed on hand. After a couple of days of hauling, cutting, sawing, thumping, and pounding, Jerryck was almost relieved to leave them when a rookie elite guard came saying that General Heston wanted him.

Just before he stepped out of the workroom, the chime went off that indicated a portal was opening. All the workers stopped, leaving deafening silence after all the noise from their tools. One of them said, "That's different than what you said was someone coming into the tower."

"Different activity," Jerryck said. "Don't worry about it."

He sent the guard to tell Heston that he would be a few minutes. Then he headed down to the room at the bottom of the tower. He kept a space there clear for just this purpose. He stepped automatically, not watching, his eyes going out of focus. The tingle of the magic grew stronger the closer he got.

Every once in a while, the Gathering of Seats needed to quickly get a message out to a particular magician. Instead of sending Gintario, their normal representative messenger, they had the option of opening a small portal, just large enough to slip a written letter through. They could send it to the court magician, or to a district magician, or to the official city magician for any particular population center.

Ressell, the Kershet City Magician, got a lot more of these than Jerryck did. Usually, the only time they sent something to the palace was when they put out a general announcement, like an upcoming convention. But the next one of those wasn't scheduled for more than a year away.

He waited outside the room, using his senses to monitor the progress of the portal. They employed some of the best portal makers known. It only took a couple of minutes for it to stabilize, a small object to come through, and then close up again, leaving the barest amount of residue from the magic.

Jerryck hesitated. He hadn't been very nice, or even remotely tactful in the last letter he'd sent them. He rolled his shoulders and opened the door. Better to get it over with.

The letter had dropped to the floor like it was supposed to. He picked it up. Broke the seal. Unfolded it.

It was formally written, addressing him with his title, and stating the governing body that had sent it. Then it got to the meat of the matter. Even that they had kept severely abrupt, getting right to the point and wasting no frivolities.

LORD JERRYCK, COURT MAGICIAN TO TERRANCE, KING OF BREND
AN OFFICIAL CORRESPONDENCE FROM THE GATHERING OF SEATS

We have received word that you have asked for, received, and followed the advice of a practitioner of shamanism concerning a pregnancy in the Coraline Palace infirmary. Consorting with shamans is strictly forbidden. You are hereby ordered to appear before the Gathering to explain your actions, or refute these accusations.

"That's not going to happen," Jerryck mumbled to himself. If he wasn't even allowed to go into Kershet, Terrance certainly wouldn't tolerate him gallivanting off two countries to the south to Kemetulla.

And how had they known about Sakila in the infirmary, anyway? Had someone there tattled on him? If so, why? Alchemical medics didn't deal with the Gathering if they could possibly help it. One of the patients? If so, even Kellos probably wouldn't be up to helping sort this out. And whoever it was, how had they gotten word to the Gathering so quickly? It had happened less than a week ago.

For the moment, the matter would have to wait. There were other more pressing concerns, such as being summoned by the king's general. Jerryck crushed the letter in a fist and left the tower, going directly to the antechamber outside Heston's office.

There, the three elites who were seen most often with Tajor lounged casually against the wall. The skinny one watched everything, as usual. The one with the cleft chin was smirking and jabbing the one with a crooked nose in the ribs, who glared at him. The nighttime sergeant of the watch paced back and forth, stopping when he saw Jerryck. He stood still, crossed his arms, and glowered.

"Lord Jerryck," Heston's aide said. He rose from behind his desk. "The general said to send you in immediately."

The office was rectangular, with the desk and two uncomfortable oak chairs near the door. Weapon racks, cabinets, and files filled the entire other half. Tajor stood near the chairs, in a beam of sunlight from the window. He wore the same expression he always did when making mischief. Heston sat dwarfing his large desk, looking as mean as ever. When Jerryck came in, Tajor said to the general, "Aww, aren't you going to play anymore?"

Heston glared at him for a moment. Then he turned, his eyes trailing down from Jerryck's face to the crumpled letter he still held. "What's that?"

"This?" Jerryck lifted it. "It's nothing. Well... I mean, it's something. It's from the Gathering."

"I thought they already sent you your letter this year."

"They did."

Heston pointed to the letter. "Then what's this?"

"They're being annoying."

"Is it sensitive information?" Tajor asked. He held up a hand. "Or can we see it?"

Jerryck shoved the letter at Tajor. Heston's scowl deepened. "You're going to simply trust him with whatever they wrote you?"

"He knows all about magical stuff," Jerryck said.

"This isn't magical stuff." Tajor chuckled and held the letter up. "This is human nature stuff."

Jerryck snatched the letter back and quickly re-read it. "They're the Gathering. They're talking about magic."

"They're men in power who feel like their authority has been challenged by a historical rival." Tajor rocked back on his heels. "What's this advice they're accusing you of getting and following?"

"Something about Shamaness Sakila, I assume," Jerryck said. "She's the only practitioner of shamanism I've talked to. And we did talk in the infirmary."

"What exactly were you doing in the infirmary?" Tajor asked.

"I helped the head medic and my wife with one of the pregnant women. The patient didn't like what the medics were telling her, and she asked for a second opinion. Mine."

"So why don't you just write them back and tell them that?" Tajor said with a shrug. "The woman was second-guessing the medics. So there happened to be a shamaness doling out some advice along with yours. So what? Unless someone was standing there listening to the entire conversation, don't you think it's rather presumptive to assume you got advice and followed it? Could you demand they tell you who's spreading these rumors about you?"

"Good idea." Jerryck stuffed the letter in his pocket and turned to leave.

"Wait," Heston said. "I called you. Remember?"

"Oh, right." Jerryck turned back to the room. "What did you need?"

Heston steepled his fingers on his desk. "The night the quepota came, did Tajor catch its magic?"

"Yes," Jerryck said.

Heston interlaced his finger so hard they turned white. He narrowed his eyes at Tajor. "Why didn't you answer that succinctly instead of leading me on a will-o-wisp chase?"

"I was afraid it would hurt your feelings?" Tajor somehow made the statement a question.

"Try again."

"Um…" Tajor rolled his ash colored eyes up to the ceiling and tapped his chin, as if trying to make himself look deep in thought. It might have worked if he wasn't also smirking. "I was afraid you would hurt my feelings?"

Heston rose from his chair, fingers splayed flat on his desktop, his anger palpable even to Jerryck. Tajor's smirk faded only slightly. "All right, how about this. It was dark. Perhaps Jerryck didn't see me react the way he thought. And if no one really saw it, not clearly, then did it really happen?"

"I could see clearly enough to know your reaction to magic," Jerryck said.

"Don't let him distract you," Heston told Jerryck. Tajor laughed. Heston shouted, "This isn't funny. You requested we keep this curse of yours secret. Then you do something stupid like this?"

"My question stands," Tajor said. "And it's similar to another question I heard somewhere once. If a tree falls in the forest, and there's no one around to hear it, does it make any sound?"

"That's the stupidest thing I've ever heard," Jerryck said. "Of course it would. Just because you don't hear sound doesn't mean it didn't happen."

"How do you know if you didn't hear it?"

"A sound doesn't require any material for it to be real. Just like there are things that you can't see that are real. You simply follow the evidence that proves it."

Heston made a sweeping motion with his hand. "This is all just more evasion."

"I think it's relevant." Tajor tilted his chin with a cocky attitude. "It was dark. The only witness was in distress. So did it really happen if no one in a calm frame of mind saw it?"

"My frame of mind was stable enough to know what happened." Jerryck raised his arms in frustration. "And even if it wasn't, you don't have to see something for it to be real. The evidence at the time pointed to the fact that you did come in contact with strong magic."

"Does any of this really matter?" Tajor shrugged. "We had to get rid of the creature somehow. I was the safest person there. It's not as if the men were killing the thing. How well are the regular guards trained for fighting in the dark?"

"They're trained perfectly well for defending the walls," Heston said.

"Oh, well then, that settles everything." Tajor used cheerful sarcasm. "Next time a quepota approaches, will just go out and set up castle walls around it. Why didn't we think of doing that?"

Heston went rigid as stone. He stood staring, using the same expression that usually had any of the guards cringing. People who weren't even under his command sometimes cringed under that expression. Not Tajor. He smirked some more, meeting Heston's eyes directly.

"Jerryck…" Heston's voice had quieted to a soft purr without erasing any of the ire on his face. "Since you interfered in the situation, making the sergeant allow Tajor to hurt himself, I need you to help me on a little exercise to make sure there are no repeat occurrences."

If talking to a shamaness in the infirmary got the attention of the Gathering, what would helping with a military exercise do? The last thing Terrance needed was them to send a representative to harass him. At the same time, Terrance had said there was chaos outside the palace walls. Heston was probably pretty busy with that, and trying to find the person who tainted the water. And yet he was taking time for this small matter anyway. Someone should ease some of the load for him.

"I can do that," Jerryck said.

"Very good." Heston stepped out from behind his desk. He went to the door and yanked it open. He pointed to the sergeant and the elite guards. "You three. Get in here."

The sergeant, Cleft Chin, and Crooked Nose all entered. Heston walked back to his desk before turning on the sergeant. "It's been brought to my attention that if your men could fight better in the dark, the quepota might not have given you so many problems."

"That thing was dangerous," the sergeant said. "Killing my men, making them afraid to move around—"

"What did they fear more?" Heston leaned his hands on the desktop. "The quepota? Or the dark?"

"The quepota."

"Prove it. Tonight. We'll do a capture-the-flag scenario out in Aconi Grove. Jerryck will use magic to make the night darker and—"

"What?" Jerryck interjected. "I will?"

Heston moved only his eyes, shifting them to look at Jerryck. "You said you'd help."

"Help, yes, but you didn't say anything about making night darker. How am I supposed to do that?"

"You're the magician." Heston stood straight, crossing his arms. "You tell me."

"Why can't you stick with something more mundane? You said you're doing it in Aconi Grove. Won't it be dark enough under the trees?"

"The grove has clearings in some places," Heston said. "Moon's more than half full and waxing. Can you make a cloud cover it or something?"

"No. Maybe with a little time to practice I might be able to make ground fog large enough to cover the grove, but not clouds to keep the moon covered tonight."

"Perfect." Heston clapped his hands once. He said to the sergeant, "You just got a reprieve of several days. Get your men ready to do a night scenario of capture-the-flag in Aconi Grove in fog."

Jerryck held up his hands. "Wait, wait, wait…"

"Can you or can't you make fog if you have a few days of practice?" Heston asked.

"Yes, but…"

Heston splayed his hands on the desk again, leaning forward to do so. "But what?"

Jerryck didn't really have a legitimate excuse. It was just coming together faster than he expected. He said, "All right, give me five days. I'll make you fog."

"Good." Heston sat down. "I've one more thing to ask you. Everyone else, out."

Tajor smirked once more before he followed the other three men out. Heston rubbed his eyes and said, "I never asked you. Do you think the poison in the water was made by one person? Or multiple?"

"I can't imagine something like that made only by one person," Jerryck said. "Poisoning an entire river takes a lot of power. But there's only one signature."

"Don't imagine," Heston said. "Follow the evidence."

"One person did this."

"Have you given any more thought to finding him?" Heston asked.

"I thought you were doing that."

Heston paused, tipping his chin down before saying, "You have better access to this field of work."

"And you're better at digging out criminals," Jerryck said. "I wouldn't even know where or how to begin."

"I can help you with that," Heston said.

"You've always done well without me before."

Heston pressed his lips together. He shuffled a couple of stacks of papers around on his desk. With a wry grimace, he said, "Fine."

Chapter 12

JERRYCK LEFT the room before Heston could come up with any other crazy things to request of him. He spent the rest of the day in his tower. Every once in a while he skimmed through a book, looking at the process of fog making. Most of the time, he agonized over a response letter to the Gathering.

He had to figure out how to explain why he couldn't come in person, without talking too much about the trouble their nation was currently having. Then he had to figure out exactly how to address the core issue. In the end he followed Tajor's advice, laying out the facts and asking who was spreading rumors about him.

Over the next couple of days, he spent his mornings out in a field practicing making fog. He took care to be in his workroom in time for the noon water test. Some of the off colors weren't showing as strong as they had at first. That should have been encouraging. Instead, the boys took it as an excuse to complain more than they already were.

They complained incessantly. They whined about having to climb the stairs three times a day. They moaned about getting through the household office to turn in the tested sample. They complained about the noise of rebuilding and workers being in the way.

It got to the point that Jerryck would just do the test and get rid of them as quickly as possible, barely even looking at the results. The day before he was supposed to make the fog for Heston, the bulk of the workers cleared out before the test. Not even that stopped the complaining. Jerryck dropped in the sugar and then turned immediately back to his books.

"Take it and go," he said.

"What happened to the other colors?" Zev asked.

Jerryck looked. The colors that were evidence of the magic toxin were absent. Only the colors of the water element and the magic Jerryck had on the sugar remained. He took the cup and peered into it, scrutinizing for any trace of the wrong colors. "Where did you get this water?"

"From the household office," Zev said.

With the shipments of water coming in from other parts of the country, more people had access. It was possible someone had put clean water in the cup by accident. Jerryck would have to double check. He sent the boys on their way, cheering that they didn't have to turn in the test. He snagged his supply of magicked sugar and took it with him to Heston's office.

"I need you to let me into the canal chamber," Jerryck said to him.

Heston shuffled aside whatever paper he'd been working through. "What for?"

"The water test came out positive," Jerryck said. "Er... Negative."

"Which is it?" Heston asked.

"There were no toxins in the water."

"Double checking is good," Heston said. "Why don't you just go to the vats?"

"I don't like the walkway at the top or climbing the ladder to get to it. Then I have to lean out over the edge to catch one of the buckets."

Heston stared at him a moment. With a droll tone, he said, "You'd rather climb the stairs all the way down to the canal chamber and back up again."

Jerryck shrugged one shoulder. "It's no different than what I climb several times a day in my tower."

"True." Heston got to his feet. He opened his desk, took out a key, then used it to unlock one of the cabinets. From that, he retrieved a large ring of master keys to the palace's many locks.

Jerryck followed him down below the palace, through the stone lined passageway to the little door near the entrance to the dungeons, which was the only way to get to the canal chamber. The guards at the dungeon entrance saluted, momentarily showing the palms of their right hands, the fingertips level with the tops of their ears.

Two torch sconces were fastened to the wall on either side of the door. One of them was empty. Heston pointed to it. "Why is one of the torches missing?"

"The pursuivant hasn't come back up yet from escorting in the change of shift," one of the guards said.

Heston grunted acknowledgment. He selected a small key on his ring and used it in the lock. He took the torch from the other sconce. Then he gestured for Jerryck to go down the stairs first.

Aside from the narrower, steeper steps, it really wasn't all that different from descending his tower at night. The torch behind him lit the way just enough. He had no missteps and navigated the loosely wound spiral down with ease.

About halfway down, probably as many steps as his entire tower, a light came up from below, growing brighter and brighter as it approached. A man toting a large canvas bag rounded up the steps. The stairs were too narrow for him to pass. And Jerryck wasn't going back up just to let him out. He wanted this test finished. The sooner they knew whether the water was clear or not, the better.

Someone spoke from below him. "Why did you stop?"

"The general and the magician are coming down," the man called back over his shoulder.

"Convenient," the voice said. The light retreated. "Come back down."

They continued down to the bottom. Four men had been coming up, not two. Three of them, dressed as workers, stood to one side. Each of them held a full canvas bag. The fourth was the pursuivant, the man Heston had put in charge of running the dungeon and managing any prisoners. He also kept watch on the canal room and closely monitored all workers that went in or out. He held the torch and called out the orders.

"I was going to send you a page," he said to Heston. "We're getting debris in the canal, like there was some big rainstorm upriver."

"That might explain my results," Jerryck said. "If a storm filled the river, that would clear it out."

The pursuivant perked up. "Water's clear?"

"We're checking," Heston said as he eyed the canal.

The three men who must have just started their shift stood at the mouth of the tunnel where the canal flowed in from the river. Two of them used long poles with nets on the ends, fishing out bits and pieces of leaves, grasses, twigs, and other debris before they could float close to the buckets on the pulley system that drew the water up to the vats. The third man took everything they fished out and stuffed it in a bag.

"I'll send crews to check the grates at either end and clean them out," Heston said. "That should cut down some of the debris getting through."

Jerryck knelt by the water flow. He dipped in the tin cup he carried. The pursuivant said, "Careful. I don't want you falling in again."

"I'm not falling in," Jerryck said. He set the cup on the stone floor.

The pursuivant pointed to the dark, arched opening where the water flowed out. "If my men have to go to the downstream grate and fish you out again…"

"I'm not falling in!"

Jerryck hadn't ever fallen in. That was just what Old Heldavio had told people. He brought Jerryck down to impress him, thinking that if he was awed enough that might help him to scry. The builders of Coraline Palace had perfectly cut the canal by scrying out its path. It was an engineering feat bragged about even outside the borders of Brend. Jerryck was supposed to scry the grate at the downstream end and then scry his way the length of the canal to the upstream grate. Instead, he had accidentally translocated himself to the downstream grate.

He stared hard at the cup, dropping in the sugar. If he concentrated enough on the present, maybe the past would leave him alone for a little while. At least until someone else reminded him of some embarrassment. The cup started glowing with the same colors as the test.

"That's it then," he said. "The water's clean."

The workers cheered. The three with the netted poles waved them around happily. Heston growled at them and they quickly dipped their poles back down into the water. Everyone else climbed back up the stairs.

Tajor's skinny, elite friend waited for them at the top by the dungeon entrance. He smiled at Heston and said, "We got him."

Heston gave a curt nod. "Very good."

Jerryck headed out after the workers with the sacks of debris, away from the dungeons. Heston stopped him with a large hand on his shoulder. He ducked out from under the hand and said, "I need to tell Terrance about the water."

"After," Heston said. "I need you to come talk to someone."

"Who?" Jerryck asked.

"Come." Heston turned to the reinforced door that led into the dungeons. "Corridors are no place for such discussions."

Jerryck looked around. The workers were gone. Aside from him, only military men were left. What was wrong with discussing military matters around military men?

The two guards on either side of the heavy door stood at attention while the pursuivant opened it. The skinny elite followed him in without hesitation. Jerryck held back. Heston nudged him through the opening.

"I hate this place," Jerryck muttered. He avoided the dungeons if at all possible, dreading the times he had to come down to maintain the magic over the place.

Heston didn't let go of him. "You say that every time you come in."

The door closed behind them. The guards wouldn't open it again unless given permission by Heston or the pursuivant. The entry room was round, with several doors leading off. Each door had a small, barred great at the top for looking through. Most of them were locked.

Heston went through the only one that was open, beckoning Jerryck to follow. The skinny guard stepped in behind them and closed the door. This room wasn't so bad. It was set up more like an office, where the pursuivant could keep records and do paperwork, and had one of the few doors that lacked a muffling spell. And the dampening spell that kept magic at bay wasn't so heavy. The rest of the place, Jerryck's skin practically itched with the weight of it.

"Some of the riots in the city were caused by a magician." Heston rested his hands on his hips. "A young one. Name of Alessandris. From Shontarra."

"That doesn't sound right," Jerryck said. "Magicians take oaths not to do anything that could cause harm."

"Regardless." Heston waived that away and gestured to the skinny guard. "I sent Cade and a few others in to dig him out, bring him here."

"Why would a magician cause riots during a time of crisis?" Jerryck couldn't quite puzzle that one out.

"I'd hoped you would tell me," Heston said. "Since you don't know, I need you to come with me to talk to him. Figure it out."

Jerryck nodded. He followed Heston and the skinny guard, Cade, back out of the office. One of the other doors was unlocked for them to enter the corridor behind it. The stone floor, walls, and ceiling made everything so stark and gray, one might expect their footsteps to echo. The doors to every room exuded a muffling spell, preventing echoes, keeping whoever was inside from understanding anything said outside, unless it was spoken directly through the grate.

Cells. Not rooms. These rooms were called cells. Even though these particular chambers weren't normally used for holding people. There were used more for dissemination, testing, interrogating... Things of that nature.

Jerryck hunched his shoulders in close. He knew the corridor was wide enough for three men to walk abreast, two guards with a prisoner between them. That didn't account for the pressure of the dampening ambience. Combined with the stunted height of the ceiling, he never could shake the feeling that the walls were closing in on him.

A dungeon guard stood outside one of the cell doors. He saluted as they approached. Heston peered through the grate. After a few heartbeats, he stepped back, returned the salute, waited for the guard to drop his, then asked, "Condition?"

"Agitated." The guard's tone was clipped, terse. "At first, he yelled a lot. Demanded to know why we brought him to the dungeons and not to the king."

"Why would he think he should see the king?" Jerryck asked.

"Probably thinks he's doing the right thing," Heston said. "Let's find out."

Heston pointed to the keyhole. The guard unlocked it. The general went in first. Cade followed, Jerryck behind him.

Chapter 13

A LESSANDRIS WAS A YOUNG MAN, older than fifteen, no older than twenty. He paced back and forth in the cell, three or four steps either direction, even after they entered. His hair was cropped to one side in the latest fashion, his boots were well-worn. He had a jaunty tilt to his head, like a lot of wealthy people from Shontarra, Brend's sister nation to the south.

"It's about time you came back." The young man's southern accent was so thick it was almost difficult to understand him. He pointed with his chin to Heston and Jerryck. "Who are these two?"

Heston stepped into Alessandris' path, forcing him to halt his pacing. "I'm the man you were brought here to talk to."

"I was brought here to get an audience with King Terrance." Alessandris' eyes roved over the insignias Heston wore. "If I'd known I was going to be locked in here, I wouldn't have come so willingly."

"The king doesn't grant audiences to people who incite riots," Heston said.

"I only told people the truth." Alessandris bounced on the balls of his feet and raised himself up an inch or two.

"And that is?" Heston still looked down on him.

Alessandris stabbed his chin in Cade's direction. "I'm sure he told you."

He settled his eyes on Jerryck again. He opened his mouth as if he were going to say something else. Heston spoke first. "I want to hear it from you."

Alessandris pointed at Jerryck, with a finger this time instead of his chin. "Who is that?"

Heston stepped to the side holding out one arm, partially blocking Jerryck from view. "I'm asking the questions here. What truth did you tell people?"

"If that's who I think it is—"

"Answer the question!"

Alessandris jumped. Then he blinked. He juggled his shoulders and said, "There's magic in the water. That's what's making people sick. Not some dead animal in a stagnant pool upstream like the proclamation said. Like the king was told."

"Where would magic like that have come from?"

Alessandris snorted derisively. "From some rogue magician, obviously."

"Bringing no harm to people is part of the magicians' oaths," Jerryck reminded him.

"That's why it would have to be a rogue." Alessandris leaned past Heston to glare at Jerryck. "And I have my suspicions who would do such a thing."

"The first person I would suspect is someone who incites riots," Heston said.

Alessandris' narrowed his eyes. "Are you trying to imply something?"

"Let me state this clearly." Heston cocked his head. "I would suspect someone who has already caused damage, like riots, before I would suspect anyone such a person accuses."

"You think *I* did this?" Alessandris' eyes widened and his mouth dropped open. "I've taken the oaths. I can't do anything that brings this kind of harm."

"The oaths don't prevent you from causing damage," Jerryck said. "They merely make you subject to punishment from the Gathering if you do."

"Same thing."

"No," Heston said. "It's not."

Alessandris shut his mouth. His shoulders hunched slightly, something most people did when they acted indignant. In this case, the hair on Jerryck's arms stood up with the prickle of gathering magic. Alessandris didn't say anything, no spells cast, not even muttered ones under his breath. It was possible he just wasn't paying attention. Some magicians had less control than others. Sometimes they gathered magic without knowing it, just as a reaction to their own emotions. It was usually also a symptom of carelessness and lack of control.

Not that any spell he cast was likely to do him much good. Most magic wouldn't work well because of the dampening effect of the charms and magic Jerryck maintained. But that was just ambiance. It wasn't a complete block. Or Tajor would have been adversely affected every time he entered the dungeons.

Alessandris pointed again. "Is that Jerryck?"

"Why?" Heston demanded before Jerryck could respond.

"It *is* him." Alessandris shook his pointing finger. "I don't want him in here. I don't want him anywhere around me."

"Why?" Heston repeated.

"I don't trust him," Alessandris said. The look in his eyes changed from angry to something more akin to an epiphany. His gathered energy dropped. He sucked in his breath and stared at Jerryck. "It was you. You're the one who did this. You made the magic to poison the water."

"*What?*" Jerryck blurted.

"You're the only rogue magician I know of." Alessandris recovered some of his composure. "Who else could it be?"

"Oh, for the sake of an orphan, I did no such thing," Jerryck said with disgust.

"Go ahead, deny it." Alessandris flipped his hair back from his forehead with his fingertips and tilted his nose up. "Did you think no one would figure out what you did? You can rest assured, I won't be the only one."

Cade, still by the door, cleared his throat. Heston nodded. Cade said to Alessandris, "You promised if I brought you to the palace, you would tell us why you think it's magic in the water."

Alessandris sneered. "And you promised an audience with the king."

"Think back on exactly what I said." Cade smiled. "I implied that there was the possibility of that happening. But first, you should tell us why you think it's magic."

Alessandris threw back his shoulders and puffed out his chest. "I'm a healer. I recognize the difference between a biological problem and a magical one. Every person I healed, I had to fight with elemental fire. This is magic."

"And why are you so sure it was Jerryck?" Cade asked.

"He hasn't taken the oaths," Alessandris said, rolling his eyes. "He's completely untrustworthy. It's obvious it was him."

Jerryck opened his mouth to retort. Cade spoke quicker. "And how do you know for certain it's in the water?"

Alessandris frowned. "Where else would it have come from?"

"If you can't answer one question with anything but your own bias," Heston said, "and you can't answer another at all, why should we believe anything you're claiming?"

Alessandris' face darkened. "Are you calling me a liar?"

"You're calling me one," Jerryck said.

"We're just trying to figure this out," Cade said. "Is there anything at all, anywhere in existence, that you've heard of or thought of, that this could be in besides the water?"

"The water is bad at the same time I'm running across this." Alessandris waved his hands around in the air. "Are you really stupid enough to think it's just coincidence?"

"Unless you can specifically pinpoint magic directly in the water and identify it," Cade said, "it's possible that it could be coincidental. I'm asking you, please, we would really like you to prove otherwise. It would make it easier for us if you give us proof this was magic in the water."

Alessandris dropped his hands and shoulders. "I tried, but I need more time. Or someone better with elemental magic."

"You'd have had more time," Heston said. "If you had focused on that instead of starting riots."

"I didn't know those people would act that way when I told them what was really wrong," Alessandris said.

"I might believe you if it only happened once," Heston said. "You started six riots before we pinned you down."

"I didn't mean to." Alessandris gathered magic around him again. Definitely someone who needed better control. He glared at Jerryck and said, "What are you making that face at me for, you charlatan?"

Jerryck pointed at his own chest. "Me?"

"You shouldn't look so smug," Alessandris said. "I hired someone to help me figure out exactly who did this to the water. As soon as we can prove it was you, you're finished. You'll never do anything to hurt anyone else ever again."

"I didn't poison the water!" Jerryck shouted.

"So what? Even if you didn't, which I don't believe, we're still going to find out who did. And I'm turning that person in to the Gathering as an example of what happens when they let anyone practice without taking the oaths. They'll have to put a stop to anyone who defies them." Alessandris jabbed a finger at Jerryck. "Especially you. You're finished either way. And they'll be so mad they won't stop there, I'm sure. How hard do you think they'll have to work to trump up charges against every woman in your family, make them look like witches, and burn them? And I'll help. I'll testify against anyone they ask me to. Just because you deserve it."

Jerryck's mouth went dry. If the Gathering had any excuse at all, they absolutely would tighten their grip on him. They would investigate his family. That would lead them to kill his niece, which would devastate his sister. They wouldn't have to work to trump up any charges. They wouldn't need any false witnesses.

Heston demanded, "Who did you hire?"

Magic gathered again, this time around Jerryck. The dampening spell pressed on him like a weight, sucking the air out of his lungs. Alessandris' haughty sneer morphed into a look of fear. He must have felt it too. He took a step back, nearly putting himself up against the stone wall.

"If you dare try anything against me, you'll regret it." Alessandris shook a finger at Jerryck, leaning to look past Heston to do so. "It'll only make it harder on you when the Gathering comes after you."

As if someone could be harder on him than killing a member of his family. The pressure of the ambient magic increased. It was a deterrent, not a preventative. And since Jerryck was the one who maintained it, he also knew how to bypass it. Normally it required enough effort that it wasn't worth the trouble. At that moment, the effort was just enough to require the kind of thought process that kept Jerryck from reacting with accidental magic.

"You threaten Jerryck or his family, he has every right to retaliate," Heston said. "Answer my question. Who did you hire?"

Alessandris stuck his nose in the air. "I can't tell you that."

"You *can* tell," Heston said. "There's a difference between can't and won't. Jerryck, demonstrate for him the difference."

Jerryck pushed a flicker of magic through the dampening pressure. It locked onto Alessandris' windpipe, swelling the tissues just enough to slowly close off his airway, like one of the gentler attacks Kendra's husband used to sometimes suffer. Alessandris wheezed. He wanted to cause distress to Kendra, he could damn well experience some of what had already caused her too much distress.

Alessandris drew in a raspy breath, labored and shallow. Jerryck pushed more magic through. Alessandris's face drooped with pain. He clutched his chest. His mouth opened and closed. His eyes bulged as he struggled to whisper out stuttered words. "Help... help... I can't... can't..."

"Can't breathe," Jerryck finished for him when his last word degraded into a struggling rasp.

"*Now* you can't tell," Heston said. "Now that you know the difference between *can't* and *won't*, let's try again. Let up, Jerryck."

Jerryck simply stopped working so hard to push magic through the dampening ambiance. He still kept it up some, crossing his arms to hide that the effort made him shaky. "He said to call him Cheber." Alissandris still wheezed, still clutched his chest, but was able to get breathy words out. "I don't think that's his real name. So I can't tell you."

"You're right on that," Heston said. "That's not his real name. We work with him a lot. He's the one who led us to you."

"And when Jerryck does something else as bad as poisoning the river?" Alessandris asked. "People like that don't ever commit only one crime. Even if you refuse to believe me, you can't protect him forever. The next time he does something like this some other magician will turn him in to the Gathering."

Chapter 14

JERRYCK SHOOK. He wrapped his arms tighter about himself and relinquished the effort of pushing magic through the dampening ambiance. Alessandris relaxed, no longer wheezing or rasping.

Heston punched him in the side of the neck, just below the ear. He dropped face first on the stone floor, sprawling limp. Jerryck gasped. "What was that for?"

"You were done," Heston said. He pounded his fist on the door. The guard outside opened it.

"What does that have to do with you hitting him like that?" Jerryck demanded.

Heston stepped out of the cell, telling Cade, "Fetch the medics."

Jerryck knelt by Alessandris. "Don't bother. I can take care of this. He'll wake up fine."

Heston came back in, grabbed Jerryck's arm, and hustled him out into the corridor before he could do anything. "The medics aren't for waking him."

"Then what..."

Heston walked up the corridor toward the entry chamber. "Don't ask and you won't have to know."

Jerryck hurried to keep up, his feet almost as unsteady from the magic usage as his hands and arms. "How's this going to reflect on Terrance when he goes back to the city and tells everyone how he was treated here?"

"He's not going back to Kershet." Heston pounded on the door at the end of the corridor. It opened too.

"Where else would he go?" Jerryck asked.

"Another cell." Heston strode into the entry. "He's never leaving this dungeon."

Jerryck's feet stumbled, betraying his weakened state. "That's rather harsh."

"Harsh is getting innocent people killed because you feel like inciting riots multiple times," Heston said. "We can't afford to be lenient. Do that once, and how many others will start causing problems and getting people killed this way?"

"I don't want to hear any more." Jerryck went to the main door and said to the guards there, "Let me out."

They looked to Heston, who shook his head. They weren't going to let Jerryck out. He screamed, "You have no cause to keep me in here."

Heston took Jerryck by the wrist, holding up his hand. Try as he might, he couldn't quite keep it from shaking where everyone could see. Heston narrowed his eyes. "Is this because of the magic you did? Or is something else bothering you?"

Jerryck blinked and looked away. Heston pulled him. "Come."

They went into the office on the side. This time, the pursuivant sat in there. Heston said, "Mace, we need a moment."

The pursuivant nodded and left, closing the door. Heston drew out a hard, three-legged stool, one of the only seats in the room. Jerryck sank onto it. Heston said, "Take deep breaths. Don't fight the shaking or try to hide it. Just relax and let it calm down on its own."

Jerryck lowered his head into his hands. "I never thought I would need healing advice for myself from you."

"You're showing the same signs as men in battle," he said. "Or any confrontation. Deep breaths. Fill your lungs. That'll help clear your head more than anything else."

Adrenaline. That was what he was describing. Jerryck put his hands on his head, raising his arms and expanding his chest cavity in the process, which allowed for more air intake. Some of the shaking calmed with each breath.

Incrementally, control of his extremities returned and he regained the ability to hold them steady.

"What bothered you more?" Heston asked. "The threat against your family? Or the accusation that you're the perpetrator?"

"If someone would poison an entire river..." Jerryck paused to shudder. "Would they do something else later on?"

"Guaranteed," Heston said.

"You sound so sure."

"This was a deliberate act." Heston paced in a circle around the outer edges of the cramped room. "No one has claimed credit. No one has stated that it was for any kind of political statement, or declaration of war. No one has even refuted the false story about a dead animal contaminating the water with a rare disease. Not credibly."

Jerryck numbly restated what he understood of Heston's words. "So this wasn't to get attention, make a political statement, or start a war."

"It may have been an attempt to cause strife between Brend and the Chemwanitz Mountains," Heston said. "That's speculation. Whoever they are, they're probably observing our reactions. Where? I don't know. I found no trail when I went upriver. I may not have been far enough up. Or maybe they're downriver. Or in Kershet. I'm searching. But I'm having trouble searching out potential magic-users, likely someone underestimated, or not well-known, or new. I need your help."

"I wouldn't even know how to start," Jerryck said.

"Start with your closest contacts," Heston said. "Tell them you're looking for someone new with high potential. You'll get a lot of false leads. It can't be helped. Bring every one of them to me. I'll have my men track them down."

"They'll want to know why I'm asking."

"You'll have to figure out yourself what to tell them." Heston stopped his pacing and stood in front of Jerryck. "Make it plausible. Have any of your associates ever contacted you with a question like this?"

"A few times," Jerryck said. "When they were looking for an apprentice."

"Tell them you're thinking of taking one on."

Jerryck dropped his hands between his knees. "The Gathering won't like me doing that."

"I'll let you in on a little inside information," Heston said. "You'll need to take one on. Terrance is planning on doing some rearranging in the household after Nita's next birthday. Everyone in a high enough position will be required to take on an apprentice. That'll include you. And Terrance won't care if the Gathering likes it or not."

"If I ever did take on an apprentice, it would most likely be my nephew Zev."

"Your colleagues don't need to know that," Heston said.

Jerryck nodded and stood. Heston led him out to the entry chamber and out of the dungeon. As soon as Jerryck got into the regular corridors of the palace, he breathed even easier. He turned to head to his tower. Heston caught his arm again. "We need to tell Terrance."

"Oh, right." Jerryck turned that way. "Of course. He'll need to know I'm sending out all these contact letters."

"And the water," Heston said. "He'll want to send word to the kitchens before they start making supper."

"Supper." Jerryck was missing something. Something about the kitchens. And supper. And... food... He'd forgotten to eat lunch again. He stopped mid-step and slapped his forehead. "No! My wife and sister are going to be furious."

"What did you do this time?" Heston asked.

"What *didn't* I do."

"I'm not helping you with women problems," Heston said. He continued on. "I'll inform Terrance while you deal with them. Good luck."

Jerryck turned back to face the way to his tower. It would be so easy to go up there and hide from everyone for awhile. It wasn't like the problem would get any worse for putting off awhile. Instead, he headed to the kitchens. Sometimes it was better just to get unpleasantness over with.

The moment he walked in, a plate flew through the air and narrowly missed his head. It whapped the door frame, the antishatter spell on it pinging and leaving a small dent in the wood.

"What the—" Jerryck looked the way it had come. Kendra was grabbing a handful of spoons while scullery maids and cooks scattered away from her in all directions.

The spoons didn't come anywhere near as close as the plate had when she threw them. Unfortunately, she was close behind them and bearing down. "You want to work yourself to death. Fine! Don't expect me to help you out. I'm not serving you hot meals at odd hours of every day when you just happen to remember that you have to eat to keep alive."

"I was testing the water." Jerryck raised his arms to fend her off. "Then I had to take care of... something else for Heston."

"I don't care." Her pitch was so high, she might have been trying to shatter the plates with her voice. By now, they were the only two in the large room, making it seem all that much more vast. She stopped just short of arm's length, close enough he could see tears in her eyes. "You can't keep doing this to yourself."

He dropped his arms, letting his shoulders sag. She had good enough aim, she might have missed his head on purpose. He bent and picked up the plate. "I'm sorry. I didn't mean to worry you."

"You never mean to." She sniffed, wiping away the tears before they could fall. Her voice dropped quiet enough he probably was the only one who could hear it, even if others had still been in the room. "Remember, please remember, you have more accidents when you don't eat right."

"That's just yours and Leanne's theory," Jerryck said, shaking his head. "There's no evidence to support that."

"There's my observations."

"Which are biased."

She closed her eyes, grit her teeth, straightened her spine, took a deep breath, and her face cleared. A couple of cooks peeked out from a side room. She said to Jerryck, still quiet, "That may be. I'll allow for that possibility. But don't think that means I won't keep hounding you. Just be glad Leanne wasn't here and I didn't tell her. It makes her cry. Now, you said you were helping out the General?"

Some of the scullery maids came out from wherever they were hiding. Leanne wasn't among them. Disappointing. Except according to Kendra, she probably would be crying if she was there. Perhaps it was best she was absent after all.

Jerryck bent to gather up the spoons from the floor. "Actually, we were helping each other. The initial water test came out clear, so he took me down to the canal chamber to test it from the source."

Staff melting out of the shadows and side rooms all paused and looked at him. Kendra held out a hand. "And?"

"And then…" Jerryck really didn't feel like telling her about what happened in the dungeon. He skipped it. "And then he went to tell the king that the water is clean and safe to drink."

Cheers erupted. Except from Kendra. She cocked her head at Jerryck. "And?"

"And what?"

She glanced around. With all the jubilant noise around them as cover, she leaned close and spoke softly in his ear. "You're as pale as when you've had an accident."

Jerryck sighed. "I didn't have an accident. There was an incident in the dungeon I had to help take care of right after the water test. And I had a chat with Heston over it, and we decided I have to help find who did this to the river. Which means pretending to look for an apprentice."

"The Gathering won't like that."

"Yes, well, I don't like that someone poisoned our water."

Chapter 15

WITH THE WATER CLEAR, Sakila decided it was time for her to return home. She paid Jerryck one more visit. He offered her the remnants of the magicked sugar as a parting gift.

"It's not a very good gift," Jerryck said. "The magic doesn't even last very long, no more than a month. Minutes, once it's activated."

"I have nothing to give you for this," she said.

"It's a gift, not an exchange. You don't have to pay for it. Think of it as my way of thanking you for visiting."

"Even after I made you destroy your workroom?" She looked around the room, at the new cabinets, new glass in the windows, new shelves with jars waiting to be filled. She brushed her fingers across the sturdy worktable, one of the only things that survived Jerryck's accidents on a regular basis. She said, "All this work and effort. And you still thank me?"

Jerryck grinned sheepishly. "That wasn't your fault. In fact, if a trade would make you feel better, then don't tell anyone that's what caused it. I'm not supposed to have accidents like that."

"I will tell no one," she said with a smile. "I would not tell anyone even if you gave me nothing. It is your business, and no one else's. But thank you for the gift. And thank you for treating me like a sister."

"I like family," Jerryck said with a shrug. If she insisted on thinking good manners were preferential treatment reserved for family, who was he to argue? "If there's anything else I can do for you, you'll let me know?"

"I do have one other question," she said. "It is not very important. It matters so little, I usually forget to ask."

"And you're remembering now?"

"So many people here are talking about your coming visitors from Shontarra, I remembered. Why are Brend and Shontarra called sister nations. I know of no other two countries called that."

"We speak the same language and have similar histories," Jerryck said.

Did he need to go further than that? He could recite to her all the boring history of the fighting the separate districts carried out before the northern two-thirds signed a unification treaty and became the nation of Brend, with the southern districts following that example about a decade later to form Shontarra. He could. But he really didn't feel like it.

Sakila nodded. She must have been satisfied with the short answer, because she said, "I thought as much."

When she left, he went back to his current project. Penning letters. He had already drafted several of them to fellow magicians, inquiring if they were aware of someone new in the field with significant potential. Not every premiere had appointed an official magician for their district, so he started with the ones who had. He also wrote a draft to the magicians officially appointed by the mayors of the five major cities of the nation. Well, four really, plus the one that was disputed, since it sat on the coast right on the border between Brend and Shontarra.

Once he started getting responses from those, he would hand them to Heston for anything that needed followed up. Then he could branch out from there, focusing on the districts where he hadn't yet contacted anyone, and some of the smaller cities.

He folded, addressed, and sealed the letters appropriately. Then he set them aside. He'd post them the next time he left his tower. Then he picked up one of his books to review fog making. Again. Bored with it, he allowed himself to browse other spells, losing himself in the pages, just relaxing and enjoying some casual reading. He certainly needed some leisure time after the stress in the dungeons the day before.

Eventually, the chimes signaled someone entering the tower. The light slanting through the window said that the morning had passed. It was now noon. He softly swore under his breath. If he didn't hurry down for lunch his wife and sister would be upset. He closed his book, put it on the shelf, then stacked his notes neatly on the counter under it. He picked up the letters that needed posting and opened the door to the workroom. A rookie elite guard stood there on the landing with his hand raised to knock.

"Yes?" Jerryck asked.

"I'm supposed to remind you that tonight is the scheduled capture-the-flag scenario," the young man said.

"Oh! Yes. Tonight. Of course it's tonight. I knew that."

"And I'm supposed to make myself available if you have any errands to run, in case you wanted to rest, or anything."

"Really? Wow. I've never had an elite to run errands for me."

"I'm just a rookie." The young man smiled with only half his mouth and turned to show his bare sleeve. "See? No stripes. So I get to play errand lad in the afternoons. You need anything I can do?"

"Uh…" Jerryck tapped his chin with the stack of letters.

If this man did menial chores, that might leave room to pursue more interesting things. Jerryck still had some ideas how to play with figuring out Tajor's curse. Which would lead to other things. He'd figured out how to make fire eat the visibility of ink, and bring it back to visibility with water. Though he probably really should use the time for a more thorough review of his responsibility to Heston. Of course, either option would require him to think up menial chores that didn't require the use of magic for this man to do. He started off with, "You could get me something to eat."

"Sure thing," the guard said. He held out his hand. "You need those posted while I'm at it?"

Jerryck looked at the letters in his hand. Instead of smacking himself for stupidity, he nodded and handed them over. When the guard left, Jerryck did shake his head at himself. He could be so dense at times.

Responsibilities first. He got his book and notes back out. Since he hadn't taken the last review seriously, he should do it again. He already knew what to do. But a little extra caution never hurt. He reran the calculations for how much energy would be required to cover the entire area of the grove. He came to the same conclusion as before. The method that provided the best efficiency would be to cast the fog spell in more than one section, then get it to spread, allowing the edges to meld together.

By the time the guard returned with a plate of food, the worktable was covered with notes and multiple open books. The young man stood there until Jerryck cleared a corner for the plate.

"Your wife and sister tried telling me you needed to come down yourself," the guard said. "I hope you don't mind, I told them it wasn't going to happen because you were trying to get things done so you could nap this afternoon."

"You really want me to sleep that badly?"

"Heston said I might need to push you," the guard said. "Anyway, the ladies weren't going to give me anything for you to eat until I told them that. Then they were happier. Anything else I can do for you?'

"You're awfully eager," Jerryck said.

"This is an easy job compared to what I normally have to do. I like this. You want me to make sure no one disturbs you while you sleep?"

"Why not," Jerryck said.

The guard ran back out and down the stairs. Jerryck stacked his notes back together. There was nothing more he could do with them anyway. He knew the magic well enough he wouldn't even need them for the scenario.

After eating he went to bed, manipulating his own aura enough to induce drowsiness. Then it was a simple matter to let his body drift down into sleep.

Jerryck met with Heston at the stables, already astride the only horse large enough to carry him. They rode out in the dark with several of the wall guards, five elites, a paddy wagon, and Head Medic Kellos with a couple of his assistants.

"What are you doing here?" Jerryck asked Kellos.

"I could ask the same of you," Kellos said.

"He's doing me a favor." Heston answered for Jerryck. Then said, "Kellos always comes on night exercises for me, to tend any minor injuries the men incur."

"What favor?" Kellos asked. "In return for what?"

"Doesn't matter," Heston said.

A couple miles down the road, they turned off in the direction of the river. They bypassed Zinrish Dell, from which many of the blooms in the palace gardens had been transplanted. A lot of people went there to access the flowers for pigments, magic, and alchemical components. Many of them had complained over the years about the lack of a road. Terrance refused to build one after Jerryck told him the construction required would likely drive away the sprites that kept the flowers in bloom longer than anywhere else.

A few more miles, and they arrived at the edge of Aconi Grove. It had been logged down to a couple of miles before being declared a preserve. Even though it was off limits to hunters and loggers, it had never expanded since. People would often venture in far enough to get to the pond. Someone had put a stone bench in there at some point, declaring it was an inspirational spot for artists. Rarely did anyone go farther in and risk disturbing the dryad. Heston claimed that need for extra caution regarding locale made it ideal training grounds.

He halted without dismounting. He pointed to one of the men and gestured him near. Even closer, it was dark enough Jerryck could barely tell that it was the sergeant he had bickered with.

Heston waved his hand at the black line of the trees. "Take your team in there and set up. You have ten minutes."

"That's it?" the sergeant said.

"Then the magician will cast a fog spell," Heston continued.

"Fog?" Kellos dismounted with his medics. "Is that really necessary? There'll be enough injuries as it is. Even with the moon out like this, it's going to be pitch black beneath those trees."

"And it'll be worse in about ten minutes." Heston stared unflinching at the sergeant.

The man grumbled something unintelligible and trudged over to the paddy wagon. He and a couple of the wall guards unlocked it and extracted a bound, hooded man. They guided him into the trees. The rest of the wall guards followed, leaving only the five elites with Heston, Jerryck, and the medics.

"Who is that prisoner?" Jerryck pointed at the men disappearing into the black. From the man's build, he looked almost like Tajor's elite friend with the crooked nose.

"That's no prisoner," Heston said. "That's Deek. He's the flag."

"The flag?"

"You have to have a flag to play capture-the-flag." Heston gestured toward the grove where the men had disappeared. "He's it."

"You don't use a standard, or a banner, or something like that?"

"Men fight harder over a fellow human than a piece of cloth."

Jerryck dropped the subject. He didn't need any more details on what men fight over. And he likely would get more than a full share of that kind of rancid information tonight anyway. He looked over at the small knot of elite guards and asked, "Where's Tajor? I half expected you to make him take part in this."

"Tajor is indisposed," Heston said. One of the guards started snickering. In the dark, Jerryck couldn't make out much. It might've been the one with the cleft chin. He silenced as soon as Heston turned his head in that direction.

"Tajor doesn't get indisposed," Jerryck said. "Unless…"

"I indisposed him," Heston said.

Jerryck dropped that subject too. Definitely more information than he needed. He stared fixedly at the dark line of trees ahead of him and waited for the ten minutes to pass. Then he gathered up his energy, concentrating it around his right hand. He shaped it with his words, then severed it, casting it away from himself to affect a section of the grove.

There, it drew moisture out of the ground and vegetation. The magic condensed the moisture, until it created a mist thick enough to grow and spread around. Then he repeated the process a few times more for other sections, making sure to keep his magic away from the center where it would disturb the dryad. Some of the fog might drift her way, but a little shouldn't be a problem.

It took more time than he wanted for the fog to cover as large an area as the grove. He didn't dare do anything to try to hurry it along. The last time he'd played with that, he'd made fog in the workroom so thick he couldn't even see the tip of his nose. Heldavio was furious. And it took days for it all to clear out.

When he finally declared the job finished, Heston turned in his saddle to the five elites and said, "You have two hours. Go."

The five of them sprinted into the trees. The medics lit lanterns as soon as they were gone. Jerryck asked Kellos, "Why didn't we light these before?"

"That would destroy vision acclimated to dark," Heston answered as he took an hourglass from his pocket.

"That group of five is less than a quarter of the men the other team has," Jerryck said.

"I can count," Heston said.

Kellos chuckled. "They're mad at him for it."

"For setting them up to lose?" Jerryck snorted. "I'd be mad too."

"After several days of preparation and planning," Heston said, "they'd better win."

"How can five men overcome more than four times their number?" Jerryck asked.

"Stealth, cunning, strategy, training, and experience," Heston said. "Those five are some of my most senior elites. I only allowed them two hours so it would be a bit of a challenge. If they win before three quarters of that time, the sergeant is washed out."

"You'd kick him out over something like this?"

"Absolutely," Heston said with a curt nod. "He's had enough training for this. If he can't hold his own for a decent amount of time, he's not worth training any further. He's certainly not qualified for leading palace defenses."

"What if his team wins?"

"They won't," Heston said. Jerryck looked over at Kellos, who shook his head and said the same thing.

After a bit, the men straggled out of the grove one or two at a time, every few minutes. Some of them limped on twisted ankles, having stepped in holes or tripped over tree roots. A few sported lumps from whapping their heads on branches or running into trees they couldn't see. Some of them had blossoming bruises, or trickling blood from meeting up with members of the smaller team. The medics treated the minor injuries. Jerryck kept his focus on the fog. Anytime part of it started to wane, he gave that area a tiny boost of energy, just enough to refresh it.

Ten minutes before the two-hour deadline, a man sprinted out of the grove straight at Heston. Gasping for breath, the man said, "Both teams are ceding to the other. One of the rookies got too close to the dryad's tree. We're trying to extract him."

Chapter 16

ERRYCK SPURRED his mount forward, heedless of Heston's and Kellos' call for him to wait. He gathered up some energy and shaped it into an illuminated orb. He adjusted that to absorb the fog within a five-foot circle around him, and to dispel the magic that had gathered it. By the time he reached the edge of the fog leaking out between the trees, he had the orb levitating about a foot over his head.

Inside the trees, he immediately slowed. The most well-worn paths were on the other side of the grove, closer to the city where the pond lay. Jerryck had never approached the dryad's tree from this side. He tried giving his horse the leeway to go where it pleased while he set up some tracking to figure out the exact location of the dryad. The animal turned around and headed back to the edge of the grove.

Heston barreled out of the dark between the boles of the trees. He reached down and snatched at the bridal of Jerryck's horse. "What do you think you're doing? I told you to wait."

Jerryck batted Heston's hand away and steered the horse back toward the center of the grove. "If they irritate the dryad too much, she'll kill them all."

"Unless they kill her first," Heston said, following.

"Not likely," Jerryck said with a snort. "Besides, if she dies, the grove dies. Then the sprites at Zinrish Dell will die. And then the flower trade from it will die. And a lot of our art trade will die, because our poets and writers and painters will immigrate elsewhere."

"Stop," Heston said.

"I know it sounds a bit dramatic," Jerryck said.

"Stop!" Heston pulled his horse in front of Jerryck's, cutting him off. "You go riding through trees on a horse, you knock your head on branches. Dismount."

Jerryck lit onto the ground. A few of the guards on foot came up behind them. Heston also dismounted, then turned both the horses over to one of the men. While that man guided the animals back the way they came, everyone else went forward heading for the center of the grove.

The fog wasn't flowing out to the edge like he expected. It was flowing in to the center, swirling and eddying as it went around the trees and the underbrush, creating ghostly shapes that reached out skeletal fingers to pluck at anything that got too close. Jerryck stopped, frowning and watching it move.

Heston stopped beside him. "What?"

Jerryck held up his hands, fingers splayed. "Do you feel any kind of a breeze?"

"No," Heston said. "Why?"

"Just double checking," Jerryck said. He pointed to the flowing fog. "It's moving the wrong direction."

Heston watched it for a few heartbeats. "What would make it do that?"

"I'm not certain," Jerryck said, continuing forward. "Maybe the dryad is pulling it in. If so, it'll get thicker the closer we get to her tree."

"Why would she do that?" Heston asked.

"She's a plant," Jerryck said. "Maybe she likes the moisture. She's also a magical creature. Maybe she's feeding off the magic that generated the fog. Maybe both."

Heston pointed at the ball of light over Jerryck's head. "Can you dim that some?"

"It won't dissipate the fog as well if I do," Jerryck said.

"That'll make it easier to see if it's thickening," Heston said.

Jerryck drew some of the energy out of the orb and back into himself. He got it down to about half the light it had originally emitted. He stopped dimming it when one of the men behind him stumbled over a root. The fog closed in on either side, flowing faster the farther they went.

The ground sloped gently upward, evidence they were getting close. Men's voices drifted their way from ahead. One of them called out something about a light. A couple of minutes later, the sergeant emerged from the fog. Water dripped off him. His wet hair was plastered to his head. His boots squished with every step he took.

Heston continued pressing forward. "What happened?"

The sergeant turned around to walk beside him. "I made the wrong choice in one of the team members."

"How did you get all wet?" Jerryck asked.

"That's from the fog," the sergeant said. "It's so thick up there, everything is wet. We tried to light torches to draw the dryad away from the tree. That's when it all billowed in and saturated everything. Now nothing will light."

The crack of a rock hitting wood resounded. The trees around them rustled, and the sergeant swore under his breath. He said, "We gathered up some rocks to throw as a distraction, just in case she went after the rookie before we could get him out of the tree."

"You shouldn't throw things at her," Jerryck said, watching the dark branches spearing the fog and waving restlessly as if there was a breeze.

"If the fog is that thick up there," Heston said, "how are you able to see enough to hit anything?"

"That's the strange part," the sergeant said. "We can see pretty clearly. I don't know if it's because the fog is condensing into water, or something else."

Another smack rang out. The trees obscured in the fog creaked and groaned. Jerryck broke into a run.

He came to another guard, his arm drawn back with a rock in hand. Jerryck grabbed his arm before he could throw. "Stop!"

"We have to do something," the man said, lowering his arm, water dripping from the sleeve of his elite uniform.

Jerryck frowned up at the tree on the pinnacle of the incline. More gnarled, twisted, and larger than any other tree he knew of. Fog swirled around it. Moonlight cast mangled shadows from it. And still, they could clearly see the man dangling from an arm and leg from some of the smaller branches, and the humanoid shape of the dryad clinging to the bole.

"She stopped moving," someone called on the right. Clarity of sight didn't extend that way. It only wrapped around the tree.

Another called on the left. "Should we try lighting the torches again?"

"No!" Jerryck raised his voice, answering them. "If you irritate her too much, she'll spear you with the branches of the other trees. Or beat you to death with them."

Heston and the others caught up. Ripples shivered across the bark of the dryad's skin. She let out the sound of dry leaves rustling, her version of hissing at them. She shifted her feet, clinging to knots on the tree, then raised her arms and splayed her twig-like fingers wide. The magic fueling the fog lurched her way and reshaped. More fog swirled in, surrounding Jerryck. It putt out his light and drenched him in seconds. At the same time, the tree became even clearer to see.

The soldier stuck in the tree called out to them. "She wouldn't really use my body as fertilizer, would she?"

"Yes," Jerryck said. He took a few steps to the right, out of the knot of fog. The dryad's fingers twitched. The fog slowly drifted after him. He kept moving while he explained to the trapped guard, "You're not a cognizant, sentient being in her view. Your best use is food for her friends."

He came to the man on the right who called out earlier. It was the elite with the cleft chin. He snickered and said to Jerryck, "You're so tactful at times."

Jerryck ignored him, keeping his focus on the magic the dryad manipulated. Heston followed him. "You used fire the last time you faced her down."

"I used the illusion of fire," Jerryck corrected him. "That way it didn't do any damage. It just startled her. If I had burned her tree, we wouldn't have made it out of the grove alive."

"Can you do it again?" Heston asked.

"She's magically clarified sight around her tree," Jerryck said, pointing to it. "That's why we can see in the dark through the fog. It'll cancel out any illusion I try to use. She remembers me, what I did."

"Can't you put her to sleep? Like you do with patients sometimes?"

"Different biology," Jerryck said. "It would take a different process."

"How soon can you get it done?"

"I'm not sure I can," Jerryck said.

Heston walked sideways, watching the dryad. The others followed. She moved with them, continually facing Jerryck, disregarding anyone else.

He stopped. The dryad stopped. The knot of stalking fog caught up and enveloped him, drenching him all over again. He walked away again, this time to the left, passing all the men who had been following him. The dryad still turned to keep facing him.

"Do plants even sleep?" the sergeant asked.

"Sometimes," Jerryck said. "Trees sleep in the winter. When it's cold. Sort of. It's not exactly the same thing."

Could he chill everything enough to make the dryad even drowsy? If he could, that would slow her down, make her lethargic. He lifted his hands, feeling the mists, letting the condensing water drip down his fingers. It connected him back to the magic that had created the fog.

He gathered up more of his own energy. Breathing in the fog, it deepened the connection. Then he breathed that out into the energy that had gathered, connecting it further. He reshaped it with words that turned it freezing. Then spoke the words that severed it, sending it out to all the rest of the magic it was connected to.

The mists crystallized into minuscule shards of ice hanging in the air. The temperature plummeted. Everyone's breath frosted, adding to the chill moisture. The dryad lowered her hands, clinging to the tree with all four limbs again. Her magic abated. The tree grew obscure in the darkness and the frozen fog.

Jerryck turned his attention to the tree. He tweaked the magic again, causing it to pull moisture out of the branches holding the man. They were young enough, thin enough, that they shriveled and snapped. The man fell.

The dryad moved sluggishly toward him. The other men rushed in, grabbing their comrade and dragging him away before she could cross half the distance. The dryad reached out again. This time, she made the mournful sounds of wood creaking and breaking.

With the clarifying magic now at its weakest, Jerryck fashioned the illusion of animals entering the grove, dying, decaying, and feeding all the trees.

Setting that in motion, it caught her attention. She settled, nestling down, the bark of her skin melding nearly seamlessly with the trunk of her tree. Jerryck motion for everyone to retreat, leaving the illusion to play out over the next quarter of an hour. That was enough time for them all to get out from beneath the canopy of trees.

Chapter 17

URING THE NEXT FEW DAYS, nobles and rich merchants came to the palace in anticipation of the Shontese delegation. Jerryck probably wouldn't have noticed if they didn't keep sending him little requests they could ask from anyone, not a magician. And if he didn't have to eat supper in the banquet hall like he did at the end of every week.

The day of the expected arrival most of the guests claimed spots outside the grand entrance hours beforehand. Jerryck watched from his bedroom window, all of them jockeying for positions. He complained to Leanne. "I don't even know why they're all here. It's not like we've never received Shontese delegations before."

"We've never received one headed up by the grandnephew of their prince before." Leanne straightened out his clothes and smoothed them down.

He'd had to dress formally. Terrance expected his entire core staff to come out and greet the Shontese Lord. Chancellor Herron and Chamberlain Malk were already out there, mingling and chatting and smiling, probably having a wonderful time. Jerryck had no intention of exposing himself to that crowd any earlier than he had to.

Leanne still fussed over him for some reason. "You look so nice when you're all dressed up like this."

He looked down at himself. His pants were pleated. The double-breasted shirt had piping along the seams. It was long-sleeved and made of thick material to make it stiff. On a warm day in early summer, with a lot of people dressed like him, that crowd was going to be stinky. Why did it matter so much what they looked like?

The high vantage of his tower let them see over the wall. The caravan bringing the Shontese delegation approached. Later in the summer, that many horses, men, and wagons would raise a cloud of dust, even though the road was paved with quarried stone. When they got to about a half-mile out, the guards on the wall rang the bell, signaling the approach.

Jerryck let out an exasperated breath. He forced his legs to carry him down all the stairs. Too bad he didn't have a way to turn himself invisible. Or at least go somewhat unnoticed. He stepped out of the shelter of the palace, into the crowd.

"Lord Magician!" The mother of the young Premiere of Plurrin strode toward him, parting the sea of people with sweeping arms as she moved. "Just the person I've been looking for."

"Lady Emmalyn." Jerryck put on what was supposed to be a smile. Hopefully it didn't look too much like a grimace. "You're a long way from home."

Plurrin was one of the smaller districts in Brend, located at the coast on the southern border of the nation. Despite its size, it was also one of the more important districts. Its location on the coast gave it access to good harbors, fishing, and trade. Technically, sixteen-year-old Wendirrop was the premiere, but everyone knew his mother was really the person in charge.

"The journey was simply wretched." Emmalyn fanned herself with one of her long sleeves. "You've traveled enough. You know how it can be. But when I heard that Prince Sanbralio's grandnephew was coming, I knew I simply had to visit. After all, he is negotiating trade."

"And tariffs," Jerryck said. He looked at the faces all around them. Surely there had to be someone he knew nearby that he could use as an excuse to get away.

"And everyone knows how important Plurrin is for trade between our two sister nations." She flung her arms out wide, nearly swiping someone's head. Then she folded her hands in front of herself. "But that's not what I needed to talk to you about. I need advice."

"You?" Jerryck nearly choked, trying to keep from laughing. "Advice?"

"My son has decided it's high time Plurrin had its own district magician. I'm gathering recommendations for the position. So far, everyone has suggested magician Bennett. I'm not sure he'd want to give up his position as Oceanside's city magician. I thought you would be up to giving me an honest opinion, since you have nothing to gain or lose, you having no credentials or anything."

"What do my lack of credentials have to do with giving advice?"

She sort of gave half a shrug. "Well, you know..."

"No, not really," Jerryck said. He caught sight of Priad Lalven passing through the crowd. He appeared to be arguing with the man walking beside him. Jerryck seized the opportunity. "I'll ask Lalven."

Emmalyn's upper lip curled. "He said if my son wants a district magician, he should ask himself."

"I'll ask anyway." Jerryck sidled away from her, hurrying to catch Lalven.

The man with him had a scarred and pitted face with a scowl to match. It gave him a rough appearance despite his finery. A couple of gold rings adorned thick and gnarled fingers that kept closing into fists. The velvet of his tunic didn't hide the build of muscle in his arms and chest. The way his eyebrows drew together gave him a glower that matched the angry tone in his voice as he talked to Lalven. "Now is perfect. The thief isn't with him to thwart me. If you'd just—"

"No, Keniv." Lallvin held up one hand. "You have my answer. This isn't the time nor the place for that sort of thing."

The man pulled up short when he saw Jerryck. "Who are you?"

"Mind your manners," Lalven said. Then his face cleared, and he said to Jerryck, "Please, excuse my cousin. He's being irritable."

"Cousin?" Jerryck looked the man up and down. There was no family resemblance to Lalven in the slightest.

Some of Lalven's frown leaked back. "Distant cousin... Very distant cousin. What can I do for you?"

"I just need an escape from the dowager." Jerryck pointed to Emmalyn, who had already found a new victim to talk at.

"Who wouldn't?" Lalven gave the woman a look of scorn he normally reserved only for the princess. "She didn't ask you how to get Terrance's romantic attention again, did she?"

"No."

"Or how to circumvent the rules of Processions and somehow get Nita to let Wendirrop court her?"

"No."

"Too bad." Lalven clucked his tongue. "Either of those would've been the perfect excuse to ask her to leave."

"She just wanted to know about hiring a magician."

"Ah, that tired story. Yes. She's been asking everyone for months now. Typical woman. Ask everyone. Do nothing."

Jerryck held up his hands and backed away. "Please don't start on that."

The necessity of socializing was bad enough. Listening to another prejudicial rant about the evils of women from Lalven would make this occasion truly torturous.

Lalven and Keniv continued on through the crowd. Jerryck ducked around a few sweating people until he was out of Emmalyn's sight. Then he bumped into Thessallim, a fellow magician, with Magician Letz standing right behind him.

"Careful there." Thessallim smiled at him. "Better to watch where you're going or you're liable to bump into someone unpleasant. Lucky for you, it's just me."

"Lucky," Letz said with a snort. "He probably finds *you* unpleasant."

"Nonsense." Thessallim laughed. "You don't, do you, Jerryck?"

"Jerryck thinks most magicians are unpleasant," Letz said. "Which might be why he's looking for someone new in the trade."

"How did you know I'm looking for someone new?" Jerryck hadn't sent a letter to either of these men yet.

"We were both with Ressell when he got your letter." Thessallim laughed again. "Lucky us."

Letz snarled at him. "Would you stop going on with all the garbage about luck?"

Thessallim's smile didn't waver. "Not as long as people keep paying me so well for it. Call it something else if you don't like the word luck. You could call it providence instead of luck. Since prayers are what actually does it."

Jerryck turned to walk away. This conversation was about as desirable as listening to one of Lalven's stupid rants. Letz put a hand on Jerryck's shoulder. "Wait, please. I need to talk to you."

"Me too," Thessallim said.

"Ressell said he'd ask around Kershet for you," Letz said. "But you may want to reconsider the idea of taking on an apprentice."

"I'm not sure I'll have much of a choice," Jerryck said.

"The Gathering of Seats isn't going to like this." Letz leaned close, speaking with low tones. "How many times have I warned you to steer clear of them, not to draw attention to yourself?"

"It won't matter if he finishes out that apprenticeship and gets his credentials," Thessallim said, louder, drawing attention from those around. He lifted an arm to Jerryck's shoulder, exposing a large, damp patch in the armpit of his shirt. "Don't you worry about a thing. I'll stay here for the next couple of weeks. We'll say it's done, and you can go take your tests."

"Get away from me." Jerryck threw off Thessallim's arm and the reek from under it. "How many times do I have to tell you? I'm not finishing my apprenticeship under you."

"And you shouldn't," Letz said. "The two of you utilize completely different forms of magic. The very idea is ridiculous. Now, if you were to consider someone like Masorno, he's much more qualified for you."

"Stop!" Jerryck backed away with his hands up in front of him. "Just stop. I threw Masorno out last time he was here."

Thessallim snickered. "We heard all about it. Every magician in the entire city heard when he came through ranting to anyone who would listen."

"I'm not taking on anyone I know as a mentor," Jerryck said.

Letz frowned. "You've said that for how many years now?"

"About ten," Thessallim said. "It still has to happen. Something will change eventually. The Seats won't stand for this to continue forever."

Another bell rang. The first of the Shontese delegation entered the gates onto the grounds of the palace. The two visiting magicians turned along with everyone else to watch.

Jerryck slipped away. He was supposed to go to the steps outside the grand entrance anyway. As distasteful as it was to put himself on display, it made him inaccessible to certain individuals, even if only temporarily. He got there the same time as the chancellor, the chamberlain, and the priad. The household steward and the General both came outside with Terrance and Nita.

By the time they all took their positions, the Shontese carriage had come to a stop. The wagons were still rolling in. Jerryck didn't bother trying to count the red and gray clad escort soldiers. There were a couple of other carriages that were already disgorging their occupants. The one that stopped in front of the steps was the one with the gold trim in the carved filigree.

Stupid nobles, Jerryck thought. They always traveled showing off so much wealth, and then had the audacity to complain when thugs tried to rob them on the roads.

Shontese servants placed a step stool under the carriage door before they opened it. They offered a hand to the man stepping out. He didn't accept the assistance. He didn't even acknowledge them at all. He looked up the steps to Terrance and Nita, putting on a smile of utter delight, an expression most nobles refused to use just after traveling.

He looked better than most nobles at the end of a journey too. Instead of frumpy, tired, and rumpled, his clothes were perfect. Made of silk draped over leather, they weren't even wrinkled. What had he done? Stopped down the road to refresh, just to make a good appearance? He looked to be in his early twenties, if even that. Young people had been known to do such silly things in the past when they wanted to make a strong first impression, as if no one would pick up on the evidence and see right through it. The people from the other carriages didn't look nearly so good. Neither did the soldiers or any of the servants.

"Lord Andreno," Terrance's herald announced for everyone gathered. "Grandnephew to Prince Sanbralio of Shontarra, second in line to the Shontese throne."

With that, Andreno climbed the steps, his smile never wavering, white teeth stark against his dark, olive skin. His eyes never strayed from the King or princess to notice anyone else around him. Following the protocols for nobility greeting royalty, he stopped just a few steps below them. He folded his hands in front of himself and bowed his head down while keeping his body straight. "Your Majesty, your Royal Highness."

"Welcome to Brend," Terrance said, finalizing the short ritual.

After that, someone may as well have opened a floodgate on the crowd. They all began talking at once, raising a cacophony of noise Jerryck couldn't make heads or tails of. It was like when he first initiated any kind of distance listening spell before he refined it down to a specific target.

Terrance led Andreno inside. Jerryck trailed them, partly because he was expected to accompany for at least a few minutes, and partly to get away from the crowd. He didn't really listen much as Terrance made pleasant small talk to his guest and explained that Nita would fill the active role of hostess.

Heston leaned over and whispered to Jerryck, "Nita is taking Andreno on a tour of the countryside tomorrow. After that, she's taking him into Kershet. You should go."

Jerryck whispered back. "I should?"

"Andreno will like bragging about how many nobles accompany him."

"Then why should I go?"

Heston paused. The side of his mouth twitched. Then he continued, "And you still need to resupply, don't you?"

"Shouldn't I go when the nobles aren't there?"

"If you go with them, it won't be questioned," Heston said.

"But…"

"You're one of them. Remember?"

"No, I'm… Oh. Right."

"And I know you sent a letter to the city magician. You can follow up. Find out if he knows anything. I'll make sure a couple of my men stay with you."

"I can take care of myself." Jerryck stopped at the entrance to the corridor where he would turn away from the group.

Heston stopped with him, closely watching everyone with the king still ambling forward. "And gather all the information they're trained to collect?"

Jerryck didn't really have a good answer to that question. They both knew he lacked social skills. Heston slowly nodded, then moved forward again. "You'll have guards."

Chapter 18

JERRYCK GRIT his teeth all the way back to his tower to keep from grumbling. He wasn't born noble. He hadn't grown up accustomed to guards following him around everywhere. Some magicians already claimed he thought too highly of himself. All he needed was a noble escort to prove them right. He could take care of himself.

Letz and Thessallim stood waiting for him outside the door to his tower. Thessallim still wore his stupid grin. Letz still glowered. He bobbed his head at Thessallim and said to Jerryck, "I told him to go away."

Thessallim was just as enthusiastic as ever. "I can be here."

"Go away," Jerryck told him.

"No, no, I can be here," Thessallim said. "I'll pretend to be your mentor. I'll go get a bed in a guestroom. Then after a couple of weeks—"

"I'll give you the same treatment I gave Masorno," Jerryck said. He'd had enough. It was probably childish that he got some satisfaction out of seeing Thessallim's grin falter.

"You didn't really, did you?" Thessallim turned his head to look at Jerryck out of the corner of his eye. "Not to someone as important as Masorno. I know he exaggerates sometimes. You didn't really sic elite guards on him and tell him never to come back, did you?"

"Close enough." Jerryck opened the door to the tower. He held up a hand to stop Thessallim when he moved to follow him in. "And you're a lot less important than he is. Think what those same elite guards will do to you if I have to call them."

Letz stepped past Thessallim and said, "At the very least, you'd lose your flapping tongue. That wouldn't be very lucky."

Jerryck allowed Letz in. Then he shut the door in Thessallim's face. He leaned his back against it, raised his eyes to the ceiling, and let out a sigh of relief. Hopefully the man left and wouldn't have to be dealt with as harshly as threatened.

Letz stood in awkward silence a few moments, staring blankly at the far wall. He was about twenty or thirty years older than Jerryck. He specialized in transportation magic and lived in a remote tower close to the village where Jerryck and Kendra had spent their childhood. He had been the magician to come to Kendra's cry for help when Jerryck had nearly killed himself with his first use of magic.

Eventually, Letz leaned against the wall at the bottom of the steps and cleared his throat. "I must say, you handle people that annoy you much better than you did when you were younger."

"Sometimes I wish I could revert," Jerryck said. "It's much more amusing to play tricks on people who deserve it."

"I'm sure it is." Letz laughed and raised his head enough to look Jerryck in the eye. "Would it really be worth it, though? Your sister would constantly be irate with you. How is she, by the way? I haven't seen her. I know she doesn't like most magicians, so I try to respect that and not bother her."

"She's doing all right considering the circumstances."

"I sent her letter of concolence when I heard about her husband. I hope that didn't offend her."

"If it did, I'd have heard about it."

Now it was Jerryck's turn to stare at the far wall. Once again, the silence grew thick. Letz had much better social skills. He could always tell when Jerryck didn't want to talk about something. Sometimes he brought it up anyway, like scolding him for never having finished his apprenticeship. Never for very long before he dropped the subject. The loss of his brother-in-law was definitely something he didn't want to talk about.

Letz shifted on his feet and pointed to the room on the bottom floor, the one with the space Jerryck kept clear for portals. "Mind if I leave from here? I won't keep you any longer. I just wanted to check on you while I was in the area."

"And see if I really was looking for an apprentice?"

"I still don't think that's a good idea," Letz said.

"I still think I may not have a choice," Jerryck said. "Not if I want to keep my job."

"A job you shouldn't have without…" Letz stopped mid-sentence. He tipped his chin down. "I'm sorry. I'll go now."

He strode over to the clear spot. Jerryck went upstairs. His skin prickled with the opening of the portal, making the hairs on his arms stand up. Reaching out his senses without even thinking, he mentally monitored the procedure. Letz was the one who had taught Jerryck to open portals. He always used the same method every time. After a quick scrying trip, he first put up a barricade to contain energy should there be any trouble. Then he punched through to the other place were the portal opened to. Then widen the opening enough for it to be used. Lastly, he reined in the energy and brought it under enough control that the portal could be *safely* used. Only at that point would he drop the protective shield.

One of the reasons he was so good at portals was because, unlike Jerryck, he was also one of the best at scrying. He claimed that he had learned to make portals because scryers didn't make enough to live off of. Kendra always laughed at that, claiming if that were true, he wouldn't live out in the middle of nowhere, but in a city with more traffic and higher demand for portals.

Jerryck reached his workroom, still monitoring. Letz stepped through the portal. Then it spiraled down to a pinpoint opening. All the energy of the spell sucked through to the other side before it closed off completely, leaving the barest of residue. That was another method that made Letz one of the best. He recuperated and conserved as much energy as possible, while others flagrantly left it lying wasted.

Shortly after Letz's portal closed, the chimes in the work room tinkled. This pattern was an alert for a magician leaving through the palace gates. So Thessallim had left as well. With everyone else's attention on the arrival of Lord Andreno, no one bothered Jerryck for the rest of the day. Which suited him just fine.

No one called on him the next day, either. Not even to accompany Nita on a tour of Kershet for Andreno. She tended to use the morning to go on different tours around the countryside, avoiding the city. It probably ran a little long. She liked doing that too. Terrance had scolded her for it on a number of occasions, claiming she did it on purpose to avoid her afternoon lessons. She would go through Zinrish Dell to show off all the flowers, visit the pond and Aconi Grove, head down to Riverbend, then take the ferry over to Unification Isle where every one of their kings had been coronated, and every royal heir took his wedding vows.

A couple more days passed, and Jerryck went looking to find out if he had been forgotten. It turned out Nita hadn't even given the countryside tour yet. And she didn't plan to for another few days. Lord Andreno had been loudly complaining about being too tired from the journey to go on any kind of tour.

After a week his supplies got so low, he figured he'd either have to go to the medics to ask for more or go to Kershet without Nita's group. Since Terrance still wouldn't let him go to the city without escort, he debated whether it would be more trouble to ask the medics or draw attention to the fact that he needed to go. He said as much to Nita, and she promised to press Andreno. The next day, she finally called Jerryck for the trip. He donned clothes suitable for traveling with the princess and other nobles. He kissed his family goodbye. Just after breakfast that morning, he rode out the gates on a horse as part of the entourage rather than get stuffed inside a carriage with Nita, Andreno, and Chamberlain Malk.

Nita's usual bodyguards rode nearest her. There was a smattering of elite guards mixed in, Tajor and his three friends among them. Andreno's bodyguards and more elite rode farther ahead and behind the cadre of other people that accompanied.

The closer they got to Kershet, the more abandoned camps lined the road. Every once in a while, a human shape flitted about the litter, trash heaps, and collapsed remains of makeshift tents. Jerryck craned his neck. How far did they go? All the way around the city?

Tajor sidled up to him. "Are your eyes going to pop out of your head?"

"What?" Jerryck turned to him. "What are you talking about?"

"Your eyes are bulging." Tajor smirked. "Should you be worried about them popping out? Or is that what you intend?"

Jerryck shook his head at Tajor's nonsense. "Eyes don't arbitrarily pop out of their sockets." He looked back out, away from the road. "What happened here? I can't even count how many times I've made this trip, and I've never seen anything like this."

"Do you remember a while back when we were having a little problem with the water?" Tajor asked. "Do you remember any discussions about chaos outside the palace walls?"

"Of course I remember," Jerryck said with a frown. "But I didn't expect all this."

"And you noticed none of it from your tower?" Tajor asked. "Don't you have a view that goes over the walls?"

"I've seen it so many times, I don't really look anymore," Jerryck said. "I hope all this mess doesn't make Lord Andreno think ill of us."

"I'm not sure he's noticed." Tajor looked at the carriage just ahead. "He tends to ignore things he doesn't think are important to him."

They pushed through the outer limits of Kershet. Groups of Garrison soldiers stood at barricades blocking the major intersections. They hurriedly move things aside for the princess and her escorts to pass through.

They took the straightest route to Bershent Fortress, the castle the city had been built around. Mayor Kyle and Premiere Kimball came out into the bailey to greet them. Kyle gestured back toward the streets and said, "I apologize for all the mess out there. We're still getting things back under control."

"You lost control?" Andreno asked as he climbed out of the carriage.

"Not exactly." Kimball cast a dark look at the mayor. He offered his arm to the princess as she also climbed out of the carriage. "We had a few people get a little unruly, some pockets of unrest here and there. Nothing we couldn't handle."

"I heard you had a fire sweep through one of the slum neighborhoods." Andreno looked over at the brown haze hovering over one of the poorest sections of the city. "I also heard you had rioters murdering entire families and stealing anything drinkable. And I heard that one of the men who lives under your roof was stabbed when he went outside the fortress walls a couple of days ago."

"Where did you hear all that?" Nita asked him as the premiere led them all inside the drafty keep.

"I sent a few men ahead to Kershet while I was on the road." Andreno shrugged as if it meant nothing. They entered a sitting room the premiere favored for entertaining important guests in the summertime. The constant breeze through the room kept the temperatures down. In the winter, the room was unusable.

"To learn more about the water?" Nita took a seat, right in the path of the breeze, along with most of the others. Jerryck remained standing by one of the flapping wall tapestries. It would be easier to leave at the first opportunity without drawing attention to himself.

"I didn't hear about the water until they came back," Andreno said. He leaned back in his seat, stretched out his legs with his ankles crossed. "I actually sent them to follow up on a rumor I heard about a man named Quillen living here."

"You know very well your cousin is here," Kimball said, his entire face growing a dark glower.

"I don't know that I'd call him a cousin." Andreno rocked his feet from side to side. "He's just a bastard."

"Did your scouts also tell you he was the man you mentioned that was stabbed?" Kimball's jaw was tight. "He drew very close to openly accusing some of your men."

Andreno's jaw went slack. "Why would I have my men make a special trip on account of someone like him?"

"You just said you had them make a special trip to check on a rumor of his whereabouts," Nita said.

"Not for him, for my granduncle." Andreno's feet stopped their agitation. "Personally, I couldn't care less about him. He was stabbed? Maybe I should assign couple of men to keep an eye on him, keep him out of trouble. That should reflect well on me back at home. For some reason Uncle always liked him."

Kimball crossed his arms. "Perhaps because Quillen is his only grandson."

"He's just a bastard," Andreno said. "Not a grandson."

Jerryck tuned them all out and inched toward the door. Eventually, he managed to slip out. No one called him back or scolded him, so it must have been acceptable.

Chapter 19

TAJOR AND TWO OF HIS FRIENDS, the skinny one and the one with the cleft chin, followed Jerryck. He asked them, "Do I still need to be in there?"

"Do you hear anyone calling you back to stay?" Tajor asked back.

The cleft chin guard snickered. The skinny one elbowed him in the ribs and he stopped. Tajor stood staring at Jerryck with that smirk he always wore when he made mischief. Jerryck shook his head at whatever they thought was so funny and walked away. They kept following.

He sought out Ressell, the official city magician of Kershet. Although there were very few page lads to point out the location, the fortress was so much smaller than the luxurious sprawl of the palace that finding him was fairly easy.

"Hello, Jerryck," Ressell said. He sat at a table counting coins and recording numbers and columns headed by the names of various magicians that lived in and around the city. "Have a nice visit with Letz and Thessallim?"

"It was no different than any other visit they've paid me," Jerryck said.

"I told Thessallim not to bother you about that particular subject." Ressell dropped a few coins into a small leather purse. "I guess that was too much to hope for. I suppose it's also too much to hope that Letz talked some sense into you?"

"About finishing my apprenticeship? Or taking on an apprentice?"

"Taking on an apprentice." Ressell wrote another figure on the parchment. "I don't think it's a good idea."

"Neither do I," Jerryck said. Ressell looked up at him, eyebrows raised, pen hovering over what he'd just written. Jerryck asked, "What are you doing? You're no accountant."

"I was given some money to pay magicians who helped here in the city while the river was sick." Ressell set his pen in its inkwell. He dug through a stack of papers off to the side. He pulled one out and handed it over. "Here. A list of names. People you should talk to if you're serious about finding some-one new in the trade. Some of them mentioned boys with potential. Some of them are new in the area and may know someone elsewhere."

"Thank you." Jerryck had been prepared for a lecture. Ressell always told everyone they had to respect the office, if not the man in it. That never stopped him from giving a piece of his mind to the king's court magician, even before Jerryck filled the position.

Ressell went back to his coins and columns. Jerryck left him to it and headed back out to the bailey to leave. Tajor and his two friends still followed him. He asked, "Did I forget something?"

"Besides us?" Tajor smirked, setting off his snickering friend again.

"I'm just going out into the city," Jerryck said.

Tajor nodded. "And we're coming with you."

"I don't take escort guards with me around the city," Jerryck said.

"Did you miss the fact that not all the chaos is completely under control yet?" Tajor sounded rather droll and his smirk faded. "Did you really think you'd be allowed to wander around through that unguarded?"

"I hadn't thought about it," Jerryck said as they went out the gate. No, he had thought the escort guard Terrance insisted on was for the road to Kershet, not for going about the streets of the city itself.

Tajor nodded. "We figured."

"Why you?" Jerryck asked. "There had to have been someone less annoy-ing than you available for this."

"How can you say such things?" Tajor gasped and put a hand over his heart. His friend's giggles turned into laughter.

"And you—" Jerryck pointed at the guard— "are almost as annoying as he is, with the way you laugh at everything."

"Almost?" Tajor emphasized the word. "You don't think you're annoying, with how you can't ever remember his name is Garret?"

"At least you can always see me." Garret grinned. He hiked his thumb at his skinny friend. "Cade's the one who disappears all the time. In fact, I'll make you a deal. If you can guess what he's doing while you can't see him, we'll leave you alone."

"How should I know what he's doing?" Jerryck demanded.

Garret laughed again. "And that's why this is a safe deal."

Jerryck threw up his hands. He wasn't going to get them to leave him alone. The harder he tried, the more they would annoy him. Better to just put up with them hanging about, watching his every move. He'd get done faster and get rid of them all that much sooner.

Surrounding Bershent Fortress, the wealthiest residents of the city walled in their properties. Their houses rose up three and four stories above the tops of their walls, giving them a view of the street and the passersby. Normally, the wide avenues between the properties teemed with carriages and pedestrians. Some of them were residents out and about. Some of them servants going to and fro about their various errands. Others were just gawkers and tourists, hoping to catch a glimpse of someone well known. Today, the carriages were absent. The foot traffic was sparse and furtive. And every person was questioned at the barricades at major intersections.

The estate style city residences of the wealthy faded into the more modest middle-class housing. A few more streets, and barricaded intersections, and houses started sporting signs outside them announcing what services were offered out of that building. Jerryck made one stop here, arranging for a service to collect all the purchases he would make, and transport them up to the palace.

The farther they got into the commerce and trade areas of the city, the less the barricades blocked their progress. More and more people filled the streets, dashing about, or strolling casually, or burdened down with bundles. Carts wheeled by, both hand-pushed and horse-drawn. Some people gawked at Jerryck and his elite guards. Others gave him a wide berth, keeping their heads down.

Cade came and went. Once in a while, he would exchange a quiet word or two with the others. More often, he was silent. Jerryck never actually saw him join or leave. Just sometimes he was there. Sometimes he wasn't.

Garret vacillated between laughing maniacally, and intimidating anyone who looked at Jerryck sideways. Tajor stuck to annoying anyone and everyone who would give him half an ear by peppering them with questions, whether they deserved it or not.

Jerryck made his way through shops, one by one, crossing them off in his mind. Some of them carried supplies he needed to restock his workroom. Some of them were names on the list Ressell had provided. The last one he almost skipped, thinking he probably wasn't going to get any information there anyway. But, best to be thorough on the off chance the owner was in a good mood.

The shop was owned by a paltry magician whose skill with magic was unreliable enough that he was unable to make a living with it. His main income lay in his retail shop. Still, he had credentials and a license from the Gathering of Seats. He always resented, loudly, that Jerryck did not.

"You can't have an apprentice," he told Jerryck.

"What?" It took a moment for Jerryck to switch his train of thought from shopping to the subject of an apprentice. "Why not?"

The man looked down his nose. "You're not a legitimate magician. You shouldn't even have the job you do. You're not qualified."

"You think you could do his job better?" Tajor asked.

"Absolutely." The man stuck out his chin. "I have credentials."

"Credentials make you better?" Tajor had that mischievous gleam in his eyes. "More skilled? Better talented?"

"Credentials prove I'm legitimate."

"I think that's licit and illicit you're thinking of." Garret snickered. "You don't even have your terminology correct."

Tajor leaned on the counter. "Do you get your magic as mixed up as your words?"

The merchant swept an arm, pushing Tajor's hands off the counter. "I don't care what words you use for it. I'm valid. That's that."

Tajor put his hands right back on the counter. "This license you speak of, it holds more validity to you than the opinions of your King?"

The merchant drew in on himself, his shoulders slowly hunching up, his face darkening. He ground his teeth. "Get out. All of you."

"Why?" Tajor asked.

"No one walks into my store and questions my loyalty to my face." He responded to Tajor, but glared at Jerryck.

"Asking for clarification is questioning your loyalty?" The gleam in Tajor's eyes turned malicious. "Or are you just pretending to be offended to try and hide something?"

"Get out." The merchant made wild shooing gestures, whirling his entire arms. "Get out. Or I'll…"

Tajor leaned back, just enough to put him out of range of the gesticulating arms. When the merchant trailed off, leaving his sentence unfinished, Tajor asked, "You'll what?"

"I'll do something you'll regret."

"Like what? Call the city guards?" Tajor looked down at his uniform. He looked over at his companion's uniform. Their double-breasted shirts had all the colors and markings of palace guards, automatically a higher rank than mere city garrison soldiers. The gold star on their collars also mark them as elite, even higher rank than the average palace guard. He leaned in to the merchant again. "How will that work out for you?"

The merchant banged his fist on the counter. "I'll use magic."

"Now wait." Jerryck waggled a finger. "The Gathering of Seats disapproves of any magic that would bring harm to someone."

"What kind of magic will you use?" Tajor spoke as if Jerryck hadn't. "The kind our illicit court magician can't protect me from? Should I get worried over that? I mean, after all, if he's not even qualified to fill a position the King judges him worthy for…"

"*Get out!*" The merchant's face turned red. He shouted so loud, people on the streets were looking into the shop then hurrying on their way. "Get out! Get out!"

139

"Let's go." Jerryck headed for the door, mentally scratching this man off the list of people Ressell had advised him to speak with, even though he hadn't gotten any information at all.

The man chased them out. "You'll regret this, Jerryck. I'm reporting your search to the Gathering of Seats. You'll never have an apprentice. *You hear me?*"

Chapter 20

JERRYCK STRODE down the street glaring at Tajor. "Do you have to annoy everyone you meet?"

"You didn't find that amusing?" He pointed at his laughing friend. "You think he found it amusing?"

"Irrelevant." Jerryck dodged his way to the other side of the street where traffic was a bit lighter. "He laughs at everything."

Garret laughed some more. "Life can be rotten. Laugh or cry about it. I choose laugh. More fun that way." He looked into the opening of an alley as they passed. "Stop here a minute."

"Why?" Jerryck asked.

Garret peered into the alley. A couple of shadows moved down at the end.

"Thought so." He maneuvered Jerryck into the opening. "Come this way."

Jerryck hesitated. "I don't really like alleys. Bad things happen in alleys. And..."

"And what?" Tajor came up behind, cutting him off from the street.

"And—" Jerryck stepped in a pile of poop that was probably several days old— "and that."

Tajor laughed. "Is that all you're worried about?"

"Oh, this is disgusting." Jerryck held back a gag reflex while using the wall to try and scrape stinky muck from his boot. "Why did you drag me in here?"

"They didn't drag you." Cade emerged from the shadow that had moved. Another man stayed behind where it was difficult to see him.

Garret nodded toward the man in the shadow. "Have you been able to talk him out of this yet?"

"No, he hasn't," the shadow man said. "Have you asked Jerryck yet?"

"He'll do it," Tajor said. "Won't you, Jerryck?"

"Do what?" Jerryck asked.

Cade waved the shadow man closer. "Come into the light so he can see."

"Who is this?" Jerryck didn't recognize the man that now approached.

"Does it matter?" Tajor replied. "Will you remember his name if we told you? Do you remember our names?"

Jerryck turned to scowl at him. "You're Tajor."

"And them?" Tajor pointed at the other two guards who had accompanied them. "How many times have you had to be reminded of their names? If I told you one of them was Deek, would you have even known the difference?"

"Uh…"

"You're so bad with names." Garret laughed. "I give you until sunset before you forget us again."

Cade reached for the shadow man, who had about the same skinny build as he did. "You can call him Cheber." He lifted Cheber's shirt and unwound some bandages to reveal a knife wound below his left ribs that looked a couple of days old. "We need you to heal that."

Jerryck bent close to examine the wound. "How did you move like you weren't hurting at all?"

"Practice," Cheber said.

"This looks only a day or two old." Jerryck waved around at the alley. "You shouldn't be in environments such as this. You could pick up an infection."

Cheber gave him a droll look. "Better than picking up another stabbing."

Jerryck straightened up. "I'm taking you to Bershent Fortress. I'll treat you there."

"That wouldn't be a good idea right now," Cade said.

"I'll clear it," Jerryck assured him.

"It's not a matter of gaining permission," Cade said. "It's a matter of proximity to the man who sent the knife."

"The palace then." Jerryck changed destinations.

"Same problem." Cheber shook his head. "I'm not going to either of those places."

"I'd make sure the General puts guards on you," Jerryck assured him. "Keep you protected."

"It's the protection I'm worried about," Cheber said. "Both those places are too difficult to get out of if I need to."

"You can't stay here." Movement drew Jerryck's eyes. A couple of rats skittered across the alley from a pile of garbage several feet away from them. He added, "And I'm not working here like this."

"Garret," Tajor said. "When was the last time you visited your family?"

Garret grew a sly grin. "Jerryck wouldn't like it there."

"Besides," Cade said. "We have nothing to pay them."

Tajor waved that away with a smirk. "You don't have to. They claim they still owe me a favor."

"For what?" Jerryck asked.

"Are you sure you want to know?" Tajor asked back.

"No, he doesn't." Garret headed for the mouth of the alley. "We'll go there. They'll get mad at me if I don't at least tell them about this anyway."

Cade kept up with him. He said to Tajor, "Give us a few minutes to clear the way of undesirables."

"Why do I have to stay behind?" Tajor asked.

"Because you're annoying," Garret called over his shoulder, and left the alley with Cade.

"I would have said because you don't fight." Cheber retied the bandage and lowered his shirt.

"I can," Tajor said.

"Only if you want your opponent broken or dead." Cheber leaned against the wall, one arm hugging his middle over the wound.

Jerryck opened his mouth, nearly telling Cheber to sit down. He checked himself just in time. Sitting in this filthy place would be insane. Skittering sounds over where he'd seen the rats set him to crinkling his nose. Definitely not the place for someone with an injury to sit down, or anyone healthy to sit down for that matter.

"You want me to ease the pain some?" Jerryck could do that much at least.

"I won't turn that down," Cheber said. He and Tajor were both eyeing the spot where the noise had come from.

"It's just rats," Jerryck told him.

He gathered a bit of energy around the fingertips of his right hand, shaping it to numb flesh. Movement flashed out of the edge of his vision. Cheber gasped and lurched to the side. At the same time, Tajor shot out an arm so fast, it was a blur. Then a knife struck the wall just passed Tajor's fingertips and clattered to the ground.

With a flinch and a startled shout, Jerryck flung the magic away from him toward the direction the knife came from, with a lot more power than he intended for it to take. Something heavy crashed to the ground with a thud behind the garbage pile.

Tajor cautiously sidled over. Then he straightened up, looking down at the ground. "Well, I doubt he's going to be throwing any more knives soon."

Cheber straightened up and walked slowly away. "I have to move."

Tajor bent down. "Can you feel anything? Or is everything too numb?"

There was some indistinguishable moaning from whoever was lying behind the trash pile. Tajor laughed. "I guess not."

Jerryck gasped. He strode over to the trash. "What did I do?"

Tajor stood straight and blocked him with both hands up. "Don't worry about it."

"There was a man there?" Jerryck pointed. His finger shook. "Is he hurt now? What did I do?"

"He's not hurt." Tajor glanced behind him. "In fact, I don't think anything will hurt him until your magic wears off. You sure stunned him pretty good. I doubt he'll be walking or talking for a while, either."

Cheber left the alley. Tajor hurried after him. Jerryck stepped out of the stink of the alley into the relatively fresher air of the crowded street. Cheber hadn't stopped. With a slow, smooth gait, he steadily made his way up the street in the direction of the fortress.

Someone bumped them as they passed by. He flinched, using a free hand to cover his wounded side again. That lurch he'd made in the alley couldn't have helped at all. Jerryck reached for Cheber's shirt, intending to lift it to

SPELL CASTER

examine and make sure the injury hadn't been exacerbated. Tajor brushed a hand in the way, nearly touching his arm, stopping him.

Garret dashed to him from the other side of the street. "What are you doing? You're exposed out here."

"I was exposed in there." Cheber pointed back to the alley with a thumb over his shoulder. "Where's Cade?"

"Working," Garret said He hovered close to Cheber's left side, nearly hiding from public view that the man was holding his ribs. "For once, I think he's more worried about you than you are about him."

They wound their way up the street through the busy traffic. Cade emerged from one of the shops and joined them. "Two out of three tails are out of the way now, if you include the one lying in the alley."

"Did you pick up his dagger?" Tajor asked.

"Of course I did," Cade said. "I used it to finish your job. Why don't you ever finish them off?"

Tajor smirked. "Is that what I'm supposed to do?"

"What do you mean finish them off?" Jerryck asked. Cade didn't answer. Jerryck grabbed his shirt. "You didn't kill him, did you?"

"Please lower your voice," Cade said, looking around at the few heads that had turned in their direction. Most of them turned and quickly went on their way rather than keep eye contact with him.

"Don't worry," Tajor whispered at Jerryck. "With your magic, the man probably didn't feel a thing."

Jerryck pulled away from him. "That's not the point."

"Keeping Cheber alive is the point," Garret said. "You might want to focus on that more than the welfare of the men trying to kill him."

The traffic tapered to a long line of people waiting to go through the process of passing through a barricaded intersection. Cheber turned to the mouth of another alley. Garret and Cade pressed against his sides, redirecting him to the barricade.

"You're not going around through the back way," Cade said. "There are too many places to lay ambushes."

"The garrison soldiers have a sketch of my face." Cheber's feet fumbled a couple of steps before evening out again. "The mayor spread one around."

145

"Then I guess it's a good thing we're escorting you quickly to the front of this long line of people," Tajor said. "It makes us look like we're just escorting you up to the fortress."

"Besides," Garret said. "Not all face sketches are well done. Maybe we'll get lucky and they won't think it's you."

The soldiers wearing the muted red and yellow uniforms of the city guard manned the narrow opening through the barricade. They snapped to attention at the crimson and gold uniforms of the three palace elite guards and gave them a salute. One of them with a rank on his sleeve said the same thing they'd heard at every barricade so far. "Sirs, I'm under orders to ask the business of everyone passing through."

Tajor waved at Jerryck. "We're escorting the king's court magician."

The soldier blinked stupidly. He looked back and forth between Jerryck and the three palace elite with an expression of utter confusion. Then he finally got out a question, "He's not riding? Someone as important as him?"

"Have you ever tried to shop on horseback?" Jerryck frowned. "It's far too bothersome. You have to find someone to hold the animal every time you go inside the shop. And the merchants in the open-air stalls don't like it if your horse poops too close to them while you're trying to browse their wares."

"You're returning from shopping without any parcels?" the soldier asked.

"They're being delivered to a shipping service for transport up to the palace," Jerryck said. "I'm not carrying all of them that far."

The soldier's face relaxed. He stepped aside. "You may all pass."

Another soldier whispered in his ear as they went by. He called out for them to wait. He looked at a cheap parchment, studying it. Then he looked at Cheber. He said, "You're the man the mayor wants escorted to Bershent Fortress."

"We found him," Cade said. "We're escorting him too."

"You didn't say anything."

"Why would we say anything?" Tajor asked with a shrug. "Who's more important? Some random person the mayor wants? Or a minor noble in the personal service of the king?"

"Right. Of course. Absolutely." The man nodded with every word.

146

They went on their way up the street past the barricade. Cheber stumbled again. A dark, wet stain leaked out from under his hand where he clutched his side. His other hand shook, and all the color had leeched from his face.

"Stop," Jerryck said.

"Can't," Garret said. They kept moving, sweeping Cheber along up the street, turning down another that ran parallel to the fortress along some of the lower cost, middle class residences.

"Stop!" Jerryck repeated. This time, he hurried out in front of them to try and block the way. Tajor caught him up and swept him along too. Jerryck said, "He's going to bleed to death if he keeps up this kind of rapid movement."

"We'll carry him if we have to," Cade said. "Where we're going is close to one of the places the pursuit can easily get through."

"I thought you killed his pursuers," Jerryck said.

"Only two of them." Cade held up two fingers. They skipped through a narrow spot between two of the houses, crossed an alley, between the next two houses, and came out on a street after another barricaded intersection. "I spotted at least one more, and only because he was out in the open, hiding in plain sight among the crowd."

"Probably a spotter posted to report sightings of their target," Garret said. "There's bound to be more of them."

Cheber tripped over nothing. Garret and Cade kept him upright, kept him going. They turned up another street, into more expensive, middle class houses, ones with a bit of yard and decorative fences around them. Cade grumbled at Jerryck, "Of all the times for you to act abnormal, this has got to be the most inconvenient."

"What are you talking about?" Jerryck asked.

"Most minor nobles ride in carriages." Cade tilted his head to get a look at the occupants of one as it wheeled by. "That's what that soldier at the barricade was asking about. Not horses."

"I don't need a carriage," Jerryck said.

Garret was constantly glancing behind them, and down every alley they passed. "It sure would have made this little jaunt a lot easier."

"Or more difficult," Tajor said. "Considering the shortcuts you're taking."

They turned into a high-end tailor's shop on a corner, nestled in among the houses. When they passed all the racks of expensive fabrics and headed straight for the back, the shopkeeper protested. Cade plucked a gold coin from his pocket and flipped it at the man as they went by. The protests stopped. They went out through the back door into another alley, this one cleaner than most. The wide avenue it opened onto ran along some of the walled off, expensive properties.

They entered the gate of the first one. Instead of leading directly into the yard, it took them into a cramped room where the residents could decide whether to admit them or do them harm. Tajor pulled on the bell rope. A square window peep opened up. Jerryck saw no more than an eye peering out at them.

"We're being pursued," Garret said to the eye.

Chapter 21

THE PEEP SLAMMED SHUT. Locks clicked behind the heavy inner gate, and it swung open. They entered a cobbled yard laid out before a wide, four-storied house. A woman came out of the front, obviously the lady of the manor in a brocaded, beaded dress, and with a jeweled clasp holding back her flaming red hair.

Cheber's knees buckled. The bloodstain on his shirt had grown. The woman rushed over to kneel beside him while guards from the wall gathered round. She put her hands on Cheber's cheeks. "Oh, dear. What happened this time?"

"Family issues," Cade said.

"Again?" The woman looked up at Cade. She stood and told the guards, "Get him inside. Quickly."

"Mama," Garret said, getting her attention as the men from the house picked Cheber up and carried him across the yard. "He can't pay you this time. And Tajor's making wild claims again about you owing him."

"Don't worry about that right now," she said to him. Then she called up to a balcony on the second floor where a few women had gathered to peer at those in the yard. "Lily, we need your healing skills."

One of the women disappeared. Jerryck followed after Cheber. Some of the men eyed him sideways, until Cade joined him and said, "He's all right. Let him in."

"Is he a new client?" The woman asked behind Jerryck. "Or is he here to help?"

"To help," Garret told her.

Jerryck entered the house and the voices of those still in the yard were cut off. The vaulted ceiling of the entry gave the feeling of spaciousness. Settees rested beneath artwork on the walls. A large book that look like a registry lay closed on the table next to a vase of marigolds, likely harvested from Zinrish Dell. The parlor that opened to the right had velvet upholstered furniture and shimmering curtains draped around a giant picture window. Boots clumped on the hardwood floor as the men carried Cheber up the broad, banistered staircase on the left.

At the landing on the second floor, the men turn left down a wide hall with several doors on each side. Small, square tables sat outside each door. Some of them were decorated with vases of flowers, each a bouquet of a single variety. The men carrying Cheber turned into the first room without a vase of flowers by the door.

A canopied, four-poster bed took up most of the large room. A vanity, bureau, and a wardrobe fit along the walls without crowding or covering any portion of the glass paned window. The rest of the floor was covered with thick rugs that stretched from one wall to the next. The woman with the red hair pushed past everyone and stripped the bed. A couple of other women rushed to put layers of towels on the mattress. The men laid Cheber on that.

Jerryck elbowed his way through the people to reach the bedside. All the color had drained from Cheber's face. His eyes were unfocused and had sunk into the dark circles under them. His breath came shallow and fast.

The other men left the room, shooed out by the redhaired woman. On the opposite side of the bed from Jerryck, Cade took out a knife and cut away Cheber's shirt. He grumbled while he worked. "I told you to go with your sister's plan."

"I would never be able to work in the city again." Cheber's words were breathless and faint.

"You won't be able to work at all if you're dead," Cade said.

Cheber tried to help peel the shirt away. His hand shook. The small effort left him gasping. Jerryck gathered some energy, shaped it with the words that would put Cheber to sleep, and released it. He went limp, and his eyes fluttered shut.

Cade grabbed Cheber by the shoulders. "No, no, no!"

"I did that." Jerryck brushed Cade's hands away. "He'll use less air, need less blood if he's sleeping. And right now, he needs to function with less blood."

"He needs stitches," one of the women said, digging into a leather satchel of the style that medics favored.

"Or magic to seal the wound." Jerryck bent close, examining the injury again. The man had definitely torn it open when he lurched to the side.

The redhead folded her hands in front of herself. "We don't have a magician on the premises."

"You do at the moment." Cade put a hand on the medic woman's shoulder. "Lily, let him work. It's faster, and less traumatic. You can keep him healthy afterward."

"No, I could use help now." Jerryck dabbed at the wound with the loose edge of one of the towels. "I need someone to keep this clear and clean so I can see."

"I've never heard of a healing magician that needs to see what he's healing." Lily kneeled beside Jerryck and worked at clearing the wound.

"I'm not accustomed to working on injuries that are purposefully inflicted," Jerryck admitted, gathering energy again.

This time, he used the words that formed it to medical purposes. He visually examined what was bleeding most and began there. He spoke the words that finalize the magic and cast a piece of it, knitting the flesh back together in one tiny spot as a kind of bandage. Then he cast another piece at a spot just next to the first. Over and over and over, he examined and knit, examined and knit, methodically, following the same line where a medic would apply stitches. All the while, Lily cleaned and washed with water at consistently timed intervals, keeping it clear enough for Jerryck to see what he was doing.

"I thought you said this would be faster," someone said. Their voice sounded like a child, until it cracked and dropped an entire octave on the third word, then back up again before the sentence finished. Jerryck spared half a second to glance up at the adolescent boy who had spoken. Large build and red hair, he reminded Jerryck of someone he didn't have time to stop and think about at the moment.

"It is going faster," Lily said. "He hasn't had to sterilize equipment, or thread a needle, or snip and tie, or anything like that. He's getting the bleeding to slow down faster than I could. Give me that water now."

The boy set a full bucket down on the floor between her and Jerryck. "Mama said Cade's going to need you when you're done here. She's trying to calm him down, but he's pretty upset."

"You can tell me that later in private," Lily said with a snap in her tone. "Remember discretion. Always."

Jerryck tuned them out, focusing on his work. Magicians with better healing skills could probably do this in half the time he was taking. Regardless, this worked. The worst of the blood flow had long since stopped. The rest tapered off enough that it clotted properly.

Now that the man wasn't in danger of bleeding out, Jerryck focused on speeding up the healing process. He used magic to probe for liquids that had spilled into body cavities and manipulated the body to reabsorb them. The clean water Lily was using, he filtered through magic that increased the oxygen content. Cloths dipped in that, were laid on Cheber's skin. Then his body was magically convinced to absorb all that liquid. The process was repeated until the absorption met resistance. A small adjustment to the magic got the body to convert most of the oxygen-rich water into the bloodstream.

Finally, Jerryck closed the outside of the wound, taking care to knit together the flesh so well it wouldn't even scar. As he finished up, his focus on his work was slowly replaced with an awareness of an ache in his knees. He looked down to where he knelt on the rug. Had he been on his knees this whole time? He must have.

He grabbed the nearest of the four posters on the corners of the bed and pulled himself back to his feet. Lily offered a hand to help. He politely declined. "I'm all right. I just need to eat and rest."

"Preston," Lily said to the boy who'd been helping her by running in and out and fetching whatever she demanded. "Take our guest to get something to eat."

The boy headed out the door, gesturing for Jerryck to follow. "This way."

They went back downstairs. To the left of the entrance, opposite the sitting parlor, they went into a dining room. Preston pointed to the chairs with padded seats around the long table. "Go ahead and take a seat. I'll be right back."

He ducked back out. Jerryck shuffled over to the closest of the chairs, sank into it, leaned his elbows on the table, and let his eyelids droop closed. He did a lot of healing magic, but not usually so intense or so long.

Preston returned with a plate of food and some wine. He set them down before Jerryck. "There's no charge, so eat as much as you want."

"Charge?" Jerryck dug into the food. He needed it, charge or not. "You normally charge your guests for meals?"

"Usually, along with all our other services," Preston said. He sat down across from Jerryck, the chair creaking under his large frame. "Mama said she's not going to charge Quil... Um... Cheber for any of this. Garret and Cade are trying to figure out payment anyway. Tajor says it can be the favor we still owe him, even though this doesn't really help him directly. She'll probably tell them that the tab is settled if they convince Cheber to go with his sister's plan."

"I go with my sister's plans most of the time," Jerryck said. "She's smart. What's stopping Cheber?"

"He could never work in the city again," Preston said the same thing that Cheber had. "And the right chance, I guess. It's not like he's going to go murder someone. He has to wait for a body to come along that would pass for him."

Jerryck choked slightly on the bite he had just swallowed. "*What?*"

"Dead bodies happen all the time in the wrong neighborhoods," Preston said as nonchalantly as an old man discussing the weather. His voice still cracked some, going from the high octaves of a child to the lower tones of a full-grown man, then back up again. "He has to wait for one that people could claim is him. He can't fake his death as easily if there's no body."

"Preston!"

Jerryck and Preston both jumped. The redhaired woman strode into the room, Garret right behind her. She stopped at the end of the table, hands on her hips, her lips pursed into a frown. Garret said to the boy, "Go out to the woodshed and wait."

Preston blanched. He slowly stood from his chair. "But you said he won't remember people, or their names, or a lot of what was said."

"Doesn't matter," Garret said. "Never break discretion. Go outside. And be glad your papa isn't here."

Preston's neck disappeared into his hunched shoulders. With a chagrined look at Garret and the woman, he left the room. The woman took a deep breath through her nose and patted her hair, the exact same color as Preston's.

"We haven't had proper introductions," she said to Jerryck. She placed a hand on her chest, just above the low cut of her dress. "I'm Marigold, the mother here at the Flower House, and we're very pleased to have a member of the king's household under our roof."

Jerryck looked past her to Garret. "What was the kid saying about needing a dead body?"

Garret sighed. His eyelids fluttered in a slight roll. He said to Marigold, "Can you give us a few minutes, please."

"Certainly," she said, and swept from the room.

Garret took the chair Preston had vacated. "Cheber was sent to live in Bershent Fortress by the Prince of Shontarra to try and keep him safe. It's not working."

"Obviously," Jerryck said. "Why would Prince Sanbralio care, anyway?"

Garret smirked at him. "If I told you, would you remember?" The humor faded quickly, and he leaned forward on the table. "His sister suggested the next time he come across a dead man that's the same build is him, he fake his death to stop the assassins. He's been rather resistant to the idea."

"Has he reported this to the authorities?" Jerryck asked.

Garret raised one eyebrow. "Of course he has. Why else would we be involved?"

"And you know who's sending these assassins?"

"Yes," Garret said. "The source is being closely monitored. Right now, as closely as possible. But you shouldn't worry about it. Sorry we involved you. Cade was just worried that if Cheber didn't get healed up, he might not get the chance to heal on his own."

"Cade was right," Jerryck said.

Garret nodded. "As usual."

"You're not worried about involving your family?"

Garret waved that away. "They're already involved."

Jerryck didn't want to talk about this anymore. He finished off the plate of food. He'd eaten it much faster than normal, just like he always did after heavy magic usage. He looked around the room while Garret watched in silence.

"I had no idea your parents were wealthy enough to afford a house like this," Jerryck said.

"They're not. And the owners are not my parents."

"Your family just works here for the owners then?"

Humor sparkled in Garret's eyes. "Haven't you heard of the Flower House? I thought every nobleman had."

"I'm not a nobleman," Jerryck said. "Oh, wait. That's right, I am."

Garret burst out laughing. Jerryck pushed his plate away and glared at the guard. "It's not really all that funny."

"Yes, it is." Garret wiped tears from his eyes. "Maybe I shouldn't tell you about it. You might not want to know."

"Then if someone brings it up, I'll have no idea what they're talking about," Jerryck complained. "I have trouble enough figuring out what people are talking about sometimes as it is."

"I doubt this will come up in any casual conversation. Especially if there are any ladies or children present." Garret's laughter tapered off, but the smile remained on his face. "This is a high-end whore house."

The food turned into a lump in Jerryck's belly. He passed a hand over his eyes. "Oh, no. This isn't right. Leanne is going to be so mad at me."

"It's not like you've betrayed her," Garret said. "Besides, if you don't tell her, she'll never know. Discretion is strictly enforced here. Currently, there are five clients in the house. Have you seen even one of them?"

"No."

"And they won't see you," Garret said. No one will even know you were here. Besides, it's not like sex is their only business. Every person in residence here has a secondary skill they market."

"People come here for other business reasons?" Maybe Leanne would be all right with this after all.

"All the time," Garret said.

Chapter 22

ERRYCK WENT back to Bershent Fortress just long enough to tell Nita he was going home. The moment his approach was spotted from the palace walls, word must've gotten to Terrance because he was outside waiting. Some people kept trying to get his attention, Priad Lalven, the steward, a smattering of others whose names slipped from Jerryck's mind. Far less than the usual number of people pestering him for his time. Heston stood off to the side, saying nothing, watching everyone.

"You came back." Terrance brushed everyone else aside and accompanied Jerryck in. "Where's Nita? Why didn't she come with you? Is something wrong? She's not hurt, is she?"

"I wouldn't have left her if she was," Jerryck said. "You should know that."

"I do," Terrance said with a sigh. "I'm sorry. Just tell me she's fine. Please."

"She's fine," Jerryck assured him.

This happened every time she left the palace to stay elsewhere. Terrance fretted and stewed. He checked security. He second-guessed his decision to let her go. He demanded constant updates on weather and road conditions in her vicinity. He'd never done that with anyone until he lost everyone else in his immediate family. Then he obsessed to the point of dragging everyone around him to the brink of insanity.

Some people, like the priad and the steward, fed him distractions. Others, like Jerryck, only had assurances to give him. Most people just gave the king as wide a berth as they could afford—something Heston encouraged.

"The conditions still aren't good out there," Terrance said to Jerryck, waving off some papers that the steward was trying to push at him.

"They're under control enough for her guards to handle things," Heston said.

"I shouldn't have let her go." Terrance stopped in the middle of the corridor. He pinched the bridge of his nose with his thumb and forefinger.

"She's fine," Jerryck repeated. He stopped walking because Terrance did. "She's having fun, from what I could tell. Right now, she's sitting down to dinner, talking everyone's ear into oblivion, most likely. I just don't do so well with all the socializing stuff. I wanted to see my family."

Terrance took his hand away from his face. "Right. Yes. Your family. Of course."

Lalven turned him away from the corridor and drew him off, talking the entire time. "And there are plenty of other things we need for you to worry about until she returns…"

Nita returned late the next afternoon, putting her father at ease. Then most of the rest of the household staff grew agitated. They kept coming to Jerryck for a number of things they didn't usually approach him for. Some who preferred magicians over medics had minor, almost superficial injuries they wanted him to heal. Or they wanted calming spells. One of them asked for a cure for nightmares. If Jerryck could do that, he'd use it on his niece.

For over a week, they dribbled in and out of his tower. From potions, to charms, to direct magic, on to advice and research. He started sending people away, refusing them service. He gave excuses for it, until a man brought a pail full of hot coals and asked Jerryck to use magic to make them stay hot in a bedpan through the night.

"No," Jerryck said, without even getting up from the table where he had books open to read from. Leanne had stopped puttering about the room and tidying things up the moment the man had come in. The evening's music in the bailey floated in through the open windows.

"B-but it's for the Sh-Shontese lord," the man spluttered.

"No," Jerryck insisted. The last time he had tried to magically heat coals for a bedpan, he'd ended up setting the bed and the entire room on fire. "What does he need warming coals for this time of year anyway? It's summer."

"Only the beginning." The man leaned down to set the bucket on the floor.

Jerryck stood, shaking his finger at the bucket. "Don't set that there. Go get rid of it. No one needs hot coals in their bed in summer."

The man straightened back up, still holding the bucket. "Lord Andreno says he's used to the warmer southern climate. He complains he's cold at night."

"Then he should wear warmer bed clothes and put on an extra blanket," Jerryck said. "I'm not heating coals for a bed."

When he finally convinced the man to leave, his wife said, "Andreno is not very nice."

Jerryck sat back down at his books, returning to the notes he been jotting down when the man had interrupted. Leanne left off her cleaning and sat across the worktable from him. "He's got the manners of a troll. And he's loony as a leshy. He should turn his clothes inside out and start doing everything exactly opposite. Then he'd be closer to acting like a rational, human being."

Jerryck paused his pen on his notes. The ink soaked out, making a spot. He lifted it from the paper and looked at his normally mild-mannered wife. "I don't think I've ever heard you talk that way about someone before."

"I have too." She looked away, her cheeks reddening. "There was that one medic that didn't want to take my advice during a birthing."

"He was soundly scolded," Jerryck said. "He apologized. And you still didn't compare him to something completely insane. And the manners of a troll?"

"It's true." She hitched her shoulders uncomfortably. "If he pays attention to the servants at all, it's because he's treating them like dung. He smacks people around just because he's feeling irritable. And he talks to imaginary people when he thinks no one is around to hear him."

Jerryck finished out his note before it left his head entirely. "That's just a rumor."

"One I believe," Leanne said. "I've talked to the people who caught him doing it. This isn't something I heard through gossip. Are you listening to me?"

"You didn't hear it through gossip," he repeated. He flipped through a few pages in one of the books and noted and a cross reference. "Andreno's crazy. He mistreats servants."

Someone else knocked on the door. Jerryck clenched his pen to keep from throwing it and yelling at whoever it was to just go away. Leanne answered it for him. A page stood on the landing. He craned his neck, looking inside the work room without stepping in.

"Lord Magician," the page said. "Lord Andreno requests you come to his chambers and give him a demonstration of the test you performed to determine the water purity."

"I'll be there shortly." Jerryck dropped the pen into the ink well. "Go make sure there some water available for me to use in the demonstration."

The page ran off. Jerryck put placeholders in his open books. He went to the counter where he kept his teapot and took out the sugar bowl. He quickly sprinkled some on a sheet of parchment, cast the correct magic on the granules, and folded it up.

Leanne caught him at the door. "Don't let him be mean to you."

"Don't worry," Jerryck said.

He left the tower and went directly to Andreno's guest chambers. A Shontese guard stood at the door, but didn't bar it. Jerryck entered the parlor of the suite. There, another Shontese guard stood, this one blocking the curtained doorway into the sleeping chamber.

A young man dressed as a noble sat on one of the chairs nibbling on some sort of sticky pastry. "He's not in."

The lad's face was covered with pimples and acne pockmarks. Jerryck knew any number of spells that would clear that up. Or at least ease it back. Medics had all kinds of creams and lotions that would work as well. Either the young man didn't care, or his parents weren't wealthy enough to pay for it.

Jerryck blinked, refocusing. He addressed the guard, "Lord Andreno requested a demonstration from me. "

"He's not yet returned from supper with the king, the princess, and the chamberlain," the guard said. He remained in front of the doorway.

The young nobleman turned his pastry to keep something creamy from falling out the center. "I told you. He must take a long time to eat."

The remainder of the pastry disappeared into the young man's mouth. He licked his fingers while he munched. Then he wiped his hand on his pants and swallowed. He looked up at Jerryck. "I'm kind of bored waiting here. I don't suppose maybe you could give me the advice I was going to ask Lord Andreno?"

"Advice?" What kind of advice could Jerryck give that would be in common with anything Andreno would advise?

"Yes," the lad said with a smile. He adjusted the cushions he was squishing in the chair behind him and stretched out his legs. "You're a lord too. You're on the core staff. You must know the king pretty well. I'm trying to figure out something for the princess' Processions."

This didn't make any sense. Nita wasn't old enough for Processions yet. That couldn't even start until she turned fifteen at the end of the summer. And very few nobles began them right away. Usually, they waited a few years, sometimes until age twenty.

"I know you were born common—" the young man studied the fingers he licked as if searching for any sweetness he had missed— "but surely you must know how the Processions work."

"Of course I do."

The lad dropped his hand and rested it on his knee. He propped one foot on the low table in the middle of the seats, using his foot to move aside a bowl of fruit to do so. "Every month an eligible noble comes to the home of an heir who is looking for a spouse and stays for a week. If someone suitable is found, they come every month in courtship. Then if the courtship works—"

"I said I know how the Processions work." Jerryck glared at him.

"Oh." The lad blinked stupidly. "I figure if they start right away and continue on into the winter, I'll get a chance. I'd really like to prepare. If I can get to the courtship stage, I'm sure Terrance will choose me to marry his daughter and become his replacement. I've studied a lot. And I have a lot of good ideas for the country. I'd make a good king. You have any advice for how best to impress Terrance?"

Angry magic flared. Jerryck took a deep breath, struggling for control. The air around him stirred, billowing his shirt and ruffling his hair. The lad's eyes widened. His jaw dropped. He jumped to his feet, over the back of the chair, and backed himself flat against the wall behind him.

The door opened. Andreno and Chamberlain Malk entered, trailed by Andreno's various guards, both Shontese and Brendish palace elite. Malk took in the room with one glance and demanded, "What is going on in here?"

Jerryck's finger shook as he pointed at the young noble. "He has designs to try and take the throne."

"I do not." The lad's voice rose an octave. "When you say it like that, you make it sound like what I asked is a bad thing."

"Remove him," Malk said to one of the elite guards. "Take him to Chancellor Herron."

"No! Wait!" The lad unsuccessfully tried to shake off the elite that grabbed him and dragged him out of the room.

"Jerryck, calm down…" Malk held up both hands to him. "What exactly did he say?"

"He wanted to know how to best impress Terrance so he could marry Nita and be the next King," Jerryck said.

Malk put his hands on Jerryck's shoulders, reassuring him. "That's not as concerning as you're making it sound. A lot of young nobleman are thinking along those lines these days. Herron is dealing with them. He'll take care of this one too. Nothing will come of it."

The swirling air died down and the gathered magic ebbed away. The palace elite eyed him warily. The Shontese guards had backed up. The one at the curtained doorway had disappeared entirely.

Andreno sauntered over to the chair and plopped into it. He flicked a hand at the door to the corridor. "Who was that, anyway?"

"The nephew of one of our district premieres," Malk said. "He has delusions of grandeur, as do most young nobles, high or minor. Enough of that. Jerryck, why are you here?"

"I sent for him," Andreno said, leaning back and draping one leg over the arm of the chair. "I expected it to take longer for him to arrive. Whenever I send for Masorno, our court magician back at home, it always takes him a long time to respond."

"Jerryck is very prompt," Malk said. "What do you need him for?"

"I want a demonstration of how he tested the water," Andreno said.

Malk interlaced his fingers and pursed his lips. "I thought you were satisfied the water is fine."

"I don't see any signs anywhere that it even happened," Andreno said. Jerryck frowned. Had Andreno missed all the garbage and wreckage and the barricades when he'd gone to the city?

Malk folded his hands in front of himself. "I assure you, it happened."

"I'm not doubting you." Andreno flashed his dazzling smile. "I'm just curious about it. I heard the magician found it, figured it out. I was hoping he would show me what he did."

"Jerryck?" Malk turned to him. "Would it be too much trouble?"

"No." Jerryck looked around for a water pitcher, a little tired now from his near accident. "I sent a page ahead to make sure there was a cup of water in here."

"You—" Andreno pointed vaguely in the direction of one of the guards— "fetch some water. And be quick about it."

A couple of the Shontese guards scurried like servants. Within a few heartbeats, they handed over a cup of water. Jerryck sat it next to the bowl of fruit on the low table. He got out the sugar he brought and dropped in a pinch.

Andreno peered at the glow it made. "How can you tell by this if the water is good or bad?"

"From the coloring." Jerryck pulled the parchment back over the extra sugar he hadn't used. He kept his fingers busy with that, acting slow and meticulous, hiding that his hands were shaky. "When the water was bad, there were other colors that shouldn't have been there. This is what it should look like."

"You just looked at the colors to figure out what was wrong?" Andreno asked.

"Basically." Jerryck stopped fooling around with the parchment and stuffed it in his pocket.

Andreno narrowed his eyes. "What exactly was wrong?"

"I've already told you," Malk said. "It was a dead animal in a stagnant pool in a tributary river."

"That's what the public was told. Commoners are stupid enough to believe anything." Andreno paused, tilting his head to Malk, giving him a droll look.

Then he looked more seriously at Jerryck. "What was the real problem? This test told you what that was?"

"Uh…" Jerryck fumbled, toying with the folded parchment in his pocket. "Well…"

"What if it was something those Chemwanee did to that tributary river?" Andreno leaned forward. "They've been treacherous before. They've got those nasty shamans, and the drugs they use. What if it was them? This test would show it?"

"Only if I knew what the colors were telling me," Jerryck said.

Andreno set up a little straighter. "It's not automatic?"

"Nothing in magic is automatic," Jerryck said. "A lot of things would turn up as the same color in a test of the sort."

"Interesting." Andreno stared back down at the cup. "I don't suppose you'd be interested in making more of this testing material?"

"What for?" Jerryck asked. "It's not something you can store up or trade in bulk. The magic is weak. It'll wear off after a while. You can already see the glow it made is fading."

"Pity." Andreno picked up the cup and swirled it around. He ran a finger through the glow as if it was something he could touch or feel. He set the cup down, still keeping his eyes on it. "I have a friend who would be very interested in what you did. He's fascinated with this sort of thing. He was going to come with me, but he was called away after we got on the road."

"Really?" The only magician Jerryck knew of in the Shontese palace was Masorno. He wouldn't have any interest in this technique at all. Jerryck could think of several magicians who might be interested, but he hadn't heard of any of them working with, or befriending Andreno.

The door opened and Heston walked in, trailed by two of his elites. He looked around the now crowded room and said, "Everyone out."

Chapter 23

ANDRENO SURGED to his feet. "Who do you think you are? You can't just barge in here without permission and start ordering people around. This is my room!"

"I'm the king's General," Heston said. "And this room is his. In his home. He's allowing you to use it."

"You behave." Chamberlain Malk scolded Heston. "He isn't just any guest."

"This room is too crowded." Heston swept a hand in the direction of all the guards. "Out."

Malk held up a hand of his own to stop them. "You can't order all his guards away."

"He may keep one," Heston said.

"Go," Andreno said to his guards, barely flicking his head at them to indicate who he spoke to.

They all scurried. Not even one of them remained. All the elites followed them out into the corridor. Jerryck tried to leave with them, but was crowded away from the bottleneck of the doorway. When the door closed, he was still stuck in the room.

Andreno crossed his arms. "Now tell me why I'm unguarded."

"Your cousin is dead," Heston said.

"What cousin?" Andreno asked.

"Quillen," Heston said. "The one that was living in Bershent Fortress with the district premiere and the mayor."

Andreno uncrossed his arms. His eyes darted around the room, flitting in and out of every corner, nook, and shadow. His breath hitched, making him sound almost afraid. He began stuttering. "I don't... see... he's not... What happened?"

"Unclear," Heston said. "He was in a pub known for violence. A fight broke out. He was one of four that were killed, according to witnesses. His body was tied to a horse and dragged through the alleys until it was unrecognizable. If not for the witnesses, we wouldn't know it was him."

That didn't make any sense. Jerryck and several other magicians could use magic to identify any body that was fresh enough. How long ago had this happened? Past the three-day mark, they'd have to rely on witnesses, not magic.

"Several were killed at the same time?" Andreno focused his eyes on Heston's face, visibly calming. "Oh. I wonder, possibly... I don't see... um, nothing."

"Three of your guards were unaccounted for at the time," Heston said.

"What?" Andreno's eyes went out of focus again.

"Three of your guards were missing," Heston repeated. "They didn't return from the city with you."

"Oh, them." Andreno sank back into the chair. "I told a few of my men to tail Quillen, make sure he doesn't hurt himself. He's kind of stupid sometimes. Gets himself into trouble. It comes from his common blood."

"Not anymore," Heston said.

Andreno chuckled. He didn't look overly upset about the loss. The initial shock was wearing off very quickly. Jerryck wasn't very good at reading individuals, but he was too familiar with the common reactions at the news of a family death. And Andreno wasn't showing the normal signs of grief.

Andreno looked around at the few people left in the room. No one else joined him in his chuckles. They tapered off. He looked down at the floor and cleared his throat. "I suppose Uncle might take this kind of hard. He liked Quillen."

"You should escort the body back," Heston said.

"What about the trade agreements?" Malk asked.

"He's not doing any of the negotiating," Heston said. "The only thing he's needed for is an official signature on the end of the documents. Someone else can come in his place and do that."

"And it would reflect better on me if I did Uncle this favor," Andreno said. "Before I go, Jerryck, May I take a sample of that substance you used for the test to show my friend?"

"By the time you got it home, the magic would be so weak you would barely be able to see the glow it makes," Jerryck said.

"It can be my souvenir." Andreno smiled as if nothing was wrong. "I don't want to leave here without a souvenir."

Heston crossed his arms. "Make it part of the trade negotiations. We'll send you some. You should be on your way by tomorrow morning, which means packing tonight. Not collecting souvenirs."

Andreno's face screwed up with anger. Malk quickly said, "There's no need for that. There's some right here. Jerryck can leave it, and Andreno will have taken no time at all from preparing for departure. Jerryck, would that be all right with you?"

Jerryck took the folded parchment back out of his pocket and handed it over while Heston glowered. Malk ushered the two of them out of the room, saying to Andreno, "You just relax for a moment while I get everything underway for you."

Out in the corridor, all the guards that had scurried were gone. None of them even guarded the door. One of the palace elite stood there instead.

Heston refused to budge more than a few feet from the door. He glared at Malk. "You're just giving away the tools we used? So they can back-engineer it?"

"They won't need to," Jerryck said. "I submitted the process for making that tool to the Gathering a long time ago. As long as they haven't denied approval, any magician can look it up and duplicate it. None of them have."

"It's an inconsequential item." Malk glared right back at Heston, meeting his gaze without flinching. "You of all people know exactly how he treats everyone around him when he's upset."

"I offered a cure for that." Heston's voice was flat.

Malk broke the stare-down by rolling his eyes. "You can't take him downstairs and whip him. Not without making his granduncle furious with us."

"You keep saying that." Heston rocked back on his heels. "My sources tell me his granduncle doesn't like him very much."

"I don't want to know any more about this." Jerryck threw up his hands and walked away.

"Wait," Heston called, striding after him. "There's something I need to ask you."

Jerryck stopped walking. "What?"

"Not here." Heston opened the door to a vacant guestroom and beckoned Jerryck in. "Some thing's shouldn't be discussed in corridors."

"There's no one around except one of your own men." Jerryck entered the room anyway.

"Irrelevant." Heston closed the door behind them. "Your search for the poison maker magician. Have you looked in Shontarra?"

"Not yet." Jerryck didn't admit that he was procrastinating that one. It was doubtful that Shontese magicians would be cooperative after how he treated their prince's court magician.

"You should," Heston said. "Andreno is far too interested in our water and our current relations with the Chemwanitz."

"What does that have to do with it?"

Heston crossed his arms. "He knows something. He's just clever enough to elude answering if he's asked about it. And he's important enough that I can't take him down to the dungeon and beat it out of him."

"Is that the real reason you're telling them to leave? Because you honestly think he's dangerous?"

"I knew he was dangerous before he got here," Heston said. "Sometimes the only way to learn about a danger is to draw it in and examine it closely. I've learned what I can. Now, he can leave."

"I'd like to leave," Jerryck said. Heston stepped out from in front of the door and opened it for him. Jerryck didn't hesitate to take advantage.

He went back up the tower. When he told Leanne that Andreno was leaving, she was so excited she ran down to tell her friends the good news. By morning he was gone, without fanfare. The rest of the delegation got down to business and the negotiations commenced. Jerryck put the whole affair out of mind.

Shipments of the supplies he had ordered in the city began to arrive at the palace. So did a trickling of responses regarding inquiries to magicians outside Kershet. Most of them only led to someone of mediocre potential. Some of them he already knew about. He sent them responses. Then he spread his feelers wider, sending letters to magicians and districts where he hadn't yet contacted anyone.

While everyone else was preoccupied with the trade negotiations, Jerryck used the time to go through the palace. He checked on every charm, every spell. He did maintenance work on any that were wearing thin.

He finished about the same time a new Shontese delegate arrived to put official signatures on the end documents. Chamberlain Malk was called on to play host to this new delegate, a role normally filled by Nita. She was excused from it while she prepared to leave the palace.

Every summer she took a few weeks for a vacation. She would travel someplace in the nation she had never visited, just to see and experience the lifestyle there. Then she would take a circuitous route, avoiding anything near the palace, and go to the Tarn District. There, she spent two weeks with her maternal uncle Premiere Grennan, and his family.

In her absence, her father would just about have apoplectic fits. Head medic Kellos stocked up on calming potions and sleeping droughts. If he ran short, or Terrance refused to utilize them, Jerryck stepped in with magic.

Every year during these preparations, Jerryck, Kellos, and others would meet. They all took inventory of the blossoms and herbs in the flowerbeds and gardens. They surrounded the various plots, arguing about which blooms were needed most, and where to plant them. Then they decided which ones to grow from seed and which ones to transplant in from other places, like Zinrish Dell.

For the most part, Jerryck and Kellos always wanted the same thing since they used very similar supplies. Jerryck rarely had to do a thing. Kellos did all the arguing and haggling. Jerryck mostly stayed out of the way and tried not to look bored.

Everything was being finalized and recorded, the arguments winding down. Jerryck and Kellos both had what they wanted. The only two still debating and haggling were the head chef and one of the top interior decorators. Several people turned to watch when Nita crossed the bustling bailey for the stables.

"Still going for her daily rides, I see." Kellos chuckled. "The priad is never going to convince her to stop doing that, not even this close to her vacation."

"She reminds me of her mother every time he tries," Jerryck said.

Kellos craned his neck, watching the last of the escort guards disappear into the stables with her. "I don't see Tajor."

"Why would you see Tajor?" Jerryck asked. "In fact, how do you even know him? He doesn't go to the infirmary."

"Which is why I sought him out and made acquaintance," Kellos said. "I was curious. As often as Heston's elite are in and out of the infirmary, I had yet to treat the man for anything. And as for your question, he's been assigned as a secondary riding escort. Several months ago. I thought you knew that."

"Uh…" Jerryck probably shouldn't admit that he didn't really pay all that much attention to such details.

"Sometimes I think she uses her daily rides to go out and talk to him, dredge out some advice," Kellos said. One of the other gardeners brought over a list for them both to sign their approval.

"Advice?" Jerryck let Kellos have the list first. "From Tajor?"

"She claims he's very reliable." Kellos looked over the list.

Jerryck snorted and rolled his eyes. "He's very annoying."

"I learned that the hard way." Kellos signed the paper. He handed it over for Jerryck to do the same.

Some of the group moved off. A few stayed to keep hashing out exact placement of items with the gardeners. Jerryck turned to head for his tower when Ressell, Kershet's official magician, approached from the direction of the palace gates. A page led him, and Tajor followed behind.

"That's why he's not with the princess," Jerryck said. "Heston finally has the perfect excuse to keep a closer eye on magicians visiting the palace. There was trouble with one during the bad water."

"I know," Kellos said. "We treated him after the guards were done with him."

Jerryck cleared his throat, avoiding anything further on that particular subject. He glanced up at his tower, where one of his alerts was surely chiming. He reached up mentally and with a muttered word, turned it off. Then he said, "Yes, well, when Andreno came, a couple of other magicians visited. When Heston wanted details, I couldn't remember every little thing. So now he wants every visiting magician escorted by an elite. Tajor, specifically, if he's available."

Ressell approached Jerryck, shooting a derogatory look at Kellos. The page ran off, his job apparently done. Tajor remained.

Ressell looked Kellos up and down. "You consort with alchemists?"

"He's very good at healing," Jerryck said.

Ressell's upper lip curled back. "He's an alchemist."

"And about half the people in the palace prefer alchemical medics to healing magicians," Jerryck said. "Besides, I never was as good a healing as my mentor. Kellos can more than make up for the difference."

Ressell glanced back at Tajor. "Isn't he the one that chased Masorno off?"

"The Shontese court magician?" Tajor smiled. "What makes you think anyone other than Jerryck or the king could chase him off?"

Jerryck blew out a breath. "Please, don't get him started. He's difficult enough as it is."

"Who? Me?" Tajor's smile widened. "Difficult? Whatever do you mean?"

"See?" Jerryck said. "What do you need?"

"I brought you these." Ressell took folded papers out of his traveling satchel. "They're the names of every boy I could find in the city with the potential to become a magician."

"Thank you," Jerryck said, taking the list. "You didn't have to come deliver them personally."

"I'm running errands outside the city and this is just one of the stops." Ressell tapped the papers. "I would advise you to read the back of the list first. Those are the youngest. That'll give you more time to go get your license."

"I have no intentions on getting a license." Jerryck opened the papers and scanned down some of the names.

Kellos looked rather consternated. "You're not seriously going to take on an apprentice while still defying the Gathering, are you?"

Ressell's sneer instantly returned. "That's done of your business, medic!"

"Behave." Jerryck glared at Ressell over the papers. "I appreciate the concern, and the personal delivery, but that's no reason to disrespect someone important on Terrance's staff."

"You're defending a medic?" Ressell raised his eyebrows. "How far? What would you do? Toss me out like you did Masorno? I'll save you the trouble."

He spun around and stomped toward the palace gates, Tajor smirking in his wake. Kellos said to Jerryck, "You shouldn't let him walk away angry like that. He just did you a favor. He didn't have to."

"He didn't have to be rude, either." Jerryck rolled the pages, making them easier to carry.

"Don't make enemies on account of me." Kellos gave Jerryck a nudge in the direction Ressell had stomped off.

Jerryck had to run to catch up, dodging around people working and moving about in the bailey. He called out, "Ressell, Wait! Wait, wait, wait. Please don't leave like that. Just... I can't... Don't..."

"Spit it out." Ressell slowed down just enough for Jerryck to catch up. He gasped from the short sprint, and Ressell stopped entirely. "You know, I've always been respectful to you, even though you don't deserve the position you have."

"I know..." Jerryck filled his lungs slowly and released it, pausing to let his heart rate slow some. "Kellos does deserve his position as head medic. Terrance hired him personally. He's not a fraud, like so many other medics. And he stands up for me when they badmouth magicians. Please, just try to respect that the same way you're respectful to me."

"Fine." Ressell ground his teeth. "Because he stands up for magicians. And for the king. Not for you."

"Then we're agreed," Jerryck said. They stood staring at each other a few moments, the hustle and bustle of the bailey continuing around them. They couldn't stay there like that. Jerryck remembered his manners and protocol. "Come up to the tower? Have some tea?"

Ressell nodded at Tajor. "Is he still going to shadow me?"

"Do shadows talk?" Tajor asked.

"Not my choice," Jerryck said.

Ressell frowned. Giggling children ran around them, trying to catch each other in some sort of game. A hammer from the smithy rang. A rider with a messenger satchel galloped through the palace gates bearing a Shontese flag. Ressell looked around at all the activity, normal for the average day in the palace bailey.

"I'll go," he said. "If your job is as busy as mine, someone will call on you the moment we sit down anyway. Besides, as I said, I have other errands to run."

He headed away again. Once he mounted his horse and left, Jerryck turned to go inside. He paused when he spotted his niece Marla sitting on a bench by the gardens all by herself. She had tucked her feet up and rested her chin on her knees. She watched the other kids playing.

Jerryck walked over and sat beside her. "You're not over there playing with all your friends?"

"I'm waiting for the afternoon class to get done so I can talk to Zev." Her head bobbed when she talked because of how she rested her chin.

"About what?"

"I had another bad dream."

"You want to tell me about it?" Jerryck offered.

She shook her head. "I'll just wait for Zev."

Jerryck wasn't sure what more to say to her. He always offered to listen. She always declined. He looked over at the other children playing around. Did other people have trouble getting kids to tell them things? Or was it just Jerryck?

Chapter 24

HESTON STRODE across the bailey along the same path Nita had. Tajor met him about halfway, and the two stopped to exchange a few words. Tajor pointed at Jerryck. Heston nodded once and continued on his way.

Tajor came over to Jerryck and gave a minuscule bow to Marla. "My Lady, I'm afraid I must take your uncle from you. Staff is being gathered for an urgent meeting and his attendance is required."

Marla giggled. "I'm not a lady."

"Are you sure?" Tajor cocked his head.

"Nobles are ladies."

"You're as pretty as any noble lady I've ever seen." Tajor grinned. "Prettier than some."

She smiled shyly and tipped her face down, looking up at him through coy lashes. Jerryck gave her a pat on the head and followed Tajor inside saying, "Thank you for that. She needed some encouragement."

They went to the large council chamber, which meant a lot of people called on to attend. Terrance usually preferred the small council chamber if it would seat everyone. It had one large table that filled the floor space, where everyone could sit facing each other. Unlike that smaller room, this one had a large table on a dais at the windowed end of the room with chairs facing everyone else. Most of the rest of the chamber was lined with long tables for people to sit, take notes, do paperwork, shuffle files, or just look busy.

Many people claimed that putting some of the staff up on the dais with the King gave them the appearance of equal authority. Jerryck couldn't see it, since Terrance rarely sat during these meetings. He normally stood in front of the table, keeping everyone's attention and reinforcing who was in charge. Having staff sitting up in front didn't put them in charge any more than the colored banners on the walls actually meant the districts they represented were physically present. All it did was make that part of the staff more conspicuous, easy for everyone to stare at and scrutinize.

Several had already gathered. More were coming in. Some of the elite guards stood casually by the walls, spread out under the district banners. Tajor went to join them while people filled the seats. Priad Lalven already sat at the table on the dais. The princess entered, still wearing her riding clothes. She headed for the dais with Heston close behind her.

Heston caught Jerryck's arm and guided him up where he was supposed to sit. "Don't try and lurk in the back again."

"I hate sitting up there were everyone can stare at me," Jerryck said. He didn't pull away, letting Heston draw him along.

"It's where the core staff belongs," Nita said to him. She didn't even hesitate to take her seat next to her father's vacant chair on the opposite side of Lalven. Neither of them made eye contact, both determinedly looking in a different direction from each other.

Terrance was one of the last people in, accompanied by Chamberlain Malk. The few people that trickled in after them scurried to find a seat. Everyone was quiet by the time Terrance stepped up to the dais. Standing before the table, he addressed everyone. "We just received a messenger with an urgent letter from the Shontese palace. Prince Yaquerro, heir to the Shontese throne, has been killed."

Whispers broke out around the entire room. People leaned over to each other, their mouths moving. Jerryck leaned his arms on the table, the smooth surface somehow not as comfortable as the pits and scars that marred his worktable. Terrance waited until the room quieted, folding his hands calmly in front of himself. "You all know he went on a hunting trip to the mountains every summer. This year, his party was attacked. There were no survivors."

"Barbaric Chemwanee," someone spewed.

The next voice was full of concern. "Are they going to war over this?"

"We don't know yet," Terrance said. "All we know is what I announced. For now, just concern yourself with preparations. We need to put together a delegation to go and bring the condolences of Brend to Prince Sanbralio."

Jerryck stopped paying attention when they started hashing out details of which people would take on what assignments. It was all generalities that didn't have much to do with him anyway. Terrance would decide with a much smaller group of people who should take on the role of delegate. Jerryck probably wouldn't be able to get out of that meeting either, though that also didn't have much to do with him.

He unrolled the papers Ressell had given him and took a closer look at the lists. Each boy was listed with his age, estimated potential, and location where to find him. None of them had any training as yet. None of them would be able to make the poison that had contaminated an entire river.

All responses he had received thus far were pretty much the same. He was going to have to spread his search outside the nation. He could ask Shamaness Sakila for help searching to the east. They also were more likely to know of any women with potential. That was information he wouldn't receive from any magician who had taken oaths to the Gathering. To the west, he'd have to mail a letter on a ship over to the archipelago. The magicians there were much sparser. Same with the tundra to the north.

He pulled his lower lip. To the south was more problematic. After he had tossed Masorno out of the palace, none of the Shontese magicians would have much to do with him. They would readily interact with other Brendish magicians. But every time Jerryck tried to interact, they asked if he had apologized to Masorno yet. It was going to have to happen. Whether he liked it or not. Which meant going to Shontarra personally. Which made it even worse. He sat back, resigned to insisting on being part of the delegation.

The people in the room started milling about. Some loitered, chatting in small groups, while others left. Terrance and Nita headed for the door that opened into the small council chamber. Most of the core staff, some of the elite guards, with Tajor among them, and a few others followed them.

Heston pulled Jerryck out of his chair. "Come. Follow-up required. You know the routine."

In the smaller room, the steward bent over the table, making lists before he even sat down. Chamberlain Malk stood off to the side, talking quietly with Priad Lalven and some other guy with a gruff looking face. Jerryck had seen that man somewhere before. But then, he'd seen a lot of people before.

Princess Nita held one of her father's hands with both of hers. She bounced on the balls of her feet. When everyone stopped talking and took a seat, he didn't start the meeting. He just stared at her, his face pinching tighter and tighter.

Lalven wrinkled his nose at her. "What are you so excited about?"

She ignored Lalven, as usual. She kept her attention focused on her father. "I could do this instead of going on a vacation!"

"Do what?" Lalven's tone dropped in pitch.

"I could go to Shontarra as the delegate!"

Chamberlain Malk rubbed his chin. "Now, that's not a bad idea."

Terrance gave him a look of abject horror. "Yes it is."

"Absolutely it is!" Lalven agreed with him. "It's a terrible idea."

"Do you have someone better in mind?" Nita challenged.

Lalven looked past her. He raised a hand to the gruff man. "Terrance, this is Keniv. He's the son of one of the land magistrates in the Flaynes District. He's been dealing with the Shontese his entire life. He's been there as a trader countless times. He knows their culture and customs better than most of the rest of us. And he knows Lord Andreno personally. That is a huge advantage, since Andreno will now be named heir."

"I know Andreno personally," Nita said. "And I'm already heir to a throne. It would be good to strengthen ties between both the heirs of our two nations."

"You're a girl," Lalven said, over-enunciating every word.

Jerryck shook his head. This was going to turn into another screaming match between the two, and this time he couldn't back out. He had to stay and make sure he was included in the delegation.

"You—" Lalven stabbed a finger at Nita— "will never rule from the throne. That will go to your future husband."

"Lalven…" Terrance pinched the bridge of his nose with his thumb and forefinger.

"How many times must I point this out?" Lalven's volume rose. "Terrance, if you'd go through that list of names I have, if you'd even look at them, you might have an idea of who you might choose. And you could send that man on this mission as the delegate. Try him out! But you haven't. And now here we are, with a dilemma. And once again, I'm offering you a solution I shouldn't have to. And just like always, she's trying to sabotage all my efforts."

"Stop." Terrance let go of his nose. "This is neither the time nor the place."

"It's never the time or place," Lalven said. "She's fifteen in a couple of months. An adult eligible to marry. You're going to have to face this long before you want to."

Terrance turned away from Lalven. "Nita, you're not going to Shontarra."

"But father," she said.

"No," he repeated.

"She's right about the two heirs strengthening ties," Chamberlain Malk said. "That's something she could have with Andreno that Prince Yaquerro didn't even pretend any interest in."

Terrance swiped his hands through the air. "She's not going."

"I'd send my best men with her," Heston said. "And whoever else you want to protect her."

"I can't think of anyone who could protect her well enough for me to let her go to Shontarra," Terrance said.

"I'd rather go with her than some stranger," Jerryck said.

Lalven turned a sneer at him. "You're not going."

Malk looked more interested. "You want to go to Shontarra?"

Jerryck grimaced. "Not particularly. But I should. And this makes for a good excuse."

Terrance sighed, long and heavy. He pinched the bridge of his nose again, squeezing his eyes shut. A slow grin spread across Nita's face for some reason.

"This is ridiculous." Lalven threw his hands in the air, his face turning red. "Nita, you're not going. That's final."

Nita's grin turned slightly smug. She put her hand on her father's arm and leaned close. "You're not going to let Jerryck go with just anyone, are you?"

Terrance opened one eye and fixed it on Jerryck. "Are you certain you need to go?"

Jerryck nodded. "Unfortunately."

"You hate going to Shontarra," Lalven spoke through gritted teeth.

"I have to find someone," Jerryck said.

"Heston." Terrance dug into his eyes with his thumbs. "Besides Nita's regular bodyguards, who else would go for security?"

Heston ticked names off his fingers. "Tad, Tajor, Deek, Cade, Garrett, Vinch, Rollard..." He listed more than a dozen of them in all. The only one Jerryck could put a face to was Tajor.

"Would you send all those same men for just Jerryck?" Lalven asked. He crossed his arms. "Nita really shouldn't go. Keniv is fully qualified to carry out this mission. And as I said, he knows Andreno. He even has some gifts to bring some of Andreno's friends. Nita's just a girl."

Terrance turned his back on Lalven. "Nita, you may go."

He walked out of the room, shoulders hunched. Nita bounced out behind him, squealing with glee. The steward, the chancellor, the chamberlain, and several others followed them out, leaving only a few in the room. Lalven and his friend Keniv stayed. So did Heston and most of the elites.

Tajor smirked at Jerryck. "That made for a short meeting, now didn't it?"

Lalven slapped both his hands on the tabletop and leaned in at Jerryck. "Why did you do that?"

"Do what?" Jerryck asked.

He lifted one hand to jab a finger in Jerryck's direction. "I have a hard enough time keeping her in her place without you interfering."

"Where exactly is her place?" Tajor asked.

Lalven ignored Tajor and continued shouting at Jerryck. "Terrance is coming up on the hardest decision he'll ever have to make. The more she gets him to give her the responsibilities of someone who will take his place, the more difficult this will be for him."

Jerryck frowned. "What are you talking about?"

"You don't believe she'll rule from the throne?" Tajor leaned on the table, putting his face right next to Lalven's.

Lalven leaned away from him. "Why are you speaking to me?"

"Because he has permission to speak his mind." Heston hadn't moved from the corner where he stood watching everyone. "As long as he's respectful to the king, the princess, and high nobles."

"I'm more important than just any noble." Lalven swished a hand against Tajor as if to brush him away. Tajor didn't move. Lalven fixed him with a pointed stare. "I have the ear of the king on a daily basis."

"Which ear?" Tajor asked. "Do you keep one in your pocket? Does he have one that's not attached to his head? Because it looked to me like he just took both of his ears and walked away from you."

"Incredible," Keniv mumbled. He said to Heston, "If I allowed this kind of disrespect from the men in my caravan, I'd never get any trading done."

Heston looked unmoved. "If the discipline of my men becomes any of your concern, I'll ask your opinion."

Jerryck picked up his things, hoping to slip out while the others continued arguing. He took a moment to roll back up the lists Ressell had given him. That gave Keniv just enough time to stride to the door, beating him there and blocking the way. Glaring at Jerryck, he said, "The priad asked you a question that you didn't answer, you cowered."

Chapter 25

"**A** BIT MOUTHY for a minor noble, aren't you?" Tajor leaned against the table with a malicious look for Keniv. "Oh, wait. Not a minor noble. Just the son of one."

Keniv clenched his fists as tight as his jaw. "Getting appointed as the delegate on this mission would have made me a minor noble."

"True," Tajor said. "Did you get the appointment?"

"I would have." Keniv opened one fist and gave Jerryck's shoulder a shove. "If *you* hadn't interfered."

"Keniv!" Lalven snapped. "Don't touch him. He's a minor noble, you're not. Whether you deserve it more or not doesn't change the situation. Treat him with respect."

"The way you treat the princess with respect?" Tajor asked.

Lalven tipped his face up, looking down his nose disdainfully. "Heston, control your men."

"I don't take orders from you," Heston said. He finally moved, stepping forward, squeezing his large frame between Tajor and Lalven. "You, however, do answer to me. Considering the way Keniv just treated a member of the king's core staff, why did you recommend him for this mission?"

Lalven stepped back. "I gave my reasons to Terrance."

Heston grabbed Lalven's shirt and jerked him close. "Give them to me."

Jerryck inched closer to the door. The confrontations between Lalven and Heston were just as bad, if not worse, than the screaming matches between Lalven and Nita. Keniv glared at Jerryck and leaned on the door, keeping anyone from leaving.

Jerryck glanced over at the door that went back out to the large council chamber. He might have to leave through there. But it was all the way on the other side of the room, past Heston and Lalven. He didn't want to get too near them, and risk them drawing him into their argument.

"He knows the Shontese," Lalven said, shaking off Heston's grip. "He knows Andreno. He has some gifts he'd like to give Andreno's friends."

"Does he have them here or elsewhere?" Heston asked.

"Here, of course," Lalven said.

"Search his room." Heston snapped his fingers at the elite guards. Two of them jumped for the door, roughly shoving Keniv out of the way.

"You can't do that." Keniv shouted after them. They were gone too quickly. He rounded on Heston, fists clenched and held at the ready. "You can't do that."

"Why not?" Tajor asked.

Keniv thumped his chest. "Those items are my private property."

Tajor put one hand to the side of his mouth, leaned forward, and whispered loud enough for everyone to hear, "Are they legal?"

Lalven slapped Tajor's hand down, barely missing his face. "Watch who you're throwing insinuations at."

"Tell me if they're legal or not." Heston rephrased it.

"Of course!" Lalven said. "Or I wouldn't have let him bring them here."

"If they weren't," Tajor said, "would you have let him take them somewhere else?"

"They aren't precisely illegal anywhere," Keniv said.

"Why are you evading?" Tajor stepped closer to him, leaving the table behind.

"They're frowned on by the Gathering of Seats," Keniv said. He looked over at Jerryck. "In fact, if they were caught in the wrong hands, the Gathering would likely take actions against that person. None of you would want something like that to happen, now would you?"

Tajor snickered. "Now who's insinuating?"

"What exactly are these items?" Jerryck asked.

"You going to stay around long enough to find out?" Keniv pushed Jerryck's shoulder again. Tajor and a couple of other guards stepped closer. Keniv ignored them and pushed a third time. "Or are you going to run like a coward?"

Jerryck stepped back. Keniv closed in. "That's right, back off. I don't care that you're a magician. I'm not afraid of you. Figured that out, didn't you. That's why you keep trying to leave."

He reached out to push again. Jerryck raised his arms to fend him off. "Stop it."

Keniv shouted in Jerryck's face. "You just took everything from me."

Tajor stuck his arm between the two of them and said to Keniv, "Step away."

"Because he's a minor noble and I'm not?" Keniv asked as he took one step back. "I needed this. I invested everything in dealing with Andreno's friends, and they won't trade with me anymore. They think I stole from them."

"Did you?" Heston asked.

"No." Keniv emphatically shook his head. "I know who did. But they won't listen to me. I needed to talk to Andreno, get him to make them to let me back in. And now I can't."

"Did they reject you on suspicion of theft?" Tajor lowered his arm. "Or did they just use that as an excuse to get rid of you?"

Keniv took a swing. Lalven shouted for him to stop. Tajor merely grinned, and leaned back, removing himself from contact. None of the other guards moved. Keniv pulled back with his other arm for another swing. Jerryck released some quick magic. It pulled at the insides of Keniv's ears, throwing him off balance. He stumbled, breaking his swing.

"Keniv? You all right?" Lalven strode to him. "What happened?"

"I happened," Jerryck said. "Try and hit my friend again, and I'll do worse."

Keniv launched. His hands lunged for Jerryck's throat. His bulk threw Jerryck backward. He hit the chair behind him, stumbled past it, then bounced off the edge of the table onto the floor.

Tajor grabbed Keniv's collar, lifting him off Jerryck with one arm. Keniv turned and kicked at Tajor's knees. Tajor grabbed one leg in mid-kick. Lalven swung a fist again. Tajor let go of the shirt and slapped him across the face with an open hand. His head snapped to the side and he dropped to the floor.

He curled in on himself, moaning in pain. One of the guards said, "Wow, Tajor. You can actually hit. I was beginning to wonder. I've never seen you do it."

"I have," Heston said. "Get a medic."

"He didn't hit him all that hard," the same guard said, while a couple of others ran out of the room at Heston's order. That left only the guard who spoke, and Tajor's cleft chin friend, who wore a grim expression for once instead of laughter.

Tajor stared down at his hands. He sighed like he was either exasperated or annoyed with himself. Heston asked, "What broke?"

"His jaw," Tajor said. He dropped his hands.

"From an open-handed slap?" Lalven pushed Tajor out of the way to kneel beside Keniv. "Impossible."

Keniv moaned again when Lalven pulled him up to sit. A bruise already blossomed on his jaw. Lalven put his hands under Keniv's arms, pulling him up. "Come. Let's get you to your room."

"He just attacked a member of the king's core staff." Heston grabbed Lalven's hands, removing them from Keniv.

Lalven pulled away. "He was provoked."

"Doesn't matter," Heston said.

"Don't you dare practice your thuggery on him." Lalven stood nose to nose with Heston. He shook a finger at Tajor. "And I insist he be incarcerated and punished!"

Heston crossed his arms, not saying a thing. Lalven waited a couple of heartbeats. Then he turned to the door. "I'm taking this up with Terrance."

"Do that," Heston said. "Be sure to mention how Keniv attacked Jerryck."

Lalven stopped short. He turned his head to glare over his shoulder at Heston. Keniv shuddered, hunkering in on himself, showing signs of shock. He wasn't acting right for a mere slap on the face. Jerryck drew close, intending to use magic to check health and ailments. Keniv kicked at him halfheartedly.

"Garret," Heston said to Tajor's friend. "Take Jerryck and help him get ready for his trip."

"I don't need a guard's help," Jerryck said.

"You have it anyway," Garret said. He plucked at Jerryck's arm, drawing him out of the room.

They headed for the tower. Jerryck kept glancing behind himself, back to the small council chamber.

"Stop worrying," Garret said. "Kellos will take care of it."

Jerryck faced forward. "Or whatever medic he sends, I know."

"Usually Kellos comes when Heston calls."

"That's a comfort," Jerryck said. They entered the tower and started up the steps winding around inside the outer wall. "He'll figure out exactly what's wrong."

Garrett followed him up. "If Tajor says the man's jaw broke, then the man's jaw broke."

"You can't break someone's jaw by slapping their face."

"Tajor can."

Jerryck stopped. He turned to stare at the guard. Some of the humor returned to Garret's eyes. "Haven't you ever wondered why he never, ever, ever hits people, like the rest of us who wear this uniform?"

"I guess I just assumed he did it when I wasn't around."

"Not even then," Garret said. "He's stronger than he looks. Stronger than he lets people believe. Fast, too. We don't spar with him anymore. We could never manage to get a hit on him, and we cracked a few too many bones when he blocked."

"Now I know you're making things up." Jerryck continued up the stairs.

"No, I'm not." Garrett followed again. "If you try and knock him to the ground, you might as well try and knock over a tree. What happens if you punch a tree with all your might? You break your hand. That's what."

Jerryck stopped a second time. He rested his hand on the stone of the outside wall. He shook his head. "No, no. This is too much. Something else would have happened by now, before this."

"It has," Garrett said. "You remember a few years ago, about the time Tajor came to the palace, there was that brouhaha in Kershet? A relative of some of the city officials went on trial as a serial rapist? He claimed it wasn't rape because his victims were just whores. He had a broken arm."

"So?" Jerryck remembered. No one could figure out how the man's upper left arm had snapped so cleanly in two. He wouldn't admit how it happened. And none of the witnesses would say, Heston included.

"So that was Tajor," Garrett said. "He grabbed the man by the arm and yanked him off his newest intended victim. Snapped the bone. I was there. I saw it. Heard the break."

"I really don't need to know all of this," Jerryck said.

"Sure you do." Garrett grinned. "He's going with you to Shontarra. It's good to know who's protecting you."

"Are you certain he's going after this incident?"

"Yes. Nita likes him. She relies on his advice a lot more than either of them will admit. And he reads people easier than an open book. Even if she wasn't going, Terrance would probably still send Tajor with you."

Chapter 26

TRAVELING HAD TO BE one of Jerryck's least favorite activities. He had never liked it, starting all the way back with the first trip he'd ever taken, when his mentor brought him to the palace from the little village where he lived. This was far worse than that first trip, or any others in the years since. Aside from the discomfort, the disruptions, and the sheer boredom, he missed his wife.

Nita's carriage, all the supply wagons, the dozens of horses and men... Everything made for a huge group traveling south. Good thing Nita refused to bring as many servants as other nobles would have insisted on. She didn't stop for niceties, like setting up a pavilion and tables for meals. She made do with eating the same road rations as everyone else. She slept in a simple bedroll on the floor of a small tent only because her bodyguards insisted on the shelter.

A portal would have been faster. Unfortunately, it wasn't reasonable. Jerryck could open one. But he had difficulty doing the necessary scrying beforehand to examine the spot where the other end of the portal would open. He couldn't sustain a portal for this many people anyway. Any magician who specialized in travel magic would have to charge an exorbitant fee just to carry him through the time he'd need to recuperate from sustaining a portal for that many people.

Most other forms of magical travel were either unreliable, like summoning a flying creature large enough to carry a passenger, or were more ideal for individual use, like transmogrifying into a bird, or translocation. They were stuck with slowly making their way south along the roads, using horses, wagons, and a lot of guards.

The flat farmlands around Kershet morphed into rolling hillocks the farther they went. Occasionally, the road curved around a larger rise that was too big to be called a hill, and still too small to be considered a mountain. More often, they would see such mounds in the distance, several miles off the road on one side or the other.

They passed through Wollock, the little town that had grown up on both sides of the bridge crossing the Flaynes River. After that, the hills became less frequent, without disappearing altogether. Sporadic groves grew more common and they passed in and out from under conifers.

Eventually, the copses conglomerated into one large forest that the road bordered on its western edge. Then an arm of the forest engulfed the land, and they traveled through a paved tunnel through trees and thick underbrush for two days. When they emerged on the other side, they came to the tower that stood on the Brend side of the border with Shontarra.

Built at the beginning of the nation, in the decade before Shontarra conglomerated into a nation of their own, the tower stood like a naked, stone finger with a bulge at the top for marksmen to shoot from. At one point, there had been a fort nearby, just inside the trees. Over the years since, the forest had taken it back, and the tower was manned by a mere handful of men acting more as border agents.

They crossed over into Shontarra. Messengers wearing the king's crimson and gold on their livery raced ahead to inform everyone on the road before them that the Royal Princess of Brend was on her way to the Shontese palace. As they approached the first village, soldiers wearing Shontese red and gray uniforms lined the road, raising banners of welcome.

Jerryck rode close to Nita's carriage. Hopefully, she wouldn't see the scraggly children lurking between the façade buildings on either side of the street. What were the chances, though? She was a lot more observant than most. She certainly put Jerryck to shame in that regard.

She leaned her arms on the carriage window, looking out at the men lining the street. "Where are the civilians? Do only soldiers live in this... Oh, there they are. Why are they hiding between the buildings?"

"Because they're poor and told to stay out of sight." The man in charge of her bodyguards rode even closer than Jerryck. He nudged his horse just enough to block her view. "Sit back inside. Don't lean out."

"I want to see," she said.

"You don't." The man shook his head. "Trust me. You really don't."

She sat back with a huff, crossed her arms, and muttered something Jerryck didn't catch. The man said, "I can give you that. You don't have to ask one of the residents."

"It's not the same," she complained.

"It's fairly simple." The man glanced back. "Even Jerryck could probably give it to you."

"Give her what?" Jerryck asked.

"She wants the history of this village."

"I could give you that," Jerryck said.

Nita leaned back out the window. "I wanted to stop and talk to some of the people here."

"The commoners here won't talk to you," Jerryck said.

Nita frowned at him. "Why not?"

"Because you're a princess." Jerryck looked at the banners they passed, the silent soldiers, and the children lurking in the shadows behind them. "That's why the soldiers are holding up banners of greeting, instead of shouting welcomes."

Nita crossed her arms and leaned them on the windowsill of her carriage, scowling at the men lining the street. "Refusing to talk to me is rather insulting."

"They think it's the other way around," the bodyguard said. "This isn't your father's kingdom, with his proprieties. Here, no commoner has the audacity to speak to a noble, let alone royalty."

"Then how am I supposed to learn about their land and their culture?"

"Their culture is similar to ours," the bodyguard said. "You know that."

"Or maybe not so similar as I was told." Nita snorted with disgust. "I talk to commoners every day."

"You wouldn't have in your grandfather's day," Jerryck told her. "Your father was the one to bury that protocol."

"As well he should have," Nita said with a curt nod.

They passed the soldiers and the last of the well-constructed buildings that made the village look good. The paving stones ran out, giving way to packed and rutted dirt for a road. The first of the children ventured up to one of the random guards riding with the caravan. Jerryck couldn't hear what they were saying, but he thought he knew what it was.

A second child came up to someone a bit closer, asking what Jerryck expected they would. "Please, do you have a morsel to spare?"

A third child dared come even closer to the carriage. "Do you have anything I could eat?"

Nita sucked in her breath. Her fingers went white gripping the sides of the carriage window. All the color leached from her face as more and more children came asking for food.

"Stop the caravan," she said.

"No," her bodyguard told her. "Sit back, inside all the way, or I'll shut your windows."

She pointed at the crutches and limps and bandages the children sported. "They're sick and injured."

"They're faking it," Jerryck said. How was it he could tell this and she couldn't? She had much better people skills than he did.

"They don't look like they're faking it," she said.

Jerryck looked over the closest of the children. With a single word, he altered his sight so he could see their auras as clearly as everything else. He pointed at the one with a foot twisted to the inside. "She's turning her foot on purpose. There's nothing wrong with it. She does have lice, though."

The other children stared at her, specifically at her head. She shouted at them, "I do not."

"And that one…" Jerryck pointed to a boy with his left arm in a sling. "He did have a broken arm at one point, the scars are there. It's long since healed. He really should take that sling off. It's so filthy, it's what's causing his skin rash."

190

The boy looked down at his arm, then up at Jerryck. Nita peered at him. "I don't see a skin rash."

"It's under the cloth of his sling," Jerryck said. He blinked his eyes, letting his sight fade back to normal. "All these kids are displaying things they're not suffering from and hiding what they are suffering from."

"Why?" Nita asked.

"What they're displaying gets more sympathy," her guard said. "Gets them more food handed out from travelers."

"So they're hungry," she said. "We should stop and feed them."

"We brought extra rations to hand out." He pointed behind them. "Look to the back."

Nita craned her head out the window, looking behind at the back of the caravan. Some of the servants she had brought were opening up a crate. They dug in and pulled out some strips of jerked meat. The children snatched at them as fast as they were produced. Until a group of Shontese soldiers marched up the street, shouting and hollering, shooing the kids away. They scattered, disappearing into the ramshackle mud huts behind the façade buildings, sucking on the jerked meat like it was candy.

Nita scowled at the soldiers as the caravan left the village outskirts behind. "That wasn't very nice of them."

"The kids here are used to it," her guard said. "And these kids are probably better fed than some of the villages we'll go through."

Nita gaped at him. "You're not serious, are you?"

"This village exists to support the soldiers stationed here at the border," the guard said. "They get food rations. Other villages don't."

Nita glared at him. "You're not going to let me stop in those other villages and feed them, either. Are you?"

"You can't feed the entire countryside," the man said.

Nita stuck her nose in the air, turning her face away from the guard. "Then I'll just tell the servants to leave food behind us as we go through. Children need fed."

The guard shook his head. "Their parents would take it all. They'd horde it and sell it. The children wouldn't get to eat any of it."

Nita looked back at the receding village. "The only adults I saw were soldiers. No parents tending to their children."

"The adults were inside," the guard said. He looked straight ahead to the road before them. "Again, it garners more sympathy for the children. They might get more from generous travelers."

"They could sell what their children could eat?" Nita asked. "Make them starve? I don't find that very credible."

"You've never been exposed to true poverty," Jerryck told her. "These people are used to going hungry. They go out in the fields and forest and collect edibles there to survive. If they get hold of something they can sell for a pair of shoes, or a winter cloak, or lifesaving medicine, they'll use it. Not eat it."

Nita sat back in her seat, nearly hidden inside her carriage. It bounced and jostled on the ruts and potholes in the dirt road. Every once in a while, she would brush back hair that had fallen in front of her face. Or maybe she was wiping dust from the road out of her eyes. She was rubbing them an awful lot. And sniffling sometimes, too. Her bodyguards closed the windows of her carriage through every village after that.

Chapter 27

THE LANDSCAPE slowly flattened out. The conifers disappeared behind them. The fields and low places turned swampy and hummed with insects. Jerryck had to use magic to repel the little blood suckers as the road weaved around, between, and sometimes through the bogs. The closer they got to denser civilization, the more the standing waters were filled in and cultivated, making way for noble estates. As they drew near the Shontese capital city of Quexintill, Nita was shut into her carriage once again, sparing her from the poverty she would otherwise have to see.

The guard with the cleft chin nudged his horse close to Jerryck's, boxing him in right beside the carriage. "Remember me?"

"Garret," Jerryck said.

The guard beamed at him. "You remembered!"

"I've lost count how many times you and several others have reminded me on this trip," Jerryck said.

"We reminded you as many times as necessary." Garret grinned momentarily. Then he dropped it, and his face turned serious. "I don't suppose we could convince you to ride in the carriage with Nita? Just this once?"

"No," Jerryck said. "Stop asking."

Garret sighed. "Had to give it one last try."

His serious expression turned into a scowl as they entered the outskirts of the city. He kept his face turned out, watching the buildings and the people as they made their way up the street. He must have somehow still kept an eye to the other side as well. Every time Jerryck tried to maneuver so he wasn't boxed in, Garret maneuvered with him, keeping him pinned.

Jerryck slumped in his saddle, keeping his eyes forward, off the poverty around them. He complained, "This city hasn't changed at all."

"Did you expect it to?" Garret asked. Some of the people close to the edge of the street jumped away as a window above them opened and someone dumped foul smelling sludge out to the street below.

Jerryck wrinkled his nose, trying not to gag on the reek. "I keep hoping it'll start looking more like Kershet."

"It looks like parts of Kershet," Garret said. He didn't look much affected by any of it.

"No parts I've seen." Keeping his eyes on the street ahead of them wasn't helping. Jerryck could still hear everything, smell everything. He swatted at a stray fly, sending it back to the swarms over piles of stink at the foundations of the buildings.

"Lots of parts I've seen," Garret said.

"You grew up behind a wall in a fancy house," Jerryck said. Garret spared him a glance. "Didn't you?"

"I was adopted," Garret said. "And I ran away a lot."

He raised his chin slightly at a beggar hobbling across the wide avenue in front of the caravan. One of the guards riding behind the carriage spurred his horse forward. The beggar wasn't quite fast enough with his limp and was within a hair's breadth of some of the people in the caravan as they passed him. The guard reached out, and jerked the man's ragged shirt, making him drop a shiv and a leather pouch of the style Brendish guards carried coins in. Jerryck hadn't seen him cut it from the person he'd nearly brushed against.

The corner of Garret's mouth twitched, a shadow of a smirk almost broke his scowl. "This city doesn't look all that different from the darker parts of Kershet. And those haven't changed during my entire life. It's been, what, a few years since you came to Shontarra?"

"The last time the Gathering of Seats held a convention in Kemetullah," Jerryck said. "And I didn't come here, to this city. I went down the coast and took a ship at the border to go around and avoid as much of Shontarra as I could."

"You still had guards that were familiar with the country."

"I told Terrance I didn't need them." Jerryck refused to look at the filthy children's faces peering at them from between the crooked, dilapidated buildings. "I don't like going through this country. I don't like the poverty."

"You could tell the king you don't need guards until you run out of breath," Garret said. "It won't change anything. He puts guards on people that are important to him. That's the only reason some of us are here. I've never been to Shontarra. Same with Deek. But since the princess is here, we're here."

"Deek?"

"Scowly man, crooked nose," Garret reminded him. He leaned a little closer. "He got it broke a few too many times by picking fights as a kid."

"I don't want to know that," Jerryck said.

Garret went back to the original topic. "You thought this city would change?"

"Wishing, more like. It hasn't changed since the first time I came through," Jerryck said. He turned at the sounds of a scuffle behind them. The guards were smacking around another couple of beggars and relieving them of Brendish marked parcels. Jerryck turned forward again. "I wasn't even an adult then. It's been more than two decades. Something should have changed somewhere."

"I'm sure the people who live this way wish it would," Garret said. "What were you doing here as a kid?"

"We were going to a convention in Kemetullah," Jeryrck said. "The only one my mentor ever took me to. We only stayed for a day, then left early. He was mad, too. Mad enough to leave in the middle of the night. I went to bed, and then woke up the next morning in a carriage on the road with him heading north. He never would tell me why."

"Interesting," Garret said. "I never knew that. I wonder if Cade knows."

"Cade?"

"Skinny guard." Garret almost smirked again. "Really good at gathering information. Disappears a lot. I expect to see him only intermittently once we get to the palace. He said something about a rumor of his favorite contact there running into trouble. He's going to want to get all the details."

The front of their procession reached the closed gates in the walls surrounding the palace, and stopped. They stood out fairly stark in the empty gap between where the walls rose up, and the space where no city buildings were allowed. About forty feet across, the strip was heavily patrolled by guards wearing the red and gray of the Shontese prince. All the beggars and cutpurses slunk back into the squalor of the city and disappeared.

One of the guards manning the gate held up one hand to them and called, "Halt!"

Jerryck looked back down the line of their caravan. Every single one of them was already stopped, most of them still back where the street was between the buildings, where they were exposed to the less desirable elements of the city.

The Brendish herald at the head of the procession sat stiff and straight on his mount, raising his voice to be heard clearly. "Her Royal Highness, Princess Nita, heir to the throne of Brend, come to bring the condolences of her father King Terrance to Prince Sanbralio, the Esteemed Leader of Shontarra."

"You may go no farther," the gate guard said.

"Did you not hear me?" The herald gaped at the guard. He waved at the crimson and gold banner carried by the man next to him. "This isn't just any nobleman's daughter. We've come all the way from Coraline Palace."

Something clattered behind them, back among the city buildings. Jerryck's horse shuffled nervously. So did several of the guards'. Tajor inserted himself right by the carriage window, so near he could have touched it without extending his arm. Garret inched closer to Jerryck, boxing him in tighter.

"Our orders are not to open for anyone," the gate guard said.

The herald pulled out an envelope with a red and gray wax seal. He waved it in front of the gate guard's face. "While on the road, we received a correspondence from Prince Sanbralio that said we were welcome to enter the palace as his personal guests."

The gate guard looked left and right, down and up, at the other Shontese guards, anywhere but at the envelope with the seal. "My orders don't allow any exceptions."

"How can your orders not allow for guests of your prince?" the herald demanded. He shook his head in disbelief. "Send someone inside to let Prince Sanbralio know his royal guest has arrived."

"We're not allowed to do that right now." The gate guard's voice was getting quieter. Jerryck had to strain to hear him above the rest of the city noise. "I'll send through the message as soon as I have permission to do so. Until then, everyone seeking entrance to the palace is advised to find lodgings elsewhere."

The window of Nita's carriage opened, and she stuck her head out. She immediately choked and slapped a hand over her nose. Tajor leaned close to her and said, "Breathe through your mouth until your nose adjusts."

"I have been breathing through my mouth." Her words sounded like she had a cold with her nose plugged by her hand. "I didn't realize how much of the smell the shutters had blocked. Why are we stopped? What's going on?"

"They're refusing to open the gates to the palace for us," Jerryck told her. "They said we need to find lodging somewhere else until he has permission to let anyone inside know that you're here."

"*What?*" Nita straightened up so fast, she almost hit her head on the top of the window frame.

"I can't see there being any lodging fit for her here." The head of her bodyguards looked back the way they'd come and wrinkled his nose. "Reports are that most nobles won't even stay in this city. They go to estates nearby."

Masorno had one of those. He likely would be delighted to host the Princess, especially if he was going to also put Jerryck in his debt by doing so. As galling as that was, it would be better for Nita than staying in the city.

"We can go to Magician Masorno's estate," he told her.

"It's bad enough that you're going to apologize for doing nothing wrong," she said. "I'm not going to put you in a situation where you have to grovel with gratitude as well."

She leaned out farther, waving her arm, shouting, getting the attention of the gate guard. He looked directly at her, instead of avoiding the eye contact. He said, "Please tell the princess—"

"I *am* the princess," Nita yelled. She pointed her finger and stabbed it repeatedly at him. "If I find lodging anywhere else, it will be on my way back home. And when you're allowed to take a message to Prince Sanbralio, you can tell him that the next time he hears from Brend, it will be a formal complaint from my father about this insult I received!"

Lord Andreno rode up on a horse from inside the bars of the gate, a small escort behind him. "What's going on here?"

"The Princess of Brend is asking for admittance." The gate guard fidgeted, and wouldn't look Andreno in the eye either. "As you ordered—"

"Why haven't you opened the gate for her?" Andreno sidled his horse up close.

"You ordered—"

"Your orders be damned!" Andreno shouted. "Are you trying to start a war? I ought to have you laid out and stretched on a rack. Open the gate this instant."

All the gate guards jumped to obey, not just the one. The moment the gate opened wide enough, Andreno beckoned them all to come through. Nita ducked back into her carriage and they moved forward.

The horrors on the city side of the palace wall made everything inside ugly by contrast. The grounds were scoured clean of filth and poverty, lying about the truth of the city that surrounded it. Everything sat immaculate and precise to the point of sterility. Flowers bloomed everywhere, delicately arranged in defiance of natural growth, their perfume masking the stench outside the walls. Water fountains tinkled perversely, mocking the quality of water the rest of the city drank and washed in. Birds in cages sang mournful melodies. Hedges stood trimmed into shapes of people and animals, frozen and trapped in place like slaves.

The carriage rolled to a stop on the raked gravel drive in front of the palace steps. Tajor acted as footman. The elite and Nita's bodyguards dismounted, keeping in close proximity to her, keeping Jerryck at her side. Not that he would be anywhere else at the moment.

"I apologize for that mess there." Andreno thumbed over his shoulder back at the gate. He dismounted too. "We've locked the palace. No one comes or goes, except me and those bearing essentials, like the letter you sent us from the road. We don't want people bothering Uncle too much right now."

Nita nodded curtly. "Understandable."

"I left the gate guards explicit instructions for your arrival," Andreno went on. "They must have misunderstood me. I'm so embarrassed about this."

"I'm just glad you were there to let us in," Nita said.

"Happy to be of assistance." Andreno gave her a huge smile. He bobbed his head at Jerryck. "Happy to see you again as well, Lord Magician. Our court magician, Lord Masorno insisted on special preparations for your arrival."

"Wonderful." Jerryck tried not to sound too sarcastic, and struggled to keep from grimacing. Knowing Masorno, it would likely be an audience to hear the apology.

Chapter 28

"**W**HERE ARE MY MANNERS," Andreno said. "We got to talking instead of the usual formalities. Welcome, both of you, to the Shontese palace. It's not nearly as fancy as yours, but it's home for us."

"I'm sure we'll be perfectly comfortable," Nita said.

"Please, allow me to escort you to your chambers" Andreno offered his arm. She placed her hand on it, and he led them all inside.

He took them to a lavish room overlooking manicured lawns. He stayed long enough for Nita to look around and say it met her approval. She went about settling in, and a servant showed Jerryck to his own guest room up the corridor from hers. Although not quite as posh as Nita's, its furnishing and décor were still richer than what he lived with at home. Surely not every visiting magician got to stay in a room like this. Was it because he came with Nita? Or was this the preparation Masorno had insisted on?

Garret followed Jerryck. He eyed the servant standing silent in the corner and said, "Leave."

"I'm waiting for his orders," the servant whispered, giving Jerryck a nervous glance.

"Please go inform Masorno of my arrival," Jerryck said. That would get it over with. And it would get rid of the servant before Garret terrorized him. The servant gave him a short bow and ran from the room. Jerryck said to

Garret, "You're not supposed to make Shontese servants talk. They think a good servant is a silent servant."

"I haven't heard that," Garret said.

"I guess it's not really all that well known in Brend," Jerryck said. "If my mentor hadn't come from southern Shontarra, I probably wouldn't know it either."

He used the canopied bed to unpack, taking things out and setting them on the thick, feather mattress. Garrett poked about the room. He looked at the walls behind the brightly colored tapestries. He opened the beveled glass window, stuck his head out, and looked in every direction. Then he pulled his head in, closed the window, and examined the latch.

"Pretty convenient that Andreno was there to make sure we were let in." Jerryck broke the quiet. It was strange, having a guard in the room when there wasn't a noble to be protected.

"A little too convenient." Garret opened the decoratively carved closet and ran his hand around the inside walls.

Jerryck watched Garret pull each bureau drawer out by their silver knobs and examine them underneath and on the sides. "What are you doing?"

"My job." Garret checked inside the bureau itself.

"Do you think someone's going to jump out and attack us or something?"

"Like Keniv attacked you?" Garret grinned. He slid the drawers back in place. "Not in here. Not now that I know there's no one in here with us, no secret doors that an attacker can sneak in through, no hidden levers or catches, the window can only be opened from inside, and an intruder would have a hard climb getting to it from the outside anyway."

"You're being paranoid."

"A little paranoia has kept a lot of people alive." Garret's grin widened. "More people should be paranoid. It's a healthy state of mind!"

"Not really," Jerryck said.

"Yes, it is," Garret insisted. "It's necessary in case there really are people out there trying to get you. Besides, if people stopped being paranoid, I'd be out of a job."

Jerryck shook his head. He took the last item from his travel pack and placed it on the bed with the others. "Is that why you think it's too convenient that Andreno let us in?"

"No, I was serious about that." Garret's grin slipped. He helped Jerryck put clothes into the bureau and the closet.

"You think he's up to no good?"

"I'm paid to believe people are up to no good," Garret said. Someone knocked on the door. Garret answered, then turned to Jerryck and announced, "Court Magician Masorno to see you."

Garret opened the door wider and stepped aside. Masorno stood in the corridor. His stomach paunch had grown. So had his double chin. He gave Jerryck a dirty look. "You have a bodyguard now? When have you ever had a bodyguard?"

"Not my choice," Jerryck said. "I can't get away from him."

"I see." Masorno stepped into the room. "I assume you accompanied the princess so you could apologize to me. But does it have to be with one of the very men you used to throw me out last time I paid you the courtesy of a visit?"

Jerryck glanced at Garret before picking up some of his toiletries to put in a drawer under the washbasin. "He was one of them?"

"Don't you remember?" Masorno said. "There were three of them. One was smart mouthed, extremely rude, and disrespectful. He kept asking inappropriate questions that were none of his business. He stayed with you while the other two escorted me out of the palace. One was very stern. This one, he laughed at me. I was very embarrassed."

"Did you laugh?" Jerryck asked Garret.

"Maybe." Garret shrugged. "I've been accused of laughing at everything."

"He laughed," Masorno said. "And the other used cuss words and crude language. Very disrespectful. Very inappropriate."

"Who was with you?" Jerryck asked Garret.

"Deek," Garret said. "He cusses at most people."

Masorno didn't even look at Garret when he said, "The man who remained with you is with the princess now. I expect an apology from him as well. I understand the other two followed your instructions, so I'll be gracious enough to forgive them. But that other man, he had no right to ask me anything, especially not with the attitude he used."

"That was Tajor," Jerryck said. He picked up some of his books. Since there was no shelf for them, he stacked them on a little table by the bed. "He speaks to everyone that way. He doesn't care who you are. He says whatever it takes to annoy you."

"He's respectful to no one?" Masorno's face went a little slack with incredulity. "How does he maintain status as a guard in the palace?"

"He's respectful to Terrance and Nita, usually." Jerryck picked up the pouch with his writing supplies. Again, there wasn't really a good place for them. He nudged his stack of books to one side to make room.

Masorno crossed his arms. "You do know we have servants here to put all that away for you?"

Jerryck frowned. He was going to have to focus more on Masorno before the man got offended and threw a fit. Instead of picking up the next few items, he turned to face his host.

Masorno let his arms drop. He straightened his shoulders. "Now, about the apology I'm due…"

"I doubt you'll get one from him without more insults."

"I meant the one from you."

"Right. Of course." Jerryck nodded. No audience. Perhaps the room really was the preparations Masorno had made. It was rather unlike him. When he wanted to humble a person, he tended to give them fewer amenities, not more.

"I'm waiting," Masorno said.

Jerryck clenched his jaw. Masorno would take an apology as an invitation to return to Coraline Palace. Then he would fall back into his pattern of repeatedly coming to pester Jerryck about finishing his apprenticeship.

There was nothing else for it. He had to speak with Shontese magicians to further his search. To do that, he had to make amends and open up that assumed invitation.

"Well?" Masorno prodded.

Jerryck squeezed out the first couple of words. "I apologize."

Masorno held out his hand, waggling fingers in a gesture that beckoned for more. After those first two words, the others flowed more easily for

Jerryck. "I'm sorry I told you never to bother coming back, and for all the insults I threw at you."

"Apology accepted," Masorno said. He sauntered over to one of the two overstuffed chairs by the marble fireplace and plopped down atop the pillows adorning it. "Now, about your unfinished apprenticeship."

"Please," Jerryck said. "Don't goad me into saying something else I'll have to apologize for."

"It's important that you get that pedigree," Masorno said. "Think of what Old Heldavio would say if he knew his last apprentice neglected finishing things properly after all the years of training he gave you."

"He complained about the Gathering more than anyone else I've ever met in my life," Jerryck said. "And I didn't come here to get a lecture on this from you."

"Of course not." Masorno leaned back and crossed his ankles. "You came to apologize and make amends to our friendship."

"I'm looking for someone," Jerryck said.

Masorno sat forward, eyes narrowed, hands gripping the arms of the chair. "Who?"

"I don't know exactly." Jerryck shook his head. "Someone new who can use magic. Someone I haven't met at all."

"And you came here?" Masorno stabbed the arm of the chair several times with his pointer finger. "Why? What have you learned?"

"Nothing," Jerryck said. "I just haven't found anyone in Brend that's caught my interest. When the princess wanted to come here, I thought I'd accompany and consult with you, see if there was anyone you knew of."

"Are the rumors true then?" Masorno let his hunched shoulders relax. His grip on the chair loosened. "Are you really looking for an apprentice?"

"Something like that."

"Hmm," Masorno grunted. Jerryck braced himself for a lecture on why he shouldn't look for an apprentice when he had no license. Instead, Masorno leaned back and pointed at the other chair.

"What?" Jerryck asked.

"Sit down." Masorno laughed. "I shouldn't have to invite you to take a seat in your own room. It's getting awkward to hold a conversation with you standing over there."

Jerryck sidled over and slipped into the other chair. Masorno said, "I tell you what I'll do. I'll send for some potentials to come in and meet you. I know of a few who are young enough to give you time to finish up your official study and take the oaths at the next convention before they come of age."

"When will they come?" Jerryck asked. "Does anyone know when the palace will be unlocked again?"

Masorno sniffed and tilted up his nose. "They'll come when I call. I can summon people through the gate. The guards won't bar someone who has an official letter of welcome."

"They barred us," Jerryck said.

"Are you serious?" Masorno dropped his jaw. He closed it again and clucked his tongue in disgust. "This sounds like something Andreno would meddle with. I suppose he's the one who came out and made sure you were let in?"

"Yes."

"Well!" Masorno slapped the arm of his chair. "I'll have this fixed."

"I don't want to cause any trouble."

"You didn't. Andreno does that quite well on his own."

"When he was in Brend, he mentioned a friend interested in magic."

Masorno snorted. "I wouldn't pay any heed to any friend Andreno claims to have. Did you know that he was treated for insanity several times before his parents died? They even took him to Coraline Palace once. Not even Old Heldavio could help him."

"I don't remember that," Jerryck said.

"That was right before he went to fetch you for his last apprentice," Masorno said. "Andreno was only five then. About a month after he returned here, his parents were murdered in their bed, suffocated in their sleep."

"Who killed them?"

"No one knows. I helped with the investigation. There was no trace of the murderer, so some speculated that magic had been employed. I found no trace of any magical activities. Andreno wept for months and kept talking to them."

A ghoulish image popped into Jerryck's head. "Even though they were dead?"

"Not to their bodies." Masorno chuckled. "You make the strangest faces sometimes. No, they were cremated and their ashes buried with all the pomp of high nobility. The servants swear that Andreno sees ghosts, and that's what he talks to. That was the insanity his parents were trying to find a cure for."

"I've never heard of that form of insanity," Jerryck said.

"Neither had Heldavio," Masorno said. The Shontese servant slipped back into the room with two folded pieces of paper in his hand. Masorno saw him, then said to Jerryck, "I should go. I need to make some arrangements for you."

He stood up and strode from the room, leaving the door wide open behind him. The servant reached to close it, just as Masorno started shouting at someone, "What do you think you're doing? You can't be here."

Jerryck shook his head and thanked the servant for closing off the rest of Masorno's words. The man held out the pieces of paper for him. One was a note to let him know the princess had gone out for a tour of the palace and the grounds. The other was an invitation from Prince Sanbralio to join him for the evening meal. Jerryck grimaced. That would be a formal affair. He would have to dress his uncomfortable best, and use the stiff, unnatural manners the nobility insisted on.

Chapter 29

A T THE APPROPRIATE TIME, Jerryck made himself ready. The servant assigned to him showed the way to the royal dining hall. The table was so large and heavy, it had to have been constructed inside the room. Silver candelabra sat along its length, adding to the light shed by the crystal chandeliers above. Padded chairs surrounded the table, many of them occupied by people dressed so foppishly, Jerryck wondered if they were a troupe of actors trying to put on a comedy.

There were no tapestries to soften the walls. No colored banners representing the districts inside Shontarra. The only wall trappings were iron light sconces between arms displays and shields in the prince's red and gray.

At the end of the table sat a striking woman, somewhere in her late teens or early twenties. Her black hair was pulled softly back in a loose bun, much like Leanne wore hers. She had a diamond on each earlobe, but no necklace or rings. She sat rigid and still, her eyes fixed on her place at the table, her face an emotionless mask. No one seated near even tried to strike up conversation with her.

A couple of women entered the dining room behind Jerryk. One of them pointed to the lone woman and laughed to her companion. "She still has no sense of style."

"Good," the companion said. "She doesn't deserve to look as beautiful as us. She can keep dressing stupid and plain."

Jerryck eyed the two women. Their hair was piled at least a foot above their heads. Baring their necks might have made them more comfortable in the heat of the southern summer. But their heavy clothes had to erase any cooling benefits of wearing their hair up. Their dresses were so stiff they couldn't possibly bend from the waist up, and so wide they would have to turn sideways to get through a single-wide door. The first woman noticed him looking at them.

"You're one of the Brendish guests, yes?" She batted her eyes at him. She flicked a wrist at the woman at the end of the table. "What do you think of the common filth there compared to our beauty."

"She puts you to shame," Jerryck blurted. "You both look kind of stupid."

The two women gasped. One of them put a hand on the wall and panted as if she were about to faint. Jerryck sensed no fluctuation in her aura, so it was likely just a show. The other woman scolded him. "How rude. Just you wait until your princess comes in wearing the latest fashions, like us. Will you tell her she looks stupid too?"

"She doesn't tolerate stupid," Jerryck said.

More and more people entered. Some of the men dressed almost as flamboyantly as the women. Nita was one of the last to enter. Her hair was done much like the woman at the end of the table. Her dress was just as simply cut. She wore more jewelry, but nothing so ostentatious as almost everyone else in the room.

People stared. Some of the women plucked at their oversized jewelry, twisting their rings around their fingers, adjusting their necklaces, touching earrings that brushed against their shoulders.

Andreno and Prince Sanbralio entered very last. The old prince's hair was a disheveled mat. His eyes had sunk in, and the rings under them were so dark they looked like bruises. His clothes hung askew and his skin sagged, a sign of sudden, rapid weight loss.

Andreno was seated on his right, in the place of the heir. Nita was on Sanbralio's left, with Jerryck on the other side of her. The meal began. Everyone dug into their plates and somehow held conversations while stuffing food in their mouths.

Except Sanbralio. He ignored his plate. Servants changed it out with every course. He always brushed it away, or leaned over it to talk to Nita, completely absorbing her time and attention.

She kept trying to shift his focus, pointing out other people in the room. He responded kindly, unless she brought Andreno into the conversation. Then Sanbralio got nasty, making derisive comments about him being ungrateful and taking everything from everyone around him.

When the meal ended, Nita invited Andreno to her room to chat. As much as the socializing left Jerryck drained, he was not about to let her have a young man in her room unsupervised, especially not one who ignored servants and bodyguards. He sent his servant to fetch him a book and tagged along.

He stood by a wall with some of the guards, until one of Nita's servants brought him a stool. He didn't even have to ask. And the stool was much more comfortable than the chair he'd used in the dining hall. The room was much like his, the floor softened with rugs, the walls hung with bright colored tapestries. Except in here, the Brendish crimson and gold was prominently displayed, and a floral scent perfumed the air.

Andreno settled himself into one of the chairs in the sitting area. "Thank you for entertaining Uncle so much. It's frightening how despondent he is. It was good to see him responsive for once."

"It was more like doting affection than responsiveness." Nita sat in front of a large vanity taking pins out of her hair. The Shontese servants in the room rushed over with horrified expressions to do it for her.

"You stood out," Andreno said. "That catches his attention. You didn't style yourself as fancy as other women, and still you stood out."

"I dressed fancier tonight than suits me for just a meal." Nita put her hands in her lap, letting the servants work. "Would you be offended if I told you the favored styles I've seen here look more like ostentatious facades than any real expression of taste?"

Andreno burst out laughing. "I think some of them dressed up more than usual just to impress you."

"They failed," Nita said.

The servant from Jerryck's room slipped in and silently handed him his book. The women attending Nita removed the last pin. One of them took a brush to her hair. Nita watched in the mirror with her hands still folded in her lap, still talking to Andreno. "I thought they looked silly. Besides you, Sanbralio, and Jerryck, there was only one other person who dressed sensibly."

"Who?" Andreno asked.

"The woman at the end of the table opposite your uncle." Nita unfolded her hands and removed her earrings. "She wasn't overdressed. She didn't look like she cared what anyone thought of her."

"Probably because no one cared enough to think anything of her," Andreno said. "That was just Charllass. She's nobody."

"Then why was she sitting in a place of honor at the foot of the table?"

Andreno shrugged. "Because Uncle likes her. She's his second son's bastard daughter. She's common and illegitimate. She's nobody."

"I didn't know Prince Sanbralio had a granddaughter."

"You might not want to say that where others can hear you. They'd take offense to that much honor being given to a nobody."

Nita's cheeks colored. "There's no such thing as a nobody. Everybody is somebody."

Jerryck glanced over at the servant. Perhaps he should have sent for earplugs as well, in case Nita went on a tirade about social injustices. If it got really bad, he could always just use a spell on his ears.

"Everybody worth counting is somebody," Andreno said. "Even minor nobles. But Charllass isn't even that. Her mother was utterly common, not even born of a minor noble. She really is a nobody."

Nita's flush spread. Her reflection in the mirror glared at Andreno, her eyes growing dark with anger. Except for the shape and color of her eyes, she looked exactly like her mother before a fit of temper. Then the moment passed. Her expression changed to something closer to her father's cool aloofness toward someone who had angered him.

"Please excuse me." She tilted up her chin and looked away. "I'm feeling tired. I would rather not entertain company anymore."

"How thoughtless of me." Andreno rose from his seat. "You just finished a long journey today. Of course you're tired. I'll go so you can rest. Good night, Princess."

As soon as he was gone, Nita said, "Someone please remind me who is in Prince Sanbralio's family. I thought his second son had no children because he had no interest in women."

She looked at the three Shontese servants in the room. None of them said a word. Jerryck couldn't help her. He didn't keep track of foreign nobility. He had a hard enough time remembering the names of the Brendish ones. She looked to the Brendish elite and her bodyguards. Then she focused in on Tajor's skinny, elite friend. "Cade, help me out here."

"You're thinking of Prince Yaquerro," Cade said. "The one that was just killed in the mountains. He was the first son."

Nita frowned. "I thought the first son was a stillborn."

Cade nodded. "Yes, so he wasn't counted as the first son. He didn't even get a name. That honor went to Prince Yaquerro, the first son to reach adulthood."

"That's what messed me up," Nita said. She went about removing the rest of her jewelry. "I was thinking Yaquerro was the second born, Chaxten the third, and the fourth died as a child when he fell from a tree."

"That was Ganthos," Cade said. "That happened when he was four. He would have been the third son if he had survived to adulthood. Since he did not, if Sanbralio had sired any other boy, that child would have been the third son once he was grown."

Nita closed her jewelry box and rose from her seat. "I think I've got it now,. So Chaxten was the second son, even though he was the third born. And he's the one who died in a boating accident ten years ago?"

"Eleven now," Cade said. "He chose a woman who was a common born servant to a district premiere on the border with us, and he was loyal to her until the day he died. She gave him two children, Quillen and Charllass. When he died, Sanbralio had the children brought to the palace to live. When their mother protested, he banished her from the country. I think she went south, across the Ahnjwat Sea, according to rumors."

Nita gasped. "That's terrible for her."

"That's lucky for her," Cade said. "Shontese princes of the past would have executed her. I think the premiere she served may have had something to do with the mercy she was shown. Or maybe Quillen. Or both. It's all rumor from that point."

Nita looked over at Jerryck, horror and disgust written all over her face. "Are things like this why you hate coming to Shontarra?"

"Something like that." Jerryck stood. He excused himself and left the room, just in case she let loose the rant she'd held back earlier.

Prince Sanbralio officially opened the palace gate. Locals poured in. Nita went out to mingle with them, claiming it was expected of her. Jerryck bit back a groan, dressed up, and accompanied.

For the most part, people left him alone and focused on the princess. There were some who tried to argue their way through the crowd by claiming they wanted to talk to him. The elites kept most of those away. The only ones they let through to him were people with ties to his profession.

A middle-aged magician was allowed to approach. He put a hand on the shoulder of a boy who had the protruding front teeth and gangly limbs of most children at about eleven or twelve. The magician smiled broadly. "Lord Jerryck, I want to introduce you to my nephew."

"I'm sorry," Jerryck said. "I recognize your face. Remind me your name?"

"Alysses," the man said. He pointed over his shoulder at a young man just behind him. "I took on an apprentice out of Kershet a couple of years ago. Then my nephew started showing talent. I've been keeping an eye out for him ever since. When I heard you were looking for an apprentice of your own, I made sure to be in the area when you arrived."

The boy looked Jerryck up and down. "Isn't he the one you used to say—"

"—is extremely talented." Alysses cut him off.

The boy shook his head. "That's not what you said."

The young man behind them snickered. Alysses snapped at him. "Quiet, you!"

"Why?" the young man sassed. "You used to complain about Lord Jerryck as much as you complain now about that foreigner."

"Foreigner?" Jerryck asked.

Masorno came up behind them. "No one important." He pointed up to a balcony where a fair featured young man watched the crowd below. He looked about nineteen or twenty. Like many, he seemed particularly focused on the Brendish group. "No one really likes him. He's from the Chemwanitz."

Jerryck glanced at Garret, who leaned and whispered something to Cade. None of the others seemed to notice. They kept right on talking. The apprentice said to Masorno, "I heard he wasn't a Chemwanee. Him or any of his friends."

Cade slunk off. Was he going to go find out more about this 'foreigner'? Or should Jerryck try and ask more? Maybe Cade was taking care of something Jerryck hadn't noticed.

Jerryck shook his head. He really should just trust the man to do his job. Masorno must have noticed the head shake. He said, "My thoughts exactly. This his ridiculous. What is this nation coming to when a mere apprentice is disrespectful enough to a full fledged magician to infer he's a liar right out in the open in front of everyone?"

Alysses bowed his head. "My apologies for the behavior of my apprentice."

"You should leave now," Masorno said. "Go teach the lad some manners."

"Of course..." Alysses quickly ushered both of his charges away.

"Sorry about that," Masorno said to Jerryck. "He was pretty far down the list of people for you to meet with. But don't you worry. I'll stay right here and make certain no one else who isn't worth your time bothers you."

"Actually," Jerryck said. "I think I'll go up and talk to the Chemwanee."

Masorno wrinkled his nose in disgust. "Why would you do that?"

"In case..." Jerryck probably shouldn't say in case Cade hadn't left to investigate him. The only other excuse that came to mind was to see if the man's tribal shaman knew Sakila. That could only lead to a line of trouble with a magician loyal to the Gathering. "In case... Uh..."

Jerryck couldn't think of an excuse that wouldn't give away that he was looking for someone who might know who had poisoned the river. Masorno just smiled and patted Jerryck on the shoulder saying, "Don't you worry about him. I've got people keeping a close watch. And I'll spend all of today with you just to make sure he doesn't bother you."

For the rest of the morning, Masorno hung over Jerryck's shoulder. When Nita finally made her excuse to leave the gathering, he tagged along with her and Jerryck, insisting on lunch. Nita declined, having already made arrangements. Jerryck was stuck for it.

Masorno babbled all through the meal. He didn't stop when it ended. After a while, he called in a couple of fellow magicians. Each of them tried to get Jerryck to slate the boy they favored as a future apprentice. At first, they touted the advantages of the boy they represented. Then they started slandering the boy the other represented. Then they flung insults directly at each other.

Masorno giggled with delight. Jerryck tuned them out. They didn't act like they noticed. He took a chance they were no longer paying him any attention at all, and slunk to the door. Since he made it out without any of them calling him back, he assumed they hadn't noticed. He headed for Nita's room, Garret chuckling as he trailed behind him.

Chapter 30

NONE OF THE GUARDS challenged Jerryck when he entered Nita's room. She paced back and forth across the floor, fists and teeth clenched. Deek and the head of her bodyguards stood over by the far wall.

"Is this why most of her guards are out in the corridor?" Garret whispered to Deek.

"I heard that." Nita whirled around to glare at him. She put her fists in her hair on either side of her head, bent over at the waist, and screamed. "I hate this place! I hate it. Hate it. Hate it."

"You were happy earlier." Jerryck backed up. "What happened?"

"The only thing anyone here cares about is their own social status." She went back to pacing. "They mistreat anyone they think they can get away with abusing. I thought maybe I could escape it for a while by reading a popular novel, and I can't even do that."

"You love reading," Jerryck said.

"The only thing they gave me to read is stupid and tasteless…" Nita pointed to a book lying on the floor on the other side of the room. With the way the pages were skewed, some of them halfway folded under, she had to have thrown it. "It started off with some stupid, vapid daughter of a nobleman out in a field picking flowers. She didn't even have any guards around. Very unrealistic. Then these noblemen kept coming up and singing to her, each of them trying to convince her to let him become her suitor. As if all that matters is how well someone sings. I tell you, if some stranger walked up to me in the middle of a field, I'd throw rocks at him. Especially if he broke out in spontaneous song."

"I could see you doing that." Her bodyguard chuckled. "You're more and more like your mother every day."

"I kept skipping chunks, flipping through the pages, thinking it had to get better," Nita continued, shaking her fist at the book. "Most of the entire plot is this stupid woman agonizing over which of her suitors will make the best heir for her father, because she's his only child, so whoever she marries will take her father's place."

"And there's the heart of the matter," her bodyguard said.

She narrowed her eyes at him. "What's that supposed to mean?"

"You don't like the subject matter," he said. "Too many people have told you that your future husband is also the future king. Personally, I agree with you. Those people are stupid. I know plenty of women who would make better rulers than most of the men in positions of authority."

"Now you're just trying to mollify me." A lot of the tension on her face melted away, a sign that her rant was winding down. Jerryck sighed with relief and inched toward the book. Nita flopped into an overstuffed chair. "Is Tajor back yet?"

"Not yet," Deek answered.

"Where'd he go?" Jerryck picked up the book. No book should be left to lie that way, not even if it really was as bad as Nita claimed.

"Cade wanted his help checking out a few people," Nita said. "Did you find anything yet?"

"No." Jerryck smoothed out the pages and closed the book properly.

Garret snickered. "You didn't find out you dislike Masorno?"

"I already knew that," Jerryck said.

"How about that Andreno is connected with foreigners?"

Jerryck set the book on the nearest table. "I didn't hear that."

"I did," Garret said. "Several times."

"So did I," Deek said.

The door opened. Cade and Tajor entered. Nita gestured them closer with the same hand wave her father used. She still partook in the ongoing conversation at the same time. "Andreno is high nobility. Of course he's connected to foreigners. Which ones are people referring to? And how specific is the information? Is it through correspondence? Is there a representative here in Shontarra? And for what purpose?"

"The only answers we have for that are rumors," Cade jumped in, getting nothing out of context, despite having missed the beginning of it. "The two things most people agree on is that they're fair featured, like the Chemwanee, and Andreno's getting gold from them. We talked to a couple of merchants who swear he's been scouring the country and beyond for leather, textiles, grains, and preserved foodstuffs to trade for gold."

Nita frowned. "The Chemwanee don't use gold as a monetary system."

"No," Cade said. "They barter."

"So they're probably not from the Chemwanitz Mountains." Nita stood from her seat. "Besides, Andreno doesn't like any Chemwanee. I think he'd have as little to do with them as possible. How reliable are the rumors that they're fair featured?"

"I saw one," Jerryck said. "He had blond hair."

"Dark blond," Garret corrected. "And Masorno only claimed the man was foreign. He didn't offer any proof."

"I'll keep digging," Cade said.

"Having our regular source of information would help," Deek grumbled. "Something I should know?" Nita asked.

"We're currently undergoing a shift in our regular information correspondent here," Cade said. "They were a father/son team, both of whom had been initiated into the elite. More the father than the son. Unfortunately, there was a recent incident that resulted in the father's death. The son is off the grounds right now, sent on leave of absence by his commanding officer for a mourning period."

Nita put her hands on her hips. "Well, you can't really blame him for that."

"It'll be harder in the future," Cade said with a glower. "The son was always more tight lipped than the father. He's more likely to send information south to Ahnjwat than to us. So, as I said, I'll have to keep digging to try and turn up information on this mysterious group of foreigners Andreno's been working with."

"Can anyone think of anywhere else they may be from?" Nita walked around the room slowly and leisurely, burning off restless energy, unlike the hot pacing she did earlier. "How about farther south than Kemetullah? Across the Ahnjwat Sea?"

"Their skin is so dark it's almost black," Jerryck said.

"What about the desert east of the mountains?" Nita fiddled with a bouquet of red roses in an etched gold vase.

"Reddish-brown skin," Cade said.

"What people live on the other side of the desert?" Nita flicked the tassels and fringe decorating the back of the chair she'd used.

"They have olive colored skin, almost yellow," Jerryck said. "If the one person I met in Kemetullah was a typical example. They have flat faces. And slanted eyes—even more slanted than the people on the northern tundra."

"Opposite direction then." As if for emphasis, Nita turned left and walked over to pick up the book Jerryck had rescued. "How about west? I know that they have light brown skin in the archipelago, not pale, and black hair usually. But what's west of them? What's west of the Makanakai Ocean?"

"I don't know," Jerryck said.

"The islanders claim they've never sailed that far," Cade added.

"What about using magic instead of sailing?" Nita asked.

"Almost everyone who uses travel magic will first scry out their ending location," Jerryck said. "And I don't know of any scryer gifted enough to see across the entire ocean."

"What if someone you didn't know did it?" Nita walked a slow circle around furniture in the sitting area of the room. "What if someone over there scryed us over here? Then they wanted to trade with us, and sent over a representative to establish a foothold? Is there even the slightest possibility that these foreigners could be from that far away?"

"I don't have enough information to support or deny that theory," Cade said.

"Keep searching," she told him. Then she folded her hands in front of her and planted her feet, much like her father when he was about to make an announcement. "On another subject, you all should know, I had lunch today with Charllass, Prince Sanbralio's granddaughter. I learned several things, one of which is that I should name someone as an advisor. That's the one servant that people here think it's acceptable to talk to."

"You want recommendations?" Tajor asked.

"I've already decided to appoint you to the position."

"No," Tajor said.

"This isn't a request." Nita's cheeks flushed. "I'm telling you to fill the position."

"No." Tajor shuddered. His aura vibrated, sending an irritating buzz across Jerryck's skin.

Jerryck reached out with his own aura, brushing against Tajor's, studying it, trying to figure it out. Once contact was made, the buzzing intensified, saturating Jerryck's skin, latching on, integrating. He tried to pull away, only to find the vibration had melded, holding him like glue.

"What is that?" Jerryck rubbed at his arms, which only made it worse.

"It's a refusal," Tajor said.

"Not that." Jerryck shuddered too. The buzzing from Tajor got worse. "*That.*"

"What are you talking about?" Nita asked him. "Are you all right? You don't look very good. Maybe you should sit down."

"I should go," Tajor said. The vibration increased again, upsetting the equilibrium inside Jerryck's ears, throwing waves of dizziness over him. Tajor kept talking as if nothing was wrong. "Cade and I were only checking in. There are several more people we could talk to."

"Be back here before I have to go back out in public," Nita told him.

"Absolutely." Tajor smiled. Some of the vibrating eased off.

"As my advisor," Nita amended.

"No," Tajor said. The vibrating increased again. Jerryck sat. Tajor shot him an irritated look. "Are you really that sensitive now? Or are you just being a hypochondriac?"

"Make it stop." Jerryck grit his teeth, not that it helped. It provided no stability, no calm, no relief.

Tajor let out a long, slow breath. "Nita, if I do this for you, please make it only temporary, ending the moment we leave this palace."

She nodded once. "Granted."

"Then I'll do it," Tajor acquiesced. The buzzing ceased.

Jerryck gasped from the abrupt change back to normalcy. He said, "That didn't feel like your curse."

Nita's bodyguard frowned at Tajor. "Curse?"

"Excuse me." Tajor spared just enough of a moment to glare at Jerryck before he turned and walked out of the room. Cade hurried to follow.

"Curse?" the bodyguard repeated.

"I'll explain," Nita said. "First, Garret, Jerryck looks a bit ill. Take him back to his room, and don't let anyone bother him for the rest of the day."

Jerryck let Garret guide him from Nita's room back to his. He didn't really need rest. The short walk up the corridor got rid of the residual reactions to the vibrating, and curiosity put a different buzz in his head. Though it did make for a nice excuse to keep Masorno away.

The next few days were spent vacillating between irritation and boredom. He got up in the mornings and spent a boring breakfast with Nita. Then he went with her to attend Prince Sanbralio's court. The necessary socializing during and afterward reinforced his aversion to ever attending court back at home. Most irritating was Masorno. He insisted on lunch every day. After that, he would parade boys with the potential for magic in the hope that Jerryck would slate one as a future apprentice.

"None of these kids are old enough to be an apprentice," Jerryck said.

"Of course not." Masorno gave Jerryck a patronizing pat on the head. "I told you they were young enough to give you time to get your credentials. Whenever you're ready to officially finish your apprenticeship so you can do that, let me know."

"Aren't there any new magicians that are already adults?" Jerryck asked. "Maybe someone who hasn't been officially trained, or hasn't gotten their license yet? Like whoever that friend is that Andreno mentioned."

"Andreno has no friends." Masorno surged to his feet. "Are you questioning what I've already told you? I allowed you in my home. I accepted your apology. And you act as if my patience and leniency mean nothing to you. Disrespectful!"

Masorno stormed from the room, leaving Jerryck with his jaw hanging open at the sudden, unprovoked anger. The next time they met, he half expected a demand for another apology. Instead, Masorno acted as if nothing had happened at all and paraded the next set of potential apprentices. Jerryck didn't bring it up again.

On the fifth day, while nobles socialized outside the throne room after court, Deek snarled and grumbled death threats under his breath. He stared up at a balcony. The man that Masorno claimed was a Chemwanee stood there watching them, focused on the princess. He wore the same expression too many young men had when they were enamored with a pretty, young woman.

Tajor excused himself and left. A few moments later, he appeared on the balcony and leaned on the railing next to the young man. The two of them exchanged a few words. The young man paled and backed away. Tajor smirked, then came down to rejoin them on the floor of the room.

"Have fun?" Deek growled at him.

"You really want to know?" Tajor still wore the smirk. "Though, if he really was a foreigner, I think I may have chosen wrong by chasing him off."

"Probably better than letting Deek spill his blood for eyeing the princess too much," Garret said with a giggle.

Nita finished with whatever noble she was talking to. She asked Tajor, "Was he really a foreigner? Did he have any kind of accent or anything?"

Tajor gave her one of his infuriating half answers. "Not really."

"You're supposed to give me more information than that." She clucked her tongue at him. "It's not like I can talk to the other guards about it while I'm here."

"Are you going to reconsider my position?" Tajor plastered on an exaggerated, exuberant smile.

"No," she said flatly. "Just tell me your impression of him."

"He spoke with an absolutely pristine and perfect Shontese accent." So did Tajor, like he was giving an example. "Every syllable of every word was exactly precise, if simplistic. He used no idiom, turn of phrase, or contraction."

"So he's perhaps a foreigner who's studied the language well enough to erase his accent," Nita said.

"Whether he is or isn't—" Tajor dropped the stupid smile— "He's one of the people Cade's been trying to get more information on."

"And you chased him off anyway?" Garret asked.

"Actually, someone called him away," Tajor said. "Or I'd have stayed longer and talked to him more before scaring him off."

At that moment, someone else called for Nita's attention, and she was swept a few feet away, most of her bodyguards following. Garret stayed right by Jerryck, still looking up at the balcony where the blond man had disappeared.

"Jerryck," Garret said. "Didn't Magician Alysses say something about him?"

"Who?" Jerryck asked.

Garret looked away from the balcony, back at Jerryck. "That first day after we got here. The magician that took on the apprentice from Kershet, but wanted you to meet his nephew."

"Oh, yes, him," Jerryck said. "He's not a very skilled magician. He keeps having to travel to find new work."

"And he complains now about a foreigner as much as he complains about you, according to his apprentice." Garret glanced back up at the balcony one more time. "That was when Masorno pointed out that blond man. You should call him for a visit."

"The blonde?"

"We've tried that. We get blocked. Call for Alysses. Talk to him without Masorno. Maybe we can get more information out of him."

"I'll see if I can arrange it," Jerryck said.

He scanned the people at the edges of the crowd. That's where the most important servants of the nobles tended to congregate. Garret steered him over by Nita and told him, "Stay with her. I'll take care of this."

He whispered to one of the other elite guards, then left. Every time Jerryck tried to leave after that, the other guard stopped him. People began drifting off, talking about getting ready for lunch. Nita wound down her last conversation.

As they were leaving the large room, Garret finally rejoined them. He said to Jerryck, "Arrangements are in process for you to have lunch with Alysses tomorrow."

"Why not today?" Jerryck asked.

"Today you already have other plans for lunch," Nita told him. "I asked Prince Sanbralio if I could eat with him, and he invited the both of us."

Jerryck pouted. "Dining with him every evening isn't enough?"

Chapter 31

SANBRALIO RARELY REMEMBERED who they were. When he wasn't doting on Nita and trying to charm her, he spent most of his time throwing nasty out comments about Andreno or bemoaning his losses. More often than not, he ended the meal by breaking down into tearful sobbing.

"You don't have to look as if you just swallowed something slimy." Nita giggled at Jerryck. "We only have a couple more days here. Then you won't have to deal with him anymore. Go get ready. Then meet me in my room."

Jerryck went. He took his time putting on something appropriate for dining with royalty. He never had figured out why people wore different clothes to court than to meals, but for now it made a good excuse for procrastination. Then he dragged his feet the short distance to Nita's room. When he entered, a hairdresser was taking mounds of Nita's hair down from where it had been piled on top of her head.

"I'd think you'd have figured it out by now." Nita sat in front of her vanity, arms crossed, scolding the hairdresser. "I don't care about the latest fashion. I refuse to show myself in public with hair so high I have to duck to go through doorways that aren't vaulted."

Jerryck dropped into a chair to wait. It only took a couple minutes for the hairdresser to come up with something different. Nita scrutinized her reflection and nodded her approval. The hairdresser left and Nita opened her jewelry box. Her reflection frowned at Tajor.

"You look amused," she said.

"Whims of fashion are fickle and ever-changing," Tajor leaned casually against the wall next to Deek. "Did you notice that when you first arrived, not one noble woman showed herself in public without her hair standing a foot higher than the top of her head?"

"A stupid way to wear your hair." Nita put on a pair of ruby earrings. "I kept watching to see if they'd fall over sideways."

"Now several of them are wearing their hair more like yours."

"Which means there are some women here that have brains." Nita latched a gold locket around her neck. "Do you have any advice before we go to Prince Sanbralio?"

Tajor smirked. "When do I ever give advice?"

Jerryck rolled his eyes. Why did Nita play this game of questions with Tajor? Why would anyone willingly put themselves through that kind of misery?

"I know you usually give riddles and make me figure things out on my own, but…" Nita turned from her vanity to look at him directly. "I don't have time for that right now. You always have something in mind. Tell me. Please?"

Tajor dropped the smirk and stood straight. "Don't get your hopes up."

She stood. "That wasn't what I expected."

"What was your true intention for requesting this luncheon?"

"I'm going to ask Prince Sanbralio to let me take Charlass to Brend," Nita said. She slowly paced, circling the furniture.

"Don't get your hopes up."

"Why?"

"Exactly." Tajor spread his hands apart. "Why is she here? Why did he take her in?"

Nita stopped pacing. "She's his granddaughter."

"She's illegitimate," Tajor said.

That set Nita to motion again. When she said nothing, he continued, "In the eyes of every noble in this country, her very existence is an affront and an embarrassment. In a land where image is everything, and nobles have had their reputations smeared just for association with a commoner, why would the greatest noble of them all take a commoner into his household?"

"She's his granddaughter," Nita repeated, passing by the vanity. "Surely that counts for something."

"It counts for everything. And nothing. It's the very reason she's here. It's the very reason he neglects her."

"Should I point out his neglect? Use that to say she'd be happier in Brend?"

"He won't understand," Tajor said. "Here in Shontarra, commoners live in misery. She lives in a palace. They dress in filthy rags. She adorns herself with jewels. They eat scraps and crumbs they've fought for. She dines at the table of the prince."

"A woman needs friends," Nita said, clenching her fists.

"A need most men don't comprehend very well," Tajor replied.

"Men need friends too."

"Not the same way, and not for the same function. Their attachment is just as strong and deep, yes, but it stems from a different facet of humanity. Sanbralio is blind and deaf to this need in her."

"I could tell him."

"How loud would you have to shout for a deaf person to hear you?" Tajor asked. "How bright does a light have to shine before a blind person can see it?"

"Jerryck," Nita turned to him. "How do your sister and wife get you to understand things. Help me out here."

"Uh…" Jerryck fumbled for words. "I'd rather stay out of this."

"But…"

"They usually just get mad at me," Jerryck said. "I can't help you. I'm sorry if that upsets you, but I really don't understand half of what they get mad at me for. Especially if they try and explain it."

Nita huffed and clucked her tongue, stomping out of her room, "Fine, I'll figure it out myself."

She wouldn't look at either Tajor or Jerryck the entire way to the dining hall. At the luncheon, the old prince ignored his food, as usual. He put his chin in his hand, propped his elbow on the table, and stared blankly at Nita's face. All the while she talked about how much companionship and friends meant to a woman. Several times, she mentioned Charlass. He never reacted.

Finally, at the end of the meal, she set her fork down and said, "When I go back home, may I take Charlass with me?"

"Charlass? Why would you want that?" Sanbralio sat back in his chair with a frown. "I thought you were a noble. Yes, I'm sure I was told you're a noble. You came to bring condolences from your father. Is this your father?"

He pointed to Jerryck. Before anyone could correct him, he shook his head. "No, no, you can't be her father. You're that magician I made Andreno do that favor to Masorno for."

"What favor?" Jerryck asked.

"Doesn't matter." Sanbralio slumped. "I don't really remember anyway. What was the question again?"

"Charlass," Nita said.

"Oh, yes, Charlass." Sanbralio picked at a loose thread on his napkin. "I doubt your father would want you associating with someone like her. What district is he premiere of again?"

"My father is Terrence, King of Brend."

Sanbralio looked up at her. "Oh, that's right. You're the Brendish princess. Then absolutely not. I'll not sully the Brendish King's home. She is my own personal shame. She stays here."

Nita spared everyone her raging rant until she was back in the privacy of her room. Jerryck considered leaving, giving her more room to pace and throw things around. But then Masorno would hear he was available. He stayed where he was, tuned out the rant, and sent someone to fetch him a book.

The next day, Jerryck used the excuse that he needed to pack. It got him out of attending court in the morning. And it got him out of the socializing afterward. Not that he did any of the actual packing. Every time he tried, the servant assigned to him just about had a silent, apoplectic fit, wincing and gasping, wringing his hands, glancing nervously around the room before snagging at the nearest thing he could pack before Jerryck could touch it.

When Alysses arrived for lunch, it was Garret who let him in and announced him. He came alone, beaming so broadly Jerryck could see his back molars. He said, "Thank you so much for this invitation."

"Glad you could come." Jerryck used a polite response. The servant left off packing long enough to quickly and silently set out a meal that he had stashed away somewhere. It was the normal amount Jerryck had been given for every meal since arriving at the Shontese palace, far more than he was accustomed to eating.

"You barely caught me," Alysses said, seemingly oblivious to the servant dashing about the room. "I stayed around in the city, even though Masorno swore you wouldn't see me again since I came out of turn. When I heard you were leaving tomorrow, I thought maybe he was right. I told my nephew and my apprentice to go ahead and pack up."

"I wanted to talk to you again," Jerryck said.

They sat down to the meal and the servant silently went back to packing. Alysses dug right in to the food, talking with his mouth full. "I assume none of the boys Masorno introduced were suitable for your needs?"

"Not really," Jerryck said. He looked over at Garret. The guard was the man who should be making this conversation. He was the one who had given suggestions for how to steer the talking. As it was, Jerryck made his first inept attempt to turn the subject in the direction they needed it to go. "I didn't really expect to find any with Masorno. This was just my first try at looking outside my country."

"Did Masorno bring in more than one boy at a time and get them bickering and fighting for his own amusement?" Somehow, Alysses was able to keep his words clear and intelligible even while chewing.

"He did, actually," Jerryck said.

"As much as I respect the Shontese court magician and his skills, I think his ego holds him back." Alysses shook his head, swallowed, and took another bite. "That's why I've done everything I can to teach my nephew and my apprentice to keep their ego in check."

"Know anyone else with an ego that's too large?" Jerryck made a second attempt at steering the conversation. Whoever would poison an entire river had to have a very large ego.

Alysses swallowed again, this time without taking a replacement bite. He stared down at his plate. "I probably shouldn't say it."

"Please, say it." If Alysses was going to name someone Jerryck hadn't heard of, that would be perfect.

"You have to have a rather large ego yourself." Alysses glanced up at Jerryck. "Or you wouldn't have gone this long without a license. I'm glad to hear that you're finally humbling yourself properly."

Jerryck leaned back in his chair with a frown. "What do you mean?"

"Surely you wouldn't be seeking an apprentice if you didn't have plans to get your license." Alysses looked him square in the eye. "Because if you don't, I won't allow you to take my nephew, no matter how good you are at pleasing your employer."

Now Jerryck was utterly confused. "Your nephew?"

The door burst open. Garret jumped between it and Jerryck. It was just Masorno, so Jerryck told him, "It's all right."

He started to rise to give a more proper greeting when Masorno put his hands on his hips and glared. "So it is true."

Jerryck stopped halfway to his feet. "What's true?"

"I ate by myself, because I thought you were packing," Masorno said. "Until someone told me you had a guest. I couldn't believe it. I didn't think you would do that to me. Yet here you are."

"Here I am," Jerryck repeated. "Doing what, exactly?"

"My last chance to share a meal with you privately." Masorno pointed at Alysses. "You're giving it to someone else."

Jerryck leaned on his hands on the table and hung his head, trying to figure out which social blunder he had committed this time. "No one told me I had to spend every lunch with you."

"Not every lunch," Masorno said. "You didn't have to. But this is the last one."

"That makes a difference?" Jerryck asked.

Masorno made a wry face. "If I didn't know you so well, I'd think you were mocking me."

Jerryck threw his hands up in the air. "I have no idea why you would think that from what I said."

"I know you don't," Masorno said. "No more than you understand how important it is for you to get your license."

"Please don't start that." Jerryck turned away. Everyone else in the room was looking elsewhere. The servant had his head bent over Jerryck's luggage. Garret kept his gaze fixed on Masorno. Alysses was staring at his plate again. The only one watching him was Masorno.

"He's getting his license soon," Alysses spoke quietly, almost a mumble.

"He told you that?" Masorno's face darkened with anger. He frowned at Jerryck. "You'll get a license after talking to him once, and not after all these times I've tried to help you along the process and offered to finish out that mentorship for you?"

"I don't need you for a mentor!" Jerryck nearly exploded. "I'm not getting my license. Ever!"

Alysses snapped his gazed to Jerryck. "What do you mean you're not getting your license ever?"

"I don't need it," Jerryck said.

"You do if you want my nephew." Alysses rose to his feet too. "Unless you thought you could steal him by deceiving me."

"Why do you keep mentioning your nephew?" Jerryck asked. "What does he have to do with any of this?"

"He has everything to do with all of this if you want to apprentice him," Alysses said.

Jerryck shook his head, trying to sort his way through all this confusion. "I never said anything about apprenticing him."

Alysses stiffened up, throwing his shoulders back. "You didn't have to. Why else would you invite me here?"

Jerryck looked over to Garret, wishing he could pick up on visual cues better, just in case the guard was giving any. Was he supposed to just come out and say that they wanted information on the foreigner he had referenced? Were they supposed to string him along and deny it? And now that Masorno was there, what was Jerryck supposed to do about that? Ask him to leave?

"You can't tell him to throw us out," Masorno said, pointing to Garret with his chin. "Not here."

"I wasn't going to," Jerryck said.

"They why are you looking at him as if you expect something?" Masorno asked.

"Are you hoping he'll help you steal my nephew?" Alysses headed for the door. "Good thing I didn't bring him. Let's see how your precious elite guards help you when I report to the Gathering what you just tried to do to me."

"You think you're the only magician who's complained to them about me?" Jerryck rolled his eyes. "You may need to wait in line to submit your grievance."

Alysses paused at the door just long enough to speak over his shoulder. "If enough of us point out how wild and uncontrolled you are, the kind of damage you're causing, maybe they might do the right thing and force a leash on you."

He slammed the door on his way out. Masorno shook his head. "You can't keep this up forever, Jerryck. There's a reason they take their time before they take action. They're very strategic that way. Eventually, they're going to find something that hurts you so bad you'll have no other choice."

"There's always a choice," Jerryck said.

"I'm sure you think so," Masorno said. "When you learn otherwise, don't say I didn't warn you. Perhaps we can discuss it more when next I come visit you."

With that, he left. Jerryck slouched in his seat. What an abysmal failure this trip was. They had dug out no information. He had agitated the magicians in Shontarra. And now Masorno felt free to return to Coraline Palace and pester Jerryck into getting a license. Worse than a failure.

Chapter 32

EVERY PERSON with half an excuse showed up in the morning to see them off. Prince Sanbralio's personal guards escorted them to the outskirts of the city. Then they settled into a regular traveling pattern.

Nita pushed for a faster pace than usual. The journey home didn't take nearly as long as the journey out. That suited Jerryck. He would see his family all that much sooner, and even the faster trip was still too long.

When they arrived at Coraline Palace, Jerryck skipped as much of the homecoming celebration as he could manage. Still weary from traveling, he had to attend meetings the next day to update everyone on everything that had happened. Fortunately, Nita took care of most of that. He didn't have to report his failure to find a magician powerful enough to poison the river until Terrance dismissed the general staff and took the core staff into the small council chamber. After that report Jerryck leaned his elbows on the table, chin in hands, and tuned everything out, daydreaming about his next experiment and what he could do with the time he could now spend with his family.

"How dare you!" Lalven's eruption interrupted Jerryck's reverie. Lalven was standing, leaning both hands on the table, his face twisted into a snarl as he leaned toward Nita. "You don't have the authority to make that kind of an appointment."

"What appointment?" Jerryck asked.

"He's mad that I appointed Tajor as an adviser," Nita said.

"Oh, that." Jerryck relaxed again.

Nita sat calmly by her father. She said, "Shontarra isn't like here. Nobles aren't supposed to talk to anyone, not even their bodyguards, unless they're an adviser. I had to do something."

"And you did something stupid." Lalven leaned closer in. "Only I can approve advisory positions, and I would never approve someone as common and defiant as that man."

"The final decision is mine, not yours," Terrance said. From where he stood, he put his arm on the table in front of his daughter. "Nita is my heir, and your future sovereign."

"Her future husband is your heir," Lalven said.

"Again, my decision, not yours."

"This is the law, Terrance. Not a decision."

"There's no law that says a woman cannot be a ruling queen," Terrance said.

Lalven drew breath to say more. Terrance tapped his fingers on the table and continued, "We're not getting into this right now. You're not going to use Nita's actions to push your opinions. Especially not when I would have done the exact same thing in her position."

"You would have chosen someone better than that man." Lalven glowered. Then he glared at Jerryck. "Why won't you pay more attention? You were there. You could have prevented this."

"Why would he prevent a good decision?" Terrance countered. "I've been watching Tajor. Heston was right to initiate him into the elite. I'm impressed with his honesty and his insights. I've already put a lot of thought into giving him an advisory position."

"Surely not," Lalven said. "He has no ties to even minor nobility. He's completely common."

"So was Lord Jerryck." Terrance flicked a hand at him.

"What? Me?" Jerryck looked back and forth between the two of them. "I'm not an adviser."

"You're a minor noble without any ties to other nobility," Terrance said. "You excel. I believe Tajor will as well."

"Please don't compare me to Tajor," Jerryck said.

"There, you see." Lalven tipped his nose up. "Even he knows better."

Jerryck frowned at Lalven. "Know better than what? Tajor's a lot smarter than I am. And hopefully I'm not nearly as annoying. And even if I am, I don't do it on purpose like he does."

"He's annoying because his questions sometimes make you dig out facts you don't necessarily like, or look at truths you don't want to face," Nita said. "Which is exactly what's needed in an adviser."

"I suppose," Jerryck admitted. "And if being annoying is what makes for a good adviser then Tajor probably would make the best one of all."

Terrance laughed and said, "After we're through in here, I'll send for him and make his new position more official."

Lalven held up a hand in a gesture to wait. "Before you do that..."

"I'm through discussing this," Terrance said. "With you or anyone else in this room. I'm moving this meeting to the next item..."

Jerryck relaxed and quit paying attention again. This time, instead of daydreaming, he turned his thoughts to his responsibilities, making a mental list of chores now that he'd return home from such a long absence. The charms that alerted him to various conditions or people would need checked. The spells in the dungeons would probably need some maintenance. Some of his regular patients would want a checkup. On top of that, a pile of requests for odd jobs had already come to him from the various residents of the palace.

The meeting ended with Terrance calling a page to send Tajor to his office. Everyone else went about their business. Jerryck tackled his chores. First, he re-energized all the charms above outside doors that were connected to his alert system. If there was a small task that wouldn't take too long within the vicinity of one of those, he got it done. Then he went around to visit with his regular patients, taking too long with some of them who seemed to just want him to listen to complaints about medics. After that, he started down the list of requests people had sent him. All in all, he stayed so busy, the rest of the afternoon flashed by. It certainly was good to be back home.

Jerryck was in the kitchen, charming a new set of plates to make them resistant to breaking, the smells of supper cooking making him salivate, when a page called him to the king's office. He set the dishes aside and went immediately.

Lalven and Nita were seated in the chairs before Terrance's desk, avoiding eye contact. Tajor stood to one side. When all the rest of the core staff gathered, Terrance sat on the front edge of his desk and spoke.

"I'm going to explain this once to all of you, and I don't want a single complaint from anyone." He eyed Nita and Lalven closely. "Tajor refuses the position of adviser."

"Why?" Nita glared at Tajor, while Lalven straightened up with a smug expression.

"Irrelevant," Terrance said. "He explained his reasons to me. That's enough for now. When you come of age, he'll explain it to you. Regardless, so far as everyone is concerned, they will treat him as though he's on the staff of the secondary advisers."

"Why?" Now Lalven glared at Tajor, his smugness gone.

"Because I want it," Terrance said. He laced his fingers together in front of himself. "Nita, he's yours. Consult with him as often as you like."

Lalven gripped the arms of his chair. "That's an adult privilege. She can't have an official adviser until she's fifteen."

"That's not very far off," Terrance said. "And he's not an official adviser. He's only acting as one."

Jerryck glanced at the door. Was he going to be allowed to leave if this turned into a screaming match between the two? Fortunately, Heston broke the tension between them with a different complication. "And his duties with the elite?"

"He's still one of yours," Terrance told Heston. "Officially, Nita's secondary riding escort, just as before."

"I don't have any say in this at all?" Lalven said petulantly.

"You had your say. What you don't have is my authority to make the decision." Terrance stood. "Only one last thing: Jerryck, Tajor is also available to you."

"What for?" Jerryck asked.

"For whatever." Terrance shrugged. "You both have complete access to each other's time and company. You listen to him. Is that clear?"

"All of the elite go through special training exercises," Heston said to Jerryck. "Please don't ask for him while he's in the middle of one."

"How long do they take?" Jerryck asked.

"Sometimes a few hours," Heston said. "Sometimes a few days."

"Then just tell me when he's doing one," Jerryck said. "Then I won't ask for him."

Terrance smiled. "Do you intend to ask for him at all?"

"I… Well… Um…" Jerryck looked around the room. There was no point in trying to hide it. These people knew him too well. "Not really."

Terrance laughed and dismissed everyone. Nita left with a smile. Lalven left with a frown. Heston left with a grip on Tajor's arm, leading him out and whispering to him. No one else seemed to care in the least.

Jerryck left the office just in time for the call to supper. He ate with his nieces and nephews at the long, pine tables in the common dining hall, then got back to work. There was so much of a backlog of tasks it took him about a week of steady, non-stop work to get caught up.

Each day he spent hours checking on the various spells in the palace, making sure to spare at least some time for various requests people gave him, and accepting still more as he tried to catch up. Each night he fell into bed in weary exhaustion. His wife and sister made sure he ate regularly, which kept his energy from flagging too low. They didn't even scold him for missing meals. They just put food in front of him and told him to eat.

Chapter 33

A T THE END of the week-long toil, Jerryck trudged up the stairs. He passed the bedroom and went up the last flight to his workroom. The evening's music lilted in the windows on the warm air. Leanne had probably gone out to dance with everyone else in the bailey.

He began to straighten up the room, putting away tools and implements he'd used earlier that day. His weariness dug in its claws, pulling him to the door that led to his bedroom. Without Leanne his bed remained empty, even when he occupied it. He picked up the last few items and put them where they belonged. Then he grabbed a random book and let it fall open in his hands. He turned to sit on the stool and almost crashed into Tajor.

"*Gah!*" Jerryck jumped back. "What are you doing here?"

Tajor looked down at his feet and said, "Standing."

"I mean—" Jerryck closed the book on his finger— "why are you here?"

"Here in this room? In this palace? In this country? Or was that a rhetorical question about existence itself?"

"Why are you in my room?"

"I've come to exercise my right to bother you whenever I please," Tajor said with a smirk.

"Please don't." Jerryck opened the book again and laid it on the worktable. "I'm really tired."

"So tired you're studying?"

"I'm waiting for Leanne." Jerryck sat and leaned over the book. The words printed on the page were blurry. He rubbed his eyes, trying to bring them into focus.

Tajor turned and looked over the shelves. "I have a question."

"Only one?" Jerryck muttered.

Tajor chuckled. Then he pointed to the sealed jar at the top of the shelves. "What would happen if the Gathering of Seats found out you have that?"

"They already know I have it," Jerryck said.

"And they haven't tried to come and destroy it for you?"

"I don't use it," Jerryck said. "They know that. It was part of a peace offering from magic-users south of the Ahnjwat Sea."

"You're not worried that something will happen to it sometime when you have one of your accidents?"

Jerryck looked up from the book. "You know about those?"

"Several of the elite know about those." Tajor smiled a little. "How else could we squash rumors every time you have workers up here to fix things you broke? What else would keep the Gathering from hearing about them?"

"I don't want to talk about this." Jerryck turned the page. It was just as blurry as the one before. He stared at it anyway.

Tajor leaned close and whispered, "How long before the Gathering finds out about your accidents?"

"They're not going to find out." Jerryck shouldered Tajor away.

"How do you know?" Tajor backed off. "Do you even know what causes them?"

"Go away," Jerryck said.

Tajor smirked. He stepped over to the counter with the shelves above it. "Is this far enough?"

"I meant leave the room."

"That's not what you said." Tajor's smirk widened. He turned and looked over the tools on the counter and the shelves again. He reached out and picked up a wand Jerryck had traded for several years back.

Jerryck jumped off his stool, lunging for Tajor's arm—too late. "Don't touch that!"

"Ow." Tajor giggled. The wand flashed and sputtered. He dropped it and flicked his hand as if it smarted. The little bit of remaining power in the tool fizzled away into nothingness.

"I used that whenever I had to do a transfiguration," Jerryck complained.

"Not anymore." Tajor shook his head. He reached for a crystal. "What do you use this one for?"

"That's for purifying some potions that get tainted if they're on the shelf too long," Jerryck replied. He snatched at the crystal, again too late. He examined it, tossed it back down on the counter. "You just made it useless."

"Oh?" Tajor wouldn't stop grinning. He reached for something else and asked again, "What's this for?"

Stop that." Jerryck grabbed Tajor's arm. "You know what these things are for. Why are you doing this?"

"I want to know how protective you are of your things," Tajor answered. He picked up a charm. It fizzled and popped. He held it in his hand with barely a twitch in his finger. "I could do this all night."

Jerryck glowered. "Do you have any idea how expensive that was?"

"Do you want to ask me if I care?" Tajor retorted. He looked over the rest of the tools splayed before him.

"Please don't," Jerryck begged.

Tajor backed away from the counter, looked up, and pointed at the sealed jar. "How exactly did you get that, anyway?"

"A summoner gave it to me at a magicians convention," Jerryck said as he pushed some of his tools close to the wall behind the counter—not that it got them far enough away from Tajor.

"Why?" Tajor asked.

"I don't know," Jerryck said with a shrug. How many things could he stuffed into the cabinet and lock it? Of course, it wouldn't do much good if Tajor took the key from him. "It was the first year the summoners were allowed back to the convention. They gave several of them away to some apprentices in a ceremony of some sort. I think it was supposed to be some sort of gesture of compliance to the Gathering."

"By giving away magic tools that the Gathering wouldn't approve of to people who wouldn't know how to control them?" Tajor asked.

Jerryck's shoulders slumped. He had no answer for that. How did Tajor do this to people so easily? At least he seemed to have lost interest in destroying the tools. Jerryck picked up the useless charm and scrutinized it. It was pretty enough, he could put it on a chain and give it to Leanne as a necklace. That would give it some use, instead of being a complete waste.

Might as well make the best of things. Tajor obviously wanted to know more about that jar and the entity inside it. If Jerryck didn't satisfy, he likely would lose more tools. Perhaps if he entertained Tajor for a while the man would give up some of the secrets of his curse, like an information exchange. As weary as Jerryck was, he could stay awake for that.

"Does everyone who received a jar still have theirs?" Tajor asked.

"I think I'm the only one who kept it," Jerryck said. "Most of the others, their mentors destroyed them. Mine told me to keep it safe."

"Would you get it down for me?"

"What?" Jerryck nearly dropped the charm. He fumbled it back down to the counter.

"If you've had that since you were an apprentice, then you've had it long enough that the entity inside should know you pretty well by now. I have some questions for it."

"Don't we have to take proper precautions?" Jerryck asked. "Draw diagrams on the floor or something?"

"Not if you know how to handle it properly. You're safe with me here."

"I don't know…"

"You want me to get it myself?" Tajor reached up.

Jerryck grabbed Tajor's arm. "No!"

He put himself between Tajor and the shelves. He slipped the jar off the high shelf and set it firmly on the worktable. With one last nervous glance at Tajor, who nodded and smiled, Jerryck unlatched the lid.

The seal broke with a small *pop*. There was the brief whistle of air sucking inside. Then it let out the reek of brimstone. Jerryck covered his nose. His eyes teared up, burning from the fumes. He backed to the nearest window.

Without moving, Tajor watched Jerryck retreat. He didn't change his breathing to deal with the stench. He didn't cover his nose. His eyes didn't water.

The jar heated so much it glowed, sending warmth all the way across the room to Jerryck. He should have put it on the floor. It was a wonder the table didn't burst into flames. Still, Tajor stood beside it, unaffected.

The glow and the heat subsided. A white mist leaked out the open mouth of the jar. It draped down the outside of the vessel, veiling it from sight. It spread in a pool across the surface of the worktable and spilled over the sides. By the time it dripped down far enough to touch the floor, the rim of the jar was visible again.

The mists continued cascading down until none remained on the tabletop. It spread across the floor, snaking over to Jerryck's feet. He pressed himself against the wall, staying out of it as much as possible as it expanded. When all of it was on the floor, it contracted, shrinking in on itself and rising up in a vertical pillar. It pressed in, solidifying to human form. In just a few seconds, the faint image of a young man took shape.

The remaining mist squeezed into the figure and completed it. It had the appearance of an adult, but about the height of a five-year-old, with pointy ears. If Jerryck looked at it directly, it seems solid. But if he looked just to the side and saw it with his peripheral vision, it was almost translucent.

"Dramatic enough?" Tajor asked as the last whiff of brimstone faded.

"The smell?" Jerryck asked.

"What smell?" Tajor gave him a funny look. "I meant the glowing and the mist."

"The glowing? You mean the heat."

"What heat?"

"Remember how mortals perceive what comes from below." The creature from the jar spoke with a high, nasal twang. It turned to Jerryck. "My apologies, Master. Those are the side effects of the magic that assists me to become solid enough in this place to act. The longer I am in the jar, the more dramatic the effects."

It looked down at the floor. Then it smiled with teeth pointier than its ears.

"Forget it," Tajor said. "You'll do as you're told and nothing else. Then you'll either go back, or go home, depending on how well you behave."

The creature dropped it smile. "Temptations..."

241

"You have enough control to resist destructive urges, or you wouldn't be able to use that jar at all."

"I don't have to resist. No compulsions are on me. And you're bound by magic that prevents you from doing anything about it if I run amok."

"There's nothing that would prevent me from going to where you come from."

"That would be a one-way trip for you at this point."

"If I have to go, I'll make you pay the price." Tajor showed none of his habitual humor. The creature somehow drew away from him without taking a single step. Tajor's face softened a bit. "This won't take long. It shouldn't be too taxing on your self-control."

The creature tipped its head differentially to Jerryck and said, "I will do as you command and nothing more."

"You will do as *I* command, not him," Tajor said. "And for now, I command you to truthfully answer my questions. What are you called?"

"You may call me Yeshiyahu."

"How does Jerryck gain strength?"

The demon smirked much like Tajor often did. "Exercise."

"I don't like you asking questions about me specifically," Jerryck said.

"Too bad." Tajor smirked too. He said to the creature, "Let me specify. How *should* Jerryck exercise to regain strength after wearying himself with magic usage? What would be most effective for him?"

"He should use his imagination in the form of experimentation with spells no one has come up with or that he's never tried."

"*What?*" Jerryck didn't like that news. He wasn't supposed to experiment, no matter how much he liked it. The Gathering disapproved. Besides, the last time he'd done it he'd blown up his workroom, with the shamaness inside it.

Tajor ignored Jerryck. "I doubt I could easily get him to do that. Does he have magic he does as a reflexive action?"

"Yes."

"Tell me what it is."

"He's never asked anything of me. Please don't make me be mean to him."

"Tell me what it is," Tajor repeated.

242

"He gains strength from his family." Yeshiyahu hung his head and averted his eyes from Jerryck. "If they come under threat, he reactively protects them."

"I should have guessed that," Tajor said. "I have a new order for you. Go get Leanne and bring her here, using whatever method you feel like."

"No!" Jerryck shouted. He pointed his finger at Yeshiyahu. "Don't you do any such thing. You stay away from my wife."

Tajor waved Yeshiyahu away. "Go get her."

Jerryck shouted at Tajor too. "Stop it."

"Are you going to make me?" Tajor challenged. He kept his eyes on Jerryck, but spoke to Yeshiyahu, slowly, over-enunciating each word, "Go. And. Fetch. Leanne."

Yeshiyahu shook its head. It started vibrating, sending an irritating buzz across Jerryck's skin. Tajor said, "Don't try and refuse. You know what I can do to you."

Yeshiyahu gave Jerryck a rueful look. "I'm sorry, Master."

It glided for the door, taking no steps. With every inch, its expression grew more malicious, its body more transparent. Panic stabbed into Jerryck's gut. Raw energy surged, exploding out of him, hitting Tajor square in his midsection.

Tajor staggered back and fell over, groaning. Yeshiyahu stopped, becoming as solid as before. Its malicious expression now tainted with sadistic humor, it hopped up and down with a maniacal cackle.

"Serves you right," it crowed, pointing with a talon-like finger. "Serves you right. Serves you right."

"Get back in the jar," Jerryck told it.

It pouted. "Do I have to?"

"Get back in the jar." Jerryck had to grab hold of the sturdy worktable to keep from falling over.

"All right, all right." It held up both hands, placating him. "You don't have to get your nose bent out of shape. Remember, it was his idea, not mine. I tried to tell him not to make me do something you wouldn't like. You're a nice master. One of the best I've ever had here. You'll do quite well for us. Even if the original plans for you didn't work out. I don't enjoy upsetting you."

"Get back in the jar!"

Yeshiyahu gave him one last smirk. Then it collapsed into a pillar of mist and shot into the jar with a sucking noise. The jar teetered one way, then the other, before it stabilized again. It sat on the table, as innocent looking as many of the other containers in the workroom.

Jerryck let out a sigh of relief. His hands shook with exhaustion as he closed the lid and clamped down the seal. The containment magic reactivated. He picked up the jar and set it back on the high shelf. Then he let himself collapse onto the floor, sitting with his back propped against the cupboard under his counter.

"That was easy," Tajor wheezed, still curled in a ball, teeth clenched together, gray eyes glazed over. "You may want to rethink how you deal with the Gathering. Avoiding them won't work if they come after your family."

Chapter 34

ERRYCK ROLLED out of bed, stretching to loosen up sleep stiffened muscles. He put his feet on the thick rug that covered the wood floor by the bed. Late morning light angled through the window. Clean clothes were set on top of the bureau for him. The fact that Leanne had put them there without waking him... or had she? He seemed to remember her humming, puttering around the room, telling him it was morning. Or had that been a dream? Either way, it was more than he remembered about how he got to his bed the night before.

He donned the clothes and went up to his workroom. The tools that Tajor had broken were still lying on the counter. He frowned at them, then chucked them in a box in the storage space behind the curtain in the back. Everything else was in order, so he headed down intending to double check everything around the palace, to make sure he hadn't forgotten anything, and to finish up the last few tasks remaining for him.

He stopped when voices floated up the stairs before he saw the people attached to them. Who was coming in his tower? And why hadn't the chimes in the workroom let him know someone had entered?

"What did you say?" the first person asked—the man's voice was vaguely familiar.

"I said he's asleep." The second voice was Kendra's. "If you tell me who you are and what you need, I'll let him know when he wakes up."

"How will you know when he wakes up? You're no page. You wear the apron of a scullery maid."

"I'm his sister."

"Oh. I apologize. I didn't realize. I should have. You look so much like him."

"I do not." Kendra's tone had a bite to it. "Just tell me who you are and what you want. And keep your voice down. If you wake him, I'll pour ashes on your next meal."

A choking sound didn't quite mask a nervous giggle. That wasn't Kendra. The man said, "You must be Lady Leanne."

"Y-you know m-me?" Leanne's voice was hesitant and filled with nerves.

"Very few magicians marry," the man said. "When they do, word gets around. It's a pleasure to finally meet you."

"Leave her alone." Kendra's tone changed to dangerous, the tone that made every worker in the kitchen hop at her command. Jerryck quickly descended, rounding the curve of the stairs to where he could see.

The man was Gintario, the messenger for the Gathering of Seats. He spoke publicly at every convention. If he traveled, it meant the old magicians filling the Seats had come to a decision on something. Gintario delivered their edict to whomever it affected. As a result, people didn't always welcome him very kindly.

Kendra's face darkened with anger at the sight of Jerryck. He said to her, "I was already awake."

Her face relaxed, her anger fading. Then Gintario said to him, "The women in your life are as lovely as rumored."

Leanne blushed, and it wasn't her comfortable, pretty blush. Bright red splotches blossomed on her cheeks, and her head shrunk down into her shoulder as she hunched up, shying back. Kendra saw it, put her hands on her hips, and bared her teeth.

"Not now, Kendra," Jerryck cut her off before she could say something he might pay the price for. "What do you need, Gintario?"

Gintario flashed a white smile, stark against his dark, olive skin. "I need a word with you."

Jerryck forced a smile. "Of course."

He led the way up to the workroom, taking a deep breath upon entering. The drying herbs up in the rafters had somehow lost some of their pungency. The air had gone stale. He should have opened the window. He glanced around at the various tools he hadn't finished putting away, the powders he hadn't finished grinding, he should have picked up more. Nothing for it now. He brushed a hand across the surface of the worktable, remembered his manners, offered his guest a stool to sit, and asked if he would like a cup of tea.

"Yes please," Gintario said. While Jerryck went through the preparations, Gintario watched him with his fingers loosely laced together, resting on the worktable. He said, "You're looking a little drawn."

"I had a busy night—" Jerryck added a portion of tea to a magically heated cup of water— "and a long workweek."

"That does have a tendency to wear a man down," Gintario said. "You don't hide nervousness well."

"Does anyone?" Jerryck set the cup in front of Gintario. He'd forgotten a cup for himself. He turned back to the teapot.

"Some better than others," Gintario said. "Most not as well as they think."

"So what society changing decision has the Gathering made?" Jerryck put the teapot back up on the shelf instead of pouring a second cup. "Who all does it affect?"

"For now, mostly just you," Gintario said. "If there's ever another magician in your unique circumstances, it will affect them as well. There's a rumor going around that you're looking for an apprentice. Some people are highly perturbed over that, since you've never taken the oaths. We've received a number of various complaints. One of them was a personal visit, who swore you were trying to steal his nephew to corrupt him."

"I did no such thing." Jerryck turned to face his guest. "And why would he assume I would corrupt anyone. I follow the safety rules. I would teach an apprentice to do the same. I don't see why this is such a problem."

"The Gathering would probably let that go if it was the only issue." Gintario leaned back slightly on his stool and crossed his arms. "They also received a report that you're working closely with the military, something about a nighttime exercise you assisted. That's not acceptable."

"That's not forbidden. And the Gathering knows it."

"Not if you've taken the oaths. Jerryck, you hold a prestigious, highly visible position. You're a public figure. An example. I honestly don't know why they've let this go as long as they have. And at long last, they've decided that every magician hired into a permanent position must have credentials. Even if they were hired almost ten years ago."

"They're going to tell the King of Brend who he can or can't hire?"

"I doubt he'd listen. He's unreasonable when it comes to dealing with the Gathering. However, we can forbid any magician from acknowledging you, or selling to you, or trading with you, or doing any other business transactions whether of goods or information. They're angry enough at this point, they could even issue an order to pull every magician from this country. I doubt your king would find that satisfactory."

They stared at each other for a few moments. Gintario broke the quiet. "I also don't know why you're so resistant. There isn't a chance you'll fail the tests. And if you're obeying all their guidelines, then taking the oaths won't even affect your day to day actions."

One of the oaths was that he would burn any woman he found who could do magic. That included his niece, even if he wasn't sure yet what kind of magic she had the potential for. Another oath was that he would never deviate from their safety protocols. It wasn't likely that the accidents he had would be included.

"I can't take the oaths," Jerryck said.

"Not until you complete those last two weeks of your apprenticeship and pass the tests." Gintario gave Jerryck a sympathetic look. "It's not meant to be demeaning. It's just a formality at this point. I'll stay here for the next couple weeks, and we'll say it's done. Then at the next convention, or sooner if you like, you can follow through and get your license. We can do it privately, or make it as complex an affair as you like. Whatever you prefer. We'll absolutely cater to your whims on this."

"What changed?" Jerryck leaned on the worktable with both hands. "After all these years. They've gotten lots of complaints about me, some of them as personal visits. I don't believe these recent ones made that much difference. And don't tell me it was a search for an apprentice. There are lots of tricking pranksters who take on apprentices and the Gathering doesn't bother with them."

"There's also the matter of a certain disrespectful letter you sent them," Gintario said. "Something about you blaming them for a death they weren't responsible for. They were not amused."

"If I hadn't had to answer their letter, I'd have been available. My brother-in-law may have survived."

"If you'd had your license, you wouldn't have gotten a letter that you needed to respond to. You'd have been available. You blamed them for something that's your fault. Which brings it to their attention that your neglect is killing people."

Jerryck stood straight. "I didn't kill anyone."

"That's not how they see it."

"And it took all this time for them to take action?" Jerryck crossed his arms. "They didn't respond. I thought they had let it go."

Gintario shrugged. "You know how they are. If you displease them, they'll sometimes take months, even years before they retaliate. It gives them time to study your weaknesses. I'm here to give you a chance. If you don't want this to hurt more than necessary, I'd suggest you comply."

"When are you going to inform Terrance?" Jerryck asked.

"Is there a need? Cooperate. Nothing will change except that you'll be legal." Gintario stood and headed for the door. "I'll stay out of your way over the next couple of weeks. If you like, you never even have to lay eyes on me."

He left. Jerryck leaned on the worktable again, gripping the thick edges, resisting the urge to pick up the untouched tea and chuck it down the stairs at Gintario's head. His eyes roved across the pits, scratches, and scars on the table's surface. Some of them he remembered how he had caused, put there through his impatience and carelessness.

He drew in a deep breath and took a few moments to calm himself. Tajor was right. He was going to have to change how he dealt with the Gathering. But change it how, exactly?

He pushed away from the table and descended the stairs. He had no idea where to find Tajor. But pages always knew where to find everyone. The first one he found told him, "Elite Tajor is in the throne room. If you want him right away, you should talk to General Heston. He doesn't like us giving summons to guards in the throne room while court is in session."

He went to Heston's office. The aide admitted him immediately. Heston didn't even look up from the mound of papers he worked on at his desk. "I have very little time to go over reports and keep records in order. Whatever you need, please keep it short."

"I just need Tajor," Jerryck said.

"Really?" Heston stopped writing and looked up at him. "Something wrong?"

"I thought I was supposed to be able to call for him whenever I wanted," Jerryck said. "Why would you think something is wrong?"

"Because we didn't think you'd ever call on him. Did your visitor threaten you?"

"How did you know I had a visitor?" Jerryck asked. Heston raised one eyebrow. Jerryck sighed. "I just need to talk to Tajor."

Heston set down his pen and went to the door. He opened it a crack and spoke to his aide. "Tell Cade he gets his wish. He can go on duty in the throne room if he sends us Tajor."

"Cade'll be suspicious you're going to make him pay for it later," the aide said.

"Good," Heston replied. He shut the door and returned to his desk. He asked Jerryck, "You mind waiting quietly?"

"I don't mind." Jerryck took one of the two chairs set by the wall.

Unlike other offices where visitor chairs were right in front of the desk, these were the only extra seats in the room. The surface was hard and tipped slightly forward. Jerryck squirmed uncomfortably. He might be better off standing.

Heston scratched away with his pen, seemingly oblivious to his guest. Every time he finished one paper, he snapped it onto a stack to his right, and snagged a replacement from a stack to his left. Once they had all been shuffled to the right, he picked up the stack, tapped the edges smartly against his desk to align them, and took them over to the wall lined with his filing system.

When Tajor entered, he didn't salute or stand at attention. Heston didn't scold him for it. He simply pointed at Jerryck. Tajor smirked a little. "Have you come to exercise your right to bother me whenever you please?"

Jerryck abandoned the chair. "You said I should rethink how I deal with the Gathering. Did you just mean it in general? Or did you have something specific in mind?"

Tajor's smirk widened. "Ever hear about something called passive aggression?"

"I've heard of it," Jerryck said with a nod. "I don't know how to apply it. And if it's something that will cause them to aggressively pursue me, I want a different option."

Heston closed the drawer to his filing and leaned his back against it. "What did your visitor say to you?"

"He essentially said the Gathering will make it impossible for me to do my job properly, unless I comply with their demands to take their oaths and get a license."

"And what did Terrance have to say about that?" Tajor asked.

"I'll tell Terrance as soon as he's out of court."

"I'll tell him," Heston said. "After I have a chat with your visitor. I'll send someone when the king's ready to speak to you about it."

Jerryck headed for the door, dismissing the matter. Then paused. He turned back to Heston, "What are you going to say to Gintario?"

Heston was already digging out another stack of papers from a different file drawer. "I'm going to ask him exactly what he said to you."

"I already told you that."

"You told me generalities." Heston snapped the file shut. "I want specifics. And if they don't match your generalities, he's in trouble. More than he already is."

"He hasn't done anything wrong. Exactly."

"He came to Coraline Palace as a representative from the Gathering, a foreign political body that Terrance frowns on." Heston slapped the papers down on his desk. "He must know that, or why else would he avoid giving his message to the king."

"One of the specifics was that the Gathering doesn't like being blamed for things they claim they didn't do wrong," Jerryck said. "They avoid Terrance because he still blames them for the trouble we had with some of the islands in the Archipelago about the time he hired me."

"With good reason. Exactly how much do you remember of the incident that set that off?"

"I remember that a couple of core staff members were killed. And that's the incident that also deposed the Premiere of Plurrin. And I had an accident protecting the king."

"So, not much of the details. Just the generalities." Heston sat at his desk and picked up his pen. "Please excuse me. I can only do this work while most of my men are at morning sparring practice or on duty in court. I have very little time left. I'll send someone for you later."

Chapter 35

ERRYCK LEFT the matter with Heston and went about his job. There were still a few tasks that required his attention. The closest one to his location was a windowpane that needed a crack repaired. It was a time consuming, if simple task, using the earth element. He headed for that one.

He finished up right about lunch time, so he went to the common dining hall. Over the rumble of the people eating and talking at the long tables, Kendra tried to wheedle out of him exactly what had happened between him and Gintario. She wouldn't accept that he didn't want to talk about it, so he ended up telling her the matter was unresolved.

Sitting and eating, his gaze wandered over to a charm he kept above the double-wide doorway to the bailey outside. It was part of a system of charms, all connected to set off chimes in his workroom, set to ring when a magic-user entered the palace. They hadn't played for Gintario.

He left his food half-eaten and wove through the tables and people to stand directly beneath the charm. With a word, he released the adhesive magic on the back that kept it on the wall above the door frame. It dropped into his hand.

It gave low energy readings, even though he had just recharged the entire network within the last week. Sometimes a single charm could go faulty. Still, the others should have picked up the slack. Taking it with him, he went to check on some of the others spread about. After the next three were in exactly the same state as the first one, he stopped.

Redundancy was the beauty that made a system like this so effective. As long as the connection between them held, they all shared power and worked together to make up any slack. They wouldn't all go faulty at the same time. And even if they did, that would trigger a different alert for him.

Holding all four charms in one hand and covering them with the other, Jerryck closed his eyes to shut out distractions. He concentrated on the connecting magic. He identified the feel of it on each individual charm. He tried following the connection from one charm to the next, and it wouldn't go through. It wasn't broken. It wasn't severed. It felt more like it was somehow disrupted.

He isolated the connection magic on each charm. One by one, he tried tracing the exact path from each charm to another. On every single one of them, it stopped about halfway between, still there, just unable to get past some sort of barrier. He went through the process a third time, just to be sure.

Still concentrating on the energy of the magic, he opened his eyes and uncovered his hand from the charms. They were a glowing mix of blue and green. His sister and wife might argue about the exact shading, calling it teal, or aquamarine, or turquoise, or some other such silly thing. He just saw them as the aura of magic.

He blinked. How had they started glowing? He hadn't cast any kind of spell for it. He looked around. The people traversing the area paid him no more attention than before. None of them stopped and stared at the charms or asked him questions. Each one of them did, however, also glow their own distinct colors. Their auras were slightly visible. He looked down at himself. He was glowing too.

What was going on? He hadn't cast a spell to adjust his sight. Why was he seeing auras? It couldn't be another accident. Those were accompanied by a drain that hadn't happened this time.

Sakila, the Chemwanitz shamaness, had altered her vision to see auras without casting a spell. It had been very purposeful on her part, nothing accidental about it. Perhaps he had simply stumbled on whatever technique she used.

Tajor approached. Every color imaginable swirled in rhythmic patterns through his aura, set into motion by his curse. It made for a breathtakingly mesmerizing, if dizzying display. Jerryck rubbed his eyes.

"Are you all right?" Tajor asked.

"Yes, I just..." He stopped jabbing his fingers into his eyelids. "I need a spell broken."

"What spell?" Tajor cocked his head. He pointed at the four charms. "Those?"

"No, no, these are fine... Sort of... I think..." Jerryck held them up for Tajor to see properly. He scrutinized them all over again. There was a paper thin line of pale blue color between all of them. "Or maybe not."

Tajor dipped his face down to Jerryck's line of sight, the colors around him obscuring the colors of the charm. "See something odd?"

"As a matter of fact, yes." Jerryck turned, holding the charm up, away from where other auras showed up behind it. He scrutinized another in the same way. "I think I'm seeing a subtle disrupting spell."

"If that's what you want broken—" Tajor said as he reached out— "prepare for the entire construct of all the charms to collapse."

"No." Jerryck jerked them all away and dropped a couple. He snatched them back up before anyone else could touch them.

"Change of mind?"

"This isn't the magic I wanted you to break," Jerryck said. He closed his hand over the charms. "I think I may have cast a spell on my eyesight. I'm seeing auras."

"There's no spell on you for that." Tajor put his hands on Jerryck's shoulders. The swirling rainbow of colors that surrounded the man didn't vanish. It didn't even react to anything, like it normally did to magic. He squinted at Jerryck. "Whatever you did, the magic is gone. Only the effect remains. Is it something that will wear off, maybe?"

Jerryck rubbed his eyes again. "I hope so."

"What exactly were you doing when it happened?" Tajor let go of Jerryck's shoulders. "Would doing the exact opposite also have the opposite affect?"

"I don't know." Jerryck opened his palms and looked at the charms. He'd been focusing on the magic there. How could not focusing on the magic clear up his vision?

"How about you figure this out later?" Tajor steered him away. "The king wants you in the White Room."

"You're doing the job of a page?" Jerryck asked, going along placidly. With Tajor steering him, he didn't have to watch where he was going.

"I'm summoned too, so they sent me to fetch you. More efficient that way."

By the time they reached the White Room, some of the auras Jerryck saw had faded slightly. Perhaps that meant the problem would eventually resolve itself, like a spell that wore off into nothingness. Only a few elites were there. Instead of straining his eyes by looking at them, he sat in a chair and closed his eyes, toying with the charms in his hand.

Before long, the door opened and a couple of people entered. He opened his eyes to see who. Tajor stood right in front of him, smirking. The shock of colors swirling around him punched Jerryck in the head, blocking out everything else.

"Tajor," Heston barked. "What did you do?"

"I stood here." Tajor's smirk leaked into his voice.

"Why did he jump like that?"

"Jerryck," Terrance said. "What's wrong?"

"Nothing." Jerryck jumped to his feet. He tried to look past Tajor, directly at Terrance and Heston.

"Why do you keep blinking like that?" Terrance asked. "Are you all right?"

"Yes. I'm just seeing auras. That's all. It's a little disorienting."

"I trust you'll take care of it." Terrance drew himself up and changed the subject. "I've already sent for Gintario, so we only have a few moments. When he comes in, I'll confront him. He'll pretend offense, I'm sure. He'll likely propose compromises. Then I'll propose a compromise of our own."

"I don't need a compromise," Jerryck said. "I need a solution."

"Do you have one in mind?" Terrance asked. "Besides ignoring and placating. That isn't going to keep working. Try making it appear that you're cooperating. Give them exactly what they demand, without the results they're after."

The door opened again. Tajor's friend, the skinny guard, led Gintario into the room. Once properly announced, Gintario bowed appropriately. "Your Majesty. This is an honor I did not expect."

"It's not for your benefit," Terrance said. He crossed his arms. "It's for those you serve, despite the fact that they never apologized to me, or made amends."

"They have nothing to apologize for," Gintario said. "No amends to make."

"And so—" Terrance continued— "this is also the last time they will receive this courtesy if they ever again try to meddle with my staff."

"Meddle?" The glowing cloud of tan and blue around Gintario shifted more toward blue, the color of manipulation.

"And this time, their action is direct enough, they cannot deny trying to manipulate my staff." Terrance glared down his nose. His mostly green aura had little movement, remaining calm and steadfast. "No one dictates to me who is eligible for hire into whatever position I choose."

"No one is dictating to you, Majesty," Gintario said. "You can hire anyone you want, as you said. But your available choices may be severely diminished if the Gathering pulls every licensed magician out of your country for fear of enabling a dangerous renegade."

"You think that's a threat?" Terrance let out a small chuckle. "I've long considered expelling every licensed magician who has sworn oaths to the Gathering. So please, pull them. It would save me the trouble of enacting it myself."

"You can't do that," Gintario said with a gasp. Now a ruddy swirl snaked its way through his aura, curling and twisting. Something about the way it moved nagged at Jerryck.

"Changing your mind?" The deep green around Terrance brightened, strengthening into almost a jewel tone. "We have alchemists that would love to fill the positions magicians hold. There are plenty of talented magic-users in the mountains, or in the archipelago who could immigrate, which would strengthen our relations with those nations, repairing old wounds in the case of the archipelago. And that's not accounting for those who've hidden their talents for fear of retribution from the Gathering. We wouldn't lack if I banished every magician they've licensed."

Gintario's aura pulsed. "Alchemists and shamans!"

"And Archipelago hydromogists," Terrance said. "And women in hiding."

"This is outrageous." Gintario fumed. "This is insulting."

"So is the assumption that the Gathering may control whom I hire." Terrance uncrossed his arms and put his hands on his hips. "And if you continue speaking to me with that tone, I will also take your attitude as insult."

Gintario recoiled, drawing back his chest and dropping his shoulders. The ruddy swirl in his aura bled over to a more bluish brown. The vibrations were far too similar to the line of color inserted between Jerryck's charms.

"My apologies, Majesty." Gintario dipped his chin down. "I'm sure we can work out some sort of arrangement that is beneficial to the both of us."

Terrance snorted. "If you're going to tell me you'll stay out of my way for the next two weeks, like you told Jerryck, don't."

Jerryck didn't remember telling anyone that. Had he?

Terrance kept talking. "You have treated me with utter contempt and disrespect by trying to go around behind my back and attempting to manipulate my staff. I'll put you up tonight as a courtesy to the Gathering. Tomorrow morning, you leave."

"Then I'll be taking Jerryck back to Kemetullah with me?" Gintario asked. "One of the Seats would be happy to play his mentor, I'm sure."

Terrance shook his head. "He just got back from Shontarra last week. I need him here."

Jerryck held up the charms. He peered at the thin line of the disruption spell with Gintario's aura behind it. The visible colors made everything easier to compare.

Gintario tapped his chin and cast his eyes up to the ceiling, giving the appearance of thinking it out. The blue in his aura strengthened. "Perhaps if you have another time to send him? Say, in a month or so?"

"Or someone else could come here," Terrance said. "It could only be one of the best."

Gintario splayed the fingers of one hand, helpless to change the matter. "I doubt any of the Seats will come."

"It doesn't have to be one of the Seats," Terrance said.

"How will we know that whoever comes is one of the best then?" Gintario asked. "Everyone claims to be the best. Very few are."

"A test then."

"I suppose the Gathering could come up with some sort of test," Gintarrio said. "Or they could use the scores of the tests the magician took to get their license."

Jerryck focused back and forth between Gintario's aura and the disruption spell. The man looked at him and asked, "What are you doing?"

"Not the Gathering." Terrance drew Gintario's attention back to him. "They'll be so happy about getting Jerryck to comply, they'll approve the first person who applies. No. He's my court magician. I want someone who meets my approval."

Gintario's eyebrows raised. "You're going to test them for qualification?"

"Jerryck's not the only one in my palace who knows a lot about magic," Terrance said with a smile.

"If you suggest one of those alchemical medics you keep around, this discussion is over." Gintario put his hands on his hips. "More than over, I'll tell the Gathering how insulting you were. How you still wrongfully blame them. How you tried to threaten to expel magicians. They'll not only pull them, they'll set them all against you."

"It was you." Jerryck burst out, pointing at Gintario. "How did you do that?"

"What?" Gintario scowled at him. "You're adding to the insults too? What are you accusing me of now?"

"You disrupted the link in my charms for my alert system without breaking the spell." Jerryck lowered the charms.

"I have no idea what you're talking about," Gintario said. He turned back to Terrance. "Tell me who you have in mind for the tests. And it better be someone good."

Terrance held up a hand to Gintario to wait. "Jerryck, which alert system? You have a few of them."

"The one that tells me when a magic-user enters the palace." Jerryck picked up one of the charms with his free hand and held it for everyone to see. "It looked like they were underpowered, but I just charged them up. There was a disruption spell in the link between them. The signature matches Gintario's vibrations. But he would have had to cast it either before he entered the palace, or just as it was about to set off the alert. And it's so subtle and light, if I had charged up the charm, it would have powered right through the disruption and broken it. I would never have noticed it was there."

"Clever," Terrance said.

"How did you do that?" Jerryck asked Gintario. "I don't know of any spell that gets that subtle."

"I still don't know what you're talking about." All the blue leached out of Gintario's aura. The neutral tan blazoned so bright, it made it difficult to see anything else.

"Tajor?" Terrance smiled. "What do you think?"

"Shamans can make magic that subtle," Tajor said.

"I'm no shaman!" Gintario nearly spat the word.

"Sorcery could also get that subtle," Tajor said.

"Sorcery?" Jerryck closed his hand around the charms again.

"A sorcerer doesn't use words to cast a spell the way a magician does," Tajor said. "He simply does the magic with nothing more than his own aura as the catalyst. In many ways it's more difficult to learn, but in the long run it's much more powerful and simpler. And it's very difficult for a mere magician to detect sometimes, because he's not looking for it."

"Does the Gathering know you have this ability?" Terrance cocked his head at Gintario. "Have you done this in the households of any other national or district leaders?"

"I… I…" Gintario stammered, looking intermittently between Jerryck, Terrance, and Tajor. "This can't possibly be. Why would any of you think such things? Everyone knows sorcery is a myth."

"Answer the question," Heston growled.

"You answer mine." Gintario put on a snarl. He whirled on Jerryck. "How would you know there's a disruption spell if it really is that subtle?"

"Adjust your sight so you can see auras." Jerryck held up the charms again. "The evidence is right here."

"Things like this are what justify him holding his position," Terrance said, looking rather smug. "This isn't the first time someone the Gathering sent has looked at him, at something he's done, some nefarious action he's disrupted or exposed, and claimed that's impossible."

"You're not referring to the incident that started your troubles with some of the islands." Gintario tipped his chin down, glaring at Terrance. "The Gathering has made it clear what they think of you blaming them for that."

"And yet their claims don't refute the evidence. Absolutely I'm referring to that. And absolutely I still blame them. And yet here I am, gracious enough to allow a compromise, whether they deserve it or not."

"Then who did you have in mind for testing? You haven't answered me that." Terrance waved a hand to Tajor. "Him."

Gintario shook his head. "It should be a magician. Someone approved by the Gathering of Seats."

"I don't need their approval." Terrance used the same hand to wave that away. "But in the spirit of compromise, I'm certain you can get them to approve."

"Why would I do that?"

"Or I could register a formal complaint with the Gathering." Terrance smiled. "And use your misbehavior as an excuse to banish any magician who's sworn allegiance to them. And warn every other national and district leader that—"

"All right." Gintario held up both hands in surrender. He sighed and hung his head. "I'll get the Gathering to agree to let this guard, this…"

"Tajor," Terrance supplied the name.

"…this Tajor," Gintario said. "He'll test applicants to mentor Jerryck through the last two weeks of his official apprenticeship. But then he has to get his license. No more delay after that."

"Very good." Terrance clapped his hands together. "We're agreed. If you need any official documentation from me, send a message to my office and I'll have it ready by the time you leave tomorrow morning."

Gintario nodded and slunk for the door. Heston blocked him. "Fix what you did to Jerryck's alert."

"I'll do it," Jerryck said. "I don't want him messing with it any more than he already has."

Heston let Gintario go.

261

"This should protect you for a while," Terrance told Jerryck.

"How?" Jerryck asked.

Terrance grinned at Tajor. "What's the likelihood you'll approve any of the applicants?"

"I might approve someone like Shamaness Sakila," Tajor said.

"I'm not accepting applications from anyone but magicians," Terrance said. "Otherwise, that gives room for the Gathering to claim we cheated and lied to them."

"Oh… well… In that case…" Tajor started chuckling. "I'm not likely to approve anyone. I haven't met any magicians who even match Jerryck's skill, let alone surpass it enough to properly mentor him."

Jerryck pocketed his charms. "Any of the Seats surpass me."

"I haven't met any of the Seats face to face." Tajor smirked and added, "And if I ever did, you don't think I could find a way to humiliate and mock them?"

"They're not going to apply anyway," Terrance said.

"How do you figure that?" Jerryck asked.

"That would be equivalent to me adopting a wayward orphan boy whose actions are in constant defiance and rebellion to my laws," Terrance said. "Trust me. They're not going to come and apply."

Jerryck frowned at him. "I obey their rules. I'm not rebelling."

"You defy their requirement for oaths to them," Terrance said. "You may not have it in your heart that you're rebelling, but in your actions you are, whether you think of it that way or not. And now you have their leave to continue rebelling. If applicants don't get so annoyed with Tajor that they just give up, he'll humiliate them to the point that they look absolutely inept."

"And when the Gathering figures out that he'll never approve anyone?" Jerryck asked.

"By then it will be too late." Terrance grew a slow smile while he spoke. "It's not wise for any governing body to rescind their own word. They lose credibility in the eyes of their subjects, and they become vulnerable to rebellion."

Chapter 36

GINTARIO LEFT without complaint. Jerryck's vision returned to normal on its own. Perhaps life would normalize too. For a while. Surely it would take some time before anyone got word about the new test and come to Coraline Palace to try for the position.

That dream was crushed when Masorno arrived just a few days later. He burst into the workroom, puffing and wheezing from his climb up the stairs before Jerryck had even bothered to check who had set off his alerting chimes.

"I came as soon as I heard the good news." Masorno exclaimed between gasps for air.

"What good news?"

"You finally agreed to finish your apprenticeship." Masorno beamed. "All I have to do is impress a certain guard. I've taken enough leave of absence to stay for those two weeks and beyond, so I can still be here for the princess's birthday gala next month. We can celebrate together. Oh, you should see how jealous Andreno was that I'll be here for the gala and he won't."

Jerryck marked the page in the book he'd been reading. "How did you get word of this so fast?"

"Gintario and I are close friends." Masorno plopped down on one of the stools, still drawing breath too fast. "He said it didn't take as long to convince you as he feared, so he had some extra time available. He used some of it to pay me a visit."

"Did he tell you who has to approve your application?"

"Who cares?" Masorno threw his hands up gleefully. "I can impress anyone I want. Gintario said it was just some elite guard. I can manage a mere guard."

"You think so?"

"I know so." Masorno leaned toward Jerryck. "You just point him out. I'll get this taken care of immediately."

"Just to be fair, I should warn you—"

Masorno sat straight and waved his hand negligently. "Don't worry about it."

"All right," Jerryck drawled slowly. No one could blame him for not trying.

They went to General Heston's office. Just as the last time Jerryck had looked for Tajor, he was on duty in the throne room during court. Just as last time, Heston asked, "Why do you need him?"

"This is Masorno," Jerryck introduced his guest.

"The Shontese court magician," Heston said. "I know who he is."

"He wants to apply to be my mentor."

"So *he* needs Tajor, not you. He can wait until after lunch."

"That's perfect." Masorno beamed, making his double chin stand out. "That will make it available for a larger audience without them being tied up in the formality of court."

"You might not want to make it a display," Jerryck tried warning him again.

"Ridiculous," Masorno said with a snort. "This will be a chance for me to show off."

"This should be interesting," Heston said.

Jerryck excused himself and left. Masorno followed him. Jerryck claimed duties to tend. Masorno insisted on accompanying and helping out. No matter where they went or what excuse he was given, Masorno wouldn't go away. And everywhere they went, he bragged about the display he planned to put on after lunch. Quite a few people said they would come and watch when he invited them. Each time, Jerryck grimaced in pity.

By the time lunch ended, Masorno had generated quite an audience. Several of the more important visitors and staff clamored to come watch the test. Terrance responded by reopening the throne room for a second time that day. That accommodated the large crowd while still giving Masorno room to work.

People arrived in the same finery they had worn for the morning's session of court. Jerryck stared at them, utterly perplexed. Hadn't they changed clothes just to eat? Why had they changed clothes again? That was a lot of extra effort just to stand around during a performance that was sure to turn into a humiliation. Of course, they didn't know it would turn out that way. So perhaps they expected a good show.

The last few people trickled in. The main doors were shut. Terrance stepped up to the marble dais where his throne rested with its gold filigrees and crimson cushions. He hadn't changed clothes from lunch or put his crown back on. Too bad more people weren't as sensible. Standing below and in front of him were General Heston and Tajor. Off to the side, by the banners and arms displays, stood the rest of the core staff. Jerryck wished he could join them, instead of standing right next to Masorno on the long carpet running up the middle of the room at the center of attention.

Terrance raised his voice loud enough for the acoustics spell on the room to catch and amplify it, sending its echoes to the farthest corners and up to the windows at the top of the two-story high ceiling. "Welcome all, to this unusual occasion. Everyone knows the unique circumstances of Lord Jerryck's credentials, or rather, the lack of them."

The crowd chuckled. There were so many people, it was a low rumble washing over the floor. Terrance allowed them a moment of amusement. Then he held up his hands. The audience quieted, and he addressed them again. "It has been decided that he will take on a mentor who can prove himself to be one of the best in the practice. The court magician of Shontarra, Lord Masorno, is the first to take up this challenge. The judge is one of my elite guards. Lord Masorno, has Jerryck given you any warning about this man?"

"No need for warning, Majesty." Masorno's smile stretched from ear to ear. "Bring forward this guard."

"He's right here." Terrance gestured to Tajor.

Masorno's smile grew taut, more like a grimace plastered on his face. His eyes bulged slightly. *"Him?"*

"I did try to warn you," Jerryck said.

Masorno glanced at him. Then he stared at Tajor. His smile slipped off his face entirely. "That's the man who still owes me an apology."

Tajor opened his mouth. Heston shook his head, so he closed it again.

Masorno lifted his chin. "I want to hear what he has to say."

"I've informed him that he may not insult you until after you begin your demonstration," Heston said.

The smile crept back onto Masorno's face. "He won't think of any insults once I begin."

Tajor opened his mouth again, with the same result as before.

Masorno cleared his throat and spoke so loudly he didn't need the acoustics spell. "Your Majesty, lords, ladies, everyone gathered. I am Lord Masorno, the man chosen by Prince Sanbralio, the Esteemed Leader of Shontarra, to be his court magician. I was assistant to the Shontese court magician before me, until it was deemed that I would do a superior job."

"Can I say something now?" Tajor asked.

"Say what you wish," Masorno said.

"You're stupid."

A few titters rippled through the crowd.

Masorno's smile slipped again. "You have no cause to call me childish names."

"Absolutely I do." Tajor held up one finger. "First of all, why should the opinions of other people impress me?" He added a second finger to the first. "And how do you know you got the job because you would do it better? Did the prince put that in writing? Or do you just claim that because it makes you feel superior?"

"I was also the first apprentice Old Heldavio ever taught," Masorno said.

"You were the person he made the most mistakes with?" Tajor cocked his head to one side. The crowd giggled. "I thought it was commonly known that a teacher practices on their first student because they don't know what they're doing as much as with later students. And what does all this have to do with your skills? Are you trying to talk everyone to death?"

"Disrespect." Masorno drew himself up and threw his shoulders back. "You're as rude as the first time I met you."

"You think I was put in this position to be polite? Or to critique?" Tajor's gray eyes glittered with amused mischief. Never a good sign. "If you don't like this, do you really wish to proceed?"

Masorno pursed his lips. He looked at Jerryck. Then he puffed out his chest and said to Tajor, "Jerryck is worth putting up with a few moments of your impertinence."

Tajor smirked. "Then how about you show what you can do?"

"I'm going to summon an elemental," Masorno announced with the same volume he had first used.

"Are you going to say it?" Tajor asked. "Or do it?"

Masorno gave Tajor an icy look. Then he held up his arms in front of himself, squeezing his eyes shut in concentration. Jerryck's skin prickled with gathering energy. Most of it concentrated around Masorno's hands, just as Old Heldavio had taught all his apprentices to do at the beginning of every spell. The amount of power fluctuated, expanding and contracting, until it eventually stabilized into the correct amount needed to summon and control a small elemental. Masorno muttered the initiating words of the spell so quietly that no one else could hear, another technique Old Heldavio had taught.

He drew it out. As quiet as he was, he spoke so slowly he had to be pronouncing each word meticulously. He shaped the power, weaving it intricately. Then he began drawing substance in the form of air.

A breeze rustled through the throne room as the spell sucked air into the space around Masorno's hands. Excited whispers broke out as people's clothing and hair rustled. This spell was utilized so rarely, Jerryck doubted any of them had ever seen an elemental outside of pictures in books. And here they were, witnessing the entire process. A treat even for a magician.

The last time Jerryck had witnessed this had been at a convention, the first one after Old Heldavio died and Jerryck took up his job. The Gathering put on a performance to show how dangerous things could get when people stepped outside their guidelines and rules. A lot of people told Jerryck the performance was for his benefit, to encourage him to get his license. At the time, he couldn't believe they would go to all that trouble just for one person. Now? He should have listened and taken more precautions.

The shape of the elemental's body took form, hovering just above Masorno's upturned palms. The insides filled, swirling round and round like a tornado's funnel cloud in miniature. Crude arms broke off the sides as the wild energy of the thing pushed against the controls Masorno exerted on it. Its eyes and mouth opened, mere slits where the swirling air left voids.

Completed, it stood about four inches tall. Masorno held it up, turning around for all to see. The crowd burst into cheering applause. Masorno shifted the elemental to one palm, swept out his other arm, and gave them a low bow. His smile was plastered back on his face, despite the sweat that now dripped down his temples and jowls from the effort he had just exerted.

"That's it?" Tajor wrinkled his nose in scorn. The crowd silenced, stunned shock now on their faces.

"This is impressive work." Masorno wheezed from the energy spent.

"You spoke untrue." Tajor sneered. "You didn't really summon it like you said."

"Yes, I did." Masorno held the creature up. "Don't tell me I didn't summon what you can see with your own eyes."

"I see what has the appearance of an elemental," Tajor said. "Yet the evidence of a true elemental is lacking. You created a body out of air and wind, but it's just a golem, under your complete control. A puppet. It can't move if you don't make it move. It has no mind. No will. Either you lied, or you incorrectly identified your own spell. Which are you? A liar? Or an incompetent?"

"You saw the effort I put into this." Masorno stuck out his chin, his jowls wobbling.

Tajor smirked. "Are you evading the question?"

"You posed the question in a way that any answer just makes me look bad."

"Evasion is acceptable if you don't like facing truth?"

"*What truth?*" Masorno's voice resonated through the large chamber loud enough that the acoustics spell actually dampened it, rather than amplifying. "That I created an elemental? By the faces of the audience I'd say I impressed everyone here."

"Except the one person you intended to."

Masorno held the elemental up higher and repeated, "You saw the effort I put into this."

"And yet it's so small."

"That's your problem?" Masorno's eyes bulged. More energy gathered. "Then I'll make it bigger."

Would Masorno be able to control something bigger? He was already straining. Jerryck expanded his aura, gently stroking the edge of the magic, monitoring in a way that Masorno wouldn't watch for.

Magic poured into the elemental. The breeze picked back up as the body of the thing sucked in more air. It got to about a foot in height. Masorno set it on the floor and took two steps back. As it continued to grow, the airflow picked up speed and strength. Women put hands on their pinned hair, keeping it in place. Men tugged at their clothing as it was ruffled and disturbed.

The elemental reached the height of the average man and continued growing. The airflow turned into a gale. Masorno panted and wheezed. His entire aura flared around the spell, struggling to engulf it, to keep it controlled. Parts of it spread too thin.

Even if the elemental didn't have a mind or will of its own, it could still pose a danger. That much concentrated wind would violently whip around if it broke free. Even in as large a space as the throne room. Wall hangings would tear from their places. Light fixtures would rip from their anchors and fall into the crowd. The crystal and glass decorations would smash into shards to fly around as sharp as daggers. People would be knocked off their feet, thrown against each other, hurled against the walls, all while flying debris pummeled them.

It was against protocol for one magician to step into another's spell without invitation. To remain professional, Jerryck should allow the slip, then help clean up afterward. He clenched his fists, monitoring.

Masorno still poured energy into the magic, either ignoring or unaware of the potential disaster. The elemental reached twice his height. His aura stretched taut. A stream of wind slipped through the thinnest part and shot through the crowd. It knocked a few people off their feet. They laughed nervously as the gust dissipated. A second one slipped through. Then a third.

Masorno shut off the flow of energy. Too late. His chest heaved, gulping breaths. His eyes showed while all around. His hands stretched out, fingers splayed, his aura around the elemental splitting like tearing cloth.

Another burst of air shot out. This time, it whipped right to where Terrance stood in front of his throne. Jerryck threw up a magic barrier in front of his king to act as a shield. Then he lunged out an arm of aura and snagged the spear of air, batting it up where it could spread out harmlessly around the ceiling.

Forget protocols. People were in danger.

He spread his aura to cover the growing gaps around the elemental. He oozed his magic inside of Masorno's, taking control.

"*No!*" Masorno shrieked breathlessly, his aura feebly pushing against Jerryck's. "It's mine."

"Not if you can't control it." Jerryck got a firm grip on the elemental and wrested it away, jerking Masorno to his knees.

The force of the magic slammed against Jerryck, nearly knocking him prone. He braced himself, concentrating on protecting Terrance and everyone else. The focus tapped into his well of strength. He funneled all the air of the body upward, squeezing and pushing from below. It raised up higher and higher, until it was level with the windows lining the top of the room near the ceiling. There, he opened one side of his control.

The air exploded out. Its force shattered the windows, spraying glass outward. Jerryck let go, allowing all of it to blow out that window and escape up into the clouds far above. The weather and the outside environment would take care of the rest.

His aura snapped back around his body, stunning him. Spent, suddenly short of breath, he sank to his knees, putting him eye to eye with Masorno.

"And you thought to mentor *him*?" Tajor laughed. "From what I just witnessed, it ought to go the other way around. Jerryck should mentor you."

Masorno pointed at Jerryck, his voice and his finger both shaking. "You sabotaged me."

"You lost control." Jerryck said.

"You interfered." Masorno struggled to his feet. "That's why I lost control. You messed it up."

"If you weren't losing control before he took over," Tajor said, "Then why were gusts of wind slipping away from you and shooting through the crowd?"

Terrance asked, "Did he impress you as someone highly skilled?"

Tajor laughed. "No."

"Judgment is rendered," Terrance announced.

"This is unfair," Masorno screamed.

"You agreed to the stipulation," Terrance said. "And I don't like guests yelling at my staff, especially not lords on my core staff, like Jerryck. Consider yourself dismissed."

People took that as a signal the show was ended. The large main doors opened, and the throng spilled out. Masorno watched everyone go with clenched teeth and fists. Jerryck got back to his feet, used one of the many side exits to avoid as many people as he could, and went back up his tower to pick up the book he had abandoned that morning.

Before long, the kids were released from their afternoon class. Zev came and interrupted Jerryck's reading. He asked so many questions about the event in the throne room that Jerryck gave up trying to learn anything from his book.

The chimes rang that meant someone had entered the tower. Then Masorno shouted up the stairs, his voice carried all the way up with magic. "Jerryck. I know you're up there. You and I are about to have some words. You better cut the attitude and straighten out. Right now!"

Zev bounced on the stool he'd taken. "Is that him?"

"Stay here." Jerryck told his nephew before the boy bounced out to see who was yelling. He descended the stairs just enough to see Masorno.

"I'll have you know," Masorno talked quieter now, "I'll see this decision overturned."

"You want a second go at Tajor?" Jerryck asked.

"That was my first thought. It would have been much easier on you. But your king refused my appeal. Wouldn't even hear me out. He insists that the judgment is final and cannot be changed or amended. So, unless you agree right here, right now, to forgo all this foolishness and finish your apprenticeship with me, I'll be forced to take this all the way to the Gathering of Seats."

"Good luck with that." Jerryck started back up the stairs.

Chapter 37

GUESTS BOTH FOREIGN AND DOMESTIC flocked to Coraline Palace. Princess Nita's fifteenth birthday fast approached, the birthday that would put her over the threshold from child to adult, the last one she would celebrate openly. Guest rooms filled in the palace, all over Kershet, and on country estates, as preparations went into full swing.

More magicians came with the guests. None of them humiliated themselves nearly as bad as Masorno. All of them failed to impress Tajor.

Jerryck did his best to stay out of everyone's way. Despite that, people kept seeking him out. Could he enhance the flavor of this spice? Could he change the color of that table dressing? Could he temporarily make this decorative piece lighter so less people could lift it? Could he strengthen the ties on that wall hanging?

Everyone ran around as if a pack of leshies had been let loose and allowed to run amok. Guests jockeyed for rooms. Every building filled to capacity, making prices soar. Tailors, jewelers, boutiques, and even souvenir shops sold wares so fast the products might have been carrion meat flung to dogs.

When the big day arrived, Nita sequestered herself in her chambers as noble traditions dictated. She had until noon to prepare. The ballroom filled. Guests mingled throughout the morning in anticipation of her entrance.

Finally, her introductory music played. The herald announced her. She entered at the top of the stairway to the balcony above and began her descent.

A necklace that spread to drape over her shoulders matched her earrings and small tiara. Her dress, simply cut, was just long enough to brush the floor. Just like every other ball she had ever attended.

Jerryck looked around at everyone else. For some reason, they all reacted differently than they ever had. Young women compared her hair, clothes, and jewelry to their own. All the young men's eyes bulged, and they practically drooled through open mouths. Older people whispered how much she looked like her mother. One person pointed out that no matter how much she looked like the late queen, she had her father's eyes.

Terrance glowed with pride as he met her at the bottom of the staircase. Following tradition, he dressed as formally as his father ever had, wearing all the trappings of his position. He took her hand to guide her last step down to the floor and said, "Welcome to the first day of the rest of your life."

Everyone else echoed him. She beamed at them all. The young men goggled even more than before. With this birthday, she became an eligible woman. Even though most women waited until they were twenty before they married, no one would call her a girl after this.

The traditions of commoners were much simpler. When a commoner reached the age of adulthood, people gave them gifts. If they could afford it, they had a feast. Then everyone got on with their workday. There was very little of the boring pomp and ritual that nobles insisted on. As much as Jerryck preferred the simplicity of commoner customs, he had learned not to say as much in as formal a setting as this. It never got him out of attending, as he used to hope for. All it ever did was upset people and earn him a scolding from Terrance or a tongue lashing from Nita. So he held his peace and let the events carry on around him.

Terrance led Nita over to the luncheon tables, where servants had laid out finger foods in aesthetic displays. She sampled a bite of her first meal as an adult. She took her first sip of wine. Then her father swept her out onto the dance floor for the first dance of her adulthood.

Throughout the afternoon, she followed tradition enough to share one dance with every unwed man in attendance. After that she pointedly ignored them all. They eventually gave up trying to impress her. Instead, they divided their time between trying to catch the eyes of other young women, bragging to each other, dodging razing comments from their friends, and stuffing as much food as possible into their mouths.

The young women grouped together to move back and forth around the ballroom in packs, like flocks of noisy, migrating geese. They giggled everywhere they went, especially if there was a young man nearby trying to impress them. They didn't hide how they mocked other groups of girls, talking about how stupid they were, and how out of fashion they were, even though to Jerryck they looked and acted almost exactly the same.

Servants kept the food and drink flowing. Musicians rotated in and out. Other entertainers performed between musical numbers and dances. The afternoon waned. Desserts, sweetmeats, and candies were set out about the time the sun set and the chandeliers were lit.

When midnight finally rolled around, everyone under the age of fifteen was sent to bed. Nita was allowed to stay up. Another first. Before a quarter of an hour had passed, she yawned, and excused herself anyway.

That meant any of the guests could also leave the party, even though the night was only half past. Jerryck took the opportunity to make his escape. With guests going to bed, some of the servants could also quit working. He snagged his pretty Leanne out of the kitchens and kept her all to himself for a few precious hours. She was much better company than anyone else in that entire crowd that had partied in the ballroom.

Normally after a large gala, the guests would linger for a week or two. This time, the weather scryers predicted the first of the autumn rains. Within two days, people packed up and left, trying to beat the weather. By the beginning of the next week, only three of the party guests remained. The pregnant wife of one of the northern premieres went into labor, so the couple stayed while Leanne took up her midwifing duties. The other guest was the highest-ranking unwed man in Brend, who was not his father's heir.

Rumors flew. Some people swore the Processions had begun with this young man. Others swore they hadn't, because noble heirs tended to wait until their twentieth birthday, not their fifteenth. The first group claimed that was the very reason the Processions had begun. The sooner someone was selected, the more time Terrance had to train the young man for the throne, making sure he was fit before he married Nita at twenty. Which was ridiculous. Terrance had always stated that Nita would take his place, not some future son-in-law. Why didn't people take him at his word?

Jerryck received a summons to the next weekly staff meeting. He usually found any excuse necessary to skip them. But when Terrance specifically summoned him for one, he had no choice.

He debated trying to sit in the back, until Heston glared at him. He went to the dais and slipped into his seat as unobtrusively as possible. There was a paper laying on the table, turned over so the writing faced down. Every seat for the core staff had some sort of paper except Terrance, Nita, and Lalven. Some people were handed papers as they entered: Head Medic Kellos, the theater director, the stable master, and the head chef, among many others.

Most of the members of the core staff entered one by one and took their seats. Chamberlain Malk looked at the Priad's empty seat and asked, "Where's Lalven?"

"With Terrance," Heston answered. He had a whole stack of papers at his seat, not just one. He hadn't hesitated to delve into them.

"I'm surprised he's not already here telling us how to proceed," Malk said.

"You've got more of a surprise than that coming," Heston said.

Terrance entered with Nita. All conversation in the room stopped. A few more people darted in behind him and quickly took seats with the general staff. Terrance strode up to the dais and dropped another stack of papers down on the table with a short snap while Nita slipped behind it to take her seat.

"We have a lot to go over, so let's get started," Terrance began. All heads turned to Lalven's empty chair. Terrance said, "I have released Lalven from my employ. He has a letter of severance from me, and a letter of recommendation to assist him in finding employment elsewhere. He is currently putting his affairs in order and has one week to vacate Coraline Palace."

Collective gasps went around the room. Terrance waited for a few moments. When the cacophony rose instead of dying down, he held up his hands for quiet. When everyone complied, he said, "When I turned fifteen, my father restructured the staff to mesh with me. I'm doing the same for my daughter."

One of the older secondary advisers stood, the gesture for requesting permission to speak. Terrance nodded at him. The adviser said, "Majesty, is this wise? Your father did that because he was old. He didn't know how much longer he would be alive, how long you would have to learn to take his place. You're not old. You should have many, many years before your daughter marries and her husband takes your place."

Terrance narrowed his eyes at the man. "I will say this one last time: My daughter will take my place. No one else."

"The law says that anyone on the throne must have the capacity to produce a legitimate heir. That means marriage. And what she inherits will go to her husband."

"I just terminated Lalven's employment because he couldn't accept that Nita will rule from the throne," Terrance said. He stood still as a statue, his knuckles whitening where he clasped his hands in front of himself. "If you wish the same treatment, by all means, continue to dispute the issue."

The whispering started back up. The old secondary adviser sat down, his jaw set. Jerryck rested his chin on his palm, hand over his mouth, covering his smile. Finally, Terrance was putting this matter permanently to rest. People could stop going on about it.

One of the steward's assistants rose. Terrance nodded at him. The man said, "What of the rumors that the Processions have started?"

"Lalven began the Processions without my permission," Terrance said. "Since no Processions have ever ceased without an engagement, they will continue. Which is unfortunate. It automatically disqualifies any of the young men visiting in the next few years. I had intended to wait until she was twenty. For now, she will be spending her time adjusting to her new, adult responsibilities. She'll have no time to be hostess to guests.

"Now, enough of that." Terrance unclasped his hands to casually wave the matter aside. "On to better things. You each have been handed documentation concerning this restructuring. While Lalven is the only person terminated at this point in time, others of you will retire. All those currently in the positions you held when my father restructured for me, you are in that category. If you wish, and if approved, there is the likelihood that you will stay on the staff in an advisory capacity to the position you're vacating."

Papers rustled louder than the previous whispers as everyone looked at their documentation. Terrance raised his voice over the noise. "Any of you not listed as retiring may have that option. If you feel incompatible with Nita, if you feel you'll be too old by the time she ascends the throne, or anything else, document your reason. Bring it to me. We'll discuss it."

Jerryck's paper said that if he tried to put in a resignation, it would be denied. Farther down it instructed him to acquire an apprentice. That was the issue Terrance addressed next. "Once we complete the restructuring, all of you in lead positions will take on an apprentice, if you don't already have one. If you have a particular individual in mind for that position, but they're not yet fifteen, you may slate them for future apprenticeship."

That made it easy for Jerryck. He could slate his nephew. That way he wouldn't have to take on any of the candidates the other magicians had pushed at him. He could probably start teaching the boy right away. Heldavio had taught Jerryck right away, even though he hadn't been fifteen.

Actually, shortly after Terrance had turned fifteen was when Heldavio had slated Jerryck for apprenticeship. He had gone to the village where Jerryck grew up and brought him and Kendra to live at the palace. It must have been due to the restructuring Terrance had mentioned.

"All personnel," Terrance was saying, "already serving or new, including apprentices, must meet Nita's approval."

"Me?" Nita put her hand on her chest, and murmurs went around the room again.

"Yes," Terrance told her. "You need to approve if they're going to mesh with you."

The meeting went on with other details while Jerryck tried not to look too bored. Nita was assigned her own office. Anyone looking for an apprentice had to submit a written request to her for approval. Anyone retiring could submit suggestions for their replacement to her.

It might be nice to have an apprentice, someone to help with mundane chores. Plenty of non-magical tasks fell under Jerryck's responsibilities. Keeping the supplies organized, grinding herbs and powders, researching recipes and methods, keeping tabs on the status of other magicians in the country, taking requests from palace residents, greeting visiting magic-users.

Wait. If people no longer believed Jerryck was looking for an apprentice, he couldn't use that as an excuse to look for an unknown magic-user.

When Terrance dismissed the general staff and the remainder of the core staff went into the small council chamber, Terrance must have noticed Jerryck's mood. He asked, "What's wrong?"

"When I started looking for an unknown magic-user, I told everyone I was looking for an apprentice," Jerryck said. He sat at the table and stared at his hand on the flawless surface. "If I already have one, I can't be looking."

"We'll address that update first then." Terrance sat in his chair at the head of the table for once, instead of standing through the meeting. "Heston, if you please."

Heston remained standing. "That group of foreigners Andreno is associated with... We have a lead on their possible location. There's an old, abandoned castle on the border between the Larksen and Shana districts. They may have taken up residence there."

"Larkeshan Castle," Jerryck said. Everyone turned to look at him. It was his job to know about things like this. So rather than try and deflect the attention, he carried on. "It's cursed."

"I know," Heston said. "So do the locals."

"They better know," Jerryck said. "Because they have to maintain it anyway. If it ever falls, so will both those districts, unless they've come back together as one. That's the only thing that will break that curse."

"If they have to maintain it," Nita said, "then why wouldn't they have people living there to do so."

"Because anyone living there also falls under the curse," Jerryck said. "Whatever endeavor they pursue will ultimately fail."

"Would that cause the locals to resist talking about someone taking up residence?" Heston asked.

"How should I know why people do what they do?" Jerryck threw his hands up. "People confuse me. Someone lives there now?"

"According to rumors just outside the immediate local vicinity," Heston said. "There's a village a few miles away from it..."

Jerryck interrupted him. "That's where they have their festival every few years when both the districts get together to make any repairs that are needed."

"They toss distractions to anyone asking about current residents in the castle and refuse to talk about it," Heston said. "No matter how many people swear its now occupied."

"By foreigners?" Chamberlain Malk steepled his fingers. "From where? Since when?"

"Working on that," Heston said. "So far, I have very little information. Most of this rumored group have fair features, like people in the Chemwanitz. But their language is strange, guttural. And they have odd, magical devices that no one has ever seen anything like before."

Jerryck sat forward. "Magic devices?"

"Can you think of anyone who works with magic on mechanical devices?" Heston asked him.

"Hmm…" Jerryck pulled on his lower lip, mentally going over different magicians and their areas of expertise. "No one immediately comes to mind. The Gathering of Seats frowns on mixing mechanics and spells. The closest I've seen to that type of magic is alchemists, or some of the magic-users south of the Ahnjwat Sea."

Malk frowned. "I thought they worked more with imps than spells that far south."

"They do." Jerryck nodded. "But some of them also work with magic on mechanical devices. I met one man who had a spell on a cheap metal slug that made it light up and glow if you spun it on its side and—"

"Understood," Heston interrupted him. "So it could be someone from there, if it weren't for the fair features these people are supposed to have. You can't think of anyone with fair features who does this type of magic?"

"The only fair featured people I know of are from the mountains and the northern tundra," Jerryck said. "The mountains use shamanism, which focuses on the magic from the land. The people from the tundra rely on totems, animal magic. No mechanical spells for either of them."

"What's the likelihood," Terrance said, "that whoever tainted the water is the same person putting these spells on mechanical items?"

"Different kinds of magic," Jerryck replied, shaking his head.

"You do different kinds of magic," Heston said.

"Every kind of magic I do is affected by every other type of magic I have the ability to do," Jerryck tried to explain. "For instance, I work best with elements and manipulations. When I do healings, a lot of times I end up manipulating the water that's carried inside a person's body to help. The taint poured into the river was a perversion of almost pure elemental magic. Putting spells on mechanical devices is something altogether different. And I didn't get any sense in the river of the kind of effect that type of magical ability would create."

"That means we're possibly looking at two different magic-users?" Terrance asked.

"Harder to hide more than one person," Heston said.

"And you have very little information on this group," Terrance said.

"Which supports my statement," Heston replied. "If that group has more than one magic-user, it makes it more likely we'd have more information about them."

"Get more information," Terrance said.

Heston nodded once. The meeting moved on.

Chapter 38

WHEN JERRYCK TRIED to simply tell Nita that he wanted Zev for an apprentice, she insisted all requests for apprentices be in writing, especially from members of the core staff. Annoyed, it took a few days, and some help from his wife before Jerryck got around to penning a formal request. It was about mid-afternoon when he brought it to Nita's new office, the same one her father had used before ascending the throne. Judging from the gossip of people in the reception area, Nita and Terrance had gone in with one of the elite guards shortly after lunch and hadn't yet come back out.

Jerryck sat and waited. It took nearly an hour more before the door to the office opened. Terrance emerged first. There was nothing in his face or demeanor that gave Jerryck any clues to anything discussed inside. When he left, more than half the waiting people followed him.

Tajor came out next, escorted by the princess, who had the wide-eyed expression of someone given a waterfall of information in too short a time period. She said to him, "You gave me more to consider than I expected."

"Take your time to assimilate the information," Tajor said. "Discuss it with your father. I'll abide by whatever decision you make."

Several people stood when Tajor left her. Some waved to draw Nita's attention. She looked around at them all. Jerryck sunk down in his seat so her eyes would go over him. Though it would be nice to get this over with, most of these people had waited longer than him.

"Jerryck—" she pointed at him— "I'll talk to you next."

He got several glares as he followed her in. He handed over the request he'd written, then summed it up for her. "I'd like to take my nephew Zev for my apprentice."

She took the letter and quickly read it over. She stood in front of her father's old desk, hers now. "You're certain he's the one you want? You've been introduced to several boys with the potential to learn your craft in the past couple of months."

"I told General Heston at the start that I'd always thought I'd apprentice Zev, not some random stranger," Jerryck said. He listed some of the attributes he'd written down. "He has a strong aura, good for working magic. He plays a few of the harmless magic tricks I used to pull off as a kid, so I know he has the potential. He's bright. Observant. He shows interest in what goes on around him. He never hesitates to ask about anything he doesn't know. And he already assists me sometimes with menial chores anyway."

"You wrote all that." Nita set the letter down. "What about all the tall tales he makes up. You wrote that's a sign of an active imagination?"

Jerryck was more grateful than ever his wife had helped him. She was the one who had insisted he include counters to some of Zev's negative quirks. "If he can harness that imagination properly, applying it to creating spells, the tall tales will probably stop. He'll have new stories that will be absolutely true."

"The general studies tutor says he needs to apply himself more."

"You know that tutor is hardest on his best students. He did it to me. He did it to you. He says that about all the smartest kids."

"All right." Nita stepped around the desk, much tidier than her father had ever kept it. She opened a tall drawer with file folders, selected a paper out of one, filled in Zev's name in a blank spot, signed the bottom, and applied her seal. She handed it over. "I approve this. Pending Zev's agreement, you may slate him as your future apprentice, effective on his fifteenth birthday."

Jerryck smiled. This had been much easier and far more efficiently handled than he had thought it would. He left the office, making room for whoever she called in next.

At supper, Jerryck went to the common dining hall. All four of Kendra's kids squeezed in by him at the long tables and chatted so much it was a wonder they got any food in their mouths at all. Between food garbling their words, and the buzz of conversation all around them, he couldn't make out much of what they said to him. As people finished their meal, and desserts were set out for the diners, things quieted down some. Jerryck took that opportunity.

"Zev, I have a question for you," He said. Zev stopped shoveling in cake long enough to look up. "How would you like to be my apprentice?"

"Great!" Zev's face split open in a huge grin. Then he closed up again. "I'm not fifteen yet."

Jerryck shrugged. "That's fine. I can start teaching you a few things anyway."

"Really?" Zev brightened back up. "You'd do that?"

"Absolutely," Jerryck said.

"Why is this coming up all of a sudden?" his sister Chandra asked. Marla had stopped eating entirely.

"Everyone's taking an apprentice now." Zev talked with his mouth full. "Darren's older brother was made an apprentice groom in the stable yesterday. And Zed's an apprentice smith now too."

"And I was told that if you agree, I could slate you for my apprentice," Jerryck said. "It would be official as soon as you turn fifteen."

Zev dropped his fork. He leaped from his seat, whooping and jumping around. Zech, the toddler, laughed and squealed, clapping his little hands at his brother's antics. Heads turned, people looking to see what the hullabaloo was about. Chandra saw that and yanked on Zev, trying to get him to sit down. He ignored her. Until Marla started crying.

Zev sat beside her. "What's wrong?"

"Are you going to move out of our room?" she said with a sniffle.

Jerryck had thought they'd all be thrilled. He stopped himself just before telling her so. Chandra hadn't been as thrilled as he thought either. So perhaps it was just another of his social blunders.

"Not right away." Jerryck tried to console his niece instead of telling her to be happy for Zev. "It just means I'm going to start teaching him a few things. He'll have to do that in addition to his normal chores and lessons, so he'll have less free time, but he'll still live in your room for a little while, until we get a few things arranged."

"It's not like I'm leaving the palace." Zev hugged her. "I'll still eat with you here. And I'll spend as much time with you as I can. If you ever need me, you'll know right where to find me."

Marla wiped a couple tears away. "In Uncle Jerryck's workroom?"

"Or in my old room behind it," Jerryck said.

"That's not really a room." Chandra looked dubious. "It's more like a closet space. And I don't care what anyone else says, I think you curtained it off to hide all the junk you stuff in there. You think Zev is going to sleep on one of those stacks or something?"

"That's part of what I meant about arranging things," Jerryck said. "I'll clean it out. And it's not junk. There's a use for every item stored in there."

"How often do you use them?" she asked.

"Some of the things in there are overflow for tools and ingredients I don't have space for in the workroom cupboards and shelves." There was no way he would admit out loud that some of the things in there he had never used. He was simply too fascinated with them to throw them out. "I'll get it cleared out enough to have a cot in there. Then it'll be in about the same state it was when I moved into it back when I was slated to be an apprentice."

"See, Marla?" Zev kissed the top of her head. "I'll stay right where you can come get me anytime you need."

Marla pushed away her dessert. "I guess that'll be okay."

It took another half a week before some of the turmoil in the palace calmed. Positions filled. People settled into their new roles. Everyone adjusted.

Jerryck received a message that he couldn't skip the weekly general staff meeting. Again. He suppressed a groan. Terrance would announce the new

Priad. And then Jerryck would be bored through the rest of the time he could be doing other, more productive things. He was attending far more meetings lately than normal. Maybe he could use that as an excuse to skip all of them for the next few months.

When he got there, almost everyone else had already gathered. He may as well have stepped into the common dining hall for all the cacophony. People discussed, debated, some even laid odds on who would be named. A few arguments sparked up, then quickly settled as they eyed the elite guards that always lined the walls under the various district banners. Jerryck spotted Tajor and his three friends among them.

The room quieted and all the secondary advisers shifted restlessly when Terrance stepped up to stand in front of the table on the dais. He said to everyone, "As promised, the first item on the agenda is the last position on the core staff. My daughter has chosen a man that meets my approval."

One of the advisers who had constantly sided with Lalven against Nita slumped in his seat. Another, who had always spoken up for her, sat straighter. He smiled as Terrance handed the meeting over to the princess.

She rose from her seat but without coming around to the front of the table like her father. She said, "I've spoken individually with each and every secondary adviser, plus many others. I received their recommendations and took them all into consideration. I took counsel with my father. I gave more weight to his recommendation than any other. That man is the one I've decided to appoint, for reasons that won't be discussed in this meeting."

Jerryck resisted resting his chin in his hands and letting his eyes glaze over. Why did people have to put so much preamble on something that could be straightforward and simple?

Everyone else seemed to enjoy the anticipation. The adviser who slumped sat up, looking slightly less pessimistic. The one who smiled, beamed even more and tilted up his chin. Almost everyone else leaned forward, sitting on the edges of their seats.

Except the guards. They might as well have been wall fixtures for all the expression they gave. Except Tajor. For some reason, he stiffened and looked slightly alarmed.

"We have decided to appoint Tajor," Nita said.

The eager adviser deflated. "Tajor?"

The slumping one curled his upper lip. "Tajor?"

"Yes." Nita didn't look directly at them.

She looked across the room, at everyone else, at the shocked expressions. Heads turned back and forth to stare open mouthed between her and Tajor. Some people came close to displaying open offense and disgust, as if the appointment were a personal insult.

As if they had any right to offense. It wasn't their decision. The fact that some of them had been consulted at all was a privilege and an honor. They ought to be pleased. Jerryck shook his head. People were confusing.

She looked right at Tajor. "You have nothing to say about this new appointment?"

All the color had leached from Tajor's face, leaving his skin nearly as gray as his hair and eyes. He pointed to the slumper. "I recommended him."

"We didn't choose him," Nita said. "We decided to appoint you. And you said you would abide by whatever decision we made."

"I wasn't referring to this."

"Whether this is what you referred to or not, you gave your word. Stand by it."

Tajor's aura buzzed, the same as it had in Shontarra. This time, he didn't acquiesce. He broke eye contact, looking only at the back of the room. The buzzing continued. Jerryck sucked in his own aura, protecting it from even coming close to touching Tajor's, even from across the large room.

The entire rest of the meeting, that was all Jerryck concentrated on. He didn't listen to anything said or done. He simply focused on keeping clear of the buzz radiating from Tajor.

Tajor refused to participate. He wouldn't respond to anyone on the floor. He wouldn't budge from the wall among the guards to take the priad's seat on the dais. And when the meeting was finally dismissed, he bolted for the exit.

"Tajor," Terrance called to him. He pointed to the door to the small council chamber off to the side. "You're going the wrong way."

The buzz increased momentarily, until Tajor stopped and hunched his shoulders. Then it went back to the level it had been at before. It went down further after all the rest of the staff had left and Heston grabbed Tajor by the arm to direct him to the small council chamber. But it was still there. Jerryck made sure to stay as far away from him as possible, even in the smaller room.

"You weren't really serious, were you?" Tajor looked back and forth between Terrance and Nita. He planted his feet just inside the door, not moving an inch farther. "I don't know how to do this. Surely you want someone more qualified."

Terrance stood behind his chair and rested his arms on its high back. "Like who?"

"I gave you my recommendation," Tajor repeated.

"This position is my primary adviser," Terrance said. "I need someone with enough experience in different situations that he understands things better than most. You think the man you recommended has more years of experience to draw upon than you?"

"This position requires decision making skills I don't have." Tajor leaned his back against the door, his hands splayed flat on its surface. "I think he has more training than I."

Nita cupped her chin in her hand, smiling innocently. "What good is training without actual experience?"

"And don't worry about making decisions," Terrance said. "You just give us your experience. Leave the decisions to us."

"No decisions?" The buzzing from Tajor eased further. "At all?"

"I can't promise *no* decisions," Terrance said.

Nita laughed. "Everyone has to learn how to make decisions. Whether we're just a few days old, or we've lost track of our years because there are too many, we have to learn how to make decisions."

"And the consequences?" Tajor asked. "What if your decision is wrong? What about the consequences?"

"Consequences are something we all face together and live with," Terrance said. "In most cases, we compensate for, or take advantage of them. We'll figure this out. Come take your seat at the table."

"Please?" Nita's innocent look gave way to a pleading expression, the same one that had worked on her father when she was little.

"Don't expect me to say something just because it's what you want to hear," Tajor said with a glower. The buzzing abruptly ceased.

"I wouldn't have it any other way," Nita said.

"I'm not letting you out of elite duties for this," Heston said, standing in his usual corner, arms crossed. "I've got other nobles in those ranks. They all do their duties."

"You've got minor nobles in the elite?" Jerryck risked getting close enough to sit. Even closer, there was no buzzing from Tajor.

"Even if he didn't before, he does now," Nita said. "As priad on my father's core staff, that makes Tajor a minor noble."

"I am *not* calling him a lord," Jerryck muttered.

Tajor cracked up laughing, color returning to his cheeks. "At least one of you is still sensible. For a while, I thought all of you had lost your minds."

Terrance laid out his agenda for the session. Jerryck grabbed some of the paper that was always available on the table and took notes. Not of the agenda. On Tajor. The buzzing happened when he refused an order. It stopped when he complied. Did it also stop when the order was rescinded?

Several theories and hypotheses flitted about in Jerryck's head. He hesitated before writing them down. What was it Yeshiyahu had said? Experimenting enervated him? Made it more likely he'd have an accident? Something like that. It explained why he'd blown up his workroom so many times. But surely, just recording hypotheses wasn't actual experimenting. He should be safe enough. He put the pen to the paper.

If Tajor was given a direct order he didn't want to obey, was that what made his aura buzz and vibrate so much it made Jerryck's teeth ache? That couldn't be it entirely. Tajor had received a number of orders he didn't want to obey. More often than not, he pestered, distracted, and annoyed the person giving the order until they didn't make him do it. Which led rise to the theory that he did it on purpose to entice the rescinding of the order.

Jerryck wrote out order after order he could give Tajor, just to see if he could get that buzzing to start up. Or perhaps he could get someone else to give the order. Tajor had a tendency to evade anything Jerryck told him to do. If he could figure out one that Tajor didn't want to do, that he couldn't evade, would that make his aura buzz? Until... when? When he capitulated? When he distracted enough that the order was rescinded or forgotten?

Before Jerryck realized how much time had passed, everyone got up. The meeting had ended. The chamberlain, the chancellor, and the steward left. Terrance and Nita followed them. Heston lingered.

"You get to keep the room you earned with the elite in their barracks," he was saying to Tajor. "But I had most of your belongings moved to Lalven's old room. You'll board there."

"You moved my things before I accepted the position?" Tajor was still standing by the door to the large council chamber. Had he actually sat down? Or had he remained there the entire time.

"Terrance assured me you'd accept," Heston said.

"Because he'd order it?" Jerryck asked.

Tajor narrowed his eyes at him. He glanced at the papers Jerryck had been scribbling on the entire time, not that he could possibly read it from that distance. Or could he? He said, "Didn't you learn recently that thinking and experimenting with new possibilities is an energy builder for you? If you haven't learned to properly control that yet, aren't you worried at all that you might have another accident?"

"What experimenting?" Heston stepped over behind Jerryck and scooped up the notes. Glancing through them, he grunted. Then he said, "This vibrating you're referring to, when he disobeys a direct order, is that part of his curse?"

"I don't think so," Jerryck said. "That absorbs magic and breaks it. This is entirely different. Almost like it's part of his very nature."

"Interesting." Heston dropped the notes back on the table in front of Jerryck. He said to Tajor. "Confirm or deny this."

"Confirm or deny what?" Tajor asked. "That there are things about me that you don't fully understand? Wouldn't that be true about every human in existence?"

"Evasion," Heston said. "All right. Explain to me why you break people when you fight."

"Break people?" Jerryck stood. "Tajor doesn't break people. I was told he doesn't fight at all."

"Because when he does, he breaks who he fights with." Heston crossed his arms, staring at Tajor. "Explain."

"You said it yourself." Jerryck rolled up his notes. "He's too strong."

"And he's given me tiny clues in the past that he believes he's weak," Heston said. "Now be quiet. He's letting you do the distracting so he doesn't have to in order to evade."

"Really?" Jerryck hadn't thought of that. He looked over at Tajor.

"Explain," Heston repeated to him.

Tajor's aura buzzed. Jerryck recoiled. He said, "You don't want to explain this."

"I've explained it to Terrance," Tajor said. "Just last week, I also explained to Nita. Isn't that enough?"

"No." Heston remained steadfast. "Explain to me. Now."

"Why don't you want to explain this?" Jerryck asked.

"Because it reveals something about himself," Heston said. "In case you haven't noticed, you get the most evasion and distraction from him if you try and dig into his personal business or his past. If I didn't know him so well, I'd have missed when he dropped the hints that he feels weak."

"How could you possibly feel weak?" Jerryck asked Tajor. "Is delusion part of your curse or something?"

"No, weakness is." The buzzing coming from Tajor ceased. "I'm at half my strength. When I'm agitated, I miscalculate how much force to apply. And no, I don't like revealing my past, for very specific reasons. Which Terrance agrees with. So, don't ask me anymore."

Heston nodded slowly. "We'll leave you be. For now."

Tajor bolted for the door, faster than he had after the general staff meeting. Heston said to Jerryck, "I'm surprised you noticed this about him."

Jerryck rolled up his notes. "It was the reaction in his aura."

"Here's a tip that I'm sure you haven't noticed," Heston said. "And it's something you'll need to watch for. When he's agitated, he stops asking questions. He starts answering them and giving orders."

"Wouldn't giving orders mean he's making decisions?" Jerryck asked.

"He makes more decisions than he realizes," Heston said. "It's just when he's aware of it and over-thinking all the possible consequences that he freezes up. In this new position, more people are going to be relying on him. He'll be in more variety of situations. Pay attention. Because if he ever flips from asking constant questions to answering and ordering, something's wrong. Do whatever he tells you."

Chapter 39

"**T**HIS IS BORING." Zev leaned away from the book so far that his arms flopped backward. If he had gone any limper, he might have melted off the stool.

"Sit up," Jerryck said. Again. He'd lost count how many times he'd said it that week. That day. That hour. "It doesn't matter how boring it is. It's necessary."

Zev didn't sit up. "It's just talking about auras and stuff."

Jerryck impatiently tapped the book. "These are your basic fundamentals."

"I already know all this stuff." Zev pushed the book away. It slid across the worktable just enough to bump the salve Jerryck had cooling there.

"Zev!" Jerryck hurried around the table to it, making sure it wasn't jostled too much. "This has to be still, or it doesn't set right."

The salve had already formed a film over the surface. That protected the fluid underneath from too much jostling. It should be fine. This time. Better to double check. He gathered just enough energy to test the congealing process, how it was progressing, whether it had been interrupted, if it was developing resistance to the magic he intended to put on it.

"Like this?" Zev asked, holding out his right hand, a wad of his aura swirling around it in a balled up, writhing mass.

Jerryck stared at the hand, as if he could see the raw magic swirling uncontrolled. "What are you doing."

"You gather energy around your hand, right?" Zev shot him a smile. "Like this?"

"No, not like that." Jerryck worked at keeping his voice calm. "Slowly absorb that back into yourself. Little by little, very slowly."

"But…"

"Very, very slowly," Jerryck repeated. "Get it started before it escapes you and blows something up and you hurt yourself and end up leaking your aura out of a tear around your hand."

Zev drew his hand back in to himself. "I can hurt myself doing this?"

"If you don't do it properly, there is the potential, yes. Now, slowly draw it back in. Not your hand, the energy you put around it."

"How do I do that?"

"The same way you put it there, just the other direction."

"You can't just tell me?"

"Everyone does it differently," Jerryck said. "If I tell you what it's like for me, it won't necessarily work for you. This is why you have to study your basics before you apply them. Now, whatever you did to collect your energy around your hand like that, go backwards, reabsorb it back into the rest of you."

Zev frowned down at his hand. His brows drew in tighter and tighter, his face squeezing more in concentration. The globule mess of energy began to ebb away, spreading out to the rest of his aura and calming down. Jerryck let out a breath of relief and leaned on the solid worktable.

"You can't jump ahead like this." He scolded his nephew. "You didn't read until after you learned your alphabet and the sounds each letter makes. You didn't learn to calculate math until you knew the values of numbers."

"What do numbers and letters have to do with magic?" Zev asked. "You mean for reading spells and knowing how much energy to use?"

"No. They're basic." Jerryck resisted the urge to tear out his hair. "You can't do more complicated things until you have your basics mastered."

The door to the workroom opened and Marla entered. She looked at the two of them and hesitated just inside the door. She glanced back behind her, and then tentatively said, "Um… Can I be here now? I… I did my chores."

"Let Zev finish what he's doing," Jerryck told her. "Then you can spend time with him."

That was the deal they had struck. Leanne woke Zev every morning and made him do menial chores around the tower. After breakfast, he attended class with all the other palace children. When he was released a couple of hours after lunch, Jerryck gave him a lesson. They had to finish before Marla completed her afternoon chores, because then she had permission to come spend time with her big brother. If they weren't done by then, Jerryck always cut the lesson short to prevent her from picking up anything that she shouldn't. It had been a week or so, and it had worked so far.

He made sure that Zev reabsorbed the mess he'd made, then turned back to his own projects to give the kids time. He was in full preparation for the fast approaching season of flu, colds, sniffles, coughs, and sore throats. If they were fortunate, perhaps they could avoid pneumonia this year.

All the preparation was better finished long before the weather turned cold, and the rains turned to snow. He preferred at least a month leeway in case it came early. That way, he was ahead of the rise in demand for the herbs and supplies required for the salves, potions, and medicines.

He measured various powders together that were general health boosters and disease fighters and mixed them. He stored that in a jar for later, to use in conjunction with magic that he could cast specific to a person's need. And that used up all of some of the powders. He fetched his stepladder from the back to retrieve herbs from the rafters above to grind more.

The kids moved out of his way and curled up under a window. Their voices carried well in the small space, getting trapped in the cone of the roof above their heads. No one ever seemed to realize how well voices and sounds carried upward.

"I don't understand what he meant," Zev was saying. "It makes no sense and has nothing to do with it."

"Sure, it does," Marla responded. "It uses the same kind of thinking. You can't spell words if you don't know which sounds to put in them, so you have to study which letters make which sounds. And if you don't know which parts of your aura to use for what kinds of spells, you don't know how to put that together right either."

"Hmm," Zev grunted, chin in hands. "That kind of makes more sense. I hadn't thought of it that way."

Jerryck stood in frozen horror on the ladder, looking down at them. Zev had the book in his lap. Jerryck had missed that when they'd moved out of his way. They weren't discussing his lesson. Were they? He said, "What are you doing?"

"She's helping me figure this out." Zev held up the book. "She's really good at it, and it makes more sense to her than it does to me. She says it the way she understands it, and it sounds like when you say it, but easier for me to get it right. For some reason, I remember it better when I share it with her."

"How long have you been doing this?" Jerryck stepped down to the floor, clenching the string of the tied herb bundle so hard his knuckles turned white.

"Since you started teaching me," Zev said.

"I've learned lots." Marla beamed proudly. "I know that magic is powered by a person's aura. And that makes sense, because now I know why you look different after you do a lot of magic that makes you tired."

Jerryck narrowed his eyes at her. "Different how?"

"I don't know." She shrugged, her smile wavering. "Just... different."

"Can you see auras?"

"I know what that is now." Her smile reinvigorated. "I used to wonder why people have color clouds around them when they got really upset, or really happy, or really... er... something. I had to squint extra hard to see it even a little, even when they shined the brightest, but I could do it. I stopped, though. I don't think anybody else can. I thought I was weird, maybe just my imagination. But now I know what it is, and I know why they couldn't see it, and it's not my imagination, so I can go ahead and do it again."

"No, no!" Jerryck waved his arms at her, nearly knocking over the ladder. He grabbed it, closing it up. "Don't do that."

"Why?" Zev asked, as his sister's smile faded entirely. "I've never met any other girl that can do this. She's special."

Jerryck stuffed the ladder in the back and tossed the herb bundle on the counter by his mortar and pestle. Then he turned around to give the kids his full attention. "Have you told anyone about this?"

"No," they both said at once. Then Zev asked, "Do you think we should?"

"No." Marla scowled at him. "They'll ask me questions. I don't want them to. It's scary sometimes."

"The questions are scary?" Jerryck asked. That wasn't the part that scared him the most. "Or what people would do if they found out?"

"Not the questions…" She turned her face away, looking down at the floor. "And I don't care what people do."

She didn't know. She couldn't possibly know what would happen if people found out what she could do. And he wasn't about to tell her. He knelt down, putting his face at her level. "Can you tell me what's scary?"

She shook her head.

Jerryck put his hands on her shoulders. "Marla, please let me help you. Tell me what's scary."

"No!" She wriggled away from him and fled the room. Zev started after her, calling her name.

Jerryck stood and grabbed his arm. "Tell me."

"I promised her I wouldn't tell anyone."

"You have to. This could be important."

"I don't see how." Zev pulled away, not quite freeing himself from Jerryck's grip. "It's not what she thinks. She's too sweet for that."

"For what?"

"She thinks that sometimes she makes bad things happen when she's sleeping."

"Like what?"

"I promised I wouldn't tell. And it's not true anyway. She loves people. She would never hurt anyone." Zev shook his arm free.

He left the room calling for Marla. When the boy's voice reached the bottom of the stairs and left the tower, Jerryck turned to his shelves and hit his books with a fury.

Flipping through page after page, he looked up every reference he could find to sleep magic. He'd only ever given a cursory study to it before. He didn't use it. He knew how to detect it while active. He knew a little about how to preemptively defend against it. He didn't know how to tell if someone was using it on accident.

The books gave him information on the advantages and disadvantages of sleep magic. They gave specifics on the types of spells, from the easiest to the most difficult. They gave information concerning what kinds of controls to apply to the person going into the sleep state. All of it assumed the magic-user did it on purpose, not accidentally.

He should have known. With as much fruitless searching and studying he'd done to try and figure out his own accidents, he should have known his books would have nothing about accidental sleep magic.

Tajor came into the workroom with a plate of food. He set it on one of the open books on the worktable. "Your wife sent this."

"Why?" Jerryck frowned at where Tajor had set the plate. He moved it off the book to the tabletop.

"Look out your window," Tajor said. "You missed supper again."

Jerryck looked. The sun was setting. He'd be trying to read in the dark within half an hour if he didn't light a lamp.

"Also, your sister is mad at you." Tajor picked up one of the books and glanced at it. "She said if you're going to upset her daughter like you did today, she's not going to let her come up here anymore."

"Did her daughter say why she was upset?"

"You'd have to ask your sister, but the impression I got was she did not." Tajor looked over some of the other open books. "Are you taking up a new line of study?"

"No." Jerryck flipped the book shut one by one.

"Looking for something?"

"No." Jerryck stacked the books to put them away.

"Anyone ever tell you that you're rotten at lying?"

Jerryck sighed. He leaned on the table, gripping the thick edge. He was reacting out of habit and fear. Tajor wasn't going to hurt Marla. And he knew as much or more about magic than any other person Jerryck had met. If there was a chance he could help, the risk to Marla was lower with him than anyone else. Jerryck asked, "Do you know how to prevent someone from accidentally casting magic in their sleep without drawing the attention of anyone around them?"

"Methods of prevention depend on the magic type."

"Sleep magic." Jerryck took the stack of books to his shelf.

"That's a method of implementation, not a type," Tajor said. He waved around the book he still had in his hand. "Not everything listed here has to be cast while sleeping. That's just when some people have the easiest time accomplishing it because of their super relaxed state. There are lots of different kinds of magic that can slip through when you're in that kind of mode. That's where control comes in."

"How can you possibly maintain control while you're sleeping?" Jerryck snagged the book from Tajor.

"The more control you have while you're awake, the more likely you'll maintain control while you sleep. Why? Have you had an accident in your sleep?'

"No."

"Your niece?"

"Of course not." Jerryck retorted a little too quickly. He shoved the last book into its place on the shelf. "My niece is no witch. She's never had anything to do with magic, and she never will."

"Did I mention that you're not good at lying?"

"She's not going to hurt anyone."

"How do you know? You can't even predict whether or not *you're* going to hurt someone, and you've had plenty of formal training. How much is she going to get?"

"She can't use magic if she's never taught how to do anything with it."

"Like tricksters don't?"

"Tricksters are taught by each other. And they only do small things. She can use enough self-control to keep from doing small things, or hide them, or cover them up. She still won't do anything serious that will expose her."

"Like you didn't?" Tajor smirked. "I heard the rumor about the day your parents died, what you did with magic, with no formal training. The rumors vary on exactly what predator it was that ate them, but everyone says you made it explode. Why do you think people are afraid of you when you're angry?"

"I can't train her." Jerryck hung his head. "Do you know what would happen if word of it got out?"

"Why would you let word get out?"

"How could I *not*?"

"When you started searching for the magic-user that poisoned the water, did you do it the normal, direct way? Or did you use a different, more round-about method?"

"What's that got to do with my niece?"

"Can't you treat her situation in a round-about way too? Teach her in ways that aren't normal, not direct? Surely you must know other female magic-users. Maybe you could get some advice from them."

"I don't know any that are alive." Jerryck crossed his arms.

"Not even the shamaness that visited a few months ago? She looked pretty alive to me."

"That's different. She's a shamaness."

"So? It's still magic. Just a different focus and method."

"It's a method I can't teach because I know nothing about it."

"Absolutely nothing? Or did she show you a little something when she was here?"

"I blew up my workroom with what she showed me!" Jerryck threw his hands up. "I can't teach my niece to blow up my workroom!"

"Has she ever blown anything up?"

"Well… no."

"Have you blown anything up since?"

"I haven't used it since."

"Not even when you touched my aura in Shontarra? When you reacted to me attempting to refuse an order?"

"So maybe I have used it a time or two since," Jerryck admitted.

"And no accidents," Tajor said. "Is this something your niece could use to exercise and gain a little control?"

"I don't know," Jerryck said. "Maybe. I would need more control over it before I teach it."

"Want some help?" Tajor offered.

Jerryck nodded.

Tajor led him through an exercise that had him purposely sensing a few of the objects around the room. He enjoyed it as much as he had when the shamaness led him through it. He would have given in to temptation again, and gone further, if Tajor hadn't threatened to start breaking his tools again.

Over the next few weeks, they slowly went through progressively more sensitive exercises. When Jerryck got good at closing his eyes and feeling objects in his immediate vicinity, Tajor started moving things around on him.

Before long he could tell what had been moved, the moment it happened, and where it was moved to.

He started casting minor spells on some of the objects. Then he had to concentrate on the aura of the spell, apart from the item it was on. As soon as he could do that, Tajor started snuffing them out one by one. Jerryck had to identify which one purely by sensing.

As Jerryck progressed, he taught everything to Marla. She practiced with Zev. That increased his control, and his interest. He began to safely cast the most minor of spells.

They fell into a new routine. Zev worked hard enough to get a spell cast before Marla came up to the tower. Then she spent time figuring out what he had done just by sensing auras. His complaints of boredom disappeared, and he developed a new fascination for studying.

Until the day Marla didn't come.

Zev said he would talk to her at supper. But when he came back, he stormed angrily through the room, and refused to talk about it.

Marla didn't come the next day either. Or the next. Zev's progress flagged. The days turned into a week, and still no Marla. Jerryck repeatedly asked Zev why she no longer came. All the boy ever did was growl about his mama's strictness and how she didn't understand what was truly important.

Chapter 40

"**K**ENDRA!" JERRYCK MARCHED through the kitchens. Everyone bent over their many various tasks or scurried out of his way. No one looked at him. Not even long enough to point him toward his sister. He called for her again. "Kendra!"

Leanne wended her way between the prepping tables, wiping her hands on a small towel and then slinging that over her shoulder as she got to him. She drew him off to the side, out of everyone's way. "You look upset. What's wrong?"

"I need a word with my sister." Jerryck looked over at all the heads turned away from him. "That's what's wrong. Where is she?"

Leanne kept him moving, turning in to a storage space filled from floor to ceiling with barrels and wooden bins of dried foodstuffs, beans, rice, lentils, and grains, among other things. She said, "Your sister is in a foul mood, has been for over a week. The only reason no one's asked you to come calm her down was because I told the head chef that you've been in a foul mood too."

"I have not!" Jerryck shouted. She hunched her shoulders, the color of a flush creeping up her face. He swallowed and lowered his voice. "All right, maybe a little."

"Did you have another fight with Zev?" she asked.

"Yes. Why? How did you know that?"

"Because that's why I had to head you off the other day," she said. "If you try and talk to her about having trouble making Zev get through his lessons, all she'll do is yell at you."

"I don't need to talk about Zev's lessons." Jerryck clenched his teeth. He glanced out into the kitchen. He didn't see anyone nearby, and there was a lot of noise out there to cover anything he said. Still, he lowered his voice even more. "I need Marla to come back. He was doing fine until she stopped coming."

"Marla's in trouble," Leanne said.

"For over a week?"

"For however long it takes until she admits why she tried to skip class and get Zev to do the same."

Kendra came to the room. She stopped right in the doorway, putting one hand on either side as if blocking the way out. Skewering him with a glower, she spoke with a low and dangerous tone. "What do you think you're doing coming into my kitchens and disturbing my workers like this?"

"Why did Marla try to skip class?" Jerryck asked.

Kendra's pitch raised. "That's why you disrupted everything?"

"I need her to come back every day," Jerryck spoke quietly again. Kendra's grip tightened on both sides of the door frame. He pressed on anyway. "Have you asked why she tried to skip class?

"Of course, I have!" she snapped. She glanced behind herself, then let go of the door frame to step inside the storage and stick her face right in his. She whispered, "She said she dreamed the Prince of Shontarra was murdered and she just wanted to talk to Zev about it."

"You don't think she dreamed that?"

"I don't think that's why she tried to skip class," Kendra whispered. "She's had nightmares plenty of times and not acted this way."

"She always had more time to talk to him before." Leanne's voice was nearly a murmur. "And she did say this dream felt bigger than any others."

"No bigger than the one she had before the water went bad last spring." Kendra somehow kept a bite in her tone even through a whisper. "And she didn't try to skip class for that one either. She didn't even act this way with the nightmare she had the day before her papa died. So why should I believe it's making her misbehave now?"

Jerryck half turned away, worrying at his lower lip with his fingers. Zev had said Marla feared she was making bad things happen in her sleep. But she hadn't caused her own papa's death. She certainly hadn't poisoned an entire river. What if she was just seeing things right before, or just as, they happened? Like a gifted scryer.

The last he knew, the Shontese prince was fine. Maybe a little crazy since the death of his last son, but physically in good health. But if someone murdered him...

"I need to check something." Jerryck stepped around his sister and walked out.

Chamberlain Malk would know the health of the Shontese Prince. He was the man in charge of foreign relations. Jerryck wound his way up through the palace to the floor where Malk's office was located before remembering the man was rarely ever there.

With all the officials and administrators that worked in this part of the palace, the wide corridor was filled with traffic. Jerryck snagged one of the many pages as the lad ran by and asked, "Where is the Chamberlain?"

"In the king's office," the lad said, turning to talk to Jerryck without stopping, making him walk backward. "With him, the princess, and the priad."

With that, the lad turned forward and ran off in the direction he'd been headed. Jerryck navigated the flow of moving people to the wide stairs at the end of the corridor up to the floor where the king's offices were. On the landing, the large vases of spring flowers had been replaced with trellises of autumn ivies. There were just as many people sitting on the benches, doing whatever it was people did while sitting in a crowd with uncomfortable, fancy clothes on. Jerryck ignored them all and moved on into the reception area outside the king's office.

"Lord Jerryck," the king's scheduler said. "Were you sent for? Or do you need him?"

The door flew open. Nita stomped out, face full of indignation. Jerryck looked inside. Terrance was pinching the bridge of his nose with his thumb and forefinger. Tajor was yawning. And Malk was covering his mouth with a hand and twitching like he was chuckling silently.

Malk saw Jerryck and motioned for him to come inside. As Jerryck entered he asked, "Is everything all right? What is she mad about this time?"

"Not what," Malk said. "Who. The answer is Tajor. She's mad at Tajor."

"What for?" Jerryck asked.

Tajor smirked. "That's a different question entirely, isn't it?"

Terrance lowered his hand from his face. "He gave very logical and sound reasons why she should stay here and continue her training, instead of going to Shontarra."

"She hated it there," Jerryck said. "Why would she want to go?"

"To attend Andreno's coronation," Terrance said. "She feels bad for him and wants to give him encouragement."

"Coronation," Jerryck repeated the word. He blinked a couple of times, letting the word sink in. "And Prince Sanbralio?"

Terrance frowned at him. "Did you not receive the message I sent you an hour or so ago?"

"I... um... well..." How was Jerryck supposed to admit that he had negligently ignored it? "The page said it wasn't a summons. I had him write it down for me to read later."

"So you didn't get the message," Terrance said.

"I was a little busy." The excuse was stupid, and only half true. He'd been busy being frustrated with his nephew. Nothing serious.

"Prince Sanbralio took ill a few weeks ago," Terrance said. "He didn't recover. We received a messenger earlier today that arrangements are now in progress for Andreno's ascension to the throne immediately following Sanbralio's funerary memorial."

"We will, of course, send an emissary," Malk added. "Nita wanted to be that emissary."

Jerryck stared at them for a few moments, still absorbing that his niece's dream had been reality. They stared back at him. Was he supposed to say something?

"Are you all right?" Tajor asked. "You're looking a bit piqued."

"This shouldn't be all that much of a shock to you," Malk said. "You were there. Surely you saw the old prince's declining health."

"He died of illness?" Jerryck asked.

"Yes," Malk said. "Specifically, pneumonia, alongside just sheer wasting away from self-neglect and depression."

"He wasn't murdered?" Jerryck double checked.

"Of course not," Malk said. "Do you have any idea what a mess there would be, the kind of investigations that would be going on, the delays in the new coronation? Why would you ask something like that?"

"No reason," Jerryck lied. Tajor raised an eyebrow at him. He backed slowly to the door. "No reason at all."

He fumbled with the handle of the door and escaped the room before anyone else pressed him for an answer. He almost bumped into a couple of people in the reception area, so he paid more attention until he got out of the press of people, up the stairs to higher floors, and into the corridor with the entrance to his tower.

The rooms here were all for guests, usually the ones with magical talents. At the moment, they were empty. Alone, Jerryck leaned against the wall and let out his breath. Marla had been correct that the Shontese prince had died. She was incorrect that he had been murdered. Had she scryed it partially, and then surmised the rest because she falsely thought she was to blame?

Footsteps approaching had Jerryck looking up the corridor. It was Tajor. He stopped in front of Jerryck and crossed his arms.

"What do you want?" Jerryck asked.

Tajor raised that one eyebrow again. "How about the truth?"

"I don't know what you're talking about," Jerryck said.

"Do you remember that time I told you that you're rotten at lying?" Tajor rocked back on his heels. "It still holds true."

Jerryck turned his back to Tajor and stepped inside his tower. "Don't you have other things do to? You're the priad now. You have to have something more important than bothering me."

"The king sent me after you." Tajor followed him in. "Did I mention that you're rotten at lying? Or do you really think I'm the only one who can tell?"

"He didn't say anything."

"You ran out of the room before he could," Tajor said. "Is this about your niece?"

"No! It isn't. You can go now." Jerryck tried pushing him back out of the tower. He may as well have pushed against a tree trunk.

"Not ready to try telling the truth yet?" Tajor asked.

Jerryck slumped. He put a hand on the stone outer wall and tried a distraction. "Why would you think this is about my niece?"

"Because her magic abilities are one of the only things I've ever heard you lie about," Tajor said. "And protecting her is the only thing I've ever seen you act this uncharacteristically unreasonable over. You don't normally get physical, and this is the first time you've ever tried pushing me."

He should have known a distraction wouldn't work. Tajor was a master at giving distractions. He wasn't subject to them.

"Jerryck. The truth?"

"She dreamed someone murdered Prince Sanbralio," Jerryck murmured. "So she's only half right."

"That's an assumption," Tajor said. "There are ways to murder someone without getting caught. Especially if it puts you in power and you can hamper anyone trying to look into it. Nita's studies aren't the only reason I suggested she stay here."

"You don't trust Andreno?"

"Not one little tiny bit," Tajor said. "He's a conniver and a schemer. He had eyes on the throne even while we were there. Some of the guards made wagers on how long Sanbralio would live after Andreno was officially named heir. And if this had happened to a noble in Brend, I guarantee you that this death would be seriously investigated with the idea of possible murder."

"But Malk said it wasn't murder."

"Which is what the public is being told," Tajor said. "It's a little outside of our jurisdiction. There's nothing we can do, except guard ourselves against him."

"It's possible that Marla saw all this correctly," Jerryck admitted aloud. "Like a gifted scryer having a dream against their will."

Tajor nodded. "Exactly like that. Which should be a relief for you. Scrying is easier to hide than some other magical talents, like making things explode."

That was true enough. Jerryck leaned his back against the wall. The smooth firmness of the stone seeped through his shirt and a weight dropped off his shoulders. Now that he knew what the problem was, he could teach her how to hide this easily enough.

"You should go talk to your sister." Tajor opened the door to step out of the tower. "And I'll go let the king know not to worry about you."

Jerryck straightened up and went back down to the kitchens. This time, people looked him in the eye and greeted him with smiles. They quickly pointed him to Kendra and Leanne. People just as quickly filled the two women's jobs when he said he wanted to speak to them privately. Kendra took them down to one of the basement storages filled with vegetable bins and the dank smell of roots.

"You're calmer," Kendra said after she had shut them in. She set the lamp she brought on one of the bins. "I assume you found whatever it is you went to check on."

"Marla is scrying in her sleep," Jerryck said. "Prince Sanbralio is dead, just like she dreamed."

"You didn't teach her this?" Leanne asked.

"I'm terrible at scrying," Jerryck said. "You haven't seen it, but I have to take a nasty potion to help me get it started. If you ever smell me mixing up that concoction, you'd understand the reason most magicians prefer to work at the tops of towers. It's so that the high breezes can carry away the stink of some of what we have to work with."

"I already figured that." Leanne wrinkled her nose. "I've smelled some pretty terrible things in your workroom."

"That potion is worse than most," Kendra said. "Sometimes, he pukes after he drinks it and has to start all over again. And the potion isn't the only reason he avoids scrying. Sometimes, he has trouble coming back. Old Heldavio, his mentor, gave up trying to teach him to scry when he kept transporting himself to the spot he was supposed to look at."

Jerryck didn't mention the void. He had never told her about it. Every time he tried to scry, that void always opened up around the edges of his vision. The longer he kept at it, the closer it got to him, the stronger it drew him. The closer it got, the more distinctly he heard pleading, screams, and cries of anguish coming up from it. That was probably why he kept accidentally moving his body with magic. It was a defense. If his body was there, he could see it with his eyes. He wouldn't have to scry it.

Kendra stared into the lamp. "I suppose I should have expected this."

"Why would you expect her to have magic?" Jerryck asked. "Just because I have it doesn't mean any of my nieces will."

"She got it from me," Kendra said.

Jerryck nodded. "Through you. From the same source I got it from, whatever that was."

"From me," Kendra repeated. "You and I both got it from our mama."

"Our mama wasn't a witch," Jerryck said.

Kendra looked up at him, the lamp casting long shadows on her face. "She was running for her life when she stumbled into that village and met our papa. Heldavio never told you all this?"

"No."

Kendra hugged herself. "Aunt Chetty told him, the night before we left the village."

"Aunt Chetty?" Leanne asked.

"The innkeeper's wife," Jerryck said. "She wasn't really our aunt. We just called her that. She was our mama's best friend. She took us in when our parents died."

"Mama had a passive ability," Kendra said. "She enhanced other people's skills. That's why Papa was so good at healing people with all his herbs. It wasn't just him. But it shielded her from anyone looking."

"Chetty told Heldavio all this?" Jerryck asked.

Kendra rubbed her hands up and down her arms. "She told him because he already knew about me."

"Knew what?"

She looked him right in the eye and said, "I have passive magic ability."

He snorted at the absurdity. "No, you don't."

"You don't know about her passive magic?" Leanne stared at him wide eyed. "I thought you knew."

"Kendra doesn't have passive magic," Jerryck said.

"Why do you think people tend to do whatever I tell them?" Kendra gave him a droll look. "Even you did, when you were a bratty little kid."

"Because you yell at them if they don't," Jerryck said.

"That's a cover." Kendra laughed. "That and I'm so used to getting anything I want. It's made me short tempered when it doesn't happen fast enough. Didn't you ever wonder why the villagers depended on me so much to keep you under control?"

"Wait, wait, wait…" Jerryck waved his hands around, shaking his head. "This can't be true. Heldavio had taken the oaths to the Gathering. And one of those is to kill any woman he finds that can do magic."

"Heldavio said one of the reasons he came north to be the court magician to King Clarrence was to avoid taking the White Seat on the Gathering," Kendra said. "At the time, I had no idea what he was talking about. He said all I needed to understand was that he disagreed with the way they treated women. His healing skills made killing anyone repulsive to him, completely against his nature. After we came here, I watched him shelter several of them, and then help them escape out of Brend."

Leanne started giggling. She put a hand to her mouth, but the giggles kept coming. In between them, she managed some words. "I'm sorry. It's not funny. We've all really gone against set traditions, haven't we?"

"You know about this?" Jerryck said to her.

"I don't keep secrets from Leanne," Kendra said.

"Just from your own brother?"

"I thought you knew." Kendra threw up her hands. "You're so good at knowing whether or not anyone has the slightest magical ability, we both thought you knew and just never said anything to protect me."

"I didn't know," Jerryck said.

"Well, now you do." Kendra smoothed her kitchen apron and picked up the lamp. "I can teach Marla what I know about keeping passive magic hidden. How do you plan to help her? And what do you need from us to help with that?"

"Keep her coming up to the tower every day," Jerryck said. "I'm teaching her control."

Chapter 41

"**I** FIGURED IT OUT." Marla grinned triumphantly. She pointed at the candle Zev had lit for her. "You tried to trick me. I thought you lit it with magic. You made an illusion that changed the color of the candle instead."

"I didn't think it would take you this long." Zev looked up from the book he was studying for tomorrow's spell. "I couldn't get the color right. That's why it's all blotchy."

"I've seen lots of candles that are all blotchy," Marla said. She leaned in and squinted at the candle. "I guess not quite that blotchy, though."

Jerryck chuckled. He hadn't had much to laugh about lately. The palace was agitated. Possibly because Nita had been moody and grumpy ever since the Brendish emissary's caravan left for Shontarra. Possibly it was just Jerryck's perception, a reflection of his own state of mind.

He had finally received some response letters from the archipelago. Not that it mattered much anymore, now that he couldn't use the excuse that he was searching for an apprentice. He had yet to open them. Instead, he sat listing every instance he could think of when his sister had changed someone's mind, gotten them to do something they didn't want to. The more the evidence stacked up, the more troubling it was that he hadn't figured this out.

"Have any dreams last night?" Zev asked Marla. He had sworn that she would respond best to him asking, so he'd been told to ask every day.

Her smile faded. She shrugged one shoulder, turned away, and blew out the candle. Jerryck looked up from his list. "What did you dream?"

"I don't know, exactly," she murmured. "It's confused."

"What's confused?" Zev asked.

"The dream was," Marla said. "I don't understand it. Some of it made sense. There were people. But they talked funny. I don't know anything they said. And they were fighting. And lying by how they were dressed."

The bells attached to the underside of the cupboards chimed. A magic-user had just entered the palace. Jerryck frowned at his list. He would have to hide it, in case whoever it was came up to his tower. Should he also try to keep them away from his sister? Kendra had done just fine on her own so far. Maybe he worried too much.

"Who is it this time?" Zev bounced up and down on the only squeaky spot on the floor. "Is it someone trying to impress Tajor, like a few days ago? That was really funny. Can I watch again?"

"How should I know who it is?" Jerryck folded the list horizontally in half, concealing the writing. Maybe making it wasn't such a good idea after all. It put him in the wrong mood to greet a fellow magician.

"Do I have to stay here again while you go greet him?" Zev asked. "Darren said a lot of apprentices greet guests for their mentors. Am I ever going to get to do that too? I want to go see who's here. When am I gonna get to do stuff like that?"

"How about now?" Jerryck said. "Why not? Go ahead."

"Really?" Zev bounced all the way to his feet. "You're not going to say I have to learn proper protocols first? Darren said there are protocols."

"Just be respectful," Jerryck said.

"I will." Zev leaped out the door and ran down the stairs.

Jerryck looked around the room. If he was going to have company, he should tidy up some. He sent Marla on her way and picked up everything from Zev's lesson. Hopefully, whoever it was wouldn't stay past supper. If they didn't leave on their own, Jerryck could always use the meal as an excuse to get rid of them. He glanced at the late afternoon sunlight angling through the window, wishing the day was closer to supper.

Much sooner than expected, the chimes told Jerryck someone entered the tower. A minute or so later, Zev burst into the workroom. "It's a lady from the Chemwanitz Mountains. Her name is, um, Kasila, or Samila, or something like that."

Jerryck thought of his shamaness friend. "Sakila?"

"Something like that," Zev said. "She came with the heir of Tarn. And I'm supposed to tell you to go meet her in the royal parlor."

"Not the White Room?" Jerryck asked. "She wants to use the royal parlor?"

"I don't know." Zev shrugged. "She didn't act like she cared. That's where the chancellor told her to go meet with you. Oh, and he said to remind you that the heir's name is Grennan."

"I know his name." Jerryck headed out the door.

The royal parlor was a cozy room near the king's private chambers. At the end of the corridor, it had large windows that let plenty of light spill across the wide, plush couches. Colorful tapestries softened the walls. This time of year, a fire always burned on the hearth. If Jerryck had thought about it, he'd have known that was where the heir of Tarn would go with any guest he brought. Terrance had only two nephews, both of them the sons of the Tarn Premiere, the late queen's only surviving brother.

By the time Jerryck arrived Nita was already there, her bad mood gone. She bubbled happily at her cousin and the shamaness. Terrance entered on Jerryck's heels. He barely had the time to get out a proper greeting for his nephew when Heston and Tajor also came in.

"I hope you don't mind, I asked your chancellor to send these two," Grennan said to Terrance. "My father sent me to inform you of an incident that took place. Shamaness Sakila helped look into it. He asked her if she preferred delivering her findings through me, or if she wanted to come herself."

"I wanted to come see all of you again," she said. "And bring better news than last time. What happened was bad, but there is something that I think might help you."

Terrance sat. "What happened?"

"One of our villages was raided," Grennan said. "The invaders were fair featured, but so are a lot of people that close to the mountains. They wore Chemwanitz war paint, but no one recognized them as anyone from any of the nearby tribes. There had been no threats, no demands for punitive payments, no disputes, no warning signs at all. They just all of a sudden attacked in the middle of the night for no conceivable reason."

"My tribe was closer to them than Premiere Grinnald," Sakila said. "We got there first to give help. My sons tracked them. They came through a portal in a box canyon, went down to the village, then back through the same portal."

"How many attackers?" Heston asked.

"Reports vary," Grennan said. "The people were panicked and confused. We're guessing anywhere between ten and twenty-five."

"How much damage?" Terrance asked.

"Most of the men are injured or dead," Grennan said. "Most of their winter supplies are destroyed. And that's another thing. Any Chemwanee I know of would take the supplies, not destroy them."

"Yes, this doesn't fit right." Terrance furrowed his eyebrows and rubbed a finger across his forehead just above them. "Does your father need assistance for his village?"

Grennan shook his head. "We have them covered. And our Chemwanitz friends have offered assistance as well. That village has strong ties with them. Family ties even. They'll be well taken care of."

Terrance turned to Heston. "I'm sure you'll ask for more details, but the generalities sound exactly the same."

"Except for the added detail of a portal," Heston said.

"The same as what?" Grennan asked.

"There was another village that was raided," Terrance said. "Much farther to the north."

"There was?" That was news to Jerryck. Could these raids be what Marla dreamed? She said something about fighting. And talking funny. "Did they say anything?"

"Not that anyone reported," Grennan said.

"Same at the first village," Heston said. "Why?"

"Just wondering." Jerryck pulled at his lower lip. Maybe this wasn't what Marla had seen. Likely it wasn't. Usually a scryer's involuntary visions were about something that would affect the seer, even if indirectly. She had seen the death of the Shontese Prince. But that affected nations. A couple of backwater villages? Not likely. Mentioning it wouldn't solve the problem at hand.

"You think it's possible it's the same group?" Grennen asked.

"They're too far apart." Nita sat forward on the edge of the couch. "I've been to that other village. Given the time frame for both the attacks, and the distance they'd have to travel, they're too far apart."

"Unless they're traveling through a portal instead of overland," Heston said.

Jerryck shook his head. "Too much power. For possibly twenty-five men? Even for ten... How long did it take them to travel from the portal to the village and back?"

"There is more," Sakila said. "The vibrations of magic... the signature... this portal was opened by the same person who made the poison that was put in your river last spring."

Heston's chin tipped down, his eyes darkening. "You're certain?"

"Yes," she said.

Heston crossed his arms. "It could be the same group. Which means we have no way of knowing when or where they'll strike next."

"Two portals, for that many people," Jerryck said. "Kept open for how long?"

"The portal was almost a mile from the village," Sakila told him. "Give them several minutes to go from there to the village, some time to attack, and then the time to get back again. I know what you are thinking. That would take too much energy to keep it open for that long, even for one person to use. I am telling you, impossible or not, that is exactly what happened. And whoever did it was messy. They left a lot of energy behind when they closed it. Or I would not have found it at all."

"Excessive power usage—" Jerryck ticked points off on his fingers— "sloppy work, too many people, too much time... It's impossible for the same person to have opened a similar portal two weeks prior."

"Why?" Heston asked.

"Too much energy. Whoever opened the first portal wouldn't be able to open another like that for more than a couple of months."

"Magicians open repeated portals all the time," Heston said.

"For just a few people at a time. And the reason that kind of travel is so expensive is because they only do it one person per day at most. If you have, say, five people going through a portal, that magician won't open another portal for about five days or more. And they close it right away. They don't keep it open for more than a few minutes. Certainly not long enough for these raids."

"Except that it happened," Heston said.

"Not twice in two weeks," Jerryck replied.

"There are ways of replenishing energy that you haven't been taught," Tajor finally spoke up.

"And if I haven't been taught them—" Jerryck said— "it's because no one is taught them. Not in any lands that I know of."

"And does this also apply to learning how to mix the elements of fire and water in such a way that it will poison an entire river?" Tajor asked.

"I'm just saying it's unlikely that these two raids have anything to do with each other."

"Unlikely chances leave room for small possibility," Heston said. "And if they're not following normal protocols, we also don't have any clue where they'll strike next."

"What reason would they have for this?" Terrance sat back, his eyes unfocused in thought. "Neither raid took any food, animals, tools… nothing in the stores. They just destroyed them. Why?"

"Vengeance, thrill, challenge," Heston said. "It could be any number of reasons. Including stirring up trouble. Someone may be trying to turn us against the Chemwanee."

"Again," Terrance said. "Why?"

"That I don't know." Heston uncrossed his arms and held his hands out. "There are too many possibilities to list. I need more evidence for their motives. Who they are would help. I'll worry about this end of the problem. You should worry about prevention."

Terrance frowned up at him. "For a small attack that will take place we don't know where—or even when?"

"The only two places we know they've attacked are villages on the border with the mountains," Heston said.

"*If* it was the same people," Jerryck interjected.

Heston didn't even spare Jerryck a glance. "They were trying to pass themselves off as Chemwanitz warriors, wearing their paint and clothing, using their type of weapons. If they're establishing a pattern, they'll attack someplace similar."

"Assemble an advisory meeting," Terrance said. He pinched the bridge of his nose with his thumb and forefinger. "We need to figure out how to deal with this, just in case the unlikely is reality."

Chapter 42

AFTER SEVERAL DAYS, and many meetings, another messenger arrived at the palace. The first village raided had actually been the second. The premiere of the first village had taken time to debate over whether or not to alert the king. The oddities of the attack finally convinced him. Then the messenger had gotten caught up in bad weather, which had resulted in the message arriving at the palace after the other two.

All discussion in the boring meetings turned to defense and prevention. Several people insisted that Heston move all available troops to the Chemwanitz border to patrol. Heston flatly refused, saying it would leave the rest of the nation too vulnerable. Every time he refused people badgered Jerryck to do something about the situation.

"Like what?" Jerryck asked them.

"You're the magician," one man grumbled. "Think of something."

"Like what?" Jerryck repeated.

The more people pressed him for solutions, the more it irritated him. Terrance hadn't told them about the attackers using a portal. As far as they should be concerned, this was a military matter, not a magical one.

"Why don't we arm the populace and teach them to defend themselves?" Tajor asked. "Don't they already fend off dangerous fauna? Why not fend off raiders too?"

"Teach them to defend against *military* operations?" The same man who pressed Jerryck the most, now gasped in horror at Tajor. "We couldn't do that."

"Why not?" Tajor asked.

Responses erupted. Jerryck couldn't make heads or tails out of them individually, but the overall cacophony was full of outrage. It took them a couple of minutes to calm down enough to go back to harassing Heston about sending troops to the border, then on to harassing Jerryck to think of something.

The second time Tajor suggested arming and training the populace, he was told his sarcasm was ill-timed and unappreciated. The third time, a few people laughed and thanked him for lightening the mood. The fourth time, people started getting the idea that he really was serious.

In times past, no king would have entertained such an idea. It would create too much danger that the populace would rise up against the local authorities and the throne.

Terrance had made many changes since his coronation, most of them in honor of his late wife's wishes for the nation. Soldiers did their job properly, instead of acting like bullies and thugs. The palace was self-sustaining, freeing up tax money for improving roads, building bridges, and digging water canals that irrigated farmlands. Better education was available to a greater portion of the populace.

Aside from a few skirmishes here and there, they had been at peace with their neighboring nations for over a decade. People had been able to raise their children in safety, and they had grown loyal and content. There was less chance of any uprising now than ever before in the history of the nation.

Jerryck said as much the next time someone annoying demanded he 'do something.' With how much trouble they were giving Tajor for suggesting it, he probably should have expected the barrage of indignation and insults that washed over him for it.

After that, Terrance cut off the general staff and narrowed the dull meetings to just the core staff, without letting Jerryck skip any of them. He ordered Chancellor Herron to send out proclamations to every town and village along the border to lock up their winter stores and guard them day and night. He ordered General Heston to send some troops to patrol around the largest populations along the border, assisted by local scouts. He also ordered the villagers armed and trained, as Tajor suggested. Then he turned to Jerryck.

"Were you just irritated?" he asked. "Or can you really think of nothing to help?"

Jerryck crossed his arms. "Won't the scouts and patrols be enough?"

"They're no good if the enemy opens up a portal behind where they're looking," Heston said.

"This can't be the same group if they're all using portals," Jerryck insisted. Again.

Terrance sank into his chair, looking weary and drawn. He tended to skip food and sleep when things were going wrong. No one had asked Jerryck for a sleep aid, so he had assumed the king was sleeping fine. Perhaps he should have offered anyway.

"Pretend the unlikely is possible." Terrance rubbed at his eyes, ending by pinching the bridge of his nose. "Is there a way to prevent portals from opening around a town or village?"

"Yes," Jerryck said. "But which villages? And how many others would want the same thing? I can't do it for all of them. Not even if all the magicians in Brend helped. Which they wouldn't. Too many of them travel from town to town by portal."

"What about some kind of alert system?" Tajor asked. "You have alerts here in the palace for various things. Can't you give villages alarms for if a portal opens nearby?"

Jerryck sat back, running several possibilities through his mind. "I could probably come up with something like that. You'd have to give me some time to puzzle it out and make sure it works right."

"Do it," Terrance said.

Finally released from all the wretched meetings, Jerryck ran back up to his tower. He slowed on the way up the stairs. Then paused at the door to the bedroom. Kendra and Leanne had Sakila in there, and all three of them were giggling as only women could. When they saw Jerryck, Leanne blushed, and Kendra and Sakila giggled even harder.

He shook his head, mentally dismissing it. He probably wouldn't like whatever they were talking about anyway. He climbed the last flight up to his workroom. After several minutes, Sakila came up. By that time, Jerryck had his entire worktable covered with open books.

"What are you studying?" she asked.

Jerryck offered her the stool Zev normally used for his lessons. "Alerts for when portals open."

"Portals." Sakila sat. "I cannot make those. When I need to travel with magic, I have to have assistance from another."

"Me too, usually." Jerryck reached for pen, ink, and a stack of cheap paper for jotting notes. "I have a clear space at the bottom of the tower I keep for portals, so if I was someplace else and needed to get back here in a hurry, I could use that. But if I want to go out, I'm so bad at the necessary scrying beforehand, I'm safer traveling overland."

"At least you can open portals," Sakila said, leaning her forearms on the worktable. "You are much more powerful than I. I can scry. I cannot open a portal."

"I have to drink a nasty concoction to help me scry," Jerryck admitted weakness, wrinkling his nose just thinking about that horrid potion. "Otherwise I can't get out of my body to go see anything."

"Your sister told me about that," Sakila said. "Why leave your body? I do not leave my body to scry."

Jerryck's jaw slackened with surprise. "You don't?"

"That is…" she paused and thought for a few moments, "…projecting, I think is the word in your language. That is more difficult. I have never been able to do it well. There is a frightening nothingness when you do that."

"Yes," Jerryck said. Had he been doing it wrong all these years?

"Your sister asked me to help her daughter." Sakila sat up. "Is that all right with you?"

"She talked to you?"

"I asked after the girl. Kendra says she can scry."

"Normally she's here now." Jerryck fidgeted with the books. "I gave her and her brother the afternoon off. They'll be here tomorrow. You can come help then if you want."

"Thank you," Sakila said. "I will."

Sakila taught both the children gathering and releasing exercises for the energies in their auras. Zev gloated that he had discovered the exercise on his own, talking about the time he had gathered a wad of untamed energy around his hand that Jerryck had made him let go. His gloat disappeared when Sakila scolded him for gathering too much energy and made him use restraint. Every time he tried to ignore her, she applied the same calming magic she had used to help Jerryck when he had blown up his workroom.

The benefits of teaching this kind of control seemed obvious to Jerryck. So he encouraged his nephew to go through the exercises by doing them with him. It was harder work than he expected, and after the first couple of times he went to bed exhausted as if he had done a day of hard, physical labor. Since he apparently also needed this exercise, he made sure to continue.

When she went through scrying techniques with the children, Jerryck had next to no progress with that skill. He couldn't get himself to both relax, and sit rigid like she did. He couldn't clear his head of seeing his immediate surroundings, especially now that he'd gotten so used to feeling things with his aura. And when he tried shaping the energy of his aura to see beyond himself, he automatically started feeling disconnected, which Sakila always put a stop to and told him that was projecting, not scrying.

She needn't have put a stop to it. He wasn't going to leave his body. The only time he did that without the aid of a potion was on accident, not on purpose. All her discipline did was make the children laugh at him.

She tried helping him along, by letting him connect his aura with hers so he could feel exactly how she did it. All he ever got were flashes of partial images, a tree, the wall of a log building, a face disconnected from any person. He had no idea if these were real things, or just his imagination.

Frustrated, embarrassed, he tried it alone late one night after everyone else was in bed. He sat rigid. He did the best he could to turn off sensing the auras of everything around him. He gathered up the amount of energy Sakila recommended. He focused on a safe spot, the clear space at the bottom of his tower. Then he let the magic loose.

There was a blur of vision. Then he viewed the clear room at the bottom of the tower. It had worked! He looked all around the empty room, incredulous. It really had worked. He was scrying.

He looked over at the tower entrance, where he had the charms that signaled when someone entered. He could actually see the aura of the magic. He had one fleeting thought that he ought to retract to his body to double check that he was doing this right. But this was just too tempting, and too much fun. There was so much he could do in this state like this.

Gleefully, he went to check some of the other spells in the palace. This was going to make his job a lot easier. Flitting around the palace corridors, ignoring all the sleeping people, passing by the few people who worked the night shifts, no one bothered him in this state.

At one of the balcony doors, he noticed clouds gathering on the horizon. They looked an awful lot like the roiling, smokey nothingness of the void. But he only ever saw that when he was doing what Sakila said was projecting. That was always accompanied with a wrenching sensation and a feeling of being disconnected with his body. He never cast any active magic to get into that state, like he had for this scrying trip.

He told himself it was just a gathering storm, common in early winter. Everyone would wake in the morning to rain. And he moved on.

Still, he couldn't keep himself from glancing out every time he passed a window. It nagged at him. He went to the opposite side of the palace and looked out. The clouds were on the horizon there too, only a bit closer. That was a bad sign.

There was one way to know for certain. He went to the highest point, a tower near the center where the nation's crimson and gold banner flew every day, and was respectfully furled every night. There, he could see all around.

The roiling smoke rising up out of the void encircled the entire horizon. And it was creeping in. Terror punched through him. He couldn't hear any screaming or pleading. Yet. It was too far away. But he remembered it all too well.

He had slipped out of his body the first time he used magic. And he hadn't been able to get back. Kendra had picked him up, weeping, and dragged him back to the village. She was so little at the time she hadn't even been able to make the trip without stopping several times. He had watched, helpless, scrabbling and clawing, screaming and sobbing. No matter how hard he fought, that smoke grabbed him and pulled him in, kept him from regaining his body.

Until Magician Letz had come. He had walked into the room where Jerryck's little body lay. He lay down. His magic flared. His body had gone as limp as Jerryck's when he had stood up outside of it. He stretched out, with a thick rope of silver trailing from him to his body. Grabbing hold of Jerryck, he had pulled him back, thrust him into his body. And the void had disappeared from perception.

It still lurked. It was still there. Every time Jerryck projected. And all those years, he had thought projecting was scrying. Every time he had seriously tried to scry, terror had gripped him, dread at experiencing that void again. And he translocated instead, if he didn't drink a potion that forced himself to project.

He had only been trying to scry the bottom room of the tower. He should have stayed there rather than taking the time to traverse the palace. Or he should have gone and checked his body. If it was limp instead of rigid, he would have known immediately that he was projecting. That was the only place he should have gone. Or just not left the bottom room. That was it. He should never have left there. In fact, he should go there immediately as the first step to reconnecting with his body.

A wrenching jerk landed him back in the bottom of the tower. The familiar magic drain of an accident washed over him, and the weight of his body dragged at him.

Translocation. So much for scrying. He dragged himself back up the stairs, stopping several times to catch his breath.

After that he avoided Sakila's lessons. Claiming he had to spend more time working out the alert system, he turned his back to Sakila while she taught the children to scry.

"There are other ways for you to experience this," Sakila said.

"Or I could just not do it and focus on my job," Jerryck refused.

She tried again anyway. "I will do all the work. Then you could just see."

That was tempting. Still, he really did need to work on the alerts. That wasn't just an excuse. He continued studying and planning those instead of letting her show him other methods.

Chapter 43

NITA'S COUSIN left after a week. Sakila stayed, continuing to teach. Some evenings, Tajor would come up the tower and bully Jerryck to go through some of the exercises he learned from the shamaness, until he started doing them every evening on his own. Then Tajor just sat and talked with Sakila in her own language while Jerryck practiced. The evenings he didn't come up, Kendra and Leanne skipped the evening dancing, and held lengthy conversations with her in the bedroom. Whatever they always talked about, it made them laugh and giggle a lot.

Every morning, Jerryck hurried through as many of his palace duties as he could get to. Any spare moments when Sakila wasn't teaching, he spent on researching how to set up an alert for portal openings. It wasn't enough. He barely started narrowing down his options a couple of weeks after Nita's cousin left.

That afternoon, Sakila's scrying trip to her tribe started like normal. Both the children followed her with ease, seeing everything she saw. Jerryck sometimes could catch a glimpse or two, now and then. He still wasn't sure if it was actually scrying or just his imagination. Until he caught a flash of someone with a broken leg and Sakila gasped. Both the children startled out of their usual, stiff posture, and the scrying trip ended.

"I have to go home now," Sakila said.

"How are you going to do that?" Zev asked. "All the passes are filled with snow."

Sakila smiled at him. "I will go with magic."

Zev looked confused. "Didn't you say you can't open portals?"

Jerryck took a breath to say he would do it. She spoke first. "Before I came, I talked with the shaman from the tribe that neighbors mine. He is good at travel magic. He will get me there."

"Do you need anything to help you contact him?" Jerryck asked.

"I need to go outside," she said. "Someplace with trees is best. I need a stick from the part of the land I will use."

Jerryck turned away from his books and notes, giving her his full attention. "There's the orchard. I'm not sure if you'll find any sticks, though. The workers always go through and clean everything after their last harvest. Outside the palace wall, there's Aconi Grove a few miles away. That's more likely to have sticks lying around."

She stood from the stool she had been using. "That should work. Will you give me directions?"

"I'll do better than that," Jerryck said. "I'll take you."

He sent Zev running ahead to the stables to get horses ready. He must have assumed he was accompanying, because when Jerryck and Sakila arrived, three animals were saddled and waiting. Instead of arguing the matter, Jerryck shrugged it off. It might be good for Zev to see different uses for magic anyway. They rode quickly and arrived at the poet's bench on the shore of Aconi Pond before half the afternoon had passed.

Their breath fogged in the chilly air as the three of them hunted around for a stick beneath the pines. After a few minutes, Zev found a small branch that Sakila said would work for her. Since it was short, she sat cross-legged, holding it with both hands. She stabbed one end into the ground and swayed back and forth, chanting.

The hair on Jerryck's arms stood up. His fingers tingled with the gathering power. It flowed up from the ground, drawn through the focus of the stick. He backed himself and his nephew out of the circumference of the building magic.

A translucent image took shape around Sakila. It looked like the inside of a small log cabin. The center of focus was a circle of stones laid out in one corner. The shamaness ceased chanting, replacing it with monotonous humming. The magic stopped flowing and went into a form of stasis.

Almost half an hour went by with her holding that stasis. Finally, another man came and sat down in the image circle of rocks. He put a wooden staff to the ground, also humming. The magic picked up on his end and connected. Then he and the shamaness looked each other in the eyes and conversed.

If only Jerryck understood their language. The man looked and sounded apologetic. Sakila looked and sounded unhappy. She nodded in acceptance. They both spoke a few more words, then they both tapped the ground with their staffs, and the magic dissipated back down into the earth.

Sakila stood and brushed herself off. "One of the babies in his tribe is ill. He spent all last night and this morning treating her. He will rest now. He should be able to perform the magic to get me to my tribe by tomorrow."

"Your patient is hurting now," Jerryck said. "The longer time goes by before that bone is set, the more difficult a time he'll have healing properly. You need to get there now."

"There is nothing more he can do." Sakila dropped the branch into a nearby pile of fallen leaves.

"I'll open you a portal," Jerryck said. "We'll need to go back to the palace, though. I'll have to drink that nasty potion so I can see where you want the other end opened."

"Who am I to you?" she asked. "You owe me nothing. You have done no wrong that needs paid for. We have no blood ties. I am not your chosen sister. We have no family ties at all. Why do you offer me and my tribe so many gifts?"

"What gifts?" Jerryck cocked his head at her. "Someone is hurt. They need your help."

"If she wants it to be an exchange of some sort—" Zev said— "why not tell her it's because she helped us learn how to scry?"

Sakila shook her head. "I did not help your uncle much."

"You helped me and my sister," Zev said.

"We shamans have sworn to help all girls who can do magic." Sakila looked at Jerryck again. "Your uncle owes me nothing for that."

"What does owing something or family ties have to do with helping someone who needs it?" Jerryck crossed his arms. "You're needed. Now. I can get you there. That's the end of it."

She put a hand on his arm. "Then at least let me help you with the scrying."

He nodded tersely. She retrieved the short branch from where she had dropped it. She sat cross-legged exactly where she had before, then pointed to the spot where the translucent image of the man had sat. "Sit there."

He plopped down on the cold ground. Zev drew close, fidgeting with excitement. Jerryck tried not to fidget, despite the cold, even when his skin started prickling with the gathering magic.

This time, when the magic had built to the point when she had started humming, instead she told Jerryck, "Take hold of the staff."

He grasped it with one hand. The magic latched onto him. She chanted, droning on until it turned into a ringing buzz through his head. Images flashed through his mind, completely overpowering his physical vision. He saw white peaks of the mountains. Groves of aspens, naked of their leaves. Meadows with ice-rimmed creeks. Slopes covered with pines. Drifts of piled snow. Deer. Sagebrush. Clouds. Then the images settled on a clearing at the end of a narrow valley.

Off in the distance, less than a mile away, stood the lodges of a winter encampment. Smoke rose from the cooking fires. People moved about their business wearing leathers and wrapped in furs. Weapons and blades adorned them like jewelry. There were a few familiar faces from some of Sakila's prior scrying trips. Then she jerked at Jerryck, taking his attention back to the clearing at the end of the valley.

The images faded. Jerryck blinked a few times, bringing his eyes back into focus. "Wow, that was... I don't even know how to describe that. It was..."

"It was scrying." Sakila dropped the branch back down into the leaves. "Can you put your portal in the clearing at the end of that valley?"

Yes," Jerryck said. He made shooing gestures with his hands at Sakila and Zev. "I'll need you both to step away. Give me room to work."

Zev grinned and bounced over to where they left the horses. "Is this far enough?"

"Take the horses all the way to the pond." Jerryck pointed at the stone bench on the banks. "Otherwise, the portal might spook them."

Normally, he would have to gather up energy for this spell. This time, Sakila opened and maintained some sort of connection between the two of them. Energy flowed from her to him. He focused on the two locations. He put up a shield at both places to contain the wild energies of the spell, until he could get them under control enough to make them safe. Then he spoke the words that initiated the portal itself.

A tiny pinprick of energy passed through the two spots, bridging the distance, binding them into one location. A dot of energy appeared in the center of the bubble-shaped shield.

Jerryck pulled, stretching the size of the portal. The deep purple colored spot spiraled outward, expanding through all the colors of the rainbow to a sharp edge of fiery red. Spears of flame shot out of it, beating against the inside of the shield. Jerryck snatched hold of them, repurposing the energy back into the portal. With that, it was mostly a matter of patience. One by one, he snagged the strands and wove them back in, calming, stabilizing.

Eventually, it settled. He cautiously lowered the shield. It held stable. The spell taking its toll on him, he turned to Sakila. "It's ready. All you have to do is step through."

"I will repay you for this kindness," she said.

"You don't have to."

"I will anyway."

She stepped through the opaque center of the portal. When she was clear, he spiraled it back down to a pinprick point. He drew in as much energy as he could from the other side and severed the connection. Then he also drew in the energy from his side of the portal as well, leaving very little residue.

He struggled to his feet. Staggering a couple of steps closer to the horses, he stopped to lean against a tree. He was definitely going to continue the aura strengthening exercises on a regular basis. Every day. No skipping. He beckoned his nephew to bring the horses to him. He scaled one of them, and forced himself to sit in the saddle instead of just lying across the animal's back as it carried him home.

Chapter 44

"**S**AKILA LEFT YESTERDAY?" Terrence interlaced his fingers in front of himself and leaned his back hips on his desk. "Why didn't you let me know?"

"I'm sorry," Jerryck said. "I wasn't thinking. She learned from scrying that there was an emergency at her home. She needed to go heal one of her tribe members, so I opened a portal for her. After that I was so drained, I just wanted to sleep."

"That's a relief." Terrence released his breath and let his shoulders drop. "Malk was concerned that you had created another foreign relations mess. I'll let him know that you strengthened ties instead. Now, while you are here, tell me how you're progressing on the warning systems for the villages."

"I've figured out which method to use," Jerryck said. "There were several different options. I studied up on each one—what it would take, how long it would last—and I narrowed it down to two. I could place a group of small wards around the perimeter of a village, similar to the system I use here in the palace. That way if one fails, the others pick up the slack. But in a village, they would be more level with each other instead of at different heights like here at the palace. So that might leave a gap in the center where they override each other."

"As far as we know, these raiders won't open a portal right in the center of town." Terrance rubbed his stubbly beard. "Still, it's best not to leave them that option."

"Which is why I chose to make one large ward to place in the center of the village," Jerryck said. "It wouldn't have the redundancy of multiple wards, so I would have to use more care in the making. But it will also require less maintenance later."

"Do that then." Terrance turned and plucked a paper from the corner of his cluttered desk. "I got another raid report this morning. The sooner we implement this, the better."

Jerryck left the king's office and went back to his workroom. He crossed through it, passed the curtain to the closet in the back. He stepped around his nephew's sleeping cot and dug through some of the boxes stacked against the wall. He brought out a handful of charms and laid them on his worktable.

He reviewed the magic in his books one more time, making certain he had the process correct. Then he picked up the first charm and carefully examined it. Even though it wasn't likely there were any spells or residual magic currently on it, he followed protocols and searched anyway.

Once he knew beyond any doubt that it was clear, he primed the charm, orienting the material it was made of to better receive the type of magic he would place upon it. Not all magicians went through this time-consuming tedium. The ones who didn't were the ones who made inferior products that required more maintenance over a shorter period of time.

The sun dropped low enough to cast long shadows in the workroom. He lit a lamp and layered a foundation on to the charm. When he finished, he could trigger it with a nudge of magic to clang with the deep tones of a large bell. Now it just needed specificity, exactly what event or magic would cause the trigger.

His stomach growled. He had missed supper again. His wife and sister would scold him. Better to face it sooner rather than later. He went to see if there was anything left to eat.

When he passed the bedroom, he stopped. He backed up a step and looked in. Leanne was already asleep. It had to be later than he thought. He stepped over to the window to get a better sense of the time. Most of the lamps in the palace were still lit. A lot of it usually darkened before people even finished the evening dancing.

Leaving Leanne to sleep, he went down to the kitchens. Music played in the common dining hall. People thumped out dance steps in perfect rhythm. What time was it really?

"There you are." Kendra snagged him by the sleeve and dragged him the rest of the way into the kitchens. "I was about to dump the food I save for you in the scrapheap. You really need to take better care of yourself, stop skipping meals like this."

He accepted the cold plate she shoved at him and asked, "What time is it?"

"After supper." She narrowed her eyes at him and pointed out to the dancing. "Do you not see people doing the same thing they do every night after supper? Or do you think they just decided to change it around and dance before they ate instead?"

"Leanne's asleep," Jerryck said. "I thought it was later than this."

"She was tired." Kendra turned to narrow her eyes at a couple of dish-washers who had slackened their pace. "More tired than usual. I told her to go to bed."

Jerryck quickly ate and went to join her. She didn't even stir as he crawled in. When morning came, she slept much later than usual. He had to wake her, and then help her out with her usual mundane morning routine. She dragged herself through it while complaining that she couldn't keep her eyes open.

Worried, Jerryck reached out and touched her aura. It moved sluggishly, like it was low on energy, as if her body was expending it on some sort of strenuous activity. But she'd been sleeping for hours. What could she possibly have been spending energy on? Healing maybe? Was she fighting a cold? He checked for that.

Her lungs were clear. Her throat was clear. Her nose was clear. No cough-ing. No wheezing. No sniffling. She wasn't plugged up in the slightest, let alone ill. Maybe it wasn't anything so sinister as illness. Maybe she had just worked too hard the day before. That was a simple, yet plausible explanation. Since she was fine, he put it out of his mind and went to work.

The moment he picked up the ward, someone came to the tower asking for a healing spell. Before he finished with them, another waited. It seemed half the palace had contracted sniffles and low-grade fevers overnight. Before lunch, he went to Head Medic Kellos for help.

"Can I send patients your way?" he asked.

Kellos didn't even look up at him, too busy measuring out dosages of medicines. "We're already swamped."

"Terrence gave me a specific task," Jerryck said. "I'm already behind because I kept the shamaness entertained."

Kellos frowned. "You did spend a lot of time with her."

"She's curious about magicians," Jerryck said.

"As curious as you are about shamanism?" Kellos spared him a doleful glance before stopping up the bottle he'd been pouring from. "The last time she was here, you blew up your workroom. You could've killed yourself."

"She's gone now," Jerryck said. "And I didn't blow anything up."

"I still don't understand why she stayed so long." Kellos snagged another bottle measured from it. "Unless she planned ahead of time to use a magician to travel back. Besides you, I don't know of any magician who would be amenable to helping her out with that."

"She'd made arrangements with another Shaman for magic travel," Jerryck said.

"Oh." Kellos stopped pouring.

"But the other Shaman was busy. I ended up helping her after all."

"You're not so good at that part."

Jerryck bridled a bit. "I can open portals just fine."

"You have trouble with the scrying ahead of it," Kellos said. He used a glass stick to mix what he'd measured together.

"She did the scrying," Jerryck said. "I just observed, saw what she saw."

Kellos stopped stirring, before he could possibly be finished. He held the stick poised above the solution. "You observed what someone else scryed? Is that even possible?"

"I guess so, since I did it." Jerryck shrugged. "I still don't think I could do the actual scrying very well. Not on my own. Observing someone else was a lot safer than the way I normally do it. Anyway, back to my original question. Can I send patients your way? I really do need some time on this project."

Kellos stared at him for a moment. He still held the stick above what he needed to finish stirring. Then he swallowed, caught his breath, and said, "Sure."

Jerryck went back up to his tower. People kept coming to him. For the most part, he could now send them away. Still, every interruption set him back. When Zev came up a couple of hours after lunch, Jerryck gave him a book and said, "Go out on the landing to read. And don't let anyone in unless they're dying. I have to work on this project."

"I want to help with that instead," Zev whined.

"Keep people from bothering me and you are helping."

Zev stuck out his lower lip in a pout. "Not that way. I want to help make the magic."

"Magic isn't all just spell casting. You should know that by now. There's a lot of preparatory work ahead of time. With some things you have to layer spell after spell just right, and you need uninterrupted time. Go make sure I get some."

Zev mumbled complaints all the way out. As soon as he was gone, Jerryck went back to work. He kept at it until supper time, when Leanne came bursting in. He fumbled the last bit of the spell. He would have to start that part all over. He tossed the charm down on the table and gripped the edges, keeping hold of his temper.

She flitted around the room, picking things up, setting them back down, idly moving knickknacks around, putting away the books he'd gotten out. She was so cheery, his irritation evaporated. He picked up the charm, examining, pinpointing exactly where he would have to pick up the magic, only half listening to her chattering away about all the babies she got to see and hold as part of her midwife job.

She stopped right in front of him and asked, "So what you think?"

"About what?" he asked.

"About babies."

He set the charm down flat and leaned over it while he answered his wife. "I think they're cute sometimes."

She leaned forward, too close to the charm for him to work properly. "You want one?"

"Someday." He moved the charm away from her.

She straightened up. Her face darkened with anger for some reason. "Someday?"

"I like family," he said. "We definitely should have more someday. I'm kind of busy right now, though. And babies are a lot of work."

She stepped back, shouting, "Haven't you heard one word I said?"

"You were talking about your job and how much you enjoy it," he said. She backed closer to the door, her lips tightening into a thin line. He straightened up from the charm, giving her his full attention. "Weren't you?"

She ran out, jerking the door open so hard it bounced off the wall and slammed shut again behind her. Jerryck winced, scrunching his face. What had he missed this time? Just how badly had he messed up?

Kendra would know what was going on. He went down to the kitchens. Leanne must've gone straight to his sister, because she yelled at him for upsetting his wife before he got one word out. He had to go out and sit down to supper with her children to get her to leave off.

When most people had finished eating, the tables were stacked against the walls and the benches were pushed up against them, leaving only a few eating spaces for stragglers. Musicians broke out their instruments. People thumped out the rhythms, whirling and clapping in time. Gossip ran amok. A few people made their way outside into the chilly night air. The majority stayed indoors with the warmth.

Jerryck found Leanne sitting on one of the benches, rather than dancing. He approached her. She turned and looked away, stiff and rigid as a stone. He sat next to her anyway.

"I'm sorry," he said.

"You don't even know what you're sorry for," she snapped.

"No," he admitted. "And I'm sorry for that too."

Her back relaxed into its natural curve. She turned and let him draw her close. Apologizing for nothing had worked once again. Why did it work? Who cared? It did.

Chapter 45

BY MORNING Leanne's grumpiness had returned. She crabbed at Jerryck for not doing anything right. She complained about being too tired to do everything for him. Then she threw up.

He checked her for the flu. Nothing. Perhaps she had eaten something the day before that had disagreed with her. Either that or she had to be fighting some sort of illness. But with all the checking done the day before with no result, there wasn't much more he could do for her until more symptoms appeared. He used magic to ease her nausea and suggested she take the day off to rest. She swore she was fine and went to work anyway.

He finished the first ward and spent the next few days testing it. He took it out to a nearby field and planted it. A short distance away, he opened a tiny portal to the corner in his tower he kept clear. The ward tolled as sharp and loud as any warning bell.

Once that first test was successful, he played with the range. Since it only worked as an alert, not a preventative, he got it to where he could extend the range to about a ten-mile radius without expending too much extra power. If he made it right it shouldn't require any maintenance for at least a couple of years. And if he made no more than one a day, he wouldn't wear himself too thin.

Nothing went as planned.

Leanne went completely crazy, distracting him from his work. She'd act happy and giddy one moment, then start crying and sobbing the next. She kept accusing him of not listening. He repeated back the last thing she'd said, proving that he was listening. Then she would stand there staring at him, or tapping her foot, or holding out her hand, as if she expected him to hear more in her words than what she'd said. Then she always got mad at him for no reason.

He tried asking his sister to talk some sense into his wife. Kendra only got mad. She told him he was stupid and needed to listen better.

Other distractions abounded as well. Tajor kept coming up to the tower and insisting he do his aural exercises and practices. Zev still had lessons to learn. A lot of people in the palace still came to him for all the ailments that compounded with the onset of early winter. On top of all that, he still had the maintenance chores and other tasks required of him as court magician.

The weather predictors announced that in a few days, the palace would get its first snowfall of the year. Everyone dashed around in mad excitement, preparing for the Winter Festival.

Jerryck hadn't made near the progress on the wards that he should have. A few of them he botched when people barged in on him in the middle of powering them up. He'd had to scratch them and start over. Then Tajor asked if the wards were going to travel to their locations while active, or if someone would activate them once they had been planted. Jerryck ruined several more trying unsuccessfully to attach a trigger that any layman could operate.

Tajor and Zev were both there for Leanne's outburst the evening before the predicted snowfall. They watched as she went on a tirade, and then stomped out of the workroom.

"Why does she talk about babies so much all of a sudden?" Zev asked.

"I think she wants one," Jerryck said. "I wouldn't have thought she'd be so eager after all the pain she's seen other women go through during pregnancy and birthing."

Tajor threw back his head in laughter. "You are one of the most inept people I've ever met when it comes to understanding hints and innuendos. She's not even trying to hide it. She's all but come right out and said it."

"Said what?"

"Good night, Jerryck." Tajor got up and left. He called back as he started down the stairs. "You'll figure it out sooner or later."

"What's that supposed to mean?" Zev asked.

"I don't know," Jerryck growled. "And I don't want to talk about it anymore tonight. Go to bed."

"*What?*" Zev slumped. "I can't sleep now. It's supposed to snow tonight. I want to see it."

"You'll see it when you get up in the morning."

"Then it'll be time for the festival."

"Stop whining," Jerryck said. "Almost everyone else is already in bed. Go on. I have more work I'd like to do. Alone."

"Fine." Zev pouted and shuffled his feet, taking twice the normal amount of time to walk the short distance through the curtain.

Jerryck worked on his current ward. With everyone in bed anticipating the Winter Festival the next day, he got several hours of uninterrupted time. His lamp nearly burned through all its oil before he finally sat back from his work and breathed a satisfied sigh at a job well done

A flicker of movement out the window caught his attention. Snowflakes drifted lazily to the ground. He smiled. Perhaps this would cheer Leanne out of whatever malaise had taken hold of her.

He went down one flight to his bedroom. He undressed as quietly as he could and crawled into bed. She was awake. She clicked her tongue and rolled away from him.

"It's snowing," he said. "Happy Winter Festival, love."

"Are you going to make the announcement in the morning?" There was bitterness in her voice.

He sat up. He never made announcements. And even if he did, it wouldn't be on the day of the Winter Festival. Not even the king made announcements then, unless he had a pregnant wife, a new baby, or a child that had become engaged to marry. Babies and wedding engagements were announced by everyone on that day.

"What announcement?" he asked.

"I'm getting really tired of that." She threw off the blanket and got up. Illumination from somewhere outside reflected off the falling snow just enough to shed light on her where she stood. She grabbed her robe and yanked it over her nightdress.

"What are you doing?" he asked.

"I'm finding somewhere else to sleep." She jammed her arms into the sleeves of the robe.

"Why?"

"You keep acting like nothing has changed." She flailed her arms around while she spoke, her open robe flapping about. "It matters so little to you that you don't even care."

"What are you talking about?"

She folded her arms over her stomach. "I'm talking about the baby."

"What baby?"

"Our baby."

"We don't have a baby."

"We will!"

"Someday, yes. Absolutely we will."

"Next summer we will!"

Jerryck leaned back, absorbing. She might as well have slapped him upside the head with a brick. "Are you… We… We're pregnant? Now?"

"Don't act so surprised." She closed the front of her robe with her hands and didn't let go. She squeezed and twisted the edges. "The shamaness figured it out. I've been telling you since she left."

"I thought you were talking about how much you loved being a midwife," Jerryck said. "You talked a lot about making arrangements for if and when we have a baby. You didn't say anything about one already here and growing."

"Are you so thickheaded that you really didn't understand that?"

Jerryck slumped. "I guess so. Look, I'm not so good at picking up on hints. You have to tell me something outright if you want me to know it. Or show me evidence if I can't see it."

"I thought magicians that can heal could also figure out when a woman is pregnant."

"If we're looking for that, yes," Jerryck said. "I checked you for illness, not pregnancy."

"You don't believe me until you do whatever magic it is that tells you?"

"I believe you." Jerryck smiled, even though she wouldn't be able to see in the dark. "You're a midwife. The best one in the palace. You know what you're doing. I trust you."

"You don't sound upset." She slipped the robe back off.

"Why would I be upset?" He reached out and took her hand, drawing her back to bed.

She lay down beside him. "You were upset before."

"I couldn't figure out what was going on," he said. "I don't like being confused. It happens too often."

She giggled and snuggled under the blankets. Within a couple of heartbeats, she had dropped into sleep. Jerryck lay awake, his mind racing in circles. There were so many things he would need to provide for another member of the family. They should make the second floor of the tower, the room below the bedroom, into a nursery. They would need a cradle, a rocking chair, clothes, blankets, diapers... lots and lots of diapers. His wife and sister would think of all kinds of details he wouldn't. He stuck to the basics. And the most basic of all, the baby would need a name.

A lot of people in Brend followed the tradition of the royal family. They gave the first son a name similar to his father, and the first daughter a name similar to her mother. Thus, Princess Nita was the first-born daughter of Queen Rita. Terrance was the firstborn son of old King Clarrence.

Would Leanne want to follow that tradition? There were a few people who didn't, claiming it must bring a curse. The last several generations of royal family had only one child. People refused to let go of that myth no matter how many magicians told them there was no curse.

Kendra had been named for their mother Lindra. Jerryck had been named for their father Jerryld. Leanne wasn't her mother's oldest daughter, so they wouldn't have to worry about repeating a grandmother's name. If the baby was a girl, they could name her Breann, or Lena, or something like that. Jerryck's father was dead, so they could repeat that name if the baby was a boy. Or maybe Derrick, or Erick. They would eventually come up with something. He hugged his wife closer and drifted to sleep happy.

Chapter 46

AS SOON AS THE SUN ROSE, children ran shrieking outside to play in the snow before they had even eaten breakfast. At midday, the feasting started. No servers dished out this meal. The cooks set out the food. Everyone grabbed a plate and served themselves. They all sat down together to eat and exchange stories of the events of the past year.

Once every belly was full, people got up one by one to announce marriage engagements. The moment they had finished, Jerryck jumped up before anyone else could. He started off the pregnancy announcements. Then he raced up to the banquet hall where the nobility held their celebrations. They were just finishing up marriage engagements, so he got to lead off the pregnancy announcements there too.

Throughout the afternoon, families and close friends exchanged gifts. Jerryck gave Leanne the charm that Tajor had ruined. He'd put it on a silver chain so she could wear it as a necklace.

The celebrations topped off with displays of sight and sound, artistic and beautiful, displayed by many. Poets read their works. Painters highlighted their most recent pieces. Orchestras and choirs gave performances, and everyone danced; the nobles in the ballroom, everyone else in the common dining hall.

Jerryck enjoyed them all. Then he lay awake again that night, his sleeping wife in his arms. By this time next year, they would be parents celebrating their child's first Winter Festival.

After the celebrations, Leanne calmed. Her happy moods lasted longer, and her irritable ones came less frequently. Jerryck walked like he was levitating. Nothing brought him down. Not even when he was summoned to a general staff meeting a few days later.

"Most of you know by now that raids have occurred within our borders," Terrance addressed the room. He pointed to maps tacked to the wall for the occasion. "You can see the locations of the incidents marked here. They all occur within about two or three weeks of each other. The attackers are all described exactly the same and use identical methods of operation."

Jerryck let his mind drift. How long before they could learn the gender of the child? It really was just a matter of curiosity. It made no difference to him. Boy or girl, it would still be his.

Tajor poked Jerryck in the ribs, leaned over, and whispered, "You keep that vapid smile on your face and people are going to think you've lost your wits entirely. Can you at least try and look like you're paying attention?"

Jerryck frowned at him. Why wouldn't Tajor consistently use the same seat in all these various staff meetings? And why, of all times, had he chosen to sit by Jerryck while he was daydreaming? Although, he probably shouldn't. He should be paying more attention. Terrance was speaking about the steps already taken.

"That will be easier done when the training for the villagers takes root," Terrance said. One of the men in the room stood. Terrance shook his head, making the man retake his seat. "Stop trying to argue this or protest training them. The decision is made and already implemented. Heston, any updates?"

"We've stepped up patrols all along here." Heston drew his finger in a line on the map along the border with the Chemwanitz Mountains. "Patrols will only do so much. We don't hope to catch anyone with them."

Lines were good. Lines did useful things, like hang mobiles to entertain babies. Jerryck stared up at the ceiling. What kind of mobile would be best? Leanne and Kendra both swore the babies could see bright colors better than dull ones. Perhaps shiny and flashy might work even better than bright colors. And what if the mobile played music? He could use magic to make it glow and play music.

Tajor poked him again. Someone standing on the floor said, "So the training of the villagers is to make up for the inefficiency of the patrols? Isn't there some other preventative we can take?"

Jerryck knew how to make small objects float for short periods. If he did that, he wouldn't have to string a line from the ceiling. Of course, he would have to stand right there, keeping the objects floating the entire time. No, it was probably better to string the line.

"Jerryck!" Terrance called.

"Huh?" Jerryck snapped his attention back. "I'm sorry. I was distracted."

"I asked how many wards you've completed," Terrance said. "And how soon they can go out to the villages."

"Only twelve." Jerryck flushed with embarrassment. "And I'm having trouble putting a trigger on them that a layman can use. A magician will have to plant and activate them individually if you want them to go out right away. I know one from Kershet that would be willing to take the job. While he's doing that, I can work on making more."

Heston hadn't moved from beside the map. "We could get them out faster if you send him out with those twelve, and then you go in the other direction to more villages."

Jerryck refrained from rolling his eyes. "If I send what I have with another magician, I wouldn't have any to place at other villages."

"You have to make them here at the palace?" Tajor asked.

Jerryck glared at him. Of course he could make them other places. That wasn't the point. He'd done more traveling in the past several months than he wanted to do in the next several years. And winter was not the best time to take a trip. Most importantly, now was the worst time to leave his family with his wife newly pregnant.

"Wouldn't it be safer to have one magician out there with these wards?" Terrance asked.

Tajor raised an eyebrow. "Safer for the villagers? Or safer for the magician?"

Terrance pinched the bridge of his nose. "If multiple people go in different directions, doesn't that increase the risk of the wards getting stolen?"

Tajor shrugged. "Who would want them? And would it really matter? Can't Jerryck just make more?"

Terrance lowered his hand from his face and asked Jerryck, "Is there anyone else who can make them?"

"There are several other magicians who could figure it out as well as I did," Jerryck said.

"Can they make them immediately?" Tajor asked. "While traveling to where they need to be placed? Or would it take them as much time to figure it out as it took you?"

Terrance scowled at Tajor. "Why are you pressing so hard for him to leave?"

"Honestly, I'm trying to figure out how you're going to decide which choice to make." Tajor interlaced his fingers together on the table. "Both choices have drawbacks. I fully understand his need to stay here. But at the cost of how many lives? Do you suppose your villagers will mind the delay in the addition to their safety?"

The question hung. Everyone looked to Terrance. Jerryck shrank down in his chair. His high spirits crashed even before Terrance said, "Jerryck, I need you to go and do this as soon as possible."

Jerryck walked out of the meeting without being excused. He grabbed the nearest page and snapped at him to fetch Leanne. Then he climbed up to his bedroom. He snagged his travel bag and shoved in the first things that came to his hand.

Leanne came sooner than expected. "I got your message. What's so urgent that you had to talk right now?" She looked inside the bag. "Are you going somewhere?"

He nodded, jamming a couple more things in.

She took one of them back out. "My festival shoes? Am I going with you?"

He shook his head.

She took the bag from him and dug through it. "Then why were you putting some of my things in here? Were you even paying attention to what you packed?"

He dropped down to sit on the bed. "No."

"Then how are you supposed to know you have what you need?" She upended the bag, dumping everything out beside him.

"I kind of don't care right now."

"You kind of will care later," she said as she sorted through the hodge-podge. "You have no extra socks, and these shirts are summer weight. You'd freeze out there."

"Or I'd have to turn around and come right back," he mumbled.

"Where are you going?" She took some of his heavier clothes out of the wardrobe. "And why?"

"Those wards I made," he said. "I can't get a trigger to work on them. I have to go out and place them one by one. And I have to make more while I'm on the road so there'll be enough of them."

"I see." She folded the clothes into the bottom of the bag. "Then you'll definitely need extra socks."

Jerryck gave her a hurt look. "You're perfectly fine with me leaving you like this?"

"Of course not." She opened the drawer in the bureau where he kept his extra leggings. "I'll have to manage. Kendra will help. It's not like you'd leave me if you had a choice."

"If it was summer, I could take you with me," he said. He scrubbed his face with his hands. Then he waved them around. "If you didn't hate travel-ing. And meeting new people. But you do. And it's not summer. And I can't take you. I won't even take Zev. I'll have to arrange for someone else to give him his lessons. And I have no way of making sure that you're all safe, and healthy, and happy. And if something happens while I'm not here to help, if you get sick, or hurt, or—"

"Calm down." She took hold of one of his hands. "I'm fine. We're all fine."

"Kendra's husband used to say that a lot, even when he wasn't fine. And look what happened."

She let go of his hand and continued with the packing. "Tell you what… Every village you go to, send me a letter. If I need you, I'll send a letter to your next destination."

"I'll still be far enough away that I couldn't get to you immediately."

"Open a portal, like you did for the shamaness," she said. "You keep that corner of the first floor of the tower cleared for it. Could you use that?"

349

A calmness settled over Jerryck with that suggestion. "Yes. As a matter of fact, I could."

Chapter 47

B Y THAT EVENING, the magician from Kershet that would take Jerryck's wards was brought to the palace. General Heston briefed him on the situation and gave him a map with a preplanned route, starting at the southeastern edge of the nation. He had two elite guards assigned to him, one of whom was native to that area of the country and would double as a guide.

Jerryck left in the morning. He also had a marked map, a preplanned route, and two elite guards, both of whom were Tajor's friends. He brought no prepared wards with him. Instead, he had several trinkets to turn into wards. When he used them all, he would have to procure more. They planned to pick up guides wherever they went. Heston thought the area Jerryck planned to cover was too large for any one person to know the terrain well enough.

Heston also went into Kershet and found magician Thessallim, who worked mainly with luck, odds, and coincidences brought on through prayer to some deity or another. Heston paid a high price for the best prayers that would cause an attack from the raiders to coincide with the time Jerryck visited their target location. That put the two guards on edge.

"Don't worry about it," Jerryck assured them. "Coincidence magicians are what give every other magician a bad reputation for being charlatans. They're notoriously inaccurate."

"Like your memory?" the skinny one asked, while the one with the cleft chin snickered. "You've done everything you can to avoid calling us by name."

"I don't remember the name of every elite guard," Jerryck said.

"Not even ones you've traveled with before?" the skinny one asked. "Or did you forget that too?"

"I remember you both went to Shontarra with the princess." Jerryck pointed to the one with the cleft chin. "And you wouldn't leave me alone."

"And do you remember our names?" The skinny one wouldn't leave it alone.

"Is one of you Dean?" Jerryck took a stab at it.

"Deek." The cleft chin one corrected him while laughing. "No, neither of us is him. He's in trouble again. He didn't get to come. Try Garret and Cade. I'll let you figure out which of us is which."

He figured it out during the first leg of the journey as they trudged their horses through the snow. They went through several villages along the route, stayed overnight with a couple of premieres as they passed through their districts, and finally reached the first village on their map exhausted and stiff with cold. Jerryck provided the mayor with the chit that allowed him to pass any expenses to his premiere, and through him to the king. The inn put them up and treated them to their cook's finest dishes, which didn't amount to anything fancier than he remembered from his childhood.

Jerryck spent the next day making the ward. He had it completed, planted, and activated by supper that evening. Then he demonstrated it to the villagers so that the sound of it would be familiar to them. During that time, Garret put on a serious face and never let him out of sight. Cade disappeared for several hours at a stretch.

The next morning, they hired a local guide to take them to the next village on the map. While the two guards restocked their provisions, Jerryck sought out a courier and sent a letter to his wife.

Over the weeks of travel, something different happened with every stop and every leg of the journey, keeping it from getting monotonous. One place tried to tally up more expenses than accurate. Another had a few soldiers who thought their village was remote enough that they could get away with bullying the citizens. In one village, they had to stop for several days to wait out a blizzard. In the village after that, every citizen had taken ill.

The roads were treacherous. The local guides knew where the most dangerous spots were and how to deal with them. They knew where the snow had drifted too deep for the horses to struggle through. They knew where bodies of water had frozen enough to cross and make shortcuts. They knew where best to shelter, and how to stave off the more dangerous fauna. Yet even with the local assistance, each leg of the trip was arduous enough that they obtained fresh mounts at every stop.

With every village, Garret and Cade kept the same pattern. Garret wouldn't let Jerryck out of sight. Cade disappeared for hours, and then came back with news, local information, and gossip. The first village where Jerryck had to purchase a charm to turn into a ward, he sat in the common room of the inn working on it. A man came and sat down across the table. He had the lighter colored hair common in villages close to the Chemwanitz border. Garret stood near and hadn't prevented the approach. So Jerryck didn't tell him to go away.

"Hi there," the man said.

"Hello." Jerryck didn't look up from the ward.

He'd already laid the foundation and spoke the initiating words for the next casting. The rest of the layering took some concentration, or the magic would slip and the perimeter of the ward would diminish. The man didn't interrupt further. He sat quietly watching, probably seeing nothing more than some magician staring at a trinket on a table.

The spell wove itself around the trinket's aura, penetrating it, melding with it, altering it. Jerryck carefully followed it all. Making these wards was the perfect opportunity for him to practice some of the exercises Tajor had told him to keep doing every day. The more he did them, the more he became aware of the nuances and changes caused by the magic he performed. He had more control over the process with less effort. He could change it, stop it, or redirect the magic in the middle of the spell before it even finished.

He had done similar things when he was younger, before he learned some of the safeties the Gathering insisted on. He knew now why he'd been so recalcitrant about learning them. Somehow this felt safer and more natural, as if he had more control. His mentor had insisted that feeling was a misjudgment due to lack of experience. Now that he was more experienced, it still felt safer and more natural. And he definitely had more control.

The magic finished. The ward lay complete on the table. Now it only needed planting, activation, and demonstration. He would do that after supper.

The man on the other side of the table still watched. There was something vaguely familiar about him. Perhaps he wanted a favor. In most villages, at least one or two people had offered to pay him for personal requests.

"Your eyes still glaze over when you concentrate," the man said.

"What?" The comment caught Jerryck by surprise. The man smiled, showing a gap between his teeth. That nagged at Jerryck's memory too.

"You don't remember me," the man said. He sounded amused. He leaned back and stretched his legs out under the table. "Maybe because we're so much farther south of the last time we talked. I'm going to be your guide through the next few villages. Name's Kent."

"We've met?" Jerryck picked up the ward from the table and stowed it in a pocket.

"Name's not triggering your memory?" Kent smiled again, eyes sparkling. "You really haven't changed all that much. How about this. My older sister's name is Indall."

Jerryck shook his head. "Sorry. How long ago was it?"

"The last time I saw you, that old court magician came with the crown prince to take you off our hands." Kent crossed his ankles and swung his feet casually back and forth. "My sister had a party to celebrate. She once told Kendra she was ugly. The next morning, she woke up with a dog's head instead of a face."

Jerryck caught his breath. That had been his first accident with illusion. He hadn't really changed the girl's head. It wore off after a day. He scooted his chair back, putting more distance between himself and Kent.

"You do remember." Kent smiled again.

"That was a long time ago," Jerryck said.

"It's still just as funny." Kent laughed. "Don't mention it to my sister if you get that far north. She'll get mad. She never thought it was as funny as I did."

"You never mentioned anything about knowing Jerryck from childhood," Garret said. His blank face had morphed into a dangerous scowl.

Kent waved that away with a lazy brush of his hand. "That village is a long way from here."

"What are you doing so far away?" Jerryck asked.

"I went exploring to seek my fortune," Kent said. "Without Kendra, the village just wasn't the same. I made my way down to this part of the country. Met a young lady even prettier than Kendra, and with a much better temper. No offense, Jerryck. I figured I wouldn't find a better fortune than her company. So I stuck around, convinced her to marry me, and I've been here ever since."

"She lives here in this village?" Jerryck asked.

"No, no," Kent said. "We'll go through the village where I built her a house. You can stay there with us, instead of the inn. She'll take good care of you. You'll love it. She's the best cook in the area."

"Is that why you wander around the area, instead of staying there with her?" Garret's serious face cracked some, a bit of his usual mirth leaking through.

"That's one of the best things about her. She doesn't mind if I wander in and out of her life. As long as I don't stay away for too long, and I bring her little presents to prove I was thinking about her while I was away." Kent stood up. "Which I should go find one for her. This village usually has the best selection. You want to come find one for your wife? Or sister?"

"I send them a letter every time I stop," Jerryck said. "Any trinkets I find go into a stash for me to turn into wards."

"Whatever makes your women happy," Kent said, and walked out of the inn.

After supper, the locals gathered in the village square. Jerryck planted the ward in its selected spot. He tested the fastenings to make certain it was secure. He activated it. Then he opened a tiny portal so everyone could recognize its ringing clang. After that, people went to the inn and danced on the common room floor. Just like in the palace, cold weather didn't keep them from this nightly ritual.

Cade showed up from wherever he had disappeared to. He said to Garret, "Finally got some news we were waiting for. There was another raid a few weeks ago, farther south, in one of the villages the other magician had already set up a ward in. It worked perfect. Saved a lot of lives."

"A few weeks ago..." Garret repeated, his face darkening to the same scowl he'd given Kent earlier.

"We're remote enough you know it's not easy to get information to us quickly," Cade said.

"If they strike every few weeks, then we're due," Garret said. "How much do you want to wager on the coincidence magic putting us in a fight?"

"Coincidence magic isn't reliable," Jerryck reminded him.

Across the room, Kent loudly regaled a growing audience with tales of shenanigans from Jerryck's childhood. Garret and Cade's faces both cleared into blank nothingness. They stood between Jerryck and the crowd, watching them with casual idleness. Every time one of the crowd would laugh and asked Jerryck if he could repeat a trick, they would glance at the guards, then quickly look away again.

What was their problem? It wasn't like the guards were threatening anyone. Not that he wanted to do any more magic. He ended the problem by excusing himself for bed.

Chapter 48

JERRYCK TOSSED and turned. Tired as he was, the reminder of his wayward childhood had caught him by surprise and thrown him off kilter. Halfway through the night, he finally floated in and out of dreams. Some of them restful. Some of them chaotic. All of them awash with color and sound.

He dreamed he was a child again, pulling pranks, some of them accidental. Then he was an adult, still pulling pranks. He reverted in age again, reliving his apprenticeship to old Heldavio. Then Leanne entered the tower and all his dreams shifted. A baby cried. She sang a lullaby. The baby wouldn't stop crying. It got louder and louder, clanging, jarring, tolling like a large bell.

He woke with a start. The bell was real, not part of his dream. The ward he'd set up that evening was ringing. He leaped out of bed and into his clothes.

Garret nearly ran over him in the hallway. Cade was already outside. Men sauntered slowly into the square carrying lanterns and muttering uncertainly to each other. They rubbed their eyes, mumbled sleepily, and milled about with their night clothes peeking out from under heavy winter coats.

"Everyone calm down," the mayor of the village said. He strode to the center of the gathering, right up to Jerryck. "I heard the stories about you last night. Did you play a trick on us and make a faulty ward?"

Jerryck took offense to the very idea. "Of course not. A portal's been opened."

The mayor looked around. "Where?"

"It's somewhere out of town." Jerryck waved his arms vaguely.

"These raiders' pattern is to open a portal about mile or less from the village," Cade said loud enough for everyone to hear. "We've got minutes at most."

"Where's your defense trainer?" Garret demanded.

"I'm here." A man with graying hair and a limp hobbled forward. "How many do you think we'll face?"

"About a dozen or two," Cade said. "We don't have a solid number."

"We've all trained for this." The mayor put his hands on his hips, puffed out his chest, and scanned around at the crowd of men. "All of you, go get your weapons."

Someone screamed in a building on the southern edge of the village. It burst into flames. Pale men wearing Chemwanitz warpaint on their faces darted around the building. They headed for others, whooping and shouting wordlessly, brandishing weapons and torches.

One of the villagers screamed, sprinting to the burning building. "*No!*"

An attacker jumped in front of him and cut his throat. The village trainer drew a short bow from under his coat and knocked an arrow. The raider threw himself to the ground. The arrow whistled by him. He scuttled away to cover.

Other buildings caught fire. Screams from women and children cut through the night. The men scattered, racing to protect their homes and families. Garret and Cade waded into the raiders, mounting a counterattack. The defense trainer kept shooting. They always kept out of his line of fire and evaded.

Jerryck stood frozen. Such carnage. Such violence. Time slowed down. Still, he couldn't take it all in. The iron reek of blood seeped into the back of his throat. Smoke choked his nostrils and blotted out the stars.

A raider approached the inn. The innkeeper stood in the doorway, framed by the light within. He held a meat tenderizer like a club. He swung at the raider and missed. The raider laughed, raising a knife.

Jerryck threw magic at the icicles on the eaves above. They broke off at the point of contact and rained down. Most of them missed. One of the larger ones speared into the raider's arm.

He cried out in shock and pain. He dropped his knife. The innkeeper swung again, bashing his head with the meat tenderizer.

Leaving the innkeeper to take care of it from there, Jerryck turned elsewhere, his stupor clearing. He took hold of the flames from one of the burning buildings. He drew it around himself, reshaping the element. Warmed by the fire, surrounded by it like a shield, he used it to send pellets of flame shooting away from him faster than any crossbow.

Garret and Cade slashed through the raiders, driving them back. Jerryck had to aim carefully to avoid them. It helped when the village trainer directed him, pointing out raiders that avoided the two guards. He could shoot them easily.

Most of the flame pellets missed their targets, pelting the ground or nearby buildings. The raiders reacted to him so fast, they couldn't possibly have any time to think about their actions. They always dove for the ground and the nearest cover. Only when they had something to hide behind did they peek out to see who shot at them.

Then they shouted at each other, the same word, over and over, *"Zauberer! Zauberer!"*

One of them shouted to all the others something different, "Rückzug! Schnell! Schnell! Schnell! Rückzug!"

With that, the raiders fought to disengage from the defenders. They picked up their wounded, struggling to retreat with them.

Garret shouted, "We need one alive."

Jerryck looked around, his stupor creeping back up on him. The raider the innkeeper had bashed still lay in front of the inn. He stirred and moaned, his hands holding his head. Jerryck flung sleep magic at him and raised a wall of flames so the man's cohorts wouldn't see him. They backed away from it. He pushed it at them. They ran, limping back in the direction they'd come.

Jerryck ran after them. Garret grabbed hold and tackled him to the ground. "You're not going after them."

Jerryck squirmed, trying to get loose. "I can study their portal."

Garret held fast. "They're running desperate. They'll turn on you like a cornered animal."

Jerryck stopped resisting. The last of the raiders disappeared into the dark.

The crackling of fires in the village, the weeping of the people, the groans of the wounded, all wrenched Jerryck's attention to them.

Garret helped him up. They spent the next several hours dealing with the aftermath. Fires were extinguished. Wounded were tended. Dead were counted. Messages and pleas for assistance were sent to the district premiere and neighboring villages. The mayor strutted around, encouraging people, handing out orders, directing activities, never actually lifting a finger to do any of the work himself.

Well after the late winter sun had risen, a band of trackers took Jerryck and Garret out to find the spot where the portal had been opened. There was so much magical refuse there, it acted like a beacon. Jerryck could have found it by himself.

He didn't have to do much examining to agree with Sakila's assessment. This magic was performed by the same person who had made the poison in the river the previous spring. He did run some tests to try and figure out the location of the other side of the portal. The best he got was a far, southern direction. No specifics. Not that too many specifics would do him much good anyway. Only if he recognized the place, or could scry, would he be able to pinpoint it on any map.

Upon returning to the village, the mayor greeted them and took them to the inn. He said, "I've arranged for an escort to take you and the prisoner to my premiere. You should probably rest today and start off first thing in the morning."

Garret shoved his face in the mayor's. "You haven't moved that raider, have you?"

"No, no…" The mayor backed away. "He's still down in the inn's cellar with your other guard friend. What was his name? Cade? I was hoping you would let him know the plans. He won't let anyone down there."

"He had us bring down their baggage," the innkeeper corrected the mayor.

"Good," Garret said. He took Jerryck's arm and pulled him to the stairs.

The moment they put their feet on the top step, Cade called up from below. "I said no one comes down. Try it, and I'll claim the broken leg you get is from falling."

"What broken leg?" Jerryck descended below the ceiling level of the cellar where Cade could see him. Garret and Kent were both right behind him.

"Oh, it's you." Cade sheathed his knife. "Nevermind."

He stood in the middle of the single room. The raider lay bandaged to one side, still under the magic that kept him asleep. The baggage sat stacked beside him. Shelves with bins, jars, and crockery full of stores and foodstuffs all sat on the dirt floor.

Jerryck looked around at it. "I thought the winter stores were all supposed to be locked up and guarded."

"These are the inn's stock for tomorrow," Garrett said with a chuckle.

"They're not going to use all this by tomorrow."

"Next week then. Look, just leave it be. The raiders have never struck the same place twice. Their winter stores are safe."

"Besides," Kent said. "We've got other, more important concerns."

Cade pointed at the raider. "We need to get him to the palace. Immediately."

"Hmm," Jerryck grunted, pulling at his lower lip with his fingers. "I can't think of any magicians in this area who specialize in portals or travel magic."

"Why don't you just open one?" Garrett said. "You keep that space in your tower just for it."

"You know about that?" Why was that surprising to Jerryck? He should have known they'd be aware of it.

"Yes." Kent snorted nonchalantly. "Can you do it? Or are we going to have to use other methods?"

"We?" Jerryck looked at him askance. "Are you even supposed to be down here with us?"

"He's elite," Garret said. "Trained to work outside the palace. Most of the guides we've hired have been."

Another thing Jerryck shouldn't have been surprised by. "I didn't know that."

"You didn't need to know that," Garret said.

"Wait." Jerryck turned accusingly to Kent. "You said you wandered around and this is where you ended up."

"Yes, well…" Kent shrugged. "I may have left out the part of the wandering where I went to the palace and ended up getting initiated into the elite."

"Why would you leave that out?"

Kent grinned. "Why would I include it?"

"He was following your sister," Cade said. "Can you open that portal or not?"

Jerryck clenched his jaw, his body rigid. "You were following *Kendra*?"

"Now, see, that's why I didn't mention it." Kent put a hand on his hip. "You're still overprotective. I didn't mention it because we were going to travel together. We had to get along."

"The portal." Cade stepped in front of Jerryck. "Can you do it?"

Jerryck turned away. "Yes."

He had to run through a couple of calming exercises before focusing correctly. Then he used all the care and precaution he'd used when opening a portal for the shamaness. When the spell was complete and stable enough to use, the warning bell tolled again in the square.

Kent and Garret looked up at the ceiling. Feet scrambled above, moving for the front door. The innkeeper started shouting incoherently. Kent said, "Maybe we should have warned them."

Cade picked up some of their gear. "I did, when I had the innkeeper bring the baggage down."

"The mayor didn't say anything." Garret helped Cade toss the luggage through the portal. Every item tugged, tightening the strain on Jerryck.

"The mayor was hoping to talk you into going to his premiere instead." Cade picked up the last bag. Garret and Kent picked up the sleeping raider.

"You're going too?" Jerryck asked Kent.

"I have to give a report," Kent said. "Then I have to get back as fast as possible, which will take longer than my wife likes me to be away. I'll have to get her a damn good present to make up for this one."

"You can handle an extra person," Cade said. "Can't you?"

Jerryck nodded and braced himself for the drain. Garret and Kent carried the raider through. Cade prodded Jerryck until he stepped through. He just about fell over to the floor in the room at the bottom of his tower when Cade came through after him.

He shut the portal down, drawing as much of its energy back into himself as he could. The raider was laid on the far side of the room. Cade and Kent both left. As soon as Jerryck finished, he sat and leaned against the wall, almost as tired as if he'd just had an accident.

Chapter 49

ARRET STOOD where he could see both the raider and the landing. If anyone entered the tower, he'd see them. If the raider stirred, he'd see him. Jerryck was too tired to tell him that the raider wouldn't move as long as the sleep magic held. And if someone entered the tower, they'd hear it because the door squeaked.

He leaned his head against the wall and let his eyes close. Home. Soon he would see his family. Sleep in his own bed. Eat in familiar surroundings. Use his own tools.

He nearly slipped over into sleep when the door squeaked open. He rubbed his face against grogginess and opened his eyes. Heston, Tajor, Cade, and two other elite guards came in.

Heston scowled at the raider. "You didn't put him in restraints?"

"He's restrained by magic," Jerryck mumbled.

"I see," Heston said. "Tajor, carry him down to the dungeon."

"You sure?" Tajor's gray eyes glittered with bemusement. "That won't create too much of a hassle just to make a point to someone who won't pick up on it?"

Heston glared at him. Then he snapped his fingers at the other elite guards. They picked up the man and carried him out. Heston grabbed Jerryck's arm and hoisted him to his feet. "You're coming."

"I hate the dungeon." Jerryck pried uselessly at Heston's vice grip pulling him out into the corridors. "I don't want to see what you're going to do to that man."

"You restrained him," Heston growled, dragging him along. "You're helping."

By the time Heston bullied Jerryck down to the dungeon, to the part without the magic dampening spell, and into a large room where the guards had taken the prisoner, they'd stripped the sleeping man naked and strapped him down to a table. The bare flesh revealed a few scars, most of them odd, like the small circular one on his abdomen. Tajor went through the man's clothing, fingering the objects he took out of the pockets.

"This man is definitely not from the mountains," Cade told Heston. "Look at these things. Chemwanee don't use these kinds of undergarments. During the winter, they usually line their clothes with down, or hair, or something else that insulates. I've never seen undergarments like these. And we can't even identify some of these other things. They're completely unfamiliar to all of us."

"Not all of us," Tajor said.

"This isn't a Chemwanitz practice, either." Kent lifted the man's right shoulder, revealing a symbol tattooed on the shoulder blade. It had perpendicular, black lines crossing each other, bending at right angles on the ends to form a square with open corners.

Jerryck leaned in for a good look. Magic-users south of the Ahnjwat Sea often tattooed themselves to aid their spells. This man had fair skin, not the blackish brown of the Southerners. And this symbol wasn't anything Jerryck had ever seen or studied.

"Tajor said it's an ancient sun symbol," Kent told him.

"What's your impression of their offensive and defensive styles?" Tajor asked as he examined a small, cylindrical object with a rounded end that dangled on a jewelry chain like a charm. It couldn't be a charm though. There was no magic on it in the slightest, and Tajor wasn't acting like he just came in contact with any kind of spell.

"They weren't very good with blades," Cade said. "More bluff than skill."

"They acted more accustomed to being shot at with projectiles," Kent added.

"Did any of them say anything?" Tajor set the cylinder down and leaned over to examine the circular scar on the man's abdomen.

"When Jerryck attacked them—" Cade said— "they started shouting '*tsow barer*.' Then one of them called '*rook zoog*' and '*shnell*' several times, and then they disengaged and retreated."

Tajor clenched his jaw and stood straight without taking his eyes off the prisoner. Heston said, "Tell me what you're thinking."

Tajor stared at the prisoner's face. "I'm thinking I'd like to ask our guest a few very pointed questions."

"How are you going to do that if he speaks a language no one understands?" Jerryck asked.

"Who told you I don't understand that language?" Tajor smirked. For once, it brought no mirth to his eyes. They remained gray and flat, void of amusement.

"What were the words Cade told you?" Jerryck asked.

"*Zauberer* means magician." Tajor pronounced the word very much like the raiders had. "The other two words were a call for a quick retreat. Did you do something that scared them?"

"Where did you learn an ancient language I've never heard before?" Jerryck demanded. With his trips to the conventions, he'd heard a lot of languages, probably more than anyone else in the entire palace.

"Who said it's an ancient language?"

"Didn't you say the tattoo is an ancient sun symbol?"

"That doesn't mean the language is ancient," Tajor said. "And with this particular combination—this language with that symbol, and the items he carried—it's a problem."

Heston's scowl deepened. "How big a problem?"

"I need to talk to him to ascertain the level of threat." Tajor sighed. "Hopefully, what I suspect is wrong."

"Jerryck." Heston pointed to the prisoner. "Can you rouse him just enough that he's only partially awake?"

Jerryck nodded. Perhaps it was good that he'd come after all. If it helped them learn what they needed without torturing the prisoner. Eager to get this over with and leave, he focused on the sleep magic.

Tajor held up a hand, stopping him. "Not until we tell you we're ready."

"Blind him," Heston said.

Kent jumped over with a cloth that he tied around the prisoner's eyes. Jerryck asked, "Why?"

"If this man has military training, we have slim chances of getting any easy information out of him," Tajor said. "Putting him in a semi-conscious state will make it easier for us. Being groggy will put his guard down. I'll catch him further off guard by talking to him in his language. Blinding him will further his disorientation, adding to our chances. Still, we'll probably only get a few good questions before he starts resisting."

"You think he'll start struggling to wake up more," Jerryck concluded.

Tajor nodded. "When I do this—" he made a cutoff gesture with a flat hand slicing vertically through the air— "immediately put him back to sleep."

Heston added, "And the entire time, you maintain silence."

Jerryck nodded. He waited for Tajor to tell him to start. Then he focused on the magic. It almost would have been easier if they had been in the part of the dungeon that had the dampening spell. He could just open it up to that. As it was, he shouldered all of the work. He lightened the strength, slowly powering it down. Easing it back. Little by little. Increment by increment.

The man groaned slightly. Jerryck stopped adjusting and held the magic at that level. The man stirred, drawing in deeper breaths, twitching his fingers and toes. Tajor started talking using a gentle voice, soft, right next to the man's ear. Slurring through sleep numbed lips, the man responded. The language was harsher and more guttural coming from him, spoken at the back of his mouth and tongue. When Tajor spoke the same language, it was fluid and almost musical.

As predicted, after only a minute or so of slow exchange, the prisoner struggled against the magic. Jerryck tightened his hold. They talked a bit more. The man frowned. His aura hit the magic so hard, Jerryck staggered with the jolt.

He put a hand on the wall behind him and broke out in a sweat. He tightened his hold again and braced himself for another hit. The man's muscles flexed, his arms and legs pulling at the leather straps binding him to the table. His speech patterns grew harsher. His heart sped up, coursing his blood, waking the man further despite the magic. Tajor gave the cutoff gesture.

Jerryck surged power back into the magic, reinstating it to full strength. It overwhelmed the man, sinking him back down into unconsciousness. His muscles went slack. His breathing deepened and evened out. His heart rate slowed back down to a normal pace. Jerryck sagged against the wall in relief.

"Did you get what we need?" Heston asked.

"I got enough to know that I need to speak with the king," Tajor half answered. "We'll need to speak with the rest of the core staff after that."

Heston glowered. "Tell me now."

"Privately," Tajor replied, tipping his head deferentially.

Jerryck went searching for his wife. With the palace nearing lunchtime, there was so much bustling activity, he couldn't find her in the quarter hour left before court ended. He left a message for her and dragged his feet to the small council chamber. He sat down, leaned his head back, and let drowsiness flow over him.

The aroma of cooked food filled the room. Dishes clanked. Heston said, "Keep him awake."

Someone tapped Jerryck's shoulder. He slit his eyes open to the kitchen server standing next to him. The man asked, "Would you like some hot tea?"

That started it. No one would leave him alone after that. Servers kept peppering him with questions about his preferences while they laid out lunch and the core staff gathered.

The steward shooed the servers out when Terrance entered. Nita and Tajor followed him in. Terrance said, "Apologies for my delay. I took the time to clear my schedule for however long we need to take in here."

He looked around the room, at everyone nodding acknowledgment, and paused when he saw Jerryck. His brow wrinkled with concern. "Are you all right?"

"Tired," Jerryck said.

"Have you seen your family yet?"

Jerryck shook his head. "They don't know I'm back. And I couldn't find them before lunch started. I left a message for my wife."

"Perhaps you should go rest," Terrance said. "I'll have her sent to you and catch you up later on everything in this meeting."

Tempting. Jerryck couldn't decide what he wanted more, his bed or his wife. A combination of the both would be bliss. But then who would verify that the portal had been opened by the very person they were looking for? And if he gave in to his weariness, how much rest would he get if he spent the time fretting that Terrance wasn't getting the service he had hired Jerryck for? And beyond that, what kind of example would that be to his sister's kids? What kind of father would that make him when his own child was born?

"I'll manage," Jerryck said. He picked up his fork, digging into the plate someone had put in front of him. Eating would help.

"Heston informed you all of the reason for this meeting," Terrance said, taking his seat for once. Heads nodded around the table. He stated it anyway. "You all know about the raids. We captured one of them alive and questioned him. Jerryck, what you don't know is that Shontarra has the same problem."

"The same group?" Jerryck paused, his fork halfway between his plate and his mouth.

"From what we can tell." Heston leaned back, not touching his own fork. "They're described the same. They're dressed the same. They have about the same number of people. And they operate the same. If it's a different group, they're answering to the same authority."

"How often are these raids occurring?" Jerryck asked.

"Once or twice every fortnight," Heston said.

"This can't be right." Jerryck shook his head and dropped his fork back onto his plate. "How is one person recovering his energy enough to do it that often?"

"What if they're a whole group of magicians?" The steward spoke with his mouth full of food, and shoveled more in.

"The prisoner referred to only one magician working with this group," Tajor said. "And considering where this group is from, the fact that they're using magic at all is incongruent. They shouldn't be making any portals. So it stands to reason, they're using unorthodox methods of energy recovery as well."

"You figured out where they came from?" Chamberlain Malk swirled his wine in his goblet with agitation. Next to him, Chancellor Herron leaned forward.

"They come from a country far removed from here," Tajor said. "It's one where science is so prevalent that most people don't believe magic exists. However, this country is under the rule of a dictator who's fascinated with it and wants to believe it's real."

Jerryck rolled his eyes and picked up his fork again. "It *is* real. Belief or desire have nothing to do with it. Can't they see the evidence of magic and know it from that?"

"They're blind to the evidence," Tajor said. "Their scientists have made excuses to explain it away. Because of the society, their leader has hidden away his belief to all but a select few. Apparently, one of that select few has found his way here. He opened a portal and brought some soldiers with him."

Heston crossed his arms. "What would they come here for?"

"Resources perhaps," Tajor said. "This nation is typically short on resources when they go through this time period."

Before anyone could question Tajor's odd statement, Terrance said, "What would they have to gain by stirring up trouble between the Chemwanitz and her neighbors?"

"If they're after raw materials, the mountains have them." Heston rose and slowly paced along the wall. "If they're a small group here, they may not have enough influence to gain what they're after. If they cause enough trouble that fighting breaks out, we may weaken ourselves against each other, making it easier for them."

"Our sister nation could be playing right into their hands," Terrance said.

Heston gave one curt nod. "Precisely."

"What else have I missed?" Jerryck asked.

"Prince Andreno is bulking up his army," Terrance said. "I sent him a letter of inquiry to make certain he has no plans to march troops across our border. He invited me to assist him in an invasion into the Chemwanitz in retaliation for the raided villages."

Jerryck's jaw dropped with shock. "He doesn't honestly think that will work, does he? Even the Gathering of Seats couldn't subdue the mountains when they warred with the shamans."

"That was a couple hundred years ago," Terrance said with a grimace. "Andreno doesn't listen to anyone saying anything he doesn't like to hear. I don't imagine any history tutor he ever had would have received different treatment."

"The Chemwanee didn't raid any villages." Jerryck shook his fork for emphasis.

"I told him that," Terrance said. "He demanded proof."

"Which means he didn't fully investigate the attacks," Heston concluded. He continued pacing.

"We have proof now," Nita said, rearranging the bits of food left on her plate. "We caught one of the raiders, and he's obviously not a Chemwanee. Invite Andreno to come and see, listen to the man's language."

"He won't come." Heston stopped pacing and faced her. "He's preoccupied with his coming military campaign."

Nita slapped her fork down. "Then send the prisoner to him." She pointed a finger back and forth between Heston and her father. "If we let him make this mistake, and he finds out later that we had proof the entire time, he could turn that army on us out of spite."

Heston said to Terrance. "She's right."

"Is there any more information you think we could get out of this man?" Terrance asked.

"Not without torture," Heston replied.

"That's not a good idea," Chamberlain Malk said. He pushed his goblet away. "Not if you want to make contact with these people and have good credence with them. If we treat one of their men well, even after what he did, that's all the more respect we can demand from them."

Terrance stroked the stubble of beard on his chin, his eyes unfocused. "And if I send him to Andreno, what are the chances we lose him?"

"High," Heston said.

"If we lose him to Andreno," Malk said, "whatever happens to him after that is on Shontarra. Not us."

"How many men should take him?" Terrance asked.

"A large enough group to keep him secure, and make the journey safe," Heston resumed his pacing. "A small enough group to travel fast. They have to get to Andreno before his campaign starts."

"Jerryck—" Terrance didn't look at him, his eyes still unfocused— "I don't suppose you could open a portal for some of the distance and shorten the trip?"

Jerryck shuddered. "Not after fighting last night and opening a portal this morning. I'm exhausted. I know a few magicians in the city who could."

Heston glared at Jerryck. "We're not employing any civilians for something this sensitive."

"Besides," Terrance said, focusing his eyes on Jerryck. "None are available. You must be so tired you're not thinking quite straight. You know very well that when winter hits, there's a rash of people paying for that kind of travel. Kershet's magicians able to do it are depleted by now. They always are every year."

Jerryck sighed. Perhaps he was even more tired than he thought. He did know that. And he was embarrassed that Terrance had needed to remind him.

"What if the prisoner stayed half asleep during the trip?" Tajor asked. "We wouldn't have to worry about him causing any trouble that way."

"For the entire trip?" Heston stopped pacing again and rubbed his chin. "Perhaps the medics might have something that would do that."

"Not really," Jerryck said, the food he'd eaten growing heavier and heavier in his stomach. "Not for that long. Not if you want him healthy at the end of the trip. And that's only if you can convince one of them to come along to give continual dosages."

"Aside from that," Tajor said. "It would mean making more people aware of the situation."

Jerryck could do it. He pushed his plate away and sank down into his chair. He didn't want to leave again. He'd just gotten back. And he hadn't even seen Leanne yet.

He scrubbed his face with his palms. He hadn't finished setting the wards in the villages. One way or another, staying wasn't an option. So really, it came down to a choice between which direction he thought had the chance of saving more lives. A few villages? Or preventing a possible war between two nations? He said, "The magician we sent to the southern villages to set the wards. He'll have to figure out how to make them."

"He already has," Heston said. "Why?"

"He's going to have to finish my route." Jerryck's mouth dried out, making the next few words even harder than they already were. "I'll help take the raider to Andreno."

Chapter 50

THE JOURNEY stretched out. Long. Boring. Cold. Monotonous. And exhausting, with the pace they maintained. Jerryck left his family again. Tajor accompanied this time, so Zev wasn't even getting any lessons. Tajor reminded him daily that Sinchet was the name of the secondary adviser under the Chamberlain who came. That drew attention to the fact that Jerryck had trouble with names. Embarrassing. A handful of elite guards escorted them. Jerryck knew none of them.

He'd been told that Cade and Garret were both tired and needed to rest. Tajor admitted that they were actually in trouble for bringing the prisoner to the palace with no restraints. They were going nowhere for a while. Their friend Deek, the guard with a crooked nose, had mouth off in their defense. So he was in trouble too, or he might have escorted just so Jerryck would know at least one of the guards.

No one would listen to him regarding the prisoner. They transported him in a supply wagon under a pile of furs and blankets, cuffed at the wrists and ankles, still blindfolded. The restraints were insulting. Jerryck kept the man under control, not the cuffs. And it took a toll on him to do it. He couldn't get enough sleep on the road to fully replenish what he spent every day maintaining the low level of magic.

All that was secondary to leaving his family again. Leanne had puked the morning he'd left. He used magic to ease her morning sickness, but it would wear off long before he returned. He should have stayed there, not gone off gallivanting around the country and beyond.

After they entered Shontarra, they turned east at the first crossroad. Andreno sent them a message telling them the exact location of his main encampment in the district of Garham so they could meet him there. They mucked through lowlands turned swampy by cold winter rains before making their way up to the higher ground that was close to the Shontese border with the Chemwanitz.

A man wearing a military uniform and ribbons of high rank met them at the edge of a city of tents and soldiers. He placed a fist on his heart and gave them a respectful nod. "Welcome, Brendish nobility. I am Commander Mirvian, military adviser to Prince Andreno representing the Garham District. Please, allow me to show you to the accommodations we've prepared for you."

He escorted them to the heart of the encampment, directing them to a tent twice the size of the one they used on the road. Still, it was dwarfed by the garish tent nearby. Mirvian nodded at it and said, "That's Andreno's. He's being informed of your arrival. Don't be surprised if he invites you to join him for the midday meal."

Three men and a woman stood in a line beside the entrance to their tent. Mirvian opened his hand to them. "Andreno has provided these servants to supply whatever needs may arise. So please, avail yourselves of them, allow them to help you make yourselves comfortable."

"We don't need servants for that," Jerryck said. He stalked past them and went inside. The canvas wall didn't block the noise of Sinchet spluttering and apologizing for Jerryck's terse words, making excuses about him being tired and cranky.

Jerryck threw himself down on one of the sleeping mats provided. It was cushioned, much more comfortable than the roll he'd been sleeping in on the road. The others came in one by one, the guards bearing some of the burdens from their supply wagon. None of the Shontese servants entered.

The guards laid the sleeping prisoner on one of the mats. They checked him, covered him, then one stood over him while the others arranged all the baggage and supplies. Before much longer, they received a summons from the Shontese prince.

Leaving behind half the guards, they stepped inside Andreno's ostenta-tious, multi-roomed tent. The garish colors of the canvas cast everything in an odd light. Andreno's skin had a false tint of orange, and when he flashed them his smile, his teeth had a yellowish hue instead of their brilliant white.

"Welcome to Shontarra." He raised his hands, throwing his arms wide. "I'm so pleased you've come. Sinchet, it's good to see you again."

Sinchet nodded in deferential response. Then Andreno turned to Tajor. "You must be the new Priad. It's a pleasure to finally meet you."

Tajor smiled and said nothing. Jerryck lifted a finger and opened his mouth to point out that the two had already met, more than once. But Andreno kept talking. "I know it's a bit early for the midday meal. I also know that while you're on the move, it can be difficult to get the time to sit down to a decent meal. Please, join me."

Servants bustled around, setting out food. They offered tasseled cushions to the guests. The elite guards that had escorted them, faded back with all the other extra people hanging about in the main room. Their eyes flicked to every face present. Tajor looked over all the extra people once, then gave Andreno his full attention.

Jerryck looked around too. Why were they all just standing there? Was watching Andreno eat with guests considered entertainment in Shontarra? People hadn't done that with Prince Sanbralio in his palace.

Most people had toned down the flamboyance of their clothes here out-side the palace. Several Shontese commanders were present, their uniforms decorated with ribbons and braids and pins, their colors coordinating with the district they represented. There were a couple of officials Jerryck had met in the palace, not that he could remember their names.

The only person that really looked out of place was a young man with dark blond hair. His boots were sturdy, polished but with scuff marks from use. His clothes looked like a uniform of some type. There were outlines on the collar, chest, and sleeves where stitches had once lay, as if all symbols or patches had been removed. On the belt at his waist, he carried a Shontese style dagger and a strange, triangular leather pouch.

One of the servants put a plate of steaming food on a low table in front of Jerryck. During the meal, he used the same stiff manners he forced himself to use the end of every week when he had to eat supper in the banquet hall with all the nobles visiting the palace. Focusing on that, he tuned out the conversation until Andreno addressed him directly.

"Jerryck," he said. "I haven't seen you since you came to visit us that time with Nita. How is she getting on?"

Jerryck swallowed his mouthful of food and said, "She's fine."

"I hear that her Processions have started." Andreno leaned his elbows on the table. "How's that going? Has she shown any interest in any of the young men in particular?"

Tajor answered for Jerryck. "Not as yet."

"It's good that she's cautious." Andreno scowled at his servant dishing him a second helping of the main course. Then he boxed the woman's ear. He kept talking as though it hadn't happened. "Someone in her position can't afford to show that they've taken a fancy to anyone if they're not appropriate for the position they'll be marrying into."

Jerryck mentally reached out and touched the aura of the servant Andreno had struck. She was going deaf in that ear from repeated abuse and injury. One by one, he checked the other servants. All of them showed signs of repeated abuse.

"Jerryck?" Andreno waved at him.

Jerryck jerked his focus back on the people at the table. "I'm sorry. What did you say?"

"I asked if the food wasn't to your liking," Andreno said, looking at Jerryck's plate. "You stopped eating."

"It's fine." Jerryck stared at the suddenly unpalatable food. "I'm tired. I think I need to rest."

"Traveling is rather hard on a man," Andreno said. "You may go back to your tent and rest."

Jerryck fled. When he got back to their tent, the guards there had let the Shontese servants in. He checked their auras and found signs of abuse in them as well. He plopped down on one of the sleeping pallets. He couldn't help them. None of them would even look directly at him.

It took almost another hour for the others to return. Tajor spent several minutes talking to Mirvian. When he left Tajor clapped his hands, getting the attention of everyone in the tent. He said to the Shontese servants, "Thank you all for a job well done. You're finished. Get out."

Several of the elite guards stared at him with surprise. Jerryck's jaw dropped open. Tajor made shooing gestures, hurriedly ushering the servants out. As soon as the tent flap closed behind the last of them, he turned to everyone else. "Pack up. We're leaving."

"We haven't delivered the king's message," Sinchet protested.

Tajor swiped his hands through the air, cutting Sinchet off. "Change of plans due to unforeseen circumstances. Pack. Leave behind anything we don't absolutely need or can pick up elsewhere on the road. We travel light."

While the guards started throwing their things back into their travel bags, Sinchet didn't budge. "We have to deliver the message."

"I did," Tajor said.

"You told Andreno we wouldn't help him invade the mountains. That's only half the message. You can't arbitrarily decide to change what the king sent you to say."

"I didn't change it. I omitted part of it."

"You can't do that."

"I can if it's superfluous."

Jerryck stood to get their attention. "What did I miss?"

Tajor turned to him. "Did you notice the blonde in Andreno's tent? The one who dressed differently than anyone else?"

"What of him?"

"He was the one I scared off in the Shontese palace," Tajor said. "He's been with Andreno this entire time. And what he wore today identified him as one of them." He pointed to the sleeping raider.

Jerryck frowned in confusion. "You weren't in the village where we caught him. How would you know he's one of them?"

"I don't know that he specifically assisted in that raid," Tajor said. "I do know he's associated with them. He comes from the same place."

"We're not going to get out of this camp if we all leave at once," one of the guards said.

"Split up," Tajor ordered. He pointed at three of them. "You go first. Make like you're wandering around until you can break out. Keep an eye on the edges of the camp for the rest of us to get out too. If we can't meet up outside, head back and make sure Terrance knows. And that goes for all of us."

One of the guards nudged the prisoner with a toe. "What do we do with him?"

"Leave him," Tajor said. "He'd slow us down. And if we're sneaking out in twos and threes, we won't be able to bring him anyway."

The guard posted just outside poked his head in. "A page just delivered a note for Jerryck. It says if he's feeling more rested, Andreno wants him."

"No," Tajor said.

"If he doesn't go," Sinchet said, "Andreno will be insulted. And it'll make him suspect we're up to something."

"I'll go see what he wants," Jerryck said. "The rest of you can leave. I'll do the same when he's done with me."

"This isn't a good idea," Tajor said.

"You have a better one?" Jerryck asked.

They held each other's eyes for a moment, the worry clear on Tajor's face. He looked away first. "No."

Jerryck left them, stepping outside where the page waited for him. He followed the lad to the prince's tent. When they arrived, Andreno whispered something to the page, sending him running off again.

"Please, sit." Andreno offered Jerryck one of the cushions from earlier. The table and all other signs of the meal were gone. Even the people. There weren't even any guards. "Tajor tells me that Terrance has decided not to punish the mountain barbarians for their crimes against his villages."

"It's his decision," Jerryck said as he sat. Then he had to readjust for comfort. That didn't work, so he fidgeted some more.

"You're right, and I shouldn't have brought it up," Andreno replied, waving that away. He took a deep breath and squared his shoulders, speaking more calmly. "I have a magic using friend you should meet. He's been looking for someone he can exchange knowledge and techniques with, someone he can teach at the same time he can learn from. I've been told you need some time with another magician to satisfy something for the Gathering of Seats. Here's your opportunity."

"That would officially be a mentor/apprentice relationship." Jerryck twitched. His feet itched, and shivers crawled up his spine. "I cannot enter into that unless the potential mentor is tested and sufficiently impresses Tajor with his skills."

"My friend won't try to mentor you." Andreno clasped his hands behind his back and paced. "He'll be learning as much from you as you from him."

"The stipulations have been publicly stated." Jerryck turned his head, tracking Andreno's movements. "A lot of people have already tried. If I go against this in any way, I'll have a few dozen angry magicians trampling over each other to get at me."

"Could you convince Tajor to come too?" Andreno crossed behind Jerryck, then back into view again. "It would only be a few days journey from here."

"I have trouble convincing Tajor of anything," Jerryck said. "I'm not sure it would be worth my time to even try."

"This is rather disappointing." Andreno circled around.

"Why don't you send your friend to the Brendish palace?" Jerryck asked. "Just warn him first that so far Tajor has only mocked and annoyed anyone trying for the position."

"He tried to come with me that time I went." Andreno stepped behind Jerryck again. "He got called away on urgent business before I crossed the border."

The tent flap opened. The young blonde entered, followed by another man dressed like him and carrying a satchel case. Andreno grabbed Jerryck and clapped a hand over his mouth.

"Quick!" Andreno shouted, holding both Jerryck's arms with just his left one. "Use your sleeping medicines."

Neither of the men moved. Their looks of sudden surprise turned into smoldering disgust. Jerryck twisted, trying to loosen Andreno's grasp. He tried screaming at him to let go. Only a muffled garble came out, completely unintelligible. That would also impede any magic spells. He couldn't cast anything if he couldn't get the words out right.

The blonde curled his upper lip. "Is this really necessary?"

"If he talks, he could use magic against us," Andreno said. He squeezed tighter against Jerryck's struggles. "And I can't hold him very long."

"Then let him go and apologize," the blonde said.

"I've had enough of your sass!" Andreno growled. Jerryck twisted one arm free. Andreno shifted his weight, pushing him down to the floor on his stomach, pinning his free arm, still yelling at the blonde. "Just do it. Or I'll have Ziegfried tell your government to kill your family."

The blonde's sneer morphed into a look of burning hatred. He turned to the other man dressed like him and spoke in the same language Tajor had used with the captured raider. The second man eyed Jerryck, sizing him up. He spoke a few more words with his comrade. He set down the leather case with a frown and extracted a small vial of clear liquid and a needled syringe.

Jerryck's energy gathered on its own. His heartbeat sped up. His stomach did flip-flops. Normally, in a bad situation, he would cast a spell, offensive or defensive. His body reacted the same, even though he couldn't get any words out for the casting.

The man filled the syringe. Andreno pressed in with his full weight, inhibiting Jerryck's squirming. His collar was pulled back. The needle poked into the muscle above his shoulder. The man emptied the contents.

The energy burst. It took the form of waking magic. Ironically, Jerryck now experienced the familiar drain of an accident. His limbs went slack. His eyes closed despite all efforts to keep them open. He started fading and drifting. Hands that moved with the competence of a practiced medic prodded him, checking his breathing and heartbeat, feeling his pulse, peeling back his eyelids one by one. Strange words floated on the air.

"He sleeps." The voice of the blonde sounded like he spoke from somewhere deep inside a cave.

Andreno let go. "Good."

Chapter 51

JERRYCK SANK. Everything went completely blank. He didn't see the abyss that sometimes loomed when he blacked out from too much magic. It always belched out sulfurous smoke, accompanied with tortured screams and pleas for mercy. There was none of that. No light. No dark. No sense of anything until he started dreaming.

Tajor and the blonde were talking. Beside them stood a large guard wearing glowing armor. It matched the armor of a second large guard that stood by Jerryck. The blonde told Tajor to hit him. From Jerryck's angle he couldn't tell if it was Tajor or the large guard who knocked him to the ground. Either way, Jerryck followed it up with fire. Good thing it was just a dream, proven by the fact than neither of the guards with glowing armor were affected by the flames. A large fire could have been dangerous in a city of tents.

Somehow, he found himself outside without any idea how he had gotten there. He staggered around a bit like a drunkard. People ran around shouting a lot. He stumbled into Tajor and grabbed him for support. Then the dream lurched and shifted.

Strange words he couldn't understand washed into his ears. Why couldn't he understand them? That wasn't right. The dream was his. He should be able to understand words in his own dream.

Periods of light and dark took turns passing. Sometimes he bounced and jostled. Sometimes everything was still and quiet. Always, Tajor was nearby.

He waited for his wife to shake him, tell him he'd overslept. He really should get up. His mouth was dry. Grit filled his eyes. Someone talked, and this time they didn't speak nonsensical syllables.

"Gerhardt wants you and the magician to leave." It was the blonde's voice. "He says you should try to connect with the three men that escaped Andreno. He has two packs with supplies for you in the other room. It is not much. But it will have to do."

"Just like that?" Tajor asked. "He's releasing us? He's demanding nothing in return? I'm supposed to believe it's this simple?"

"It is why he did not allow our medics to dose the magician again," the blonde said. "He does not want war with Brend. He will not be part of this. Help me with your friend."

Jerryck tried opening his eyes. Light stabbed through them. He groaned. Hands gently shook his shoulders. Tajor said, "Wake up. Open your eyes. We have to move."

"Move where?" Jerryck asked. At least that's what he tried to ask. What came out of his mouth was so slurred he couldn't even make out his own words.

"Anywhere but here." Tajor must have understood it anyway. "Open your eyes."

Jerryck slitted his eyes open. He groaned again. This time, he kept them open long enough to see Tajor's blurry face looming over him. Someone hooked their arms under his shoulders and heaved him into a sitting position. The world spun. He closed his eyes against the vertigo.

"Where's Leanne?" Jerryck still had trouble understanding himself.

"We'll go find her," Tajor said. He and the blonde pulled him to his feet. "Open your eyes again."

"Need sleep." Jerryck got much closer to enunciating the words that time. He tried more. "Need Leanne."

"Who is Leanne?" the blonde asked.

"His wife," Tajor said.

"He's *married*?"

"Why sound so shocked?"

"I was told magicians did not marry because—"

"Are we leaving or not?" Tajor sounded irritated. "Jerryck, move your feet. Walk forward. Put one foot in front of the other. Good. Now do it again. No, with the other foot."

Jerryck's body did not want to follow the commands, no matter how hard he tried. They moved anyway. He managed a little of it. Mostly, Tajor and the blonde dragged him through. He strained until he got his eyes back open. The memory of the blonde hit Jerryck. He was the one who had brought that wretched medic to Andreno's tent. Jerryck twitched with revulsion where the man was touching him.

The twitch must have been more of a lurch, or a jerk. Tajor shifted his grip, supporting more of Jerryck's weight and saying, "It's all right."

"There are the packs," the blonde said, pointing at something on the ground. He let go of Jerryck. "I will go make sure no one is outside."

He left. Jerryck looked around at the drab canvas walls of their small enclosure. "Where are we?"

"In a tent." Tajor didn't help. Jerryck sagged. He didn't have the energy to ask for clarification. Tajor sighed and gave it anyway. "We're in the mountains."

Jerryck let go of Tajor and leaned on a small, sturdy table. He couldn't think with all the fog in his head. He gathered his energy for magic to clear it up.

"Careful," Tajor said. "Make your spell something that has no lingering magic so I can help you if you need it."

Jerryck nodded. The motion set the world to spinning. Had he heard right that some medic had dosed him with something? Stupid medics. He set his spell to cause a chain reaction in his body that would purge itself of the effects of whatever they had used on him. His alertness would be slower than a quick spell that kept hold of him. But the magic wouldn't linger.

The blonde re-entered from the outside. "We are clear for now. We should go while we can. How is he?"

"He'll manage." Tajor hefted a pack on his back and lifted another.

The blonde took the second pack in his hand and led the way outside. Jerryck leaned heavily on Tajor, still prone to dizziness. He staggered at the drop in temperature the moment they left the meager cloth structure.

They moved in halting bursts. They ducked behind tents. The blonde would check an open space. Then they'd cross it and duck again. A couple of times he left them, talking to someone else, or something. Then Tajor would call him Adam and he would come back and they would move forward. Or did that happen only once? Twice? Once. Maybe. No, it had to be multiple times, because one of the times Tajor had to call him to come back when he took too long away.

After several hours... or was it only a couple of minutes? After some time, the blonde let Jerryck have a rest. Either that or something had distracted him. Tajor said, "Adam, how far can you get us?"

The blonde turned his head at the name and pointed in the direction they were heading. "To that line of trees over there past where the tents end. You will have to move quickly over where we cleared away the brush to where the trees start. The faster you are, the easier for me to make sure no one sees you. After that, you are on your own. Try and find those three men..."

He stopped talking mid-sentence. He was looking past Tajor to a large lump on the ground, halfway behind one of the tents. Jerryck rubbed his eyes. If only that would bring them into better focus. The blonde dropped the pack he carried and headed for the lump with a frown.

"This can't be good," Tajor said, his nose flaring.

Jerryck sniffed and caught the coppery scent of blood mixed with excrement. He shuddered, then checked to see if he was the one bleeding. He didn't find anything. He wasn't hurting anywhere. Just groggy and addled. This was the smell of death. And he was very much alive.

"Stay here," Tajor whispered. He let go of Jerryck and left him.

To his credit, he didn't fall over. To his discredit, it took all his concentration. There was some sort of commotion over by Tajor, the blonde, and the lump. There were more blurs over there that might be people wearing crimson and gold. Someone shouted in that harsh language these people used. Jerryck looked around, hoping no one else heard it. He didn't see anyone running their way. Of course, with how blurry his vision was, he couldn't really see much of anything at all. He rubbed his eyes again.

"You can't kill him," Tajor said.

"He'll raise the alarm," someone responded.

"You can't kill him," Tajor repeated.

"We can't leave him here to send everyone after us," the same voice argued.

"Problem solved," a different voice said.

Tajor came back to Jerryck. With him was a somewhat tattered and bedraggled elite guard. The guard picked up the pack the blonde had dropped.

"On your feet," someone said over by the lump. Jerryck checked his feet. He was still on them. And he'd done pretty good to stay that way. The same person said, "Let's get out of here."

They walked. Uphill. Of course, Jerryck might have felt like he walked uphill even if he'd sat on his butt and slid down a slope. He put one foot in front of the other, over and over, trying not to fall. Tree roots and rocks and bushes kept throwing themselves in front of him, tripping him up. When they crossed open spaces with no trees the very ground worked against him, slipping out from under his feet. And every time he tripped someone was right there, pulling him back upright and prodding him forward.

His breathing labored with the exercise. His vision cleared. The ground slipped because they walked on shale. They really did climb uphill. The trees were conifers interspersed with groves of aspens. The bushes were sage. And his breath was labored not just because he exercised, but because the air was slightly thin.

There were six of them altogether: Jerryck, Tajor, the blonde, and three disheveled and dirty elite guards. One of them walked with Tajor and the blonde. The other two helped Jerryck.

The group entered another stand of aspens and came to a small dell. They descended to the bottom and stopped. One of the guards with Jerryck stayed at the lip and disappeared back into the trees. The one with the blonde said, "Sit."

Jerryck sat. The guard remaining with him tugged on his sleeve, whispering at him, "Not you. You won't like this part. Come over here with me."

He refused to budge. He was still slightly groggy, still had difficulty piecing everything together. He needed to catch his breath and figure things out. Drawing up his knees he rested his arms and face on them, trying to even out his breath before he hyperventilated and brought all the dizziness back.

After a few moments, Tajor asked, "Got your breath back?"

Jerryck nodded.

"Good," Tajor said. "I have a few questions for you."

Jerryck couldn't possibly answer any questions in his current state. He lifted his head. Tajor's focus was entirely on the blonde between him and the third elite guard. The young man sat on his knees facing Tajor, his hands behind him, his face a grim mask of resolute acceptance.

"Oh, come now, Adam." Tajor clucked his tongue. "No need to look at me like that. It's not difficult. I ask a question. You answer the question. Simple. And the first question is, what year is it?"

Confusion flitted through Adam's eyes. Understandably so. Who were they? Where did they come from? Why were they here? How had they come? What weapons did they use? What types of magic did they use? Those were all logical questions. Why ask what year it was? As if every culture even used the same count.

The guard smashed a fist into Adam's face. Jerryck gasped. Adam didn't put his hands forward to catch himself or straighten back up. Tajor helped him with that and said, "Oh, I didn't tell you that part. If you don't answer fast enough, he'll hit you."

"You do not count years the same as my people," Adam said. "Why do you need the year?"

The guard hit him again. His nose bled. Jerryck swallowed down the nausea that rose up. The guard next to him stepped in his line of sight, blocking his view. He leaned over, unable to tear himself away.

"That's another thing," Tajor said to Adam. "I ask the questions. You don't get to, unless I give permission. Let's try this one more time. What year is it?"

Adam hesitated. The guard raised his fist. Jerryck inhaled to tell him not to hit, just as Adam flinched and said, "1949."

The guard lowered his fist. Tajor sat back with a slight frown. Maybe because the number was ridiculously high. What kind of nation was nearly a couple thousand years old?

"What year did the war start?" Tajor asked.

"1942," Adam said.

Tajor's frown deepened. "It wasn't in the late 1930's?"

"No."

"When did the Great War end?"

"1925."

"So late…" Tajor murmured.

None of this made any sense. The last great war had been back when the districts had all joined under the banner of the man who ended it and became the first King of Unified Brend. But then, Tajor wouldn't have any cause to ask after Brendish history. Of course he wasn't. Jerryck still had cobwebs in his head. Tajor would be asking about the nation Adam came from.

"Have the Americans entered the war?" Tajor continued, asking this time about something Jerryck had never even heard of. How did he know to ask?

"Yes," Adam said, his expression getting more and more confused.

"What provoked them? And when?"

"In 1945, when the Japanese sank their fleet in San Francisco Bay."

"*San Francisco?*" Tajor straightened up in surprise, startling Jerryck. "They didn't sink the American's Pacific Fleet in Pearl Harbor? Why did they skip Hawaii and go all the way to California?"

"They were in control of Hawaii at the time. They would not attack themselves. How do you know these names and places?"

The guard struck. He left a reddening, swelling ring around Adam's left eye. Someone had to stop this. Jerryck pulled his feet under him to stand. The guard with him gently gripped his shoulders and whispered, "Leave it alone. It's part of the job."

Tajor glanced in Jerryck's direction. Then he grabbed Adam's coat front and sat him up straight. Blood still dribbled out of his nose. He sniffed. Jerryck clenched his hands, itching to get over there and work some healing magic.

"You remember when we talked about you being from another world than this one?" Tajor asked.

"Yes," Adam answered quickly, his eyes flicking momentarily to the guard's fist.

"If there are two worlds," Tajor said, "doesn't it stand to reason that there are bound to be more?"

Adam's eyes unfocused. He frowned and shrank back slightly. He didn't answer the question. The guard raised his fist. Tajor held up his hand. "That question was only to make him think."

Adam's focus snapped back. He warily watched the guard lower the fist. Tajor poked him in the chest and said, "Something you should know, and you can pass this on to your leader. Your people, in this war, you lose. Always. One way or another, something happens and you lose. Sometimes it's a major event that turns the tide, like the storming of the beaches of Normandy by the Allies. Sometimes it's sabotage of the war machine from within. Sometimes it's a slow process of attrition, everything winding down due to lack of resources. Sometimes with that one, your leaders go underground, feigning surrender and leaving the populace to the mercy of your enemies. Sometimes it's a sudden halt, such as a fire weapon dropped on Berlin that's so hot and destructive it razes buildings to the ground and melts people's flesh from their bones."

That was the most horrific thing Jerryck had ever heard of. Adam gulped, but didn't look shocked or surprised. Or confused. Just how bad was this war his people were embroiled in?

Adam opened his mouth. Then he looked up at the guard and closed it again. Tajor said, "You may ask a question."

"Why do you talk like my country is in many different worlds?"

"It is."

"How?"

"Some events are so large, they splash across many worlds. It's like echoes in a canyon, or ripples in a pond. They spread out from where they originate, bounce around, and touch everything around them. And just like echoes are sometimes distorted, or ripples are broken, as the event spreads out into neighboring worlds, variations occur. The biggest distortion in your world seems to be the timeline. Your dates are all late. It's throwing off the major events. Let me guess. When you invaded Russia, it wasn't the worst winter they'd had in over a century."

Adam shook his head.

Tajor nodded. "Usually by the time the Americans enter the war, your people are running out of resources and supplies. That was four years ago?"

"Three and a half," Adam said.

"Why haven't you run out of resources?"

Adam clenched his jaw. The guard hit him, splitting his lip open. Tajor kept him from falling and asked, "Who's winning the war?"

"No one," Adam slurred his words. Even with Tajor holding him, he tipped a little to the side revealing the cords around his wrists. The guard grabbed the back of his collar, tipping him back fully upright. He and Tajor both let go.

"Is it because you're getting your resources from another world?" Tajor asked. "Like this one?"

Adam clenched his jaw again. He flinched right before the fist smashed into him, knocking him over completely.

Jerryck couldn't take any more of this. He shouted, "Stop it!"

"Now look what you've done," Tajor said, sitting Adam upright. "The scary, fire-throwing magician is upset. You should answer the question before he gets any angrier."

Adam closed his swelling eyes and braced. Jerryck stood speechless. If he said anything more, Tajor would twist it again. The guard raised his fist. This time Tajor held up a hand, stopping him.

He leaned close to Adam. "Your silence speaks volumes."

The third guard who had disappeared into the trees came sliding on his feet down the side of the dell. "Visitors coming. About ten of them. We have less than two minutes."

The guard who had done all the hitting drew his sword. Adam's breath hitched and he cringed. Tajor jumped to his feet, holding up both hands. "You can't kill him."

"We can't take him with us," the guard said.

"Leave him," Tajor said.

"So he can tell them what direction we went?" The guard didn't lower his blade.

Tajor shrugged. "How? If he can't see or hear us go?'

Jerryck would have to use magic to make him sleep. He focused, gathering energy. The guard brought the hilt of his sword down with a sharp crack on the base of Adam's skull just under his ear. He fell over, motionless.

"Hey!" Jerryck shouted.

"Don't argue." Tajor took him by the arm and ushered him up the opposite side of the dell. "We only have seconds before he starts coming around."

"I could have done that in a way that would have been a lot better for him!" Jerryck moved his feet where Tajor directed him.

"I don't care what's better for him," the guard growled.

"Stop talking," Tajor said. "Focus your energy on walking fast, not on needless spell casting."

He tossed a triangle leather pouch off to the side. The guard bent to pick it up. "What are you doing?"

Tajor grabbed him, stopping him. "Two things will make them pursue us. One, if we kill their interpreter. Two, if they think we have one of their weapons. Leave it."

The guard left it. So did the other two. The three of them and Tajor all hustled Jerryck farther away from the dell, sticking to the cover of trees.

Chapter 52

ONE OF THE THREE surviving guards specialized in knowing the mountains. It was the very reason he'd been sent with them. After making certain they weren't being followed or hunted down by Adam's friends, he headed them for the nearest group of people he knew of, a Chemwanitz tribe in their regular winter camp.

Tajor lagged behind, loudly proclaiming, "This isn't a good idea."

"Neither was leaving that interpreter alive," the hitter said.

"You think his friends would have stopped following us if they'd found him dead?" Tajor asked.

The hitter wouldn't turn to look at Tajor while he spoke. "How did you know to ask all those questions anyway?"

"How do I ever know to ask any question?" Tajor pulled his customary evasion. "How do you know it's a good idea to go to this winter village?"

The hitter stomped his feet as he walked. "What else do you know about those people?"

"The villagers? Not much," Tajor said. He pointed to the guard who had become their guide. "Shouldn't you ask him what he knows about them?"

"Not the Chemwanee." The hitter swept a hand over his shoulder back behind them. "Those men back there. You were asking questions none of us could have. What more do you know about them?"

"Why do you get to ask all the questions?" Tajor frowned at him. He nodded to Jerryck. "He doesn't even know where we are or how we got here. Don't you think he should get to ask a question?"

"How did we get up here anyway?" Jerryck asked as they skirted around a clump of sedge. "The last thing I clearly remember is Andreno attacking me in his tent."

"You and I were transported in a wagon under guard," Tajor said.

"How many guards?" Jerryck asked.

"Why would you ask that? There were enough that it would've been difficult for these three—" Tajor waved to the men wearing tattered crimson and gold elite uniforms— "to extract us with you in a drugged state."

"We would have tried anyway," the hitter said. "If we'd caught up before they reached that second camp."

"You see?" Tajor said to Jerryck. "They did the best they could. You shouldn't ask how many guards there were."

"I asked because you're strong enough to overwhelm people," Jerryck said. "Were there too many for you?"

"Back to your previous question," Tajor evaded again. "When you were in Andreno's tent, I knew something had gone wrong when the raider started waking up. I tried to get Sinchet to leave with more of the escort guards. Only these first three we sent when you left made it."

"Sinchet didn't make it?" Jerryck's foot slipped on another patch of shale where the ground rose again.

"He refused to go," Tajor said. "Andreno's men killed him."

The hitter also slipped on the treacherous ground. He screwed up his face into a snarl. "And they left you alive."

Tajor's feet didn't slip at all. "They took me outside first. I thought maybe I could talk them down. Until they went inside and started killing everyone."

"Except you and the raider," the hitter said.

Tajor shook his head. "They killed the raider too."

"Why would they keep you alive and no one else?" the hitter asked.

"They kept Jerryck alive." Even though Tajor didn't lose his footing on the rocky slope, he still lagged behind. He asked Jerryck, "Did you tell Andreno you can only work with another magician if I approve?"

"Yes," Jerryck said. The slope was growing steeper and he was getting short of breath. "Why?"

Tajor wasn't running out of breath. "Because that means Andreno believes these foreigners want something from you. That could be the reason they're here. They're looking for magic. And someone rogue enough to teach them to wield it."

"You asked about resources." The hitter was short of breath too. "Not magic."

"And he didn't answer," Jerryck muttered.

"That doesn't mean what you might think," Tajor said. "If he was told they're here for resources and he found out differently, he might not say a thing to the contrary no matter how much you beat him. Where he comes from the truth can get you killed. And your family killed. And your pets killed. And your house razed to the ground as if none of you ever existed."

"And we're back to you knowing too much about them." The hitter picked up a sliver of shale and chucked it in Tajor's general direction. "How can you possibly know all this?"

"I still would like to know why you didn't escape before today," Jerryck said. "You're strong enough. How many could you have killed? How many were there?"

"Don't believe all rumors about his strength." The guide had stopped in front of them at the top of the incline. He panned the landscape, his gaze roving over the peaks and valleys.

"Most of the rumors run toward the ridiculous," the hitter said.

Jerryck leaned his hands on his knees, desperate to catch his breath. "He can break a man's jaw with just a slap."

The hitter jutted out his own jaw. "As I said, ridiculous."

"I watched it happen," Jerryck said.

All three of the guards turned and stared at Tajor. The hitter crossed his arms. "Tell us why you didn't escape before we caught up. And don't give us the excuse about the magician being drugged."

Tajor shuddered at the direct command. He stepped past them all, looking out across the landscape. "You're sure we're going in the right direction? I still don't think we should go to any group of people in this area."

The hitter clenched his fists. "Explain!"

Tajor shuddered again and glanced back over his shoulder. "You wouldn't believe me if I told you."

"Are you in league with these people?" the hitter asked.

"No," Tajor said.

"Are you from the same place?"

"No."

"Then how do you know so much about them?"

"I explained to the king and princess." Tajor turned fully around to face them all. "That should be enough for you."

"They're not here." The hitter tipped his chin down, deepening his glower. "We are. And we are risking our lives. What else can you tell us that could lessen our danger?"

"Besides telling you to avoid any villages in this area?" Tajor cocked his head at the man. "You won't listen to that. Why would you listen to anything else?"

"What more do you know that kept you from trying to escape?"

"I did try." Tajor threw his hands up in the air. "Jerryck set fire to their tents."

"So that's how that fire started," their guide mumbled.

"I thought I was drugged," Jerryck said.

"You had magic on you," Tajor told him. "I can only assume you cast a spell right before you lost consciousness. The magic was set to keep you awake, but it was fighting with the drugs. You weren't really coherent. Just standing with your eyes open and moving your lips enough to cast the fire spell that set everything to blaze."

"That was in Andreno's camp." The hitter put his fisted hands on his hips. "That doesn't explain why you didn't try to escape while you were transported up here. Does it have something to do with the real reason you wouldn't let us kill that interpreter?"

"He's valuable," Tajor said. "We can communicate through him. He speaks both our language and theirs."

"So do you," Jerryck blurted out.

All three of the guards frowned at Tajor. His shoulders slumped and he gave Jerryck a dirty look. The hitter said, "Tell us the real reason why."

This time when Tajor shuddered, a whiff of his aura brushed up against Jerryck's. The buzzing of a thousand hornets vibrated. Whether it was the close proximity, or the buildup through continued resistance that caused the contact, Jerryck didn't care.

"Stop it." Jerryck stepped back, hoping more distance would help. "Please don't resist. Just tell the real reason why."

"He has a veiled guardian," Tajor said. The buzzing stopped.

"A what?" Jerryck asked.

"I told you you wouldn't believe me," Tajor said.

"It's not disbelief," Jerryck said. "It's lack of understanding. What's a veiled guardian? I didn't see anyone else there."

"That's what the veil is for. The veil was dropped just enough for me to see. Adam likely doesn't even know he has one. But if you kill him, that guardian will kill all of you." Tajor turned back to look across the landscape in front of them. "Are we pushing forward or not? Which way are we going?"

The guide sat on a rock. The hitter said, "You gave us a reason for not killing him, whether we understand it or not. That still doesn't explain how you know so much."

"I know a lot because I've studied," Tajor said.

"Tell us where you studied," Jerryck ordered.

Tajor glared at him. "I studied at the place I come from."

"Tell us where that is," Jerryck said.

"It's everywhere around you, like the next step up in a fractal," Tajor said. "You can't see it because it's too big. It touches this place, encompasses the entire world and many others besides. Including the world those foreigners came from. As I explained to the interpreter. Some events are large, and they splash across world boundaries. Those are the kinds of events I studied."

The hitter finally unclenched his fists, only to rub his fingertips on both sides of his head. "Now you're talking complete gibberish."

"If that man has a guardian we can't see," the guide said, "then why did you have him beaten?"

"There are many kinds of assignments for guardians," Tajor said. "One of them is to encourage a certain level of violence for the individual they're guarding to go through. It tempers them. Prepares them for something worse."

"Why would you think that's the kind of guardian that man has?" Jerryck asked.

"Because he hit Adam," Tajor said. "In Andreno's camp. Just as you were igniting the place. Adam probably thinks I did it. But I didn't touch him. Guardians are really good at making things look like a coincidence, or like someone else did it."

The hitter shook his head. "You're still not making any sense. And the less sense you make, the less reason we have to listen to you telling us not to go to any village in this area."

"Agreed." The guide started down the other side of the slope, pointing between two of the peaks. "This way."

Going downhill was much easier than going up. The slippery ground actually aided their progress instead of impeding it. And Tajor still lagged behind.

The guard who hadn't said anything finally spoke up. "Do you think these are the same group of foreigners?"

"Same group as what?" Jerryck asked.

"I tried to check out a group of foreigners at that abandoned castle between Larksen and Shana," the quiet guard said. They passed beneath a copse of trees that blotted out the sky. "The nearest villagers were... less than cooperative."

"Are they still there?" the hitter asked.

"As far as I know," the quiet one said.

"They might have split up," the guide said. "Keep a force there to maintain their foothold base. Send the rest up here to spearhead an invasion. Then Andreno can bring in his main army to occupy once the dirty work is done."

"Gerhardt, their leader," Tajor said. "He's none too pleased about the situation from what I could tell."

"Because you overheard him talking when he didn't know you can speak his language?" The hitter sounded bitter for some reason.

"Because he let us go," Tajor said. "And told the interpreter to ask us to find someone to threaten them so they could have an excuse to leave."

The hitter glowered. "I don't remember the interpreter saying that."

"Things didn't quite go according to plan," Tajor said. "I guess he just didn't get around to it, what with us kidnapping, interrogating, and beating him and all."

"And it's all the more reason to go to the nearest group of people," the guide said. "So we can tell them to send threats to those men so they can leave."

Tajor sighed and shook his head.

Chapter 53

"**W**E SHOULD HAVE RUN into people by now." The guide had slowed considerably over the past hour or so, moving with more caution. "We're close. There should be gatherers, workers, hunters, kids playing around. Scouts at the very least. Where is everyone?"

"Are you sure they're still there?" the hitter asked.

"Spring isn't quite here yet," the guide said. "There's still snow in the highest places. Not enough fresh greens to support a whole tribe on the move. They should still be here."

They crested another small rise and came to the edge of the aspens they had been trudging through. Several earsplitting shrieks pierced the air, something halfway between a screaming woman and a bird of prey. A cold chill shivered up Jerryck's spine. Tajor stopped and looked up at the sky.

Several large creatures circled through the air, just over the next rise. Most of them had a wingspan wider than the height of a tall man. They slowly descended lower, the bottommost ones disappearing over the hill. Higher up, two of them came so close together, they nearly collided. The larger of the pair let out another bloodcurdling shriek and slashed at the other with its talons. The smaller one beat its wings, gaining some distance before continuing its descent.

The guide watched them. "Something's wrong."

"Those birds keep circling like carrion eaters," the hitter said.

399

"They're not birds…" Jerryck took a step backward, ready to bolt back into the aspens behind them. "I've never seen so many of them together all at once."

"They fly like vultures," the hitter said.

"They're volashes," the guide said. Another shriek reached them. The smaller one was getting picked on again. "They're usually solitary. Territorial. I've never seen them act like this."

Jerryck took another step backward. "They're in a feeding frenzy."

"They're eating the encampment," the guide whispered, tension crawling up his back, hunching his shoulders, darkening his expression.

"You must have made a mistake," the hitter said. "There must be a herd of animals here. People would be fighting back."

"Dead people don't fight back," Tajor said. The smaller volash disengaged from the main group.

"If their prey was alive, they wouldn't be congregated like this," Jerryck said. "And they'd be whistling, not frenzied. They draw in their prey with audible magic, then terrorize them like a cat with a mouse until their victim's bodily fluids flavor the meat to their liking. Unless their meal is already dead. Then they just eat."

"This is where those men went this morning," the guide still whispered, now craning his neck, looking every which direction. "They could still be in the area."

"We're at least a couple of hours behind them," Tajor said. "They'll be gone, on their way back, avoiding the carrion eaters."

"Who are you talking about?" Jerryck asked.

The guide backed farther toward the trees. "This is why you didn't want to come here."

The smaller volash soared several feet in their direction. Jerryck threw up an illusion of the field and trees, so that would cover them visually. It wouldn't do much good if it scented them.

The creature came close enough for them to see how its body undulated beneath the layers of skin flaps that gave it the appearance of a feathered creature. It cocked its flat, snake-like head to one side, its face fixed on something it had sighted on the ground. Then it opened its beak.

Jerryck started the words for an ear-blocking spell. The volash's whistle hit him, piercing through everything. His vision blacked out. His entire body went numb. He couldn't even hear his own voice as he fought to speak the last word. If the magic behind the whistle hadn't been spread between so many of them, he might not have succeeded. He severed the magic from his aura and cast it away. He came back to his senses, several feet closer to the volash, his legs having moved while he was unaware, drawn by the whistle. The three guards stumbled mid-step once Jerryck's deafening magic hit them. They blinked sleepily and looked around as if awakening from a confused stupor.

Jerryck reached out with his aura, trying to sense whatever had caused the volash to start whistling. First, he felt everything nearest to him: the men, the field, the edge of the aspens. He spread forward from there, creeping over the next rise. The grass grew sparse, the ground cold and hard, the sagebrush abundant.

There was movement. Someone walked straight for the volash in its continued descent. Jerryck focused, brushing against the aura of the victim: a wounded little girl.

The child walked headlong into the middle of the bramble of sedge. The bush caught her up and impeded her progress. The volash stopped whistling and dived, its long body stretching out more like a serpent, streamlining it for speed.

The girl shook her head and put both her hands on her temples. The volash flew over, bypassing her, flexing at the last moment to spread its faux feathers. Their razor-sharp edges slashed open the girl's shoulder. She screamed. The sound didn't penetrate the ear-stopping spell. The vibrations of it flowed back through the contact with her aura.

Jerryck reeled, his senses snapping back to normal. Tajor had to have heard the scream. He was already passing hand signals to the three guards. They drew their swords and move forward.

They came upon the girl as the volash swooped for another strike. Jerryck threw a wad of raw magic, stunning it. It faltered in the dive and crashed to the ground hard, stunning it further. The guards quickly dispatched it from there.

Tajor and Jerryck disentangled the girl from the bush. She was ashen and limp. Her shoulder bled where the volash had struck. Blood oozed from a small, circular wound in her side. The hitter scooped her up and they all ran back to the cover the aspens provided.

Jerryck let go of the magic that stopped their ears. The sounds of the volashes feeding, gorging, and dickering among themselves reached them. It spurred them farther into the trees, putting more distance between them and the vicious creatures.

As soon as they were out of earshot, they stopped. Jerryck examined the girl's wounds. She sobbed, talking rapidly, frantically gesturing back the way they'd come.

The guide leaned in, staring at her intently. Then he shook his head. "I can't figure out what she's saying. She's talking too fast. Something about a sister."

"She says she stuck her younger sister under a bush to keep her hidden," Tajor said. The guards stared at him in surprise. Tajor continued, "She wants to go back and get her."

She wouldn't calm down until Tajor got the exact location of the sister. He left with two of the guards. The hitter stayed with Jerryck and the girl.

Jerryck focused on the wounds. He sealed up the gashes where a medic would use a needle and stitches. He stemmed the blood loss from the wound in her side. Then he probed with magic.

Inside the wound he found a blunt-pointed lead slug. He could seal the wound, help along the girl's healing well enough. The question was, did that slug have to come out or would it be detrimental to leave it in? Plenty of people walked around with bits of foreign objects inside their bodies. Smiths got slivers of metal embedded all the time. But that was near the surface. And slivers. Not a large slug deep in the body like this.

It should come out, just to err on the side of safety. Now the question became how to do that without causing more damage? He didn't have enough experience with extracting foreign objects from penetration wounds. He knew of one time, when a large splinter of wood had speared a builder's leg. Jerryck's mentor had used purely white magic to force the body to expel the wood.

Jerryck concentrated all his attention on the wound and the lead slug. He cobbled together a spell as best he could. He kept his grip on it tight, his control high. He got a stirring of response. Just a stirring. The lead slug stayed in the exact same position. He backed off and let go of the magic. He had either gotten the words wrong, or this technique simply lay beyond his skill. He would have to do this the way a medic would.

"I need some help." Jerryck grit his teeth while the girl whimpered. He used magic to put her to sleep, then said, "There's a lead slug inside her. I need a sharp knife, and you'll have to hold her side open so I can reach in and dig it out."

"She's already lost a lot of blood," the guard said.

Jerryck gathered energy for magic. "I'll control the blood loss."

He would control more than blood loss. His hands would need to be sterilized before and after the procedure, along with the knife. He would bespell swollen tissues into relaxing. Magic would also have to close and seal the wound. Over the next several days, he would have to keep a constant vigil against infection. All while they traveled.

"You're lucky I have this." The guard handed him a Shontese style dagger. "I lost mine."

"Where?" Jerryck took the blade.

"Between the ribs of some guy trying to block our escape from Andreno's camp," the guard said as nonchalantly as if discussing the weather. He pointed at the dagger. "I got that from our blonde friend when he pulled it on us."

"I don't remember him doing that," Jerryck said.

"You were so befuddled I'm surprised you remember anything." The guard actually looked slightly amused, as if there was anything funny about all this. "The way he held it makes me think he's got more talent than skill. Easy to get yourself in trouble that way. Makes you overconfident."

"I don't want to know any more about it," Jerryck said.

He refocused on the girl and spoke the magic words that sterilized everything. With the guard's help, he managed to cut in and dig out the slug. It looked almost exactly like the one that the raider had worn on a necklace chain. Jerryck closed and sealed the wound. the guard kept looking around, his attention everywhere but on the girl. Jerryck ended up finishing the final steps himself.

"I could have used a little more help," Jerryck complained. "What's got you so distracted?"

"Just keeping watch," the guard said. "Don't want to get sneaked up on."

Jerryck picked up the girl and held her close, sharing his body heat and wrapping her in warming magic. "The volashes are distracted. We're far enough away we should be fine here until bigger predators come along."

"The bigger predators are what I'm watching for." The guard stood and slowly circled them, facing outward. "Including the ones that fed the volashes."

"Fed the… What are you talking about?"

"We were going to wait a day or two before penetrating their camp to try and rescue you and Tajor," the guard said. "Wait, watch, study, lay low, strategize, pick off a few loners if we could… Then about half of them formed up and marched out of camp, loaded with weapons and supplies. This winter encampment, this is where they went. They did this."

Jerryck squeezed the girl tighter. "*Why?*"

"Tactics for spearheading an invasion." The guard tilted his head back, scanning the treetops. "Slash and burn, some call it. You move a powerful group into an area and kill every living person until everyone else backs away from you. Then you bring in the occupying army to hold territory."

Leaves rustled in the direction of the slaughtered people. The guard spun around to face it, dropping into a fighting crouch, dagger in hand, eyes glittering. He relaxed when Tajor and the other two guards stepped into view through the trees, carrying a sniffling toddler.

The child caught sight of the girl in Jerryck's arms and wriggled down to the ground. Tajor quickly caught her back up before she could throw herself on the patient and reopen the newly closed wounds. She started wailing and saying the same word over and over. "Khata! Khata! Khata!"

"Shh, shh," Tajor rubbed her back and stroked her hair. He spoke gently in the Chemwanitz language until her cries eased back down to sniffles.

The quiet guard plucked the girl from Jerryck's arms, careful of her freshly sealed wounds. Jerryck checked the toddler. She had no injuries other than a few scratches, nothing even a medic would say needed stitches.

Then they moved. As quickly as they could. Putting as much distance between them and the volashes as they could manage before the sun set. The creatures would be sleepy after their meal. But where volashes gathered, other predators tended to follow.

They spent a restless night in another grove of aspens. Jerryck put wards up. The guards kept a constant watch. Tajor didn't sleep the entire night. When they arose, Jerryck checked the girl's wounds and magically nudged them toward healing. She let him do everything he needed to without question or protest.

When he finished, the girl and her sister babbled at Tajor, both pointing off in the same direction. The hitter asked, "What are they saying?"

"Senka is just copying Khata," Tajor said.

"What? Who?"

"Their names…" Tajor squatted beside them. He patted the toddler on the head. "This is Senka, and her big sister is Khata."

"I don't care who's copying who," the hitter snarled. "What are they saying?"

"Does it really matter?" Tajor asked.

"Something about the next nearest tribe," the guide said. "Her mother's brother lives there. And something about shamans gathering. We should go there. Get help."

"From shamans? With a magician for a companion?" Tajor glared at him. "Besides, I had thought the state of that last village proved me correct. We shouldn't go to any encampment or winter village in this area."

"I already headed us in that direction," the guide said. "We need supplies. And if shamans are gathering, we can talk to them."

"You can get killed." Tajor bared his teeth. "If they're attacked while we're there, what do you think the chances are that you'll survive? And even if they're not attacked, we won't be able to keep from telling them what happened to Khata's tribe. We'd be the bearers of bad news. Very bad news. What will they do to us to extract payment?"

"If her mother's brother lives there, she can pass that information to him through the family tie without payment," the guide said. "We would be doing her a favor. Jerryck saved her. She owes him life debt. If we bring her to let her pass the information on anyway, we'll be paid, not punished!"

"What's life debt?" Jerryck asked.

"You're discounting human nature," Tajor said, completely ignoring Jerryck. "The tradition you're clinging to for hope is missing some pieces."

"Why can't you ever say anything that makes *sense?*" The guide picked up a clod of dirt and threw it at Tajor's head. Tajor ducked. The dirt missed.

Khata asked a question. Tajor said something to her. She started crying.

The guide said to Tajor, "You're truly horrible sometimes."

Khata crawled into Jerryck's lap and clung, sobbing as if her life were ending. The toddler saw her sister's distress, and her eyes welled up. She looked around to each of the men in turn, probably expecting them to fix whatever was wrong.

"Tajor," Jerryck said. "Tell us what you said to her."

"I told her we shouldn't go to where her uncle lives," Tajor said.

Senka's tears fell. She looked between them all more and more frantically, the more her sister carried on. Khata's breath hitched in sobs so hard, she was in danger of reopening the wound in her side.

"I can't handle this." The guide rubbed his eyes with his thumbs. "I don't care what the rest of you do. I'm taking these two where they want to go."

Chapter 54

UNWILLING TO SPLIT UP, all of them went with the guide. Even Tajor. Though he continued protesting the entire way, even after all three guards told him to drop the matter. Khata directed them, jabbering most of the way. Tajor refused to translate. The guide told them what he was picking up on.

Her uncle wasn't the only one there she wanted to see. The shamaness from her tribe was also there. An entire group of them had gathered to discuss things. Khata hadn't known what they were talking about, but with the attack on her village she guessed.

"Ask her if she knows if Sakila is there," Jerryck said.

The guide spoke a bit with the girl. Then he said, "She doesn't know who Sakila is."

The girl definitely knew the area. Over the next several days they went through cold valleys. They struggled through a couple of passes that still had remnants of snow trying to clog them. She knew where to find water and which of the early spring shoots were edible, even though they were so young Jerryck couldn't identify them properly.

They saw the smoke from the fires before they came anywhere near the winter encampment. A scout stopped them. He eyed them. Then, using Brendish, demanded, "Who are you and why are you here?"

Khata talked to him. Then the scout eyed Jerryck and said, "You asked about a shamaness?"

"Sakila," Jerryck said. "She's from a lot farther north than here."

"What tribe is she from?"

"Urgh," Jerryck grunted, passing a hand over his eyes. "I forget the name she used. I know it means the Jagged Finger Peak."

"Chempagquin," the guide said.

The scout called out in his language. Another one popped out from hiding and ran for the village. They waited. Khata sat down at Jerryck's feet. Senka mimicked her.

After several minutes, the second man returned. He exchanged a few words with the scout who barred the way. Then the scout stepped aside, saying to them, "Follow him."

The man led them down into another small valley. The winter encampment was huddled up against a steep rock face with the buildings growing smaller the farther it stretched down the gentle slope of the valley. Every building was much sturdier than a tent, but still had the cobbled together look of a temporary shelter. Other than that, the place was very much like any outlying village in Brend. People bustled about. Children played, tending warming fires, chasing domesticated animals, or reluctantly doing chores. Groups of women huddled around laundry racks or cooking pots. Old men sat in doorways watching everything.

They weren't allowed any farther than the outermost buildings from the rock face. Khata sat by Jerryck again. Her sister mimicked her again. Jerryck rested his feet and sat next to them. They both giggled like little maniacs over that.

Sakila approached them from the center of the village, still wearing winter furs against the chill of the dawning spring. She spoke to Khata, who giggled through her entire response. Whatever she said it made Sakila chuckle.

"They keep a hut for strangers to sleep in," Sakila said to all of them. "You have permission to use it. Follow me."

She took them to a small structure on the far side of the village along the outer rim of the buildings. She stopped just inside and beckoned them to enter. Then a man came running up. He skidded to a halt a few feet away. Senka ran to him with squeals of delight. He caught her up and held her close, saying something to Sakila.

"He asks your permission for time with the daughters of his chosen sister," Sakila said to Jerryck.

"Why is he asking?" Jerryck wrinkled his forehead with confusion. "It's one of the reasons we brought them here."

She said something to Khata, who followed her little sister with the same squeal. Sakila led Jerryck inside saying, "The child owes you life debt. That is why he asked."

"She doesn't owe me anything," Jerryck said.

"Khata said you saved her life."

"So?"

"So she owes you life debt."

"No," Jerryck insisted. "She was hurt. I helped. Any decent person would. She doesn't owe me."

"I will think on this, how to explain it better to you later," Sakila said. "For now I must ask, what are you doing here?"

"That's a long story." Jerryck sank down onto one of several sleeping pallets in the one-room building. The others had already tossed down what little they carried. "We could ask you the same. What are *you* doing here? Khata said something about a gathering."

Sakila also sat. "When the attacks started on the winter encampments, we shamans agreed to gather. The closest ones came over land. Those of us farther away chose a few to speak for many. We used magic to travel here."

"The last gathering of shamans I know of was when they fought with the Gathering of Seats a couple hundred years ago," Jerryck told Tajor and the guards. "I know some people don't believe it now, but they made the volcano of the southern tip of the mountains erupt. It nearly destroyed the city of Kemetulla. The Gathering barely survived. And it was several years before anyone knew for certain that they wouldn't disband entirely."

"Most of the shamans who did that were killed," Sakila said. "The apprentices took up their tasks before being fully trained. Much knowledge was lost to us. We have never again had all the shamans gather all at once. That is why those of us farthest away have only sent a speaker. This is how we have done it ever since then."

"We haven't heard of any other gatherings," the guide said.

"We have taken no action that affects anyone outside the mountains," Sakila told him. She drew her knees up and hugged them to her chest. "This time, I fear they will."

"They?" Tajor raised his eyebrows. "You're not including yourself?"

"The few of us from the north keep reminding our southern brothers that Brend is not attacking." Sakila stared at the dirt floor of the hut. "We want no part in striking out against our neighbors. We want to ask King Terrence for help. But these tribes here in the south, the ones in the greatest danger, they do not want to listen. They keep demanding proof that your king means us no harm."

They spent the next few hours telling her everything. They told her about their efforts to defend their villages and placing the wards. They gave details about capturing one of the raiders. They described their attempt to turn Andreno aside from the military campaign. Tajor filled in the parts Jerryck couldn't remember: their capture, their transport up to the foreigners' camp, their escape. He mentioned that he thought the foreigners' leader might be looking for an excuse to abandon the campaign. Last, they told her about the volashes feeding on the dead.

"That is bad news." Sakila said. She hadn't moved during the entire recounting. Now she let her knees drop back down to the floor and hung her head.

"Bad news?" The guide screwed up his face in fear. "What do we need to pay?"

Sakila shook her head. "I will accept no payment from you. Not after Terrence treated us so well when we brought him such bad news last spring. I will have to think on how to pass this information on to the others."

"Do you need help paying them?" Jerryck asked.

"As a shamaness, I can give the information to my fellow shamans. The problem is, they will reject it. Even the good news you brought."

"What good news?"

"Other than your king trying to stop Andreno," Sakila said. "The attackers' leader wants to leave."

"Why would they overlook that?"

"The tribes in this area are very angry," Sakila said. "They want to make the attackers pay."

"Getting retribution will likely lead to their own deaths," Tajor said. "You all need to get out of this area. This village is next over from the one they just slaughtered. It could be the next target."

"Couldn't Khata pass it along through the family tie?" the guide asked.

Sakila drew her knees up again. "It will not do any good. Her mother's chosen brother is very low in this tribe. No one will listen to him."

"Chosen?" Jerryck frowned in confusion. "How did Khata's mother choose a brother? Either you're born that way or you're not."

"We Chemwanee choose a sibling of the opposite sex who is a member of a different tribe," Sakila said.

"Why can't you give this information to your chosen brother?" the guide asked. "Couldn't he pass it along?"

Sakila hesitated. She looked at Jerryck, then looked down the floor again. "That will not work."

"Because he's not here?" Tajor asked.

"He is here," she said. "This is complicated. The first brother I had chosen died several years ago. I have chosen another since. But we have not gone through the ceremony. I have not even spoken to him about it."

"Why not?" Jerryck asked.

"Because you are not a Chemwanee." She looked at him again. "I did not understand. So I did not think you would. I thought I would try it your way."

"What do I have to do with it?" Jerryck asked.

"When did you choose Jerryck for your brother?" Tajor asked Sakila.

"What?" Jerryck sat up straight. "Me?"

"Was it last spring?" Tajor asked.

"I chose when I last visited the palace a few months ago," Sakila said. "When he still treated me like family even with no blood ties or bond. I still do not understand how that works."

"And you decided it anyway?" Tajor cocked his head, face screwed up with confused curiosity. "How? Why?"

"It seems to work for him," Sakila said with a shrug.

"What if you talk to him and he doesn't agree?" Tajor asked. He turned to Jerryck. "Would you agree to something like that?"

"Sure I would," Jerryck said.

Sakila grinned. Tajor looked more confused. "You just threw out an answer without even thinking it over. You can't possibly have considered what all it would require, what kind of consequences it could have. How do you make such important decisions so quickly like that?"

"What's to decide?" Jerryck said. "I like family. If she wants to think of it this way, that means more family. More is better."

"No, Tajor is right," Sakila said. "You should know more about this. For others of my people to recognize it officially it requires a magic ceremony. If your Gathering found out you took part in a shaman ceremony they would kill you."

"They don't have to know," Jerryck said.

"You really think you could keep something like this from them?" Tajor asked. "And have you considered what this would mean for your job at home?"

"Terrence would support it," Jerryck said. "He likes the Chemwanee a lot more than the Gathering."

Someone called from outside. "Visitors! Come out. We will speak now."

"The shaman of this tribe," Sakila explained as she rose to her feet.

Jerryck got up too. "He speaks Brendish."

"Most shamans do," Sakila said. "So do most hunt chiefs, though they do not let it be known much."

She led them all outside. Both the hunt chief and the shaman stood there, with many other shamans ringed behind them. The hunt chief wore an intricate collar of beads interlaced with tiny, sheathed knives. The shaman carried a staff. He stood straight and tall without leaning on it, despite his age lined face. His hair might once have been blond. Now it was so gray and wispy, it was difficult to tell.

And he had nothing but contempt in his eyes when he pointed a bony finger at Jerryck. "Why do you come to us?"

Tajor stepped between them. "King Terrence sent us to Andreno to try and tell him not to attack you. He attacked us instead. We escaped to here."

"Why should we believe you?" The shaman sneered. "You have a filthy magician with you."

"He is a good man." Sakila threw her shoulders back. "I told you, my tribe now has strong ties with him and his king. For good reason."

"I do not believe you." The shaman turned his head and spat on the ground. "Filthy magician. Sakila, I would never have thought you, of all people, would stoop to this. You have no ties, no blood between his people and yours. You keep claiming you have turned around completely from the person I used to know, as if you think he would be fine with any of our magic or ceremonies. I tell you, he would never be part of a single one of them."

"Yes, I would," Jerryck said. Every shaman stared at him, boring holes with their eyes. Some curious. Most blatantly hostile. He swallowed. What had he gotten himself into? He added a caveat, "If I knew how."

"You do not need to know how," the old shaman said. "You say that now to try and take back your words. You would not do one."

"Yes, I would," Jerryck repeated.

"Prove it." The old shaman tipped up his nose and stuck out his chin. "Sakila, you have no brother. You claim ties. Make it real. Or do you not believe him?"

"I believe he would," she said loud and clear, glaring at him and the shamans behind him. "I do not believe any of you would treat him right. Even if we did go through the ceremony, you still would not listen to me or to his message."

"Go through the ceremony," the hunt chief said. His words were more fluid and less accented than even Sakila's. "You can present his message to us in the morning."

Chapter 55

THE HUNT CHIEF turned and walked away, leaving the old shaman spluttering. The others muttered and whispered to each other in their own language. Sakila frowned at them and said, "That is very rude."

"I don't care if they say rude things," Jerryck told her.

"They know your language." Sakila still glared at them. "It is rude of them to speak around you in a language you do not know."

"They're not saying rude things," Tajor told him. "They're trying to figure out if you're serious or not."

The old shaman narrowed his eyes at Tajor. "You speak our language?"

Tajor smirked at him. "How else would I be able to tell him part of what you're talking about?"

The old shaman tilted his head at Jerryck. "You are a magician. You are lying when you say you would do one of our ceremonies. You're Gathering of Seats would kill you."

"I've taken no oaths to the Gathering," Jerryck said. "They have no binding spell on me. I can go through whatever ceremony I want."

All the shamans stared at him again, this time in stunned silence. Some of them turned that stare to Sakila. She lifted her chin, threw back her shoulders, and returned their gaze without flinching. Jerryck had seen others who'd worn that expression, used that body posture, right before they said something like, "I told you so."

Jerryck shuffled his feet. "So what ceremony is it?"

"A brother/sister binding." Sakila put a hand on his shoulder. "It calls up magic that would change us both. You and I, we would become brother and sister as much as if born to the same parents."

"I like family," Jerryck said with a smile. "The more, the better."

The old shaman tapped his staff on the ground. "Do not look to me to do this foolishness."

One of the few male shamans in the group behind him smiled and said, "I will."

"As will I," a shamaness said. Both the volunteers turned and walked away.

"Where are they going?" Jerryck watched them both go off into some nearby conifers on the valley floor.

"To find branches to use for staffs," Sakila said. The other shamans took out some of their weapons they wore like jewelry and scratched in the dirt with them. Sakila also took out a small knife, about the length of Jerryck's index finger. "We will stand in circles. When the magic is right, I will tell you. Then we will use this to prick each other's finger just enough to bleed. You must let a drop of your blood fall to the ground between us. Then I will do the same. Whatever happens, do not fight the magic. Do not play with it. Do not shape it. Do nothing with it. Just let us shamans do that part."

Tajor laughed. "You don't want a repeat of what he did to his workroom?"

"No," Sakila said, giving Tajor a baleful look. She turned back to Jerryck. "I will sleep in the visitor hut with you tonight to make sure the magic settles and holds right."

"Has that ever been a problem?" Tajor asked.

"Not for many generations," Sakila said. "It is more just tradition now."

The two volunteers returned with long branches after a few minutes. By then, the others had two circles marked in the hard, packed dirt. The old shaman of their host tribe crossed his arms, his staff crooked into one elbow. He glared at Jerryck. "Now we are ready. Now everyone will see you are a liar when you do not do it. And Sakila will stop acting so foolish."

Jerryck went over to the circles. Sakila pointed at one of them. "Stand here."

"Last chance to back away and think this over," Tajor said.

415

"Get far enough away that you don't interfere with the magic," Jerryck told him and stepped inside the circle.

The old man's jaw dropped open. Sakila stepped into the other circle. The old man started shaking his head. The rest of the shamans ignored him, stepping back as the two volunteers began waving their staffs and chanting.

Jerryck's skin prickled. "They're calling up magic."

"For the binding," Sakila said.

Jerryck turned to make sure Tajor was moving far enough away. He already had, watching from many paces off, seemingly not even affected by the magic. The energy rose up from the earth inside the circles. Ancient. Powerful. Intoxicating. It swirled and eddied, following the movements of the staffs.

The woman changed her pattern, waving differently from the man. The magic wove around Sakila. The man changed his pattern and the magic wove around Jerryck as well. It covered them. Penetrated them. Rooted them where they stood. Then the man and woman slowly brought their movements into sync, eventually waving together in the same pattern again. The magic roots under Jerryck and Sakila's feet intertwined.

"It is time," Sakila said. She held up the little knife and took his left hand. She gave him a sharp jab in the ball of his middle finger. A tiny amount of blood welled up onto his skin.

He turned his hand over and let one drop fall to the ground. The magic latched onto it, sucking it in, tuning itself to his aura, making him part of it. It sang, and he floated on the melody.

"Jerryck," Sakila said. She handed him the small knife. "You have to prick my finger for the binding to complete."

She offered up her left hand. He held his breath, took her middle finger, and jabbed into it. She turned her hand. As soon as her blood touched where his had the melody of her aura meshed and melded with his, creating several eddies of harmonies. This was better than any orchestra performance he had ever attended at the palace. Never before had he equated magic with music. He stood as still as he could, letting it play out, letting it sing for him as long as possible.

Eventually it faded. The song quieted. The flow ebbed. The ripples and eddies played themselves out. He breathed in the last remaining wisps. The shamans stopped chanting. The sounds and smells of cooking took the place of the magic. The sun had dropped low. Dusk was settling in. Everyone stared at him again. The old shaman bared his teeth in a snarl.

"What has happened to you?" he demanded of Sakila. "I asked for you to represent your area because I was sure you would understand our needs. A year ago you swore all magicians should die, that if you ever met the one who brought that summoner involved with the death of your last chosen brother—"

"He knows nothing of that," Sakila interrupted. "Just because the summoner was seeking him doesn't mean he brought it about. And nothing is as I thought it was. I was wrong. That summoner was right. I should have listened. And so should you."

He thumped his staff on the ground and stalked away. Sakila looked smug watching him go. She stepped out of the circle to the other shamans and thanked them. Jerryck scrutinized the ground.

One circle. They had started with two. Hadn't they? He looked up at Sakila. "One circle?"

"The magic," she said. "You followed it. You did not know it did this?"

Jerryck looked down again. "I wasn't watching the ground."

"You followed the magic," one of the shamans said. "Not what you saw with your eyes. You should have trained in the mountains. As a magician, your talent is wasted."

He headed into the encampment, the same direction the old shaman and the hunt chief had gone. The others slowly followed him one by one.

"Go inside," Sakila said. "The sun will go down soon. I will get something for everyone to eat."

Jerryck passed Tajor on his way inside and told him, "Don't touch me."

"Don't worry," Tajor said. "The magic is gone. Only the change remains."

Inside, the quiet guard sat by the entrance watching outside. The guide took some kindling by a primitive hearth and worked on starting a fire. The hitter took off his belt and used the leather to strop his stolen Shontese dagger.

Before long, Sakila and the little girl both came. They brought a loaf of hot bread, a steaming pot of stew, bowls and wooden scoops for everyone, and a skin of cold water to wash it down. The girl served Jerryck and sat by his feet without getting anything for herself. He gave her the bowl, served himself, and sat beside her. She flushed and smiled. After he took a bite, she dug in, eating voraciously.

"She sits at your feet to show that she is your servant." Sakila broke off a chunk of bread for herself. "When you give her your food and sit beside her, you show favor."

"Her name is Khata, by the way," Tajor said.

Jerryck shot him a dirty look. "You already told me that."

"And did you remember?" Tajor asked.

"Of course!"

"For how long?" Tajor asked.

"I'm not answering that," Jerryck said, and shoveled in more stew.

"That's what I thought." Tajor went over and sat by the quiet guard at the door. "I'll watch a bit. You eat."

"You should eat too," the guard said.

"Why?" Tajor asked. Then he laughed at the guard's expression. "Later, maybe. Go eat."

The quiet guard slipped over to the food and helped himself. He looked over at the hitter, ignoring the food, still stropping the dagger. He squinted at the weapon and moved closer. "That's Dalrien's."

The hitter paused, his hand frozen with the dagger halfway down the leather. He lifted it, turning it in the light of the fire. "You sure?"

The quiet one nodded. The hitter said, "But I got it off that foreign interpreter. Wouldn't it go to Nolrien? Inheritance after death and all?"

The quiet one sat back and scooped into his bowl. "Shontese tradition."

"What is?" The hitter lowered the blade back down to the leather belt.

"When a weapon is used to attack someone," the quiet one spoke with his mouth full. "If the attacker dies in the fight, the weapon is inherited by the person he attacked."

"You think Dalrien attacked that interpreter? That's how he died?"

"Nolrien wouldn't tell us how he died," the quiet one said.

"Tajor," the hitter said. "Are you sure that was the same man you scared off in the Shontese palace?"

Tajor didn't even turn around to face them. "How much detail do you want in your answer?"

"Forget it," the hitter grumbled.

He set the weapon aside. He ate with the others then went back to stropping the dagger. The hut fell into sullen quiet. Khata took all the dishes and left. When she came back, she brought her little sister. The two of them lay down on a pallet and cuddled themselves to sleep.

"Now that's a good idea," Jerryck said, and picked a pallet for himself.

Chapter 56

ERRYCK SAT bolt upright before he even registered what had awakened him. Sound still reverberated, shaking the wall of the hut. The hitter crouched in the doorway, silhouetted by the gray light of early dawn, looking out. He slowly backed inside the hut, still crouching while he moved, his face set in grim lines, his hands on the hilts of both the dagger and his sword.

The guide had also jerked upright out of sleep, along with everyone else in the hut. "What was that?"

"Explosion," Jerryck said.

Another one went off somewhere in the middle of the encampment. Senka let out a wail of terror. Khata clapped a hand over her mouth, quieting her. Not that it made any difference, so many screams and cries were resounding throughout the village.

Short, percussive *rat-a-tats* started up. The screams intensified into anguished terror and gurgles of death. Sakila jumped to the doorway. Tajor and the hitter grabbed her, holding her back.

Jerryck looked out into the growing light. A stick, one end bulging like a ball, twirled through the air, flipping end over bulging end, from somewhere above on the other side of the encampment. It hit a building that exploded into flame and splinters of wood. A heartbeat later, the percussion shook the visitors hut.

People sprinted past the entrance of their hut. More ran around in utter chaos. The snappy *rat-a-tats* continued. Dirt splashed like water around running feet. Individuals fell to the ground, bleeding or dead.

"They're missing a weapon," Tajor said. He had his head cocked, his ear toward the rock face on the far side of the encampment, the source of all the short percussions.

Sakila struggled to get free, staring out the door at the bleeding people. "I have to get out there."

"You need cover," the hitter said.

"Or a distraction," the guide added.

"Distraction," Tajor said. He dipped his finger into the cold ashes of the fire and hastily drew rune symbols in a ring on the floor of the hut. "Jerryck. That jar on your shelf. Get Yeshiyahu."

"How?" Jerryck asked.

"The spells in the jar enable the owner to call the entity from within no matter what." Tajor finished his symbols and wiped the rest of the ash from his fingers.

"What am I supposed to do?" Jerryck demanded. "Just say, Yeshiyahu, come and get in that circle of symbols there?"

The moment the words left his lips, his hair stood on end and magic ignited the runes making them glow. With a puff of sickly yellow smoke and a hint of sulfur, the little creature appeared in the circle. "Master called."

"That was fast," Jerryck said.

"A shorter time in the jar—" Yeshiyahu's words were cut off when a series of small holes opened up in one side of the hut. Whatever caused them flew over their heads and out through the opposite wall. "Gunfire? Here?"

"One of the worlds with Nazis figured out how to open portals," Tajor said.

Yeshiyahu cocked its head and flicked its pointy ear. "I don't hear any *machine-gewehren*."

"Which means they'll likely treat the Schmeissers like the heavy weapons and support them with Mausers. You go find the Schmeissers. Wreak some havoc and hamper them."

"You're not my master!" Yeshiyahu snarled. "My cause here... is..."

The runes flared. Yeshiyahu's eyes bulged. It made some sort of choking, gurgling noise. Its knees buckled and it fell, bringing its nose close to one of the symbols. It glared at the symbol. Then up at Tajor.

"We don't have time for power struggles or games," Tajor said. "Obey."

Yeshiyahu hissed. It vanished with a little *pop*.

The toddler whimpered. Khata trembled, silent tears streaming from her eyes, so wide they showed white all around. Another building exploded. More screaming people died. Sakila wept, begging to go out and help them.

The hitter still held her back. "You need cover."

"We are not any safer in here." She pointed to the holes in the walls. They shook again as yet another building exploded, this one closer to them.

"The entire encampment needs a cover," the hitter said, so quietly it was hard to hear him above the cacophony of the attack.

"I could make fog," Jerryck said. "If I had more time."

"I can help you with power." Sakila stopped struggling and leaned closer to him.

She reached out and put both hands on his temples. Her aura connected with his. Her energy flowed into him. He shaped the magic faster than all the practices he had done getting ready for Heston's military game. When he spoke the words for the spell, it didn't grow so much as it sprang from the ground, all at once, through the entire encampment and beyond into the trees. The sounds of the attack tapered off, with shouts of startled surprise coming from the rock face.

"Jerryck," Tajor said. He pointed outside. "I can't go into that fog unless you want it dispelled everywhere I go."

Jerryck threw up a bubble shield around Tajor, much like he did when opening a portal. This one, instead of containing the magic within, it would keep the fog without. Weeping and wailing continued, more apparent now that there was less noise. Sakila stepped outside, her energy still flowing. The guide stepped out with her.

A smattering of shots still fired. The guide yanked her down into a crouch. He turned back to the hut. "We need more of a distraction."

More shouts from the attackers. One of the weapons stopped. Someone over there screamed. Then maniacal laughter floated through the mist.

"Yeshiyahu found a target." Tajor smirked, stepping outside, carrying the toddler and bringing Khata by the hand.

A few human shapes ghosted past them toward the trees. One of them stopped, stumbling their way. The girls' uncle coalesced into sight. He saw them and caught them up, weeping frantically. Tajor said something to him in his language. The man took both the girls and ran for the trees with them, vanishing into the mist.

The weapons fire picked back up. The quiet guard pulled Jerryck out of the hut. The guide said, "We still need more of a distraction. If I were them, intent on eradication of the populace, I wouldn't rely on blind range weapons."

"No, they'll come down into the fog and sweep the place," Tajor said. "How about an elemental?"

Magic pushed at the far edge of the fog, probing it, countering it, clearing it. More than one person behind that magic. Jerryck pushed back, holding it in place. Tajor snapped his fingers a couple of times in front of Jerryck's face.

"Distraction," he said. "You handled that fake elemental your friend tried to make in the throne room last summer. Make a real one."

Jerryck opened up his senses, monitoring, checking whether or not he could handle that much extra magic. More shots rang out. The other magic-users still pushed and tugged, fighting his fog spell. Sakila still supplemented his energy. Over all that, there was some kind of a shadow, a whisper of magic from at least two other people. It was small enough, he couldn't grasp or identify it.

"Elemental!" Tajor shouted in his face. "Distraction."

Jerryck refocused. With the assistance from the shamaness, he could do an elemental and still maintain the fog. He went over the words in his head a couple of times. He gathered his energy and concentrated.

He opened his mouth. The spell initiated before he uttered a single syllable. The first word hung on his tongue, melting into a long moan of shock and surprise.

The air around them drew itself together and solidified. The consciousness of the entity rose up, coalescing as the body took shape, impatient with the desire to destroy, yet awaiting his command.

Someone grabbed Jerryck by the shirt and yanked him off to one side, behind the building next to the visitor hut. He glimpsed Sakila, stumbling off in the opposite direction with the quiet guard. The fog engulfed them. The guide stayed by the visitor hut, face down in a growing pool of blood.

"What are you doing?" Jerryck slapped at the hitter, who was pulling him farther away and making his concentration on the elemental slip.

"Your distraction worked." Tajor followed closely. He hiked his thumb behind himself back the way they'd come. "Why did you make it right over our heads?"

"I didn't think about that," Jerryck said.

The hitter gave him an irritated glance. "Obviously."

The exploding pops of the enemy weapons had picked up again. Tajor had to raise his voice to be heard. "Can you move it?"

"Where to?" Jerryck looked around, blind to anything further than a couple of feet in any direction.

The hitter pointed. "Slowly across the village toward the attackers."

"How slowly?" Jerryck concentrated, mentally issuing the order for the elemental to move.

"Inch by inch," the hitter said. "Make them nervous watching it come."

He pulled Jerryck along, farther into the encampment. The reek of blood and excrement increased with every step. They came across a wounded woman, weeping over a dead child. Jerryck reached for her without thinking. The moment he took his focus off the magic he already maintained, the spells tried to slip. Whoever pushed the fog made headway, clearing some of the space of the far side. The elemental gleefully smashed into the nearest structure.

The only part of the magic that remained constant was the energy flow still pouring from Sakila, even though they had lost visual contact. It centered him. Enabled him. He pulled back, using that stability to refocus on the two spells and get them back under control.

He couldn't get the fog back to cover up the small part of the encampment now exposed. He did get it to stop retreating and revealing more buildings. He also got the elemental to stop smashing up whatever it came across and restart its slow progression toward the attackers.

They shot at it, using two different sizes of slugs. The smaller ones had a rounded end, like what he had extracted from Khata's side wound. They flew through the air at regular spaced intervals, as if machines fired them one after another after another, less than seconds apart. The other slug was larger, longer, more pointed. Those came one at a time, as if individually fired.

Every time one of the projectiles ripped through the elemental. It disrupted some of the air that made up the body. The creature started shrinking. To replenish and sustain it, Jerryck drew in currents of air. That disrupted the fog. He turned his focus back, trying to keep what air the creature had. It still leaked and continued shrinking.

The head of the creature rose well above the fog's ceiling. Jerryck drew air down into it from higher up. That left the fog intact. He still maintained his attempts to keep air escaping. Both methods together maintained equilibrium with its size.

"Finished?" Tajor asked.

"Huh?" Jerryck looked around.

He had paid no attention to where Tajor and the guard led him. The two of them ducked low for some reason. Why? It wasn't like making themselves less visible would make a difference in the fog.

Another explosion went off. A second echoed, much closer to the ranks of the enemy. Yeshiyahu's maniacal laughter floated through the air.

The hitter looked in the direction of the sound. "How does that thing laugh so loud we can hear it over all this noise?"

Jerryck didn't have an answer. Tajor didn't give one. He started forward again, still crouching low.

"Where are we going?" Jerryck asked.

"To check on the shamans," the hitter said.

"Have you felt the magic from any of them?" Tajor asked.

"No," Jerryck said. He followed the two of them, walking normally, trying to puzzle out why they moved so laboriously low to the ground.

They passed a central open space with a large fire pit. A sort of gathering area? On the other side was one of the largest structures in the entire encampment. Still small compared to an inn at a Brendish village, it could have given shelter to at least a couple dozen sleeping people. If it was still intact. Half of it was gone. Holes riddled the remains of the walls. The roof lay smoldering in pieces on the ground.

The popping of the weapons stopped. Jerryck should use the quiet to go over there. To peer in. Search through that smoldering rubble. Look for someone alive who might need help. His feet froze in place, refusing to go any nearer.

The hitting guard did. Tajor did. Staying in Jerryck's sight, they both went to the ruins. Tajor gave no indication of what he saw in there. The guard shook his head and turned away. They both returned.

"Are any of them still alive?" Jerryck asked without hope.

"It looks like they got hit first." The guard passed Jerryck, heading back the way they had come. "If they'd heard the attack start up, they'd have reacted. At the very least, they would have jumped out of bed like everyone else."

Jerryck followed him closely. "So that means they can't rally and defend the people."

"It means this place was under observation," Tajor said. "They knew who was most dangerous, where they were, and got rid of them first."

"Wouldn't that mean they knew we were here too?" Jerryck asked.

Shouts in the guttural language of the foreigners rang out, close by, down inside the encampment rather than up on the rocks above. The guard uttered a few foul words.

"Time to go." Tajor sped up, almost disappearing into the fog. The guard hustled Jerryck after him.

Yeshiyahu let out a feral, raging battle shout that rang everywhere. There was another *pop* from one of the weapons up on the rocks. The little creature made a gurgling, strangled noise. Then a loud *whump* echoed, bouncing off the buildings. A burst of air blew down, driving away more of the fog on that edge. Jerryck held it tight, struggling to keep it in place.

The guard looked back toward the enemy. "What was that?"

"Yeshiyahu won't harass the enemy anytime in the near future," Tajor said.

The sound of another explosion, accompanied by a red glow through the fog, came from the direction of the elemental. The last shred of it burned away. The entity that inhabited the body sank back down into nothingness. The magic that summoned and held it disintegrated.

Jerryck staggered with shock. He had never had a spell torn asunder with such violence. His eyes rolled up. His head spun. His knees turned to jelly. His arms and legs shook. A chill ran through his entire body, his energy pouring out of a fresh wound in his aura.

Sakila's energy flared around him, concentrating on the aural wound, soothing it. The bleeding sensation eased. Then it ceased. It left him weakened. But at least his life was no longer draining away.

"You want to move faster, you can damn well help me out," The guard said to Tajor, half dragging, half carrying Jerryck over the cold dirt.

"No, I can't." Tajor walked backwards ahead of them, watching both them, and the way forward. "I told you, I can't touch him. It would nullify the magic he's working. That includes the little bit left of our visual cover."

"It's already thinned to the point it's almost useless," the guard growled, dragging Jerryck a few more feet.

Jerryck looked around. The fog was rapidly thinning. His skin prickled with magic again. He opened up his senses to it. There was still that wisp of something he couldn't quite identify. More prominent than that, magic-users pushed at the remains of the fog, clearing it, pushing it away, dispelling it. The edge would reach them soon and expose them. He turned to face that way, probing for the location of those magic-users. If they were close enough, perhaps he could throw some offensive spell of them.

"You back with us again?" the guard asked.

"Keep moving," Tajor said.

Jerryck caught movement out of the corner of his eye. The guard must've seen it too. He sidestepped, putting himself between Jerryck and whatever it was, dropping low in a wide stance.

Two men came into view through the remains of the fog. They wore hard, round helmets with curved flanges at the bottom. Long, belted coats hung to their knees, brushing the tops of their boots. One had a knitted scarf around his neck. The other wore gloves with the fingers missing.

Both carried mechanical devices, a long metal tube attached to shaped wood with other metallic accoutrements sticking out here and there. Both the men held the wood end of their device firmly to their right shoulder, keeping their instruments pointed in whichever direction they turned. Both now pointed at Jerryck, Tajor, and the guard.

Fear pulled through Jerryck. Magic rushed to his fingertips. The end of one of the devices flashed. The *pop* it made was much louder from this close. The device jerked. The magic escaped Jerryck. Both men's heads turned into small spheres of heat and flame.

At the same moment, the guard's neck exploded. Blood and flesh spewed everywhere, spraying all over Jerryck. A bone fragment struck him in his left shoulder.

The influx of energy from Sakila cut off, severed as if with a knife. The fog spell shattered. The last of it whisked away so fast a tornado may as well have ripped through with him at the center. He didn't feel as wounded as when the elemental had been destroyed, but it still left him shaky, and even weaker than before.

Some of the blood that had spattered him dripped down his side. It was warm compared to the chill that surged through his extremities. He looked down at himself. There was more blood than he expected. A lot more.

His shoulder hurt. A dull, throbbing pain that gripped him, similar to a crushing vise. His left arm went numb. He wiggled his fingers, trying to get some sensation from them. He saw them move. He didn't feel it. He bent his elbow to make sure his arm still worked.

The pain in his shoulder sharpened. With a hot stab, it overwhelmed. He dropped to his knees. He sucked in air through clenched teeth. That was no bone fragment that had struck him.

He wilted further. The pain weighed him down. He kept himself from falling prone with his good arm. His training at healing kicked in. He spoke the words of a spell that numbed the injury. Then he magically immobilized that part of his body.

Other magic probed. Observing. Searching. Pinpointing the exact location of the magic he worked. One of them had the same signature as the taint in the river, as the portal for the raiders.

Chapter 57

TAJOR STRODE over to the bodies of the two attackers. He picked up one of the long metal and wood sticks. Jerryck felt no magic on these devices. They were purely mechanical.

Using a metal protrusion on the side, Tajor pulled back some sort of bolt on the top. A metal cylinder popped out. He looked down inside the device, then pushed the bolt back into place.

He raised it straight, the wood end held tight to his right shoulder, exactly the way the attackers had carried it. He tilted his head and looked down the length, pointing in the direction of the magic-user with the correct signature. He released his breath without taking another. With a finger, he squeezed the small metal piece on the underside. The same loud *pop* resulted. The device flashed and jerked. Jerryck felt a brief flash of natural magic from the element of fire.

The searching stopped. The magic withdrew around the caster and morphed into something different. Jerryck couldn't quite make heads or tails of it. Trying to focus on it, too many other distractions demanded his attention. The pain in his shoulder alone was nearly enough to overwhelm him. And what had happened to Sakila? Was she hurt too? Or was she safe?

Two more men dressed like the enemy ran up. One of them shouted in that harsh, guttural language, pointing another, smaller device at Tajor. The other was the blond interpreter, carrying another of the long weapons, also pointing it at Tajor.

"Put it down!" the blonde yelled. "And keep your hands where we can see them."

Tajor slowly complied. Jerryck looked over to the rock face, clearly visible now with the fog gone. That strange magic hadn't stopped, and now someone was dead from it. What exactly was going on over there?

The blonde put down his long device and knelt by Jerryck, examining the shoulder wound, his bruised face pressed with concern. He exchanged a few guttural words with his comrade, who still pointed his smaller device at Tajor. Then the other man raised a black box to his face and talked to it.

The box responded.

The voice that came through it was scratchy. They must have understood it anyway. The blonde whipped his head to look behind himself at Tajor. "You shot Ziegfried in the chest."

"The *chest*?" Tajor put on his malicious expression. "That's too bad. I missed. I was aiming for his head."

The other man and the box kept exchanging words. It had to be a device for communication. There was no magic on it. How did they make something like that without magic? Jerryck had never even thought of making something like that *with* magic.

Though he probably could. His brain whirled, blocking out his attention on the strange magic still going on at the rock face. If he modified some sort of traveling spell to translocate sound, rather than an entire object, that might work. Of course, he would also want to perfect a translation spell. That way the box would speak intelligibly no matter what language was used by the person on the other end of the communication. Nevermind that no one had ever perfected a translation spell. Surely it could be done. Look at what these people had done without the help of magic.

And yet they had a magician. Jerryck turned his focus back to the strange magic on the rock face, reaching out with the ragged remains of energy left in his aura.

The magic was worked by one man lying on the rocks, wounded, bleeding, unable to hardly breathe. The man had pierced another's aura with hooks like a quepota, but through physical contact. He sucked the last bit of life out of his victim. That was the second man this strange magic had killed. Then the man let go, grabbed a third victim, and latched the hooks on again.

Was he an animal that he consumed other humans like one? If this was the kind of man these people followed, was it any wonder they were attacking villages and killing innocent people? This was unacceptable. This had to stop.

Without thinking, Jerryck started to roll to his side to get up. The pain that shot through his shoulder, despite the numbing spell, had him hissing and gasping. The interpreter put a hand on Jerryck's chest, holding him down. "Lie still."

"That man has to be stopped." Jerryck's voice sounded wheezy.

"You are safe," the interpreter said. "I will let none of our men hurt you more."

"No, not me." Jerryck tried to point to the deadly magic on the rocks. "That man."

The interpreter glanced over that way. He shook his head in confusion. He wouldn't be able to see magic. Jerryck snorted, frustrated, disgusted with himself. He was going to have to be the one to do something about it. And at the moment, magic was his only option no matter how dangerously low he was.

He shaped some of his meager supply of energy. Then he whispered the words that detached it. The spell hit the other magician, forcing his muscles to go slack. The spell was so weak, it lasted only a moment. It was just enough. The physical contact was lost. The hooks contracted.

And turned on Jerryck.

While part of Jerryck's mind screamed at him not to do it, he reflexively jerked his aura back to himself. The hooks dragged at the other man. The connection combined both their energies, washing over Tajor as it translocated the rogue magician down into the village to lie right at Jerryck's side.

"Ziegfried!" The blonde fell back, scuttling away a few paces in shock and alarm.

The other man shouted, at him, at Magician Ziegfried, at the box. The box shouted back. Tajor groaned, gritting his teeth, kneeling on all fours in dirt. Ziegfried turned his head, looking at Jerryck out of eyes glazed over with pain. Reaching out a hand, he grabbed hold of Jerryck's arm.

The hooks dug in. This time, Jerryck pushed like he should have done the first time. The surge drove Ziegfried away. His body rolled over to his side. His aura stretched beyond that, washing over Tajor all over again.

Jerryck's energy was too depleted. It stretched taut, too thin. The hold on his body snapped. The recoil shot him away. He latched onto Ziegfried now out of desperation to stay and regain stability. Ziegfried's connection to his body snapped as well. The two of them went tumbling in just their projected aural forms.

They disengaged. For a moment they just stared at each other. Jerryck had only seen one other person in this form. And he had been a child, terrified and unable to understand what was happening. He very likely had worn the same expression that Ziegfried now did.

Ziegfried's eyes refocused looking past Jerryck and out across the village. The terror on his face intensified and he drew back. Jerryck looked around.

Everything was awash with color, as it always was when he was out of his body like this. Everything's aura glowed as bright and real as if he could touch it. Fire flowed everywhere. Humans writhed in death throws by what was left of their bodies. Black smoke roiled across the ground, reeking of sulfur.

Not smoke. The void. Jerryck gasped and stumbled desperately toward his body. He had never stood right over the void. Always, he had done all he could to avoid it, keep it at bay, far off near the horizon. Now, he couldn't see his own feet, lost in the stinking smoke rising up out of it. Now it pulled at him, keeping him from his body, from his physical form.

Then he noticed the shafts of light piercing down from above. People moved up and down those shafts, collecting some of the dead, singing to them, cradling them, soothing them. Others among the dead screamed in agony and torment as the black smoke from below engulfed them, dragging them down. Many of them left behind wisps of energy. The wisps took on the shape of the original person, without the ability to attain wholeness or stability.

Ziegfried whispered, magic flaring, interpreting his one word into the language Jerryck understood. "Ghosts."

A translation spell? Jerryck looked at him again. He hadn't ever even thought of talking while in this form. What more did this magician do that

Jerryck had never thought of? Or did he even want to know? If it included more ways to kill people, he probably didn't.

A malicious light pierced through Ziegfried, discoloring his entire being. He smiled with hunger, staring at the energy spilling everywhere from the carnage of the battle. The translation magic flared again as he said, "So much to draw from!"

He reached for the nearest 'ghost'. Jerryck stopped trying to get to his body and whipped out a tendril of his aura, an arm of himself in this form. He grabbed onto the 'ghost' himself and altered the energy, shifting it into a wall. Ziegfried smacked up against it.

He reached for the next one. Jerryck did the same thing. Ziegfried scowled at him, color as black as ink curling through him like the smoke below. They circled around each other. Ziegfried crept tendrils out, almost as if testing. Jerryck blocked every one of them with walls.

"You're fast," Ziegfried said.

Jerryck wasn't fast. He was experienced. He wasn't even thinking about the actions. In this form, he didn't have to shape the energy, or speak words to sever the magic from himself. He just reacted as if he was going to go through all those processes, and it happened. Good thing, too. He was so weak right now, if he had to go through the entire process, it would be at the pace of a slug.

Ziegfried looked over at Tajor. The mass of colors in his aura swirled so fast and thick they could hardly see the man where he had curled up in a fetal position. It pressed in on him, crushing, squeezing from every side, every angle, pushing him toward the void below.

The hungry look intensified on Ziegfried's face. He glanced at Jerryck. They both were thinning, their own colors fading with every action they took.

Many live men milled about now. A few of them looked up at the sky, where a volash circled high above. They brought makeshift litters to pick up their own wounded and Jerryck and Tajor. Then energy from the sun flashed briefly on a silver thread stretching between Jerryck and his body. He had never seen that before.

Ziegfried's hooks shot past, straight at Tajor. Jerryck lunged. He couldn't redirect Tajor's energy into a wall. So he grabbed Ziegfried's reaching arms, and yanked them back.

The hooks dug in. He couldn't tell if it was on purpose, or accidental. It didn't matter. He pushed again.

In this form, that moved his entire being. He ended up tackling Ziegfried, and they both fell. Instead of hitting the ground, they went down beneath the roiling, stinking smoke.

And fell, and fell, and fell. Tumbling. Twisting. Turning. The agonized cries from below blocked out all other sounds. The black smoke pressed in on all sides, crushing his entire being, pushing him further down.

Ziegfried clung, still latched on with hooks. Jerryck didn't have enough energy left to push with his entire being, so this time he pushed with only an arm. Ziegfried stretched too thin, just as when they had snapped out of their bodies. When his connection to Jerryck broke, the recoil tumbled him further away. The smoke swallowed him up out of sight.

Alone, Jerryck still tumbled. Despite the crushing press pushing at him, he instinctively reached out, grasping for anything that might help.

It couldn't end this way. There had to be some way back. He couldn't leave his family like this. Who would care for Leanne? And what about the baby? He didn't even know if he was having a son or a daughter. He had to get back.

It wasn't fair to make Kendra lose another family member in less than a year. And who would help take care of her children? And now Sakila was another sister to worry about and care for.

His hand brushed against a thread so thin, it might have been a spider's web. He closed his fingers around it, even as his mind told him it was just going to break.

Except that it didn't. Echoes of his fear and desperation rippled up through it. He needed help.

Tajor was not going to be able to help. With all the magic that had washed over him, he likely couldn't even help himself at this point.

Maybe Sakila? If she was still alive. And unhurt.

The vibrations going up the thread changed, tuning to his intentions. Nothing else changed. He still fell and tumbled. The smoke still crushed him. And his plea for help was lost in his ears among all the cries coming up from below.

Light raced down the thread, the same energy that earlier had flowed to him from her. The smoke withered back, away from it. It pulled at him, drawing him up. It was just enough to counter the pull from below, checking his fall. The chaotic tumble ceased. His motion stabilized.

Holding on with one hand, he reached up with his other. Then he crossed his hands, reaching up to grab hold again. And again. With each new hand-hold, the crushing pressure released incrementally, the easier he gained the next handhold.

The smoke thinned enough he could see more light through it from above. Then he was above it. Tendrils of the stink clung to him, threatening to drag him back down. He did the only thing he knew that had ever held the void at bay before. He willed himself to return to his body.

Sakila drawing him along had more affect now. He flew so fast that everything was a blur. Just one heartbeat later, he slammed into his body.

Chapter 58

PAIN FILLED all of Jerryck's senses. With every breath a hot knife stabbed into his shoulder. He couldn't draw in enough air, and his lungs burned for the lack. His body felt only half solid, trying to tremble and quiver, without the energy to pull it off. It was so weighty he couldn't really move anything properly.

At least the void no longer crushed him. He was alive. He would recover. Especially since Sakila was still out there somewhere. She must be safe. He could still feel an influx of energy from her.

It was just a trickle at this point, slow and measured. That was a good thing. He was so depleted, if the influx had been too strong it would have put him further in a state of shock. He struggled with that as it was.

Lying on his back, nauseated, he turned his head in case he puked. Then he had to wait for his head to stop spinning and the ground to stop swaying beneath him, increasing the nausea.

"Jerryck?" Someone put a hand on his good shoulder. "Lay still. Try to relax."

Opening his eyes didn't help. At first everything was blurry. As his eyes slowly focused, nothing made sense. He was surrounded by the enemy. None of the village's buildings were in sight. And where was the sky? He saw only rock.

The hand on his shoulder belonged to the blond interpreter. Someone else spoke to him, and he leaned in close to Jerryck. "Do you remember me?"

"I'm sorry we hit you so much." The words came out. Jerryck heard them. It sounded a lot like his voice, but breathless, slurred, and he didn't feel his mouth moving.

"Do not worry about that," the man said. He exchanged a few words with the other person, a large man, almost as large as Heston, almost. Then he talked to Jerryck again. "Do you remember my name?"

Jerryck shook his head. That was a mistake. The ground swayed again and he shut his eyes against the nausea. The blonde squeezed his shoulder gently, reassuringly. He said, "It's Adam. Do you know where you are? What happened?"

"Village," Jerryck said. "Fighting."

"The fighting is over," Adam said. "And we are not in the village. We moved under an overhang of rock to shelter. A day has passed. We have stayed the night here. It is almost morning. You were injured. And we cannot figure out what is wrong with Tajor."

Magic was wrong with Tajor. Jerryck could feel it better now. They lay side by side. The magic flowed at only a trickle because it was spread out, which dissipated some of it, but affected everyone in Jerryck's immediate vicinity. Tajor's curse acted almost as a filter, dissipating it further, which kept it at exactly the level Jerryck needed.

Khata sat behind him, wrapped in a coat and watching silently. A coat? It looked like the one Adam was wearing, and like the man beside him wore.

Adam pointed at Khata. "Do you know her? She asked for you by name."

"Why is she here?" Jerryck asked. Khata saw him looking at her and she smiled briefly, just a flash before she went back to staring wide-eyed at everyone.

Adam exchanged a few more words with the large man before answering Jerryck. "She came to us in the night."

"You didn't kill her?" Jerryck was just being sassy now. He knew it. And yet, he somehow couldn't stop. Maybe because he was hurting and weak?

"Such a pretty little *Goldlöckchen*?" Adam smiled at her. She gave him the same brief flash of smile she had given Jerryck. He said, "And so brave, to come to us after what we did."

"There were a lot of other little kids in that village," Jerryck said.

Adam clenched his jaw and looked down at the ground before meeting Jerryck's eyes again. "There is nothing that can make good what we did in that village. Or any of the other villages. But understand, we were ordered to come to these mountains by people who will kill the families of these men if we do not obey."

He waved a hand to encompass everyone around them. Jerryck spoke again before thinking, "Does that include the raided villages in Brend and Shontarra this winter?"

"Ziegfried did that," Adam said. "Without permission. We have stopped him. And if we could talk to your king, we could give him an apology. We should have figured out what he was doing long before we did."

"Would you also apologize for the poison in our river last year?"

Adam sat back with a frown. "Poison?"

"The poison he made with magic," Jerryck said. "That was put in our river."

Adam blinked at him a few times, saying nothing. Then he turned to the large man. With the tone he used, it sounded like he was asking a question. As the two exchanged words, the large man's expression went from confusion, to dark anger. Then Adam turned back to Jerryck. "We do not know of any poison in a Brendish river."

"I know his signature," Jerryck said. "He did it."

"We believe you. It sounds like something he would do. You can tell us more later, when you are more healed. Maybe after we get back to our camp."

"I'm not going to your camp," Jerryck said.

Adam gave him a droll look. "There are dangerous animals around. You are injured, and it is our fault. We will keep you safe, and make sure you heal enough that you can return to your home safely."

"Why would you care for our safety?"

"I cannot give you a short answer for that." Adam sighed. He rubbed his eyes, then winced when he pushed at one of the bruises the guard had given him. He dropped his hands, looked at Tajor, then at Khata. "Some of us, we are tired of all the fighting, all the killing. Too many people have died."

"So you're going to risk King Terrence attacking you by making us go back to your camp?"

"We will not make you. We are hoping." He spoke again with the large man. Then he pulled out a piece of soft leather with words written on it in what looked like charcoal. "Khata brought us this."

Jerryck rubbed his own eyes with his good hand. "I can't read that."

"It is in your language," Adam said. He nodded at Khata, "Not hers."

"My eyes won't focus right," Jerryck said. "The letters are blurry."

Adam handed it back to the large man. "It says that your sister demands we release you and Tajor, or she will gather shamans from everywhere and kill us all. We are waiting for morning when it is light before we send Khata back with our answer."

"That you're making us go to your camp?"

"That you are injured, and we want to heal you."

For half a moment, Jerryck was actually tempted to leave them to the mercies of the shamans. They certainly deserved it. But only for half a moment. While he had taken lives as a defensive measure in times past, he couldn't purposefully refuse to save people, even if they didn't deserve it. Not without at least warning them first.

"They'll kill you," Jerryck said.

"With what? Their shamans? We just killed them all."

"No, you didn't."

Adam paused for a moment. Then said, "There are more than what had gathered in that village?"

"A lot more."

Adam didn't look very surprised. He simply nodded his head, then spoke with the large man. Jerryck looked over at Khata. She flashed another smile at him. Then she reached out her hand and placed a button on a string beside him. Then she pulled out some little sticks of wood with a bulb of red on one end and set those beside him too. Then a couple of pieces of what looked like wrapped candy. And some kind of biscuit.

"Where did she get all this?" Jerryck asked.

Adam interrupted his conversation with the other man to say, "I gave them to her."

Jerryck picked up the button, trying to figure out why anyone would think a button was a gift. Adam said, "I made it a toy for her. You wind up the string, and see how long you can keep it spinning."

"And the coat?"

"I gave her that too. She was shivering when she first came, like she was cold. So I took my coat off and gave it to her."

"You're wearing a coat."

"After this last battle, we had a few extras."

Jerryck picked up one of the little sticks. Adam said, "We call those *Streichh*ölzer. We use them to make fire."

Jerryck put the stick back down. "In her culture, a gift is an apology."

Adam's eyes bulged. "It *is*?"

"They have some sort of system to measure how sorry you are," Jerryck said. "I don't really understand it. I do know that a Chemwanee never threatens anything they won't actually do. So maybe my sister hasn't killed you because you gave Khata gifts. Maybe? I don't know."

"You really do have a sister here in these mountains?"

Jerryck nodded. He didn't feel like explaining it right at the moment. All this talking was making him tired. Not sleepy. Just tired.

"And you really do think she could get shamans together to try and kill us?" Obviously Adam still felt like talking.

"She can get all the other shamans together."

"Would that not put them in danger of us killing them?" Adam looked away, presumably out from under the overhanging rock. "Perhaps we should ask her not to gather them so we do not have to."

"You might not even know they're in the area," Jerryck said.

"We knew about the shamans in that village."

"They were talking. Not acting. You killed them. The next group will act, not talk."

"What will they do?'

"I don't know for sure." Jerryck almost shrugged. The mere start of the motion nearly sent him into twitches of pain.

"You do not know, but you are certain they will kill us?" Adam just wouldn't let it be, wouldn't let Jerryck just lie back and give in to misery, kept him focused. But was that really such a bad thing? At the very least, it was a distraction from how much he hurt. A distraction was good right now.

"One way or another, they will kill you all, if you can't convince them to let you leave." Jerryck said. "They work with earth magic. They could uproot trees on your head... Break a natural dam and flood a creek you're trying to cross... Make a mountainside slip and bury you... I don't know exactly what they'll do. When they fought with the Gathering of Seats, they made that volcano erupt."

"Volcano." Adam pronounced the word very slowly. "I do not know that word."

"A mountain that blows up," Jerryck said. "Spews out fire rock that flows like water. Burns everything in its way. And that's what doesn't get buried by all the ash raining out of the sky from the explosion."

"Oh! *Vulkan*! I know what that is." Adam repeated the word a few more times under his breath.

"*Vulkan*?" the large man asked. Adam talked to him. As the two spoke back and forth, a slow smile spread across Adam's face. Then the large man stood, and moved further back under the overhang.

"I think that will work," Adam said.

"What will?" Jerryck watched the large man moving away until he was out of sight from where Jerryck lay. "Work for what?"

"That is enough of a threat, I think we can stop killing, and leave these mountains." Adam grinned. He looked in the direction the other man had gone. "We will make it work."

To Be Continued

About The Author

REBEKAH OLSON is a Story Grid Certified Editor who lives in Salem, Oregon. Her earliest memories are her love for stories. When she couldn't get 'big people' to tell her enough stories, she would fill entire sheets of notebook paper with squiggles writing stories of her own. Unfortunately, she couldn't read yet and so had no idea what the story was. Since none of the 'big people' would tell her what the squiggles said, those stories are lost. So now she makes up new stories. When she's not writing, she's reading, watching movies, playing piano, knitting or crocheting.

Please help the author by leaving a review where you purchased this book. You can visit here for a list of retailers where this book is available https://www.authorrebekaholson.com/books.

If you liked this story, visit her website at https://www.authorrebekaholson.com/ or you can visit her blog https://www.authorrebekaholson.com/blog and read chapters for free. While Adam struggled in Shontarra, find out what was going on in Brend from Court Magician Jerryck's point of view.

www.ingramcontent.com/pod-product-compliance
Lightning Source LLC
Chambersburg PA
CBHW071733110726
47908CB00006B/1580